Ashacan

The Vhanian Remnants
Catherine Vino

Dwellwater Books

ASHACAN

THE VHANIAN REMNANTS: BOOK I

CATHERINE VINO

Contents

A Brief Glossary

THE PRONUNCIATION OF THE elvish *a* is often soft, resulting in an "ah" sound. *Ae* shares the sound of a long ā.

Necessary terms:

Nhuaela – /Nhu-ay-la/

acan – /ah-kon/ hunter

Ashacan – /ahsh-ah-kon/ honored hunter

Ashan – /ahsh-on/ honored lead

vashte – /vah-sh-ta/ shield

vashte'rae – /vah-sh-ta-ray/ shield tribe

For Andrew
I'll finish the campaign for you.

Rendara

MY FATHER STANDS WITH his back to me. His fair hand presses the black bark of a *vashte*. He tilts his head downward, listening through the sounds of the settling tribe to the Gatewood beyond.

"What do you th—"

"Shh..." he hushes me. His hand carefully drops to rest upon the dagger at his hip. For a moment he looks ahead into the depth of the forest, and then he turns.

His brow softens, and his eyes meet mine. He nods approvingly, causing wisps of silver hair to fall over his shoulders. "This is a good spot, *Ashacan*."

I bite the inside of my cheek to keep from grinning at his use of my rank rather than name. He has no obligation to call me by it, and yet his approval means more than anyone else's.

"Your mother will like the trees," he muses.

"They're close. Humans won't think to look beyond them."

"That is exactly what she told me. *They're tactical, Selejor*," he imitates.

He lifts his face toward the canopy above. Shafts of sunlight emphasize the sharpness of his features and the fine wrinkles that stretch outward from the corners of his eyes. He opens them briefly, and their blackness absorbs the light.

"Yes," he says again. "Yes, this will do." He looks over my shoulder. "And the *vashte'rae* seems content."

Beyond me, the Rendara adjust to the new location. A narrow stream cuts through the camp. Families reconstruct their tents along the banks just under cover of the encompassing trees. Horse-master Egen unburdens our forest ponies of supplies. A rope pen is strung between the trees. Firepits are dug. Sleeping arrangements made. Children chase each other, avoiding their chores in favor of a game of disappearing within the low-hanging boughs of fat gaea. *Acans* walk the perimeter with their bows at the ready, should our intrusion on the space rouse beasts nearby. It shouldn't. I made sure to scout the area days ago to startle any carnivorous creatures away. The acans—*my* acans—followed. We discerned a perimeter, studied the trees, ensured there were no lingering threats awaiting our arrival.

"I was worried they would think this place too near the humans," I admit, relieved that the Rendara have taken kindly to the new space.

"They trust your judgment, my Ashacan. You should too."

This time I allow myself to grin, pleased by my first success as Ashacan. Relocating an entire *vashte'rae* is no simple jaunt through the woods.

"There's a village not a day's ride to the south," I continue with my report, hoping to distract from my elation. "I suspect it's where the trespassers are coming from. They've cleared the strongwood trees on the outskirts."

"Well," my father sighs. "Humans will be less inclined to trespass once they stumble upon us. Perhaps in their shock, I'll be able to dissuade them from thieving the trees."

I roll my eyes. "When have they ever cared to hear the words of an elf?"

"When have you ever cared to hear theirs?"

"They test our borders. They steal our trees. Poach our animals." I cross my arms. "I don't want to hear them. They think we want to kill them anyway."

"Ah," he says flippantly. "Then we may as well follow through."

I give him a look.

"You are Ashacan now, Nhuaela," he says. "The shield of the Rendara, and despite what you think that rank means, there's more to it than just leading acans and smiting threats."

"I know." My reply is sharp. "That's why we're here—to speak with the humans, although you know diplomacy is not my talent."

He comes near. A long white claw hangs from a leather strip around my neck. It curves like a bony finger, sharper than any blade. The scars on my torso and calf prove as much. My father takes it in hand. Wisdom gained through time shows in his soft smile as he gazes upon the claw, and suddenly, he looks incurably tired.

"This..." he says, lifting the claw between us, "this tells me you are very talented. And those talents don't end at the reach of your ax."

"What—"

Before I can ask what he means, a sharp whistle interrupts us.

"It's Halstaer," he informs me, looking over my shoulder.

"Who else whistles like that?"

"Should I stop him?"

"No."

"Are you sure? I could give him stern warning that you are *not* to share tents."

"Don't you dare," I hiss, tugging my necklace from his grasp. "Go away. He's bringing report."

With a wry smirk, my father glides around me to greet my second.

It was Halstaer who we all thought would be named Ashacan, and until recently, it was he who kept me warm on chill mornings, he who hunted at my side, he who knew my thoughts before I needed to say them—who still knows my thoughts, infuriatingly enough.

I've kept him at a distance since becoming Ashacan, although there are no stated rules against our partnership aside from common sense. Acans die to protect the vashte'rae, and it is now my duty to order them to if need be. Sending any of my hunters into danger regardless of necessity is an ill thought. I have been taught by them. Some, like Halstaer and I, have grown up together, trained, and hunted with each other for decades. Perhaps if I were a commander in the north, circumstances would be different, and I'd never hesitate to send soldiers to their deaths.

But we are not in the north, and there is not one Rendara who I do not cherish, particularly Halstaer—my own fault. We have been in difficult situations before—deadly situations—but in those moments, it was not I who gave order. I'm still not sure if I would be able to hold back personal emotion in favor of defense, and I'm not convinced Halstaer could either. Perhaps that is why Evoriel's *caracosh* dragged me into the night instead.

I watch as Halstaer clasps my father's arm and indulges his reaching questions regarding our relationship with vague answers.

Deterred, my father asks a simpler question. "Have you settled in?"

"Not quite." Halstaer's gaze moves over my father's shoulder and lands on me. "But I'm thinking this bank looks nice enough for a tent."

"Excuse us, Father," I interrupt.

He takes my meaning and pulls away from Halstaer. "I suppose I'll leave you two to discuss your sleeping arrangements then."

"*Father.*"

"I'm going, child. Off to help your mother. She looks far too calm *not* to be annoyed about something."

He offers us his most diplomatic smile as he departs for the center of camp.

"Ashacan..." Halstaer says once we are alone. He draws the word out. It has been weeks, and he has not grown used to it, nor have I adjusted to him calling me by rank.

It is not out of disrespect. Likewise, I have not been successful in referring to him as strictly an acan—a hunter. *You go by your rank,* my mother told me when I confessed my aversion to formality. *They respect you by name but may distance themselves through rank.*

Halstaer turns his attention south, looking warily toward imperium territory. His fine black hair is braided and bound down his back. The breeze picks up a few loose strands. They brush against his cheekbones and curve along the rigid angles of his face to catch upon the bow he keeps slung over his shoulder. He wears patched hide pants and a dark green shirt that clings to his lean torso. The shade compliments the flecks of green in his amber eyes. I clutch the claw atop my chest to keep myself from turning his chin in seek of his gaze.

"It doesn't help to stare," he tells me.

I avert my eyes at his words, embarrassed to have been caught. "I wasn't staring."

"I know you like this shirt, Nhu."

"It matches your eyes."

He grins, flashing the edge of a fang. "I thought I'd dress nice to impress an honored member of the Damicus. Flustering my Ashacan, though...I suppose that's a bonus."

It pangs me to hear him say it like that. *My* Ashacan.

I firmly change topic. "How is our perimeter?"

"Established and well-guarded, just as you left it."

"And all are ready to receive Elder Tolorian, whichever direction he may come?"

"You know he'll sneak past our watch. Old *rihar* treats it like a game."

"Let him. Maybe it will keep him in a good mood, and he'll have nothing negative to say."

"Want to take bets on what issue it'll be this time? Judging by our border, I'd wager it's human expansion."

"Could be dwellers," I suggest.

He shakes his head uncomfortably. "Better not be dwellers. I never stayed long in the north because of those things."

There was a time when Halstaer considered becoming one of the *vatanukro*, the elite soldiers stationed in the north at the Shadowed Threshold, but after a stint of time there, he preferred the usual threats of the Gatewood. He has never spoken in depth about it, only that he couldn't sleep so close to the Deep.

In the woods before us, sunlight shines through the branches and lights Rendaran land in a shade of warmth. I struggle to imagine a dweller shattering the calm. And that is exactly what one would do—beyond shatter our peace. A dweller would devour it, leaving nothing behind but unchecked magic and a wave of darkness.

"Could it happen?" I ask, suddenly doubtful.

"What? A dweller? Here?"

"Do you think we could handle one?" I press.

"You're not serious."

"As Ashacan, I'd like to know our chances."

He sighs. "Depends. We might be able to take down a moderately sized one." He hesitates and then corrects himself. "No. *Chief* might be able to take down a *small* one if we all pitch in as fodder."

I nod, agreeing to the notion. My mother spent time in the north as all chieftains are expected to do. She fought and survived dwellers, and could surely do it again, but like all who have ventured north, she does not want to face another.

Halstaer continues, adamant. "If you really expect to fight one and win, you need magic. Powerful magic." He inspects me more closely. "You have any abilities you're hiding from me?"

"If I did, you would have found them by now."

"Mm, *sai*," he agrees. "But it's magic that stops them. It was always the mages that dealt the killing blows. The rest of us were just there to buy them time."

"My mother has no magic."

"Well, Chief is a bit more talented than me. I suppose you don't need magic. But it will save you casualties." He puts an assuring hand on my shoulder, catches my eye. "Don't worry about dwellers, Nhu."

I grip his forearm.

"And if there is a dweller," he says, "you won't have to fight it alone."

I pull away from him before I decide to move closer. "I suppose the current worry is setting camp before Tolorian gets here."

"The true enemy," he teases. "An old fairborn sneaking past our guard."

Together we enter the main camp, or what has been set up thus far. Families work to construct their tents, most consisting of hide strategically strung from tree trunks and pinned by wooden stakes. Halstaer and I pause to assist those we can. Other acans swing themselves upward by low-hanging branches to tug the tents upward into soft peaks. Below, Rendara stretch tanned hide as bases to keep out morning dew or rain, then they haul in their belongings, largely consisting of fur blankets. Some have soft fabrics from various visits to Daerva'Tor: richly woven blankets in shades of blue or green, or fine linen clothes mismatched with articles of leather and hide. Many families own a mirror and brush to regularly untangle knotted braids. Each is unique and often valuable, passed through generations and inlaid with gemstones, scales, or carvings. My mother's most prized possession is her brush of plated green and gold dragon scales. It was gifted to her by my father, and aside from him, it is the only thing she loves from Daerva'Tor.

Halstaer and I continue our walk, drawing curious looks. There are no secrets to be kept when living in the close-quarters of a *vashte'rae*, a shield-tribe. The changes between us have not gone unnoticed. I find it easier to embrace the stares than shy away from them.

As we approach the main tent, my mother pushes aside the flap and stands with arms crossed, awaiting me. She is an imposing elf, taller than most and twice as strong. Her lips are set in a firm line and her gold eyes level all. Her dark hair is freshly braided in an intricate plait. Black ink climbs her arms in the pattern of vines that coil up the sides of her neck to the very tips of her sharp ears. Around her neck is a regal necklace of dark bone, fragments of deepdweller teeth arranged in order of size. All were collected by previous chieftains as proof of their worth. At its center is my mother's addition, a jagged tooth still shadowed by blood.

I do not possess the elaborate inkings of a vashte'rae chieftain, but I resemble her far more than my father. I only wish I could mimic her unshakeable countenance.

"*Ashacan,*" she addresses me, lengthening each syllable of the title in heavy Rendaran style.

Halstaer steps away from my side, dismissing himself. "I'll see you later, Nhu—I mean, Ashacan."

"Check on Serin for me, will you? He needs to hunt before tonight."

"Sure. Say hello to Chief for me."

My mother's stern eyes follow Halstaer at a distance until he disappears into the sea of tents. Then her gaze snaps back to me when I'm in speaking range.

"Mother," I greet her with a respectful tilt of my head. I can see it is stress, not anger, adding lines to the corner of her eyes.

She uncrosses her arms and motions me forward. "Where have you been all morning? I haven't seen you since we arrived."

"I was with Father."

"Was he keeping you from your duties?"

"He was giving me his opinion of this place."

"And?"

"He likes it."

"As do I. The humans are closer than I would prefer, but perhaps it will be more effective to be close. It's bold."

"We need to be bold when it comes to humans," I say.

She nods and puts a gentle arm over my shoulder, guiding me on a new path through camp. "Have we a perimeter?"

"I walked it this morning. It's solid. The trees are thick. We are well hidden."

Her relaxed arm tells me she is pleased with my answers. She would have already walked the perimeter herself, and double checked every detail of the location before seeking the correct answers from me. If something were wrong, she would have never allowed the Rendara to pitch tents.

She stops nearby the main cookfire as she is pulled into a conversation regarding Elder Tolorian's arrival. The shallow pit is dug into a dry patch of bank. Several of the older Rendara encircle it. They stoke the warming embers and ready a spit of metal. Serin's younger sister, Sil, makes clusters of gathered herbs and separates them into baskets. The little girl smiles up at me with the same innocence as her brother, the same wide, yellow eyes. I await the day she is old enough to draw a bow. With luck, she will share in Serin's talent.

She slyly holds a closed hand out to me. I crouch and humor her by offering my palm. She drops a clump of wittleweed onto it and turns away in a fit of giggles.

I feign shock. "Does my breath smell?" I demand of her.

"You and anyone else who walks by," Zanil, her mother, says tiredly.

I tap the girl's nose with the minty weed in retribution.

"Ash'can smells!" she giggles.

I take a large bite from the wittleweed. The bitter herb cleanses my mouth with a mild burn. For effect, I smash the green leaves against the front of my teeth before I bare them to her.

"Etter?" I ask through them.

Zanil offers me a soft smile as Sil gleefully shrieks. Behind me, my own mother clears her throat, less amused.

I quickly run my tongue along my teeth to clear them of wittle and spit it into the fire. Even Sil knows to return to her chore under the glare of the chieftain.

"Come, Ashacan," she orders me.

I follow her to the stream's edge, wondering what strains her tone.

"I saw you with Halstaer earlier."

The claim is more curious than accusatory. A false curiosity to be sure. She likes Halstaer. *So long as he treats you well*, she has always said, although she has never forgiven him for teasing me about my sloppy swordsmanship. If not for him, I would never have learned to favor axes instead of swords. *Crude weapons*, she calls them. But axes hit harder, lodge deeper. And I like to think I wield them with finesse.

"He walked at your side as an equal," my mother resumes her thought, "not a step behind."

"We are equals."

"No, you are not. You are Ashacan. He is an acan, your hunter, your soldier," she reinforces, as though I did not know.

I glance over my shoulder to ensure no one is listening—at least not obviously. When I speak, my words are terse. This conversation is one we have had before, and it is not one I care to have.

"He respects me," I tell her.

"Perhaps in words, but not in action."

"Father walks at your side."

She gives me a sideways look. "Your father is my mate. We *are* equals." She steps nearer in warning. "You are *not* mated to Halstaer."

I'm quiet for a moment, knowing my retort was weak and wrong. Part of me wishes it was not.

"If you were, you would know it," she says, this time softening her tone.

"I can still love him."

"Yes, and I love every member of this tribe. Even so, each Rendara has their place. If we did not, we'd be a senseless rabble." She puts her hand in mine. "As Ashacan, you must love your people, but certain relationships cause rifts. Weaknesses. If you are partial to every other acan under your command, you'll never be able to think clearly."

"And how do you think with me as Ashacan, mother?"

She squeezes my hand. "You know the difference between your chief and your mother. I know the difference between my daughter and my Ashacan."

"Halstaer knows I am Ashacan."

"I don't think either of you know you are Ashacan. Not yet." Another squeeze of my hand, and then release. "But you will. Prove it to me. You are to come to the meeting tonight."

I look at her in surprise. When I was young, I tried to eavesdrop on one of her meetings involving members of the Damicus. I pressed my ear to the backside of their tent. They had not started to speak before her hand burst through a thin seam and grabbed me by my braids. I was scolded for listening. The experience ensured I never went near her meetings again.

Her voice is firm. "You are Ashacan, therefore you will report to the elder as you would to me."

I grasp my claw necklace. She notices the anxious movement.

"Or perhaps you are not ready?" she challenges.

"I am ready," I assure her, dropping the claw. "Elder Tolorian doesn't frighten me."

"No, but whatever he has to say might. You must be ready for it, without fear, as Ashacan. *Sai?*"

"*Sai.*"

Fractures

SERIN HOISTS HIS DEER upward so it hangs from the lowest branch of a sturdy tree. His lanky arms strain against the deer's weight. He is still young, a boy eager to prove himself as an acan. His muscles remain undefined within his lithe frame, and he could stand to gain a few inches in height. The black braids upon his head are randomly placed and haphazardly tied, as though he has not quite mastered the technique or patience for them. One is woven with a string of feathers that mimic a style once favored by Halstaer. Favored until the boy began to copy him.

Serin smiles proudly at his hanging deer, beaming similarly to Sil as the carcass sways from the branch, already sliced and gutted. Blood drips in a neat line down the animal's neck.

"Is it right?" Serin asks me, his yellow eyes seeking approval.

"Is it?" I ask in turn.

Halstaer passes by with a string of rabbits over his shoulder. He studies the beginning of Serin's work. "It's upside down," he criticizes.

"It is not!" Serin rebukes.

"Look at it. Head is down. Tail is up. Even the insides are gone!"

"They're supposed to be."

"You sure?"

Serin looks at his deer, less confident.

"Serin, don't listen to him," I say. "You know what is right. Now show me. You have your knife?"

The boy removes his blade from his belt. Using a flat rock as a stool, he angles the deer carcass toward himself and makes an incision at its back, inner leg.

Halstaer gasps loudly, and Serin flinches.

I grab Halstaer's shoulder and shove him to the ground. "Mind your own game."

"Apologies, Ashacan."

"Where's your deer?" I inquire. "An acan of your standing has no excuse to not have one, especially on the eve of a party."

He jabs his knife toward Serin's work. "Right there. That little *rihar* shot it."

"Norveh un diil," Serin snaps back without looking at his accuser. "You weren't making any move to shoot, so I did."

"I was waiting for a better angle."

"We had the same angle."

I give Halstaer a quiet look. He rips the fur from his rabbits and shrugs. "Kid's good," he says. "But it's only because—" The smile slips from his face as his eyes shift to Serin.

The boy stands motionless on the high stone, one hand lightly gripping a swath of deerskin. He stares toward the stream. I follow his gaze to the far bank where a pair of elegant horses walk.

The Rendara watch. I recognize Elder Tolorian instantly. From the distance, he is ageless and glowing. His fairness is intensified under the orange rays of sunlight along the stream. His white robes and perfectly alabaster skin make him a beacon of light. He rides a bay warhorse—the only elf I have seen do so. The tribes prefer hardy forest ponies. Most fairborn favor agility and speed, which I see in his companion's mount.

"Is that...?" Halstaer drifts.

"The Ashan," I answer.

Serin drops his knife.

I expected Tolorian to have a guard. It would be senseless for a member of the Damicus to go wandering the forest alone. Many times before, he has arrived with five or six fairborn soldiers, but never the Ashan. One might call it excessively cautious to bring the leader of elven ranks as a bodyguard.

He follows Tolorian like a shadow. Unkempt white braids fall over his dark cloak and reach down his back. His travel clothes are well-worn and plated with patches of strategically placed leather meant for easy movement. His frayed and mud-stained cloak is swept around himself so as to not tangle with the two swords across his back.

He could be mistaken as any roughened soldier; one of the *vatanukro* who wield two swords instead of one and spend their days weathering the harsh lands of the north. But two details set him apart from the rest. On either arm he wears bracers of deepdweller bone. They are meant to be his official insignia of rank, just as my talon necklace is mine. It is what we are not privileged to see that defines him. Just below his eyes is the beginning of a gray, close-fitting mask. It hides most of his face—the worst of his rumored scars.

Halstaer sidles up beside me. "What in Evoriel's name is he doing here?"

"I don't know."

"You don't know?"

"Obviously not. My mother never mentioned *he* was coming."

I have met the Ashan before. For no longer than a moment, and never in the close setting of the *vashte'rae*. My meetings with him have been impersonal and contained within Daerva'Tor during gatherings of the vashte'rae where all acans are addressed.

"Perhaps your father invited him," Halstaer suggests.

I shake my head. "He would have told me."

My father was born and raised in Daerva'Tor, although he did not live the usual life of a fairborn elf. He was a diplomat until he met my mother, and when he departed the city for her, the Damicus was left shaken. Without him, the fragile Daerv-human relations frayed. Elder Tolorian was the only one to remain my father's friend, and through him, my father came to know the Ashan.

I elbow Halstaer. "Stop staring. Help Serin finish with his deer."

"What are you doing?"

"My duty."

I take long strides through the camp. My steps disrupt the gawking Rendara, and they return to their work. I move quickly in attempt to avoid their questions but end up deflecting them just the same.

I head for the main tent, keeping track of our encroaching guests as I do so. With the Ashan accompanying him, it's no wonder how Elder Tolorian slipped past our guard. Together, they cross the shallow river. Their horses effortlessly jump up to our side, and my father appears just as suddenly to intercept them.

Both Elder and Ashan slow their horses. My father politely takes their reins but offers no formalities. They do not appear to mind.

My mother pushes aside her tent flap and joins me at the short distance. As she takes note of the Ashan, her under-eye twitches. Without word or glance, she points to the ground beside her.

I move as instructed. "Am I to stand at your side?" I provoke. "As an *equal*?"

"Do not think I won't demote you here and now," she warns. "Before the entire vashte'rae and Evoriel himself, *child*."

"Do you have that power?" I genuinely ask.

"Use that tone with me again, and we'll find out."

I settle beside her, suddenly more wary of her side-eye glare than any visitor. "Did you know about the Ashan?"

"I did not."

"What about father?"

"He made no mention of it, but if he did know…" she clenches her jaw heatedly.

"They're earlier than expected."

She composes herself. "It is no matter. It will give us more time to speak."

Between tents, the Rendara poorly hide their eavesdropping. Dinner preparations and tidying of camp have ceased for them to watch us welcome our guests. I hear whispers amongst them. A few of my more trusted acans catch my eye with supportive nods or amused grins. My father stands in the clearing before the main tent, his differences more apparent than ever in the presence of other fair.

He is a fairborn elf dressed as a member of a vashte'rae, not looking quite like either sect. His gray hair is scandalously loose with only two thin strands tied back from his temples. With his back to me, I imagine the stark contrast of his eyes to our guests'. His, solidly black, lacking the crystalline pureness of the fair. Yet the ashen paleness of his complexion is akin to many fairborn, as are his mannerisms and Daerv accent. Even so, he has always been held as something odd. He is more accepting and thoughtful than any fairborn I have met. I've often wondered if that is what led Evoriel to pair him with my mother.

Tolorian and the Ashan dismount. Egen arrives to take the horses to pasture. Finally, my father gives proper greeting. He takes Tolorian's hand and bows his forehead to the Elder's frail knuckles. The Elder returns a hint of smile before tipping his head, releasing my father.

I expect to see a similar exchange with the Ashan. A lesser rank would take a half step back while briefly lowering their eyes to show submission. I have seen my father do so before, but that was when we did not meet the Ashan in the privacy of our own vashte'rae.

He takes the Ashan's hand as though he means to bow, and then embraces him. The Ashan, surprisingly, reciprocates.

"Do *not* do as your father does," my mother warns.

I cast her a horrified look, but any further explanation is lost in the Elder's approach.

"Elder Tolorian," she says in an inviting tone.

Fine wrinkles crease the corners of his crystal eyes and thin lips. His white robes drag atop the brush of the forest but are not dirtied. He extends a hand to my mother.

She takes it, curling her fingertips with his in a display of equality. "Welcome."

"I am honored to be present amongst the Rendara once more," he replies in Daerv. It is quick and elegant, not as gruff as vashte'rae dialects. Hearing it makes me more aware of my Rendaran, and dwelling on the matter causes me to hesitate in taking his hand.

With our fingers clasped, he turns his hand, angling it to be above my own. Veins ripple beneath his thin skin, showing his age. He is nearing eight-hundred years. It is a rare feat. I have never known an elf to live beyond seven-hundred, let alone eight. Only the Vha from the North were truly immortal.

"Elder Tolorian," I greet.

"Nhuaela," he answers, flipping our hands back to a neutral position. "Stand, let me see your face."

His eyes are pure white, the same shade as the caracosh claw around my neck. He gently places his fingertips upon it, as if to confirm it is real.

"You are so grown," he remarks with the same, reserved smile. "A true Ashacan, I see. It seems the last I visited you were sparring in patches of mud."

"My favorite pastime," I return. My mother glares. If he were any other Damicus member, I would not be so foolish, but it is hard to maintain decorum when I have known him since I was a child wrestling in mud pits.

"Perhaps this time it will be the river," I reply. "Often that is what these parties devolve to."

"Indeed, although I think I shall forgo such revelries at this age."

My father catches the Elder's last statement. "You are not that old, my friend. You can spar with the best of us."

The Elder chuckles. "Selejor, you know as well as I that I was never acan material."

The two jest, but the Ashan's presence keeps me from relaxing with the conversation. He approaches my mother, who clasps his hand as she did to Tolorian. As a chieftain, her rank falls equal to theirs. It is a momentary connection, released just as quickly as it was performed.

In Daerva'Tor, the ranks are straightforward. A soldier is a soldier. They have no dual rank of being a soldier and an acan. For the shield-tribes, an acan is foremost a hunter, but we are also soldiers.

As Ashacan, the Rendaran acans answer to me, but we all answer to the Ashan. With him standing before me, the true height of my new rank becomes suddenly apparent. Excluding the chieftains, I am a single rank below the leader of the Undecayed.

Our etiquette differs from that of a chieftain or elder. I am not his equal, but as an acan, it is inappropriate to clasp his hand. But what *is* proper slips my mind.

Overwhelmed, I stupidly meet his eyes, and once I meet them, I cannot look away. They are striking. Not white, not shimmering fractals, but silver. Beneath them is the start of his mask. It covers his face to the base of his throat where it melds with the rest of his dark clothes. It serves its purpose, but not everything can be hidden. The space beneath his right eye is etched by a series of scars. The taut red lines slice upward to the corner of his eye, across his temple, and beneath his braids. His ear is completely lacerated, torn at its edge. A single white braid hangs in front, doing what it can to conceal even a fraction of the marks.

His gaze sharpens at my lingering stare. As his eyes narrow, their shade darkens, and his visible scars upraise. I have only stared a moment, but a moment too long. I quickly glide my foot back and drop my eyes, remembering how to execute the half-bow of my rank. From my periphery, my mother briefly sucks her cheek before composing herself.

"Nhuaela," my father interrupts.

I straighten at the sound of his voice. He comes to my side and puts a steady arm around my shoulders. I lean into him, taking what strength I can.

Elder Tolorian and my mother enter the main tent, leaving the three of us in what would be a private moment if it were not for the tactlessly listening Rendara.

I try to angle my father toward the tent, but he stands rooted in place. His hand squeezes my shoulder, facing me back toward the Ashan.

"Nhuaela," he says my name again, this time more firmly. "I'd like you to officially meet the Ashan of Daerva'Tor, Rolan."

"*Iesh*, I know who he is."

"Then where are your manners?"

I briefly roll my eyes upward so as not to stare again. "Forgive me, Ashan. I did not expect your presence. I forgot myself."

He tips his head in acknowledgment and proceeds to shift to the Rendaran dialect with ease. "The fault is mine for giving no warning, but I thought I should meet you myself."

"Why?"

My father's grip on my shoulder tightens again at my reaching question.

The Ashan does not hesitate. He gestures at my necklace. "To see if that was real."

"Of course, it's real."

"Yes, and now I have no doubt of your legitimacy."

I feel the sudden spark of temper I inherited from my mother and shrug out from under my father's arm. "You thought I was not truly an Ashacan?"

"Considering your relation to Chief Elendira, the thought had crossed my mind, yes." He looks to my father. "No offense intended, Selejor. You understand the caution I must take after the Nishtari tried to instate their own Ashacan without proper trial."

"You compare us to the *Nishtari*?" I say defensively.

"It is nothing personal, Ashacan. You would do well to realize that. Now, this is not a conversation to have in front of your people, is it?"

A portion of Rendara have encroached, obviously hearing the words tersely pass between us. Amidst them I see Serin. His hands are still bloody from the deer, and he watches intently.

I push my anger down and try to salvage decorum. "You're right, Ashan. It's time we join the others."

* * *

Elder Tolorian sits on the roots of a strongwood. Its sturdy trunk rises behind him like a throne, and its roots flow outward into the space of the tent. It is the only tree perched upon the stream bank, overlooking the center of camp. I knew my mother would choose it to anchor the main tent. The hide roof is strategically strung from the strongwood branches above Elder Tolorian's head. The walls are framed by their own supports with sunlight winking through the seams of stretched hide. In the center is a small table only large enough to display a tattered map of the Gatewood. Like our mirrors, the table is one of our permanent possessions. It was crafted to cleverly fold to make our moves more efficient, and its sole purpose has always been to hold the map.

"Our Ashacan joins us," Elder Tolorian says from his roots. "It will be refreshing to hear your words, Nhuaela. I look forward to your take on matters."

I smile at him but remain silent until I can grapple my thoughts. My mother covertly gestures to the space beside her, indicating for me to take it. I fall in line at her side, this time without comment. My father takes the head, and the Ashan the place across from me and my mother. It seems instinctive for him to observe the map. He lightly touches it with one hand and draws it toward himself.

"All settled?" my father asks Tolorian.

"Quite," he replies, relaxing against the strongwood. "The chairs of the Damicus Hall are not nearly so comfortable."

They continue their conversation with Elder Tolorian launching into a recount of his journey south. At a leisurely pace, it is a two-week trip from Daerva'Tor to the edge of Rendaran land, and the Elder spares no detail of their uneventful ride.

Rather than listen, I too take solace in the map, wishing I could see the path of the Ashan's thoughts.

The parchment is divided into five sectors; at the center lies Daerva'Tor. A rough circle surrounds the city, marking the portion of land patrolled by the fair. The Rendara are charged with protecting the southern border from the western Mountains of Zurranis to the river Uduro in the east. A small stone shows our current location at the southernmost tip where the Wood bows outward. A second stone plots the human village just over the border.

The eastern edge of the Wood runs up along Imperium territory. It is protected by the Nishtari. To the west are the Elesaan, whose territory bleeds into the Zurranis, and with whom we maintain a close friendship. Tucked away in the north are the Teur. For them, sharing the border with the North is a constant battle. The dangers of that fractured land seek entry to the Gatewood, and the Teur kept watch over the north long before the army of Undecayed was stationed alongside them. Now, they work together to defend against the conjurations of the Deep.

The Ashan fixates on the north, which comes as no surprise. The threats at all other borders are trivial compared to the north, but still I wonder what could possibly bring him away from his post. He is not known for leaving his soldiers while they are exposed to threat.

"Tell me, Lizana, what has brought you to this particular location?" Elder Tolorian asks.

With the niceties finished, I give ear to the new conversation and look away from the map.

"Humans," my mother gruffly replies. "I'm sure you caught trace of the vashte prevalent in these parts. Should you venture southward, you'll find only remnants of them, pillaged by those *rihar* humans."

My father clears his throat at her crass word. "But as in any case, they may not know what they do, which is why I mean to pay them a visit soon."

"They know exactly what they do," my mother retorts. "They have done so before and they will do it again. Now is the time we use greater force than mere words."

"Violence, then?" My father does not shout or force anger into his words; he simply adds a questioning lilt to his tone that implies disagreement. He shakes his head and looks down at the map. "Aggression does not solve a problem. It ensures the continuation of it."

"As do diplomatic words," my mother points out. "You are infuriatingly good at cajoling humans, but here we are, once again needing to remind them where they should and should not swing their axes. I only mean to scare them."

"They are already scared of us."

"If they were scared, they would not be taking our trees."

Elder Tolorian lifts a silencing hand to my parents. "Ashacan, what do you think of this?"

I pick my words carefully, aware of the distinction between my bickering parents and arguing leaders of the vashte'rae. "I chose this location because it ensures confrontation," I say. "The manner of the confrontation, though..."

"How would you handle it?" the Ashan presses.

"I'm inclined to talk to them first," I admit, glancing at my father. His dark eyes warm approvingly.

"And should they offer threat?" the Ashan poses.

I angle my head at him. "I suppose it depends on what kind of threat."

"The kind that puts your people in immediate danger, such as you have done by choosing a camp so near humans, I might argue."

"The Rendara are well guarded," I assure him, "and if it came to it, not one of them would balk from a fight."

"A fight should never come to them when they have an Ashacan to defend them."

For an instant his comment causes me to hesitate, as if I made a poor decision, but then I realize the intent behind his interrogation. "I don't knowingly put my people in harm's way, Ashan. This is a strategic location. I do not regret choosing it."

"Good," he says dismissively. "It'd be a hassle to backtrack on the decision now."

"These humans are hardly a threat," my mother adds. "They're more of a nuisance."

"They'll grow with time," says the Ashan.

"Which is why we have come to stop them in whatever way is most appropriate," my father puts an end to the discussion. "There will be time to revisit our plans regarding the humans later. I do not mean to intrude upon them until *after* we have found our footing here. There are other matters to be settled first, like that of your visit."

"Yes, what news from Daerva'Tor?" my mother asks.

Tolorian sits forward to share. "The city is fine as always, although council squabbles have heightened since Elder Creeva has begun to argue for the Nishtari-chosen Ashacan to be recognized."

There is a tense silence only broken by my father's laugh.

"*Nishtari*-chosen?" my mother inquires, less amused. "Did they not encounter the caracosh?"

Tolorian shifts under my mother's gaze. "They claim Ashacan should be an elected position—elected by the vashte'rae. Not one to be dictated by—"

"Their own god?" my father poses.

"...By needless slaughter, Selejor."

"Needless?" my mother's tone grows heated. "Dying in defense of one's tribe is not *needless*."

"They do not see why the risks of facing the caracosh are needed when an Ashacan can easily be appointed," Tolorian replies.

"An Ashacan can only be appointed by Evoriel," she returns.

"At the loss of acans and kin. The Nishtari wonder why such losses are necessary."

"Because if acans did not face the caracosh, the vashte'rae would be eviscerated. They do not needlessly die, nor do they fight with the intention to die, but should they fall, it is in honor—because they were *protecting* their own. As an acan should. As an Ashacan should." Her thumb works the ring of her finger in a controlled fashion. "Ashacans are not appointed. They are not chosen. They prove themselves. And any who circumvent that process dishonor those who have given their lives."

If I could fade into the tent's side, I would. The rank does not fit. It never felt like it fit and hearing them speak reminds me of its weight. Acans more skilled than I were massacred before my eyes. I was just the one who got dragged instead of disemboweled, who caught the beast at a good angle with a lucky strike.

Tolorian patiently waits for my mother to finish speaking. He lets her frustration hang a moment before addressing her more calmly than before.

"We know this, Lizana," he says, "and we do not agree with the Nishtari's actions. However, since the Teur, Elesaan, and now the Rendara all have established Ashacans, the Nishtari presume they should have one as well."

"If they are in need of one then the caracosh will present itself," she snaps. "Likely to grab their hunters in the fringes of the night."

"The Teur and Elesaan have held Ashacans for centuries," my father says. "It appears the Nishtari have only reacted because the Rendara now have one. This smells of jealousy."

Tolorian nods. "That is likely part of it, but you must also consider the implications of three vashte'rae discovering Ashacans in their midst. An Ashacan is established when there is need of one, when acans alone will not suffice. The Nishtari think themselves at a disadvantage being the only tribe without one." Tolorian meets my eyes. "Unprepared for whatever you forewarn."

"I can't imagine I forewarn anything for them," I say, perhaps too flippantly. "I'm still trying to determine what I forewarn for the Rendara."

"Which still should not matter to the Nishtari," says my father, "and we should not waste energy concerning ourselves with what they do. Even if they appoint an Ashacan, the caracosh will eventually come, and they will have to endure just the same."

The Ashan nods. "I agree. However, there is a reason they are tense—the same reason we have come."

"What is it?" I ask, like a *rihar*.

The Ashan briefly looks at me, as though to silently call me a rihar, and then he continues. "Our borders have been quiet save for the occasional human conflict such as yours, and we trust they will easily be driven back to Everwatch territory. The reason we are here, *Ashacan*, is because of the situation in the north."

To call it a situation is to put it lightly. I almost say as much.

"Dwellers?" my mother asks, prepared to strategize a defense.

I dare not look at the Ashan now. Over a century ago, a dweller breached the border to the Gatewood. It would have reached Daerva'Tor if the Ashan had not stopped it, enduring grave injury to himself. Few likely know how he has recovered behind his mask, but it is common knowledge that he reduced the offending dweller to the bracers along his arms.

"The fractures are increasing, and dwellers of all kinds are crawling from the Deep in stronger numbers," he says. "For now, the border is secure, and we are working on ways to temper the rifts. I have no doubt we will continue to hold out as we always have. However, should the worst happen, the vashte'rae must be on alert."

A tense quiet follows his report as we consider solutions to a problem that has none. A knot of anxiety forms in my stomach at the idea of a deepdweller crashing into camp, and I break the tent's silence as a fracture would break the fabric of our realm.

"Then why are you here?" I ask.

The Ashan's eyes turn flinty at my demand. Looking down in a show of submission would quickly absolve me for speaking out of turn, but my mother taught me to keep my eyes forward. *Do not look for safety in the dirt,* she would say, so I steel myself and await an answer. The Ashan swiftly provides rebuke.

"Why are you not outside, circling the Rendara like a wolf?" he poses, clearly not seeking a response. "Have you no defenses other than yourself? Are there no acans here but you?"

It would be wise to simply bow to his point, but somehow, that feels worse. "Our acans are very capable," I say, "but there are also no deepdwellers here. No fractures."

"Not yet."

"But you just said it would be unlikely for the border to fall. As of now, there is less threat to us than there is to the north."

He tilts his head. "So, you think I should be permanently tethered to the north because there is more threat?"

"I think you are the greatest defense we have, Ashan. With more dwellers crawling from the Depths, shouldn't you be there to help stop them?"

His tone relents, but his words do not. "Once you have successfully protected the Rendara for a season, then you can criticize the way I do things, Ashacan."

If he were anyone else, I would not hold back my reply. Instead, I finally avert my gaze, abashed.

After a moment's silence, my father moves the conversation forward. "Have you had the chance to warn the others about the fractures?"

The Ashan elaborates. "The Teur, of course, know the state of things. I have sent riders to the Elesaan, and we plan to meet with the Nishtari upon our return to Daerva'Tor. This dispute regarding their appointed Ashacan needs to be...resolved."

"Then to what do we owe the pleasure, Ashan?" my mother repeats my prying question with tact. It also does not hurt that she is equal in rank to the Ashan, and such a question is within her power. "You go to the Nishtari to resolve a conflict. I cannot help but think you assume there is conflict here as well." Her eyes shine cleverly. "Aside from humans, that is."

He speaks plainly. "I'm here to ensure that your daughter legitimately earned the rank of Ashacan. Considering the state of things, I need to know our borders are protected by those who were meant to defend them, not by favoritism or cowardice."

A slight narrowing of my mother's eyes turns their cleverness to offense. "And do you contest my daughter as Ashacan?"

"No. I do not."

I see her relief as she glances at me with the briefest smile.

"And it is not my intention to frighten your people," the Ashan says to her, "but should the worst happen, I'd rather you be prepared."

"We will be ready."

I glance at her as though to ask how.

Tolorian collects us. "For now, your focus should remain on the humans. I am confident you will resolve the situation just as we will manage the fracturing in the north. Let us not fret over it now. Lizana?

Would you be so kind as to show me my accommodations? I am quite ready to rest before the festivities begin."

My mother offers Tolorian her arm and together they exit, the Elder inquiring about the well-being of the Rendara until his voice fades away. I make to follow when the Ashan's voice stops me.

"You are not dismissed, Ashacan."

I turn back but look to my father instead. He sighs tiredly and momentarily lays a comforting hand on my shoulder.

"I will meet you outside," he says and then leaves me with the Ashan.

I stand tall and face him. Since he has requested my stay and we have already formally met, it is not inappropriate for me to meet his eyes. I hold them firm, as though I never made any stupid mistakes.

He says nothing for a moment, and in the quiet, a breeze rustles the leaves in the tree outside. The walls of the tent quiver. When they settle, he speaks.

"You may be Ashacan by Evoriel's standards, but that does not mean you have proven yourself to me. Your skills mean nothing if you are filled with doubt, and I have no need for doubtful Ashacans." He steps around the table to close the space, halting a pace before me. "Understood?"

"*Sai, Ashan.*"

He measures me with his gaze. "And next time you question me, at least think through the question first."

I nod, wincing inwardly.

"Dismissed."

I take a half step back and leave before he can see me bite into my cheek.

Worthy of Drink

MY FATHER MEETS ME outside as promised. He looks thoughtfully back at the tent. It would not have been a strain for him to hear my brief conversation with the Ashan. Still, he asks.

"Well?"

"Well, what?" I question back.

"He's right, you know."

The Ashan, likewise, can certainly overhear our conversation through the tent. One would need assured distance or a spell to deafen elvish ears. I embrace the lack of privacy and speak my mind.

"I want to say he's an ass."

"But?"

"But he's forgiving, so I'm the *rihar*."

"Lesson learned. Watch your tongue, just don't bite through it."

"Why not? Then I won't be able to say anything stupid."

"I'd rather you say something stupid than nothing at all. If there is one area where you do not doubt, it is in matters of speaking your mind."

"Am I meant to speak it in a formal meeting?"

"If you determine it wise." He chews on the word and then back-tracks. "That, I think, is what you need to work on, my acan."

"Wisdom?"

"And patience. Don't worry." He kisses my temple before I can take offense. "They will come with age."

"What are you doing?" I ask as he moves to reenter the tent.

"I have some catching up to do. Meanwhile, maybe you should attend to your acans. They've been staring for quite some time."

I linger a moment after he disappears into the tent and listen. He and the Ashan are both too clever, though, and either wait me out in silence or seal the tent with magic until I give up and head for the trees.

Clustered in a small clearing are a group of my acans joined by Serin. None of them attempt to pretend they did not see my missteps in etiquette. Serin waves me toward them excitedly.

"Did you finish with your deer?" I ask, trying to dissuade the questions he clearly wants to ask.

"C'mon, Nhu," Halstaer groans. "Give him a break."

I give him a stern look.

"*Ashacan*," he corrects himself. "You expect him to skin a deer while you and the Ashan are having a secret meeting?"

"Yes. I do. Where's your deer, Serin?"

He shifts his yellow eyes, obviously weighing the risk of a lie.

"That's far too much hesitation for the truth."

"Frae finished skinning for me," the boy confesses. "Well, specifically, he said he'd seen the Ashan enough times to no longer give a—"

I cut him off. "That old man is too soft on you. You're going to find another deer tomorrow, and you're going to skin it yourself."

"Fine," he huffs, "but can you at least tell us why the Ashan is here?"

The gathered acans eagerly await my response, their expressions ranging from curious to wary. Halstaer leans back against a root. The slight narrowing of his eyes inquires more of me than the others notice. It is a look that already knows I intend to hold something back, but now is not the time to frighten them with news of dwellers.

"The Ashan is here to approve of this," I say, holding up the caracosh claw from my chest.

"You've got to be kidding," Lya, an acan only a few years younger than myself laughs. "Since when did the Ashan start approving Ashacans?"

"Since the Nishtari tried to appoint their own without trial."

Lya's smirk fades. The two of us have never gotten along, but we can agree upon the Nishtari's shameful actions.

"I suppose it does look questionable when your mother is chief," Halstaer poses, "but if he knows Chief at all, then he also knows you are the last acan she would want as Ashacan."

I nod, fully aware of that truth but doubting the Ashan's knowledge of it.

"Fortunately, caracosh claws can't be forged," I say in a lighter tone. "All is well."

"You mean all is well aside from you nearly falling over when greeting the Ashan," Halstaer mentions, drawing smiles from the others.

"I lost my balance."

"And as we all know, Ashacans are known for falling over flat surfaces."

"You would, too, if you had to meet him without warning."

"Those scars look different up close, don't they?" he teases. "I've always wondered how he looks under that mask..."

"You should be on rotation," I remind him, putting an end to his musings before the Ashan can sneak up on us. "You too, Lya."

"Expecting trouble?" Halstaer asks.

"So long as you're not guarding your portion of the perimeter? Yes. Or have you forgotten how near the humans we are?"

I know he sees through the reason behind my concern. Humans pose no real threat to us, but he does not push for more.

"As you command, Ashacan," he says while standing up. "Let's go, Lya. No insubordination while the Ashan is lurking about."

If he were anyone else, I would immediately admonish him for such a comment, but like Serin, I hesitate too long. The moment passes and my silence draws looks from those gathered. An embarrassed heat climbs my neck at his disregard for my authority and my inability to act.

I resist the inclination to leave or slump my shoulders. With more difficulty, I fight my want to yell after Halstaer as the shock following his comment turns to anger. With other acans watching, I do neither, knowing both actions would make me appear weak. It is Serin who saves me from the silence.

"Ashacan?" he prompts, coming forward from the group. "Can we walk the perimeter now? Or I could walk it, and you can tell me when I'm wrong."

I smile, grateful for his rescue. He would have already walked it by now, likely with Halstaer to guide him. But the others don't know.

I jerk my head in the opposite direction of Halstaer's path. "Let's go. Maybe we'll find a new deer trail along the way."

Having moved beyond Halstaer's comment, the off duty acans turn their gazes away, and Serin joins my side as I head for the trees.

*   *   *

We return late. After walking the perimeter and checking on each posted acan, Serin wanted to know more about the humans. We ventured south, although not nearly far enough to encounter any danger. Serin memorized the surroundings and asked various questions about humans: *What if they come too close? Are we going to confront them? Will I be allowed to join the fight?* He already knew the answers, but I gave them anyway, happy to be away from camp. I'm far more useful on the perimeter, teaching Serin and keeping watch than I am at preparing dinner or entertaining fairborn guests.

As we reenter camp, I keep an eye out for the Ashan. It occurs to me he was likely assessing the state of camp or scrutinizing my acans all day. My absence may have looked bad, as though I were shirking my duties, but Rendaran acans have kept the same traditions for thousands of years without fail. What brief moments there has been an Ashacan, their duty was not to hover or cook dinner. If anything, my absence was perfectly normal.

Fires glow bright under the darkening sky with Rendara gathered around them. The stream runs slow and steady, its ripples glinting in the dusky light. Along the bank, a stretch of dirt has been tilled and tamped by a series of spars. Dust rises under the agile movements of two acans as they attempt to push one another into the stream or simply knock each other flat.

Serin smiles at the event and leaves my side to join the jeering audience, but then he pauses and turns back.

"Can I go, Ashacan?" he remembers to ask.

"Only if you're going to win."

He takes off at a run.

"No matches!" I shout after him, hoping he did not mistake my sarcasm as a challenge. "Fair play only!"

"Oh, you've done it now," my mother says, joining me to watch Serin enter the fray. She offers me a wooden cup of averlin wine.

I drink it at once.

"How is he?" she asks about Serin. "Holding his own?"

"He's going to make a wonderful acan, but he's still not ready to spar with the likes of Halstaer."

She raises her brows while drinking deeply from her own cup. There are no Rendara close enough to hear us, nor do I think they would care to listen. They busy themselves with drinking, dancing, sparring. Even Elder Tolorian sits cross-legged at the main cookfire, purple wine spilling onto his luminous robes as he laughs heartily at something healer Shayv said. Still, I don't want anyone to hear whatever it is my mother clearly has to say.

"I heard about what Halstaer said to you." The bitterness in her voice is sharper than the wine. "Lya told Giama who told Beshtel, and of course Beshtel told me." She shakes her head, unable to say more.

"I didn't expect it," I admit. "Not from him."

"Ashacan or not, it doesn't matter. You know better than to let someone speak to you that way, so why did you let him?"

My eyes fall to the ground.

"You see it now?" she asks.

"He's walking at my side?"

"He's walking over you."

"You think he's resentful?"

"No, he's scared."

"Of what?"

"Losing you."

"And does he think I'm not scared?" I demand. "I did not ask for this rank."

"But you *do* have this rank. And it's your job to allay your peoples' fears." She puts her hand firmly on my shoulder and tugs me into her line of sight. "Show him that *you* can do better, and he will follow."

I nod at her order, tired. After my acknowledgment, she pulls me close to her chest and draws her hand down the back of my head, briefly cradling it as she held me the night I returned from the caracosh. I remember how openly fearful she had been, how my father took on the role she could not. I hug her back.

"Go on now," she tells me, gently pushing me away. "Settle this."

I head for the space alongside the stream. Two younger acans push each other across the dirt, forgetting proper sparring technique as they lose themselves in laughter. I take up space at the edge of the ring and drop my axes on the ground. Their heavy clank alerts the group that I intend to take the ring next. I carefully remove my boots and the knife I keep tucked into my belt while the acans finish their brawl.

When they fall outside of the ring, an older acan shoos them away. The air of excitement quiets the longer I stand alone, rolling the sleeves of my shirt. Waiting.

A fresh murmur ripples through the crowd, and then Halstaer steps forward. He grins at me. His fangs slip over his bottom lip—a move that would have tempted me before.

I smile back, assuring everyone I bear him no ill will, but it does not fool him. He hides his fangs, and in the exchange of a glance I know he knows exactly why I stepped into the ring. My mother taught me how to fight, and as a result, there are only a handful of acans who match me as a sparring partner. Tonight, there is only one I want to lay flat.

If he doesn't succeed in doing it first.

"Friendly and fair?" Halstaer habitually asks.

"Always."

He takes his stance and crooks a finger, beckoning me to fight. The moment I step forward, those nearest to the ring back away.

Halstaer welcomes my opposition. He opens his arms as I run forward, not anticipating the true intensity of my first strike. It is a careless move, one that could have landed me directly in the water if he had not underestimated my seriousness.

His mischeivous expression shifts to surprise the instant I make contact. I do the courtesy of withholding the full force of my fists, elbows, and kicks. After I nearly knock him to the ground in the first minute, he responds with more focused energy, cutting close and quick. Our feet trace patterns in the soft ground as the aggressive dance continues. He lands a hit and I land another until we are evenly bruised. I slide backward to take a breath, and he unexpectedly follows. His arm arcs low to swipe my abdomen. I block it and angle around his side. He keeps his footing, ducks behind me, and tugs one of my braids.

Our audience hollers at his audacity. He circles away from me, instantly regretting the public display. His eyes widen as I lunge forward, seething. My shoulder collides with his torso, and I hear his lungs expel. The bank dips out from under us. Cold water rises upward. In a fit of splashing, Halstaer attempts to roll over me, but he is slow moving and breathless. I scrabble against the shallow water. My hands dig into the mud below. I almost throw a clump, but that would be no better than pulling hair. I catch one of his wrists, halfway pin a leg.

"Yield! I yield!"

He stops thrashing and hangs his head, signally submission.

"*Iesh*!" he coughs. "I said yield, Nhu. Depths."

I let him go but do not leave him. The acans on the bank, either seeing the fight has ended or sensing their intrusion, steadily return to the party. Halstaer finds his feet.

"That did not feel very friendly," he accuses.

"You pulled my hair."

He sheepishly wrings out his braids. "A regrettable reflex."

"Get it in check. Along with your tongue."

"You're mad about earlier. About what I said."

"We're not standing in a stream because I'm pleased with you."

Water drips down his throat, highlighting the movement of a heavy swallow. "I'm sorry," he tells me. "Truly. I didn't mean to undermine you like that. I didn't mean to say anything at all."

"But you *did* say something."

He thoughtfully nods.

"Look," I say, "I love you, but—"

"—But you're my Ashacan," he realizes. "That complicates the love part."

Weaknesses. Rifts.

"I get it," Halstaer continues. "You need to be able to order me toward danger, and believe me, that's not a problem. I'd run into a dweller's mouth if it would protect you and everyone else."

"Then what is the problem?"

He spreads his hands. "You're the one who has to deal with the consequences."

"I can handle consequences."

"Alone?"

"I'm not alone. I have a vashte'rae."

"A vashte'rae that needs to see your strength, which means any weakness, any moment of doubt you have must be kept private. That's what you have to deal with alone—the darkest moments. It *will* change you, Nhuaela. The idea of that..." his tone softens. "I don't want you to face it alone."

I look at the water. Its gentle current grows chill around my thighs. I hide a shiver and hear my mother's order resound in my mind. *Show him you can do better.*

I wade to him. "As long as you're my second, I won't face anything alone, but I need you to trust that I'm going to be fine. Because if I

couldn't handle being Ashacan, the caracosh would have grabbed someone else."

After a moment he comes forward. He takes my hand. Lifts it. Kisses
it quick. It is a formal display, like my mother kissing the hand of Elder
Tolorian, but it feels private.

"C'mon," Halstaer says, dropping my hand. "It's cold. I can still have
a drink with my Ashacan, can I not?"

"You can have one."

Together, we climb up the bank and gather our things from the dirt.
I carry my boots, not wanting to pull them onto my wet feet. The spars
promptly ended following ours, and the party turned to dance instead.
Over the din of voices cut the rapid notes of Beshtel's fiddle. I catch a
glimpse of her twirling through the dancers. The gold streaks in her hair
glimmer in the firelight.

At the edge of dancers, we meet Frae, the oldest acan. He drinks from
a cup and upon noticing me, offers a drink. I take a swig of the biting
wine before passing it to Halstaer. He hangs onto it for a time, sipping
generously.

"Gods and dragons," Frae observes us. "You're soaked to the bone."

"I fell into the stream," Halstaer replies. "Thankfully, our Ashacan
was there to rescue me."

Frae turns to me. I shrug. My shirt and pants cling uncomfortably to
my skin.

"The Ashan see that happen?" he asks.

"Wasn't paying attention to who was watching," I say.

"Almost forgot he was here," Halstaer adds. "Where's he been?"

"Haven't seen him since midday," Frae answers. "He made his rounds
then vanished into the woods—doesn't seem the type to enjoy a party,
though, being Daervish and all."

"My father is Daervish," I remind the old hunter. "He likes a party."

Frae chuckles. "Selejor isn't Daervish."

"I think I would know."

He huffs in disagreement.

"Nhu!" Beshtel calls, skipping to the edge of dancers. She holds her fiddle and bow like extensions of her arms. Some of the hairs of her bow have snapped from the intensity of her playing and sweat dampens her temples. She tucks her bow under arm and teases the cup of wine from Halstaer's grip while looking at me. Not being an acan, she can call me by name. I remember a time when I was saddened that she had no interest in being a hunter. Since becoming Ashacan, though, I'm glad to have a friend detached from formalities of rank.

In one gulp she swallows whatever remains in the cup. Then she sighs and moves to rest her head on my shoulder. She does not care to ask why my hair drips water onto her cheek. "Your father's gonna kill me," she says. "Can't keep up with the man. I finish one song and he asks for another."

"Stop playing, then," Frae suggests.

Beshtel answers the old hunter without lifting her head. "I *like* fiddling with my bow, just as much as you acans like to fiddle with yours."

"Rest a moment. Ignore my father," I tell her.

"I am resting," she mumbles into my shoulder. "Nudge me when everyone begins to look bored."

It is not long before my father cuts through the mingling tribe. His hair is wildly loose from dance. Only the two thin braids keeping it from his face. His confused expression breaks the moment his eyes land on Beshtel leaning on my shoulder.

"Ah," he realizes. "I've done it again, haven't I? I'm sorry, I get so caught up in your music I forget how exhausting it must be."

"Just a little more time," Beshtel replies, "then you may have another song."

"Nonsense. We have voices, do we not?"

"You're going to keep dancing? Without my notes?"

His eyes dart to me, reading my wet hair and tense muscles in a glance. "Some of us need a good dance still."

"Mm..." Beshtel grunts as he peels her away from me.

"Have a nice rest right over here," my father says, guiding her to Halstaer. She leans into him just as she did to me, equally comfortable with both our shoulders. My father gives a diplomatic nod to Halstaer, seeming to understand why he and I are wet and standing with Frae between us.

Then, my father addresses everyone nearby. "Get a song going!" he encourages. "Giama! I want to hear your fine voice."

It takes no more convincing for her to clear her throat and find a tune. She picks a familiar song known to all the vashte'rae, one with a swift tempo. My father disregards the rhythm as he leads me, soaked and shoeless, to the center of the clearing. He lets me choose a slow, swaying pace although the song calls for a quicker step.

"You look just as tired as Beshtel," he notes.

"It's been a long day."

"You can stand on my toes if you'd like."

"And break them?"

"You're not that heavy, my dear. Although, I have heard you know how to throw your weight around." He pinches the tight muscle at my collar bone, and I feel it loosen. "It must have been a hard hit."

"I feel bad."

"He'll be fine," he says about Halstaer and then adds, "You'll both be fine."

We dance quietly for a time. The singing continues, lacking the swift elegance of the fiddle, yet sounding far more pleasant to my ears. The swirling dancers around us bring me comfort, my father's hands a steady warmth. He takes the lead and guides me in a larger arc opposite everyone else. As we spin, time seems to slow. I catch sight of Halstaer laughing, one hand on Frae's shoulder while the old man sloshes lickthorn from his cup. Beshtel tunes her fiddle beside Elder Tolorian who has taken rest beside her. He leans near her deft fingers and smiles widely when she plays a fresh note. Children run between the dancers and scale nearby trees to gain a better vantage point.

"You've found your step," my father mentions between breaths, and I realize I have taken the lead.

I slow our pace.

"Oh, don't do that," he protests.

"I should return to my duties. What will the Ashan think if he sees me dancing instead of guarding against dwellers?"

"He'd think you sensible."

I bring us to a halt near the treeline. Just beyond the trees an acan calmly paces. I look back to my father's dark gaze, happy to have had a dance. "There are monsters out there that need watching."

His smirk fades, and for an instant, the creases at the corners of his eyes appear deep with age.

"What is it?" I ask.

"Nothing. I'm only sad our dance has ended. But you are quite right." Quickly, he kisses my forehead. When he pulls back, his smile has returned. He humbly gestures toward the woods. "You have monsters to hunt, my acan."

I find my axes and boots before heading to my tent to exchange my wet pants for a dry pair. The dirt and forest debris easily brushes off my calloused feet. As I ready myself to walk the perimeter, I keep watch on the distant dancers. My mother soon joins my father's side. He pulls her into an intimate dance, and the music slows in response.

The sounds and light of camp become muffled behind the layers of trees as I walk the first length of the camp. The dark of the forest is alive, breathing in the wind that rustles the high canopy. What moonlight seeps through the branches illuminates my eyes. I see through the thinner shadows to the crevasses between—the depth of the wood, the hidden life within it. The *vashte* are black slashes in the dark, and the meager moonlight catches on their jagged bark like dew upon thorns.

I take a hunter's step, silent and careful while listening beyond the usual sounds of the forest. It's not uncommon for our presence to draw the interest of beasts, but this close to the southern border, I'm more concerned about humans. They know well enough not to venture into the Gatewood at night, but in two hundred some years, I have learned humans are not averse to risk.

An irregular rustling of undergrowth instantly calls my attention through the dark. Ahead of me on the path, a shadowed acan steps toward the sound, equally alert.

I whistle low in her direction, and she turns her head to me. I lift a hand, telling her to wait. She acknowledges with a nod.

For a moment, the rustling continues, followed by the heavy snap of twigs. The clumsiness of the racket does not speak of a predator, and after a moment, I hear the cadence of hushed voices.

The acan and I share a look. Her shoulders slump with a sigh and she shakes her head, likely disappointed with the false danger. I wave her back to her post and silently pursue the voices—young voices, two boys and a girl, hushing each other louder than they speak.

They are just far enough from the perimeter to be of concern, bickering beside the edge of utter darkness where the forest canopy thickens, preventing any moonlight from permeating. I recognize Elik, Giama's son, clutching a wineskin while the other two look warily into the trees.

"Go on," the girl—Daiva, now that I see her face turn—presses Elik. "You said you weren't afraid."

"I'm not!"

"Then prove it."

"You said you're gonna be the next acan," the other boy accuses, "but you're scared of the dark!"

"Shh—shut up!" he stumbles over the words, then takes another drink from the wineskin, knotting his face as he does so. "I don't see either of you...going in there."

Daiva bravely takes up the challenge and puts one toe into the real darkness. From deep in the forest comes a low, echoing roar. All three children freeze.

I snap a stick in hand.

They startle at the sound from behind and spin toward me. Daiva shrieks. Elik stumbles and falls into shadow. The second boy backs against a tree.

"It's only a rhougl," I inform them of the noise, letting my snapped stick fall. Their expressions shift from terror to relief and then worry at my presence.

"Asha..." Elik rights himself. "Ashhagon?"

"What are you doing out here?"

"Elik said he wasn't scared of the forest at night, but we didn't believe him, so we came out here to make him prove it," the second boy blurts out.

"We also thought maybe we'd find some humans," Daiva adds.

I walk closer to them. "And how did you get past the perimeter?"

They all share a quiet look.

"You're already in trouble," I remind them.

Daiva sighs. "We waited for the acans to change shifts, and then we used the trees."

I nod, inwardly admiring their cleverness, and remembering a time when I would use the same tactic.

"You all know better than to be outside the perimeter at night. You *should* be afraid of what lives in the dark."

"Like..." Elik lowers his voice. "Like the caracosh?"

I lean forward, ignoring his question. "What's in the wineskin?"

"...water."

I take it from him and smell its contents. "How much of this have you had?"

"Hardly any," Daiva answers for Elik.

"But hardly any was plenty," I note.

Elik nods.

"C'mon," I say, pulling him to his feet. "Head back. And if I catch any of you out here again, I'm going to make you spend the night in the dark."

I point toward camp and watch them until they are out of sight. The moment I'm alone, I take a drink from the wineskin, enjoying the lickthorn.

"Is drinking in the woods at night part of your duties?"

I tense at the voice that comes from behind. Unsure of what to say, I bid him good evening. *"Ai'shtanu, Ashan."*

"Ai'shtanu."

With the lickthorn filled waterskin in hand, I turn to face him. He stands a few steps off, only just visible at the edge of moonlight. A portion of his braids are messily knotted at the back of his head. Their tension highlights the sharp angle of his eyes and exposes the torn cartilage along his ear. He shifts and the shadows play across his face, briefly making his eyes appear like two slashed sockets in a skull.

"I was scouting southward," he explains before I can form the question. "It's been some time since I was this near the southern border. On my way back to camp I heard voices. Thought I'd investigate."

"Have you been standing there this whole time?"

"Yes, but dealing with disorderly children is not my specialty."

"They can't be that different from dwellers."

Between his mask and the darkness, his expression is lost to me. Uncomfortable with the silence, I experimentally offer him the wineskin. "Drink?"

A reprimand would suit his glare.

"You've been away from the festivities," I try. "I figured you might like a drink."

To my surprise, he pushes away from the trees, and takes the waterskin as he walks by. He looks in the direction of camp.

"I hope you recognize the inappropriateness of offering alcohol to your Ashan," he says, and with his back to me, he lifts a hand to tug his mask below his jaw. The hilts of the swords on his back block any view of his face as I try to sneak a glance. When he drinks, he tilts his head slightly left. Then he caps the wineskin and pulls his mask back into place.

"Is something wrong?" I ask.

"It has been a long day is all." He angles back to me, extending the wineskin.

"Keep it."

His arm lowers.

My feet remain rooted in place as I press for more. "Will you be returning to camp?"

"Yes, I need to rest. We leave early tomorrow."

"But you've only been here a day—not even."

He narrows his gaze in a curious manner. "Do you *want* us to stay?"

"No—I mean, sure. I don't mind. Elder Tolorian usually visits longer, is what I meant."

He nods thoughtfully. "Unfortunately, this is not a reprieve for us. We still need to pay the Nishtari a visit, and then I return north. As you said earlier, that is where I need to be."

I cringe, doubting he will soon forget my missteps.

"You should be on your way, Ashacan," he tactfully dismisses me.

Not wanting to mess up again, I take a few steps ahead of him. But then I stop and turn back. "May I ask—"

"You've been asking."

I hold back my words, realizing I've been far too informal.

After a pause he urges me to speak anyway. "What troubles you?"

"Do you think...could my becoming Ashacan relate to the increase in fractures?"

His eyes move between my face and caracosh necklace. "You are drawing parallels where there are none."

Something about his tone is wholly confident and reassuring, and yet it does not convince me. I step back in a half bow before leaving.

"Enjoy the lickthorn, Ashan."

The Long Hunt

THE SUDDENNESS OF THE Elder and Ashan's departure leaves me feeling dazed, as though they were never really here. In the coming days, the vashte'rae settles into routine, and I continue my duties as Ashacan. It is during the early hours of a foggy morning that I choose to wake Serin. I stand over his sleeping form as acans from the night watch return for an early meal. Some of them pause at the sight of me hovering near Serin, excitedly reading my intention.

Serin sleeps on the bare ground without bedroll or tent, away from his family. He has been doing so for the last year as part of his training to become an acan, and like any good acan, he manages to find comfort in the dewy underbrush of the Wood.

He has curled himself upon the drier ground against a branch. His arm is bent as his pillow, and his knees fold to his chest. Last night I excused him from his usual training, knowing he would need his strength for today.

With my boot, I give his leg a hearty shove. He startles awake, seeming to realize he should have done so when I first approached.

"Ashacan!" he blurts from sleep. He clumsily feels for his bow and quiver as he sits up. His instinct to grab his bow is self-taught, and I'm sure he will have no trouble proving himself.

"Ready yourself," I order. "It's time."

His tired eyes widen in understanding, and he rushes to obey. I turn away and begin to count the time it takes for him to prepare. My order sparks a new energy throughout the camp. Those who did not take the night to sleep quickly recognize the reasoning behind Serin's zeal. Excited whispers fall on sleeping ears. The Rendara wake at the sound of Serin's hurried steps. He scrambles to ready himself with catlike precision, running to his family's tent and then surefootedly weaving between obstructions of camp. A few Rendara cheer him on.

I'm halfway to the enclosure of our forest ponies when he emerges from his tent. He has changed his raggedy hide vest for a doeskin shirt and patched leather jacket. He wears a belt over his hide pants. From it hangs a scabbard and short sword. The strap of his quiver cuts diagonally across his chest, hugging his bundle of arrows in place between his shoulders.

He meets my scrutinizing gaze as I pass the center of camp. The pony pen is near, just beside the small clearing we used to dance. I lengthen my stride in challenge, and with bow in hand, he sprints. Little Sil toddles after him, shouting his name in encouragement.

It would be easy for me to beat him to the ponies, but that is not the point. This portion of the trial is for me to observe his efficiency and speed, his organization under pressure, not to prove I can outrun him. Still, it would reflect poorly on him if I were to reach the enclosure first. His goal is to be ready for me, not I for him.

In the past, the duties of Ashacan were divided between chieftain and several older acans. Together, they oversaw Long Hunts and decisions were made unanimously after discussion. Now, full responsibility falls to me. It is no other's business what I decide, when, or how. As Ashacan, I am guided by Evoriel to make the right choice, and the vashte'rae trusts in that choice.

Serin ducks through the ropes of the pony pasture as I drop a hand upon the entrance. Once inside, he frantically searches for me. He exhales with a relieved laugh once he sees me outside of the ropes. I take my time unknotting the rope entrance that crosses tightly between two closely grown trees. When I step into the pasture, Serin slings an arm through his bow and looks for a suitable pony to retrieve.

Nearby the pasture entrance, Halstaer waits with my pony's reins balanced over his shoulder. He is the only one I told that Serin's trial would begin today. I knew he would be willing to help. He agreed to meet me here, agreed to saddle Lo. Most importantly, he agreed to watch over the vashte'rae in my stead.

He smirks at Serin, who tries to catch a pony to no avail. They sense his nerves and dart away. At the edge of the pen, I notice horse-master Egen shaking his head at Serin's clumsy attempts to coax a pony into his reach.

"Whose job was it to teach him to properly catch a horse?" Halstaer asks me.

"He knows how. He just needs to realize it."

"He better realize it quick."

"Give him a moment. Do you remember when we took the trial? How we thought we were prepared, but when it came to it, we could hardly manage our adrenaline?"

He nervously knots Lo's reins. "I just want him to do well."

"You helped train him," I say, teasing the reins from his stiff grip. "He will be fine."

Lo steps toward me. He pushes his grey muzzle against my chest and takes in my scent. My father named him Lo for *sunlight*. Over the years, his coloring has tinged with white, and like all our faithful ponies, I will miss him when he is gone.

"Thanks for saddling him," I tell Halstaer. Normally, I would have done so myself, but I can better focus on Serin without the distraction of readying a horse. My saddle is laden with provisions to make my travel easy. Serin, however, is tasked with surviving without aid. His saddle will carry nothing but himself and the weapons he has chosen to bring.

Halstaer sucks air between his teeth. "Oh, depths. He caught Speckles."

"I told you he would figure it out."

"But Speckles likes to bite."

"He knows how to handle her."

The dark pony has a blanket of white spots upon her flanks and a tendency to pin her ears. Halstaer has scars in his forearm from her flat teeth. He worriedly looks on as Serin leads her.

"She's going to take off his arm," he frets. "Then you'll have to make her an acan instead."

I swing into Lo's saddle. "Her gait is smooth. He can easily shoot an arrow from her back. It's a wise choice."

I need to move on. Every moment I spend with Halstaer buys Serin extra time, but Halstaer rests his hand on my boot, keeping me from leaving just yet. He looks up at me from behind the loose strands of his hair.

"Take care of him, Ashacan," he says, and then squeezing my foot adds, "Take care of yourself."

I lightly touch his cheek. *"Zashtavah m'hash acan."*

The reverential phrase brings a dignified blush to his cheeks. In full, it means *go bravely, honored hunter.* It is the first time I have said it—the first time it holds weight.

Halstaer steps away and bows his head to me. I nudge Lo onward to the stream. Serin has until I reach the far bank to catch up. It will be a mark against him if he makes me wait. He has already saddled Speckles by the time I reenter the camp. The entire vashte'rae is now awake. They do not care for my progress as much as Serin's, although they are intrigued by the suddenness of the trial.

Before me, Long Hunts were planned and generally known amongst the Rendara. Keeping their imminence secret was nearly impossible when more than one acan knew about it. The tasks would be divided. When I completed my trial over one hundred years ago, I raced Frae to the ponies. On the hunt, an elder and another hunter observed. Upon my return, the three deliberated my success. As chieftain, my mother would normally take part in the discussion, but when I was the subject for debate, she abstained from all decisions. Still, she knew when the day for my trial would arrive and by extension, so did everyone else.

Today, I have taken them all off guard. I'm dressed for the part. My hatchets hang from either hip. I carry my bow and quiver on my back. My armor is leather and hide, the garb of an acan. I bathed in the night, knowing I will have no time to wash during Serin's hunt. I brushed my dark hair and braided it in a single, tight plait down the center of my scalp. I keep it pulled around one shoulder to avoid it snagging in the feathers of my arrows. My caracosh claw rests noticeably white against my chest. Lo plods along. He tucks his head and perks his ears, looking every bit the formidable pony I need him to be.

I hear Speckles' quick hooves encroaching from behind. My worry dissipates at the echo of cheers that lift Serin's name and wish him blessings on his hunt. With the vashte'rae at my back, I let slip a brief smile. Serin has trained tirelessly for this day. I anticipated this moment before I knew I would be the one to oversee it, and now that I have the privilege to do so, I cannot contain my excitement.

My father steps into my path. There remains a short distance to the stream, but with Serin following close, there can be no question of stalling as I halt Lo.

I sit tall on my pony, as tall as my father holds himself. He nearly stands in a sparring stance. One foot is slightly back, his body is angled, his hand rests on the hilt of his dagger. He is more stoic than I have ever seen him as he studies my place atop Lo.

"What are you doing?" he asks, the inquiry ending in his disapproving lilt.

"I'm overseeing Serin's hunt."

He looks behind me to where Serin waits and then back to me, one brow raised. "Is this really the best time for a hunt?"

"If I say so."

"I thought you wanted to handle the human conflict first."

"They will still be here when we return."

His black eyes glint in opposition. "I don't think this is wise."

I mean to demand why. He has never stood in my way so rigidly, and now of all times, is more than an annoyance. But then I hear my mother's voice.

"It is not your decision to make." She stands at the edge of the path, unaligned with my father or I. Her words are resolute. "The Ashacan has decided. We will trust that decision."

After an uncomfortable silence, he lowers his eyes. First to my mother and then to me. "Of course," he concedes. "Forgive me. I am being selfish."

When he steps aside, I feel a pang of guilt from the sorrowful smile that creeps onto his face.

"What kind of father would I be if I did not worry over my daughter's safety?" he proposes to those within earshot, drawing a response of hushed agreement.

I keep Lo still, unable to leave behind the disheartened look in my father's eyes.

"I'll be okay," I assure him, my irritation dissipating. "Serin will protect me."

"Will he now?" he wonders, eyeing the boy on his spotted pony.

Serin gives a confident nod.

My father gestures onward. "In that case, lead on."

Serin takes a breath before sending Speckles forward. Across the way, my father joins my mother's side. He rests one hand on her shoulder. The other remains on his dagger's hilt. He'd look very nonchalant if I did not know he was leaning into my mother for strength. I nearly ask what's wrong, but that is a question for his daughter—not the Ashacan—to ask.

"Evoriel guide you," my mother bids us farewell.

Lo instinctively follows Speckles. I put my focus fully on Serin, we cross the stream, and the Long Hunt begins.

* * *

Serin has seven days to prove himself worthy of being an acan. Within that time, he will demonstrate the extent of his skills in survival, his knowledge of Evoriel's land, and his mastery of it. He must track and hunt one of Evoriel's beasts, whatever it may be. My duty is to observe and ensure his survival, although should I need to interfere with the hunt, he will have failed with no chance to repeat it.

He rides ahead of me, making every decision. The only trail we take is the one he creates. In some places, the trees grow farther apart; but here, everything is close. Our ponies crush undergrowth and snap thin branches. I duck in my saddle to avoid scrapes from needly leaves or spider webs. Serin clears what is necessary from our path, but he wisely avoids the thickest of brambles or uneven slopes. Occasionally, he halts Speckles to listen or smell. He looks to the sky and shadows. There is no particular direction he must go. The hunt is his to command, but Evoriel will not present a worthy animal until the time is right.

I follow quietly, studying the choices Serin makes and those he does not. Lo is content to be on a simple journey. He gladly trails Speckles, head low, ears forward, a veteran of many hunts. Serin spins his pony within a gap of trees. She jerks her head and dances on her front legs. He keeps hold of her reins with one hand. His fingers clench and his hand shifts with minute movements, encouraging the feisty pony to spin as he surveys potential paths. His hold is firm but not harsh as he keeps her within his control, and when he decides a new path, he allows her to take the bit and continue on.

"This way, Ashacan," he shouts back to me, grinning with all the confidence in the world.

"Are you sure you don't want to go right?"

"Toward Nishtari land? Depths, no."

It's not a response for me to judge, but I'm proud of him just the same. His path turns northeast toward the territory of the red-toothed-king.

* * *

It's late night by the time we make camp. While I tend to Lo, Serin scouts the woods nearby and establishes a perimeter, taking over my usual duties. His chosen resting place is decent. We have long since entered the dark of the Wood. In its depth, moonlight struggles to penetrate the canopy and only a few specks dot the blackened waves of ground. Branches of strongwoods swoop downward, tremendous black tendrils

dashed in the faint glow of stars far, far above. At their tops are splotches of giant-winged rhougls, bat-like creatures that scavenge the forest's
dead.

Serin clears a patch of ground and builds a small fire. The few flames
push back the immediate dark, and the ponies shift toward the comforting light. There is a chance an unwanted threat could be drawn
toward the light, but it seems unlikely. I've listened closely to the Wood
all day, took in its scents and sounds. The ponies have not stirred at the
unknown, and neither have I. Once Serin settles, I look at him from
across the fire.

"So, you want a king-bear," I say.

His eyes dart to me as though I've discovered a well-guarded secret.

"They're dangerous, you know."

"I didn't come on this hunt planning to kill a deer," he insists.

"I'm not criticizing. I just want to make sure you're aware of the risk,
so I can know if I must prepare to rescue you or not."

He scowls. "I know what I'm doing."

"Good. I don't want to get near one of those things unless I have to."

I turn my attention to the cluster of averlin buds I plucked earlier,
giving Serin a moment to hide his concern for my comment. It's not my
place to console him now.

"Do you not think I can do it?" he presses.

"I'll think nothing until I've seen it done. Anyone can kill anything,
but whether you can or cannot kill a very lethal predator when you've
never killed one before remains to be seen."

His annoyed tone turns curious. "What was your target during your
hunt?"

"An echoer."

"Oh."

"Does that disappoint you?"

"I just thought you'd have hunted something more...grand."

I repress a laugh. "You're not old enough to have ever encountered an echoer."

"Aren't they just big cats? Up in the Zurranis?"

"They are *just big cats* about as much as a redtooth-king is *just a bear*," I tell him. "They perch high on the cliff walls camouflaged against the stone, and you don't know they're about to leap until there's a dusting of pebbles falling from above. Those little rocks echo so loud in the quiet." I pause, reminiscing before locating my words again. "By the time you notice, it's too late. They can't be outrun or outclimbed, and they'll snap your spine by crushing or catching you in their bite. You have no choice but to fight."

"All right, I get it."

"I might have killed a king-bear," I admit, "but at the time, we were camping with the Elesaan. Echoers were closer, and there were plenty of them."

"So, it wouldn't make sense for *me* to try to hunt one," Serin notes. "But a king-bear..."

"There are plenty of suitable beasts in this forest. Why is it you want a king?"

He looks down at the toes of his boots. "Well, they have the most impressive teeth and..."

"And?"

"You're going to laugh."

"I'm an unbiased Ashacan. I will not laugh."

He leans forward and rests his chin on his knees. His yellow eyes lock onto me like an echoer's in the night. "Halstaer killed a king during his Long Hunt. He told me about it the first day he showed me how to string a bow. Ever since then, I've wanted to do the same. I want to go home and have my mother be proud. To have Sil wonder at the size of a king's redtooth. To have her look up to me the way I look up to—" he stops himself and looks away, abashed. "Don't tell him I said that."

"I think he already knows that."

Serin lifts his head.

"It's why he knew how to prepare you so well."

"He told me where to find king territory," Serin confesses.

I nod.

"Are you mad?"

"No, because he also taught you how to shoot."

"Does that mean you think I can do it?"

"If I did not think you could manage, we would not be here. Now get some rest, or you'll never kill a king."

* * *

One must be very brave and a bit stupid to hunt a king bear without extensive experience. Evoriel decides what beast is presented during the Long Hunt. If a young hunter is unworthy of their chosen prey, it will not show. By the end of Serin's fifth day, I begin to worry a king bear is not his destined target.

His gradual loss of excitement tells me he shares the same fear. His shoulders grow tense, and he pushes the ponies hard to our final camp deep in redtooth-king territory. It's my wish to warn him away, to advise him to seek easier game, but it is not my place to say. He must come to that realization on his own.

The trees grow thicker, unrulier. Dark mosses cover their bark. Their roots rise above ground looking like fat, roiling snakes. The ground swells in mounds as though the tree roots have gripped too tightly. No tall grasses or pleasant flowers grow. Not enough light breaches the blanket of leaves to provide for such pleasantries. There is a chill in the air and a clamminess to everything I touch. The ponies lift their heads to the shadows of the woods. Just off our chosen path, the multitude of greens, mosses, and creeper vines seem to move in enchanted motions. They vaguely pulsate, smothering what lies beneath.

An old power stirs. To me, a familiar power. I have sensed it before, or rather, it sensed me. In my periphery, leaves rustle and roots stretch. Branches groan. The wind whispers. I keep a vigilant eye, waiting. When I faced the caracosh, it came to me in a similar manner—summoned by the old power through the unperceivable partition of realms. It existed as god and beast. Hunter and hunted.

Serin does not seem to sense Evoriel's presence as I do. His hold on Speckles has become too hard, agitating her. Ahead, the ground rises in a treacherous wall, and she refuses to find footing upon the steep rise. The roots are firm but the mosses between may crumble into leg snapping shallows. Speckles rears slightly, snorting her disapproval.

"*Iesh!*" Serin swears at his pony. "Stubborn *rihar!*" He turns her away, circling her around the small space of flat ground before the impassable lichen wall.

Lo shifts uncomfortably from one hoof to the other. I put a calming hand to his bony withers.

"Aagh!" Serin huffs, finally coming to the obvious conclusion. Speckles calms the farther he retreats from the wall.

"What's the plan?" I ask, keeping my voice low.

"I guess we'll camp here," he decides. "It should do for the ponies. I suppose I'm meant to complete the hunt on foot, anyway."

"Perhaps that is Evoriel's way of reminding you," I say, nodding at the mound.

His shoulders slouch. He hasn't eaten enough in the last days, nor given thought to Evoriel's wishes. The exhaustion has caught up with him.

Rest, I want to order. *Recover and rethink.*

He dismounts.

I follow his lead. Lo exhales at the absence of my weight. From one of my saddlebags, I pull a sweet carrot. Halstaer wisely packed the treats, and they instantly brighten Lo's mood. He momentarily forgets about the eerie forest around us.

Serin longingly stares at the decadent treat. Personally, I have never cared for the taste of sweet carrots, although if I had not eaten more than the sap from bark in the past days, I imagine any morsel of food would look tempting.

I give Lo a second carrot and then a third to Speckles. It is cruel but necessary. Serin should have known better than to forgo meals simply because he could.

"You torture me, Ashacan," he mumbles.

I rummage through another bag and pull out a bundle of pink-veined leaves. I offer them to him. "Here. Have a snack."

He takes the bundle, examines it, and glares. He throws the leaves across the clearing. "Halstaer tricked me into eating scratch-weed once, and I'll never do it again."

I laugh, distinctly recalling the evening Halstaer shared the story of his prank.

"You're meaner than I thought," Serin says.

"I'm just checking to see if you still have sense in your head."

"I'm hungry, not delusional."

"Scratch-weed *is* edible," I inform him.

"Yeah, if I want to feel like there's sand in my throat. Not to mention the way it itches...uh...everything else." He begins to untack Speckles. "I'm going to hunt. Do you have to come with me?"

I'm not worried about his ability to find dinner as much as a king bear picking up his scent.

"I trust you can hunt your own dinner," I tell him, sensing he needs some time alone, "but stay close, and be back before dark. And remember, it won't count if you kill a bear without me there to see it."

"I *know*."

I mean to reprimand his tone, but he quickly vanishes into the woods.

* * *

It may not have been entirely right for me to send Serin off alone, but he would not be on the Long Hunt if he did not know how to handle himself. Even in the darkest corners of the wood, it's important he experiences moments alone. Should a king bear or another threat arise, he is well-equipped to properly react. At the very least, he has two good legs to run on. Still, I made note of which direction he went.

In the meantime, I try to connect with the essence of the Gatewood. There are many magics in the world. Certain places are rife with power. While I have no intimate understanding of such things, I still sense the presence of them as one would feel a breeze on their face. Under the ancient branches I am small, less like a protector of Evoriel's forest, and more like another link within its composition.

I keep our camp confined within a dish of roots and tie the ponies near a modest fire. Flames will not dissuade a curious beast, nor will they change a bear's ability to smell our presence. Light or dark, the same danger remains. For two hours I wait with my bow in my lap, an arrow nocked. My hatchets lay within reach. I hate to leave the ponies without protection, but as darkness closes in, I regret letting Serin hunt without me.

A whistle reaches my ears before the sound of footsteps. The pitch is not as loud or piercing as one of Halstaer's notes, but the tune is the same. I set my bow aside as Serin announces his presence. A moment later, he comes into view of the firelight.

A squirrel hangs in his hand. He sits down heavily, drops his bow, and tears into the animal with his knife. Not all the fur is stripped before he skewers the squirrel and balances it over the fire. He watches it cook in anticipation.

"You're late," I say.

"It's only just gotten dark."

I judge the ratty quality of his squirrel. "It's been several hours. All that time just to kill one measly squirrel?"

He avoids eye contact. "I may have been scouting too."

"So, doing what I told you not to do?"

"You said no hunting," he retorts, "I wasn't hunting."

"You were tracking."

"Yeah, but that's not the same."

"Tracking leads you to a target, and once you find that target what happens? A deer will flee. So will a squirrel. But you weren't looking for a deer or squirrel, were you?"

He does not answer.

"Serin, if you had tracked down a king bear, it would not have fled. You are in its territory with an intent to kill, and it knows. Once you meet one, that will be it. No hesitation. No backing down or sneaking back to camp. Your first encounter will also be the last and attempting it without me is both reckless and invalid."

His frustration boils over. "I had to try!" he shouts. "It's been five days. Five! I thought I would have found a king by now, or at least caught a trail, but there's nothing. I only have two days left, Ashacan, and right now I don't know if I can do it. I...I feel like I've already failed."

"Two days is plenty of time." *Plenty of time to reevaluate and hunt an easier beast.*

He shakes his head, seeming to understand my unsaid advice. "It has to be a redtooth-king."

"Says who?"

He stubbornly sets his jaw. "I kill a king, or I kill nothing."

There are several things I want to say in response, ranging from annoyance to words of comfort. All are too biased for an overseeing Ashacan, so I keep silent and allow him a moment to be angry. I can understand his stubbornness. It is a common trait for acans to be a bit pigheaded.

"I thought I was going to fail my trial to become Ashacan," I confess to him.

He has pulled his squirrel from the fire and chews the undercooked meat from feeble bones. Over the glistening carcass, he looks at me in disbelief. "No, you didn't."

"I did," I insist. "Now that I think about it, it was very similar to completing the Long Hunt. There was more risk involved, but I went into it the same. I was excited and desperate to prove myself, especially since my father is the one who accompanied me. Turns out I completely underestimated Evoriel's task, and even after I had killed the caracosh, I was positive everyone would somehow be dismayed."

"Why?"

"I didn't feel I deserved it."

"But you killed the caracosh, right?"

"Yes."

"Then how could you feel like you failed?"

"I imagined it going differently. I thought I might fight valiantly without doubt, without fear, but the reality was quite...messy."

It felt wrong, like I had committed an atrocity rather than a predicted kill. But I do not tell Serin that detail. I don't mean to frighten him. Recounting the story awakens the memory of the caracosh. Not just the hunt, but the weeks of terror before Evoriel's menace deigned to show itself to one of the Rendara. In those weeks, we rarely slept. We did not move and built our fires high. The vashte'rae huddled close day and night. Children did not play. Beshtel did not fiddle. Giama did not sing. Hardly any words passed between us. No laughter, no jokes, only the shrill hunting whistles and an occasional, muffled gasp followed by the retraction of claws from flesh.

The summoned creature lurked in the shadows. It moved too quickly to distinguish and had the cry of tormented elves. Half our ponies were snatched from their corral. Anyone who ventured too far into the forest did not come back. It seemed every night another acan was lost in the creature's endeavor to find a suitable opponent.

My mother ordered the acans to stay close to camp, within sight of the fires. The caracosh had an aversion to flames, although the light did not stop it from testing our defenses. We guarded at the edge of shadows, each of us waiting for it to show itself. It toyed with us, seeking the one who could wound it and signify their worthiness to hunt. I was certain it would be Halstaer. In many ways, he seemed more fit for the rank. Many looked to him for guidance, even the older hunters. I was eager to see the caracosh show itself to him and was distracted from the section of forest I was meant to be watching.

"I saw when it dragged you into the trees," Serin interrupts the memory.

I meet his eyes, not having realized I shared the terrifying moment with another.

"It was quick," he continues. "I had been arguing with my mom. I wanted to join the acans in guarding the camp, and she refused to let me. She even told Chief I was trying to sneak into the acan ranks; you know how protective she's become since my dad died." He pensively rolls a squirrel bone between his forefinger and thumb. His father was killed while serving in the north not long before the caracosh arrived. For him, it was a dark stretch of time. "It was humiliating," he continues, "so I stormed off. Well, as far as I could go without leaving the camp because at that point, Chief was watching me like a hawk."

"I know the look."

"I remember seeing you standing guard. Pacing, actually. I wanted to talk to you. I thought maybe you could convince Chief to let me help."

"I certainly would not have," I tell him firmly.

"I guess it was a good thing she was watching me. If she wasn't, it would've just been me that saw you get snatched. All I saw was a glimpse of a clawed hand and then you were gone. Believe me, after seeing you vanish, I realized I would have made a useless guard. If it could grab you, it probably would have killed me.

"For a time, we thought you were dead. Chief tried to follow, but she couldn't find you, and your father had to bring her back before she was taken too. Not much later, you emerged from the trees far from where you were guarding. You were limping and dazed, but you seemed so calm."

"It was shock, not calm," I say, remembering little of my return. Aside from the most pertinent details, much is a blur due to my head hitting the ground as my legs were yanked out from under me. I had no time or thought to break my fall. The full weight of my body slammed against the ground, and then I was dragged into the night. I was lucky not to have been knocked out, otherwise I would have had no chance at all.

One of the caracosh's claws had wrapped around my ankles, but I never managed a good look at the creature until it let me go. It was unlike any of Evoriel's worldly creations. The caracosh was a monster from a nightmare summoned to test our strength—our ability to overcome fear.

As I laid on the Gatewood floor, the caracosh allowed me a moment to look upon it. Its form was vaguely elven in that it had two arms, two legs, and a haunting elegance, but it certainly was no elf. The monster was larger than any king bear or echoer. Its limbs were unnaturally long and crooked. Two elongated arms clutched the trees. Its white claws gouged into the bark, splintering the trunks like twigs. The legs were thin and disturbingly bent, its body emaciated and long, and the head was a flat shell atop a wide jaw that glimmered with countless silver fangs. Its face was featureless aside from two fractured slashes in place of eyes. They were hollows of darkness, and yet I could feel them watching me intently.

I tug at the claw necklace, lift it, study it for a moment. It's not the white of bone, nor does it possess the thin cracks of horn. The surface is smooth like a polished stone with a dull sheen. It seems smaller than it did upon the hand of the caracosh.

"How did you escape it?" Serin asks.

"I shot it in the eye."

It lunged at me an instant after I saw its full form. I dodged aside and drew my bow. I was lucky to have not dropped it. The arrow pierced through the back of the caracosh's skull, but it was not a wound suffi-cient enough to kill. For a caracosh, the first wound is only an acceptance of the challenge. Whether the rank of Ashacan is desired or not, surviving an attack by the monster establishes one's worth to hunt it. It is an honor bestowed by Evoriel, and no acan would turn it down.

"It retreated with my arrow through its skull, and I was free to return to camp."

Once the caracosh abandoned me in the forest, I made the disorienting walk back. I remember stumbling over the uneven ground. One of my ankles was sprained from the grip and pull of claws. There were neat slices around my calves. I'm not sure how I knew what direction to go. It must have been instinct. When I returned, healer Shayv ran to meet me. He took my face in his hands to dull my pounding head. My mother came next, and then Halstaer and the rest of the vashte'rae, each demanding to know what happened until my father took my hand and ushered me away.

"You still killed a caracosh. That doesn't sound like failure to me," Serin reasons. The bitterness in his voice brings me back to the present, away from memory. Remembering why I brought the story up, I drop the claw and refocus on the tired boy across from me.

"I made many mistakes on my hunt," I tell him. "Clumsy mistakes. Things I had done a thousand times before but suddenly couldn't get right."

"And how did you fix them?"

"I realized my task was not all about hunting or fighting, my knowledge of how to build a fire, ride a pony, skin a deer—knowing what plants would burn my throat," I say with a pointed look. "None of it mattered to my Hunt. They were important things, yes, but they were also things anyone could learn. But the trial was not meant for just anyone."

"It was meant for you."

"For an *acan*," I correct. "Evoriel wasn't simply testing to see if I could kill another beast. He was waiting for me to prove I understood the true mark of an acan, that I could recognize it and trust it."

"What was it?"

I let his question hang in the firelight. The ponies swish their tails. Somewhere in the branches a group of rhougls growl. The old magic of the Wood breathes, and I remember what my father told me as I held my punctured abdomen after slitting the caracosh's throat.

"This hunt is not about killing," I repeat his words to Serin. "You do not survive by killing your enemy, but by enduring while they still live. That is what you must remember."

He sinks back, and I see myself in him. Mere months before, I was similarly frustrated against the roots of a strongwood with my father, the Rendara's Witness, sitting across from me. Silent and perfectly impartial, his countenance haunted me more than the caracosh. Even when the caracosh had me pinned to a tree, its claws slicing into the sides of my neck, I saw my father in the distance, leaning against a dark *vashte*, unblinking.

I lay back upon the bed of the Gatewood, eyes closed and return myself to the dance when my father held me steady, spinning me away from my troubles. And I hide away the memory of the caracosh once more.

* * *

The fire has flickered out by the time dawn breaks. The ponies begin to stir, made restless by the silent forest. I wait for Serin to give an eventual order for us to move on.

During the night, he paced around our camp, pausing for long amounts of time at various positions. He spent most of the time standing at the base of the mound of forest floor. He scaled it from various angles.

His nimble hands and feet had no trouble finding purchase in the nooks of slippery roots, but the dexterity required is not within our ponies' abilities. I half expected him to risk leaving our mounts unattended in favor of seeking more promising ground, but he carefully returned to the cold fireside and has not moved since.

The sound of wings rustles the leaves above. A quail flaps its wings in distress, as though it has just realized it is lost in an unfamiliar part of the Wood. Almost without thought, Serin raises his bow and shoots the bird from its branch. The time it takes for him to ready an arrow, aim, and make a clean shot happens quicker than my tired eyes can see.

The bird hits the ground at my feet. I try to keep an impressed look off my face as Serin claims the quail and wordlessly begins to gut and pluck it. Most elves know how to wield a bow. It is a required skill for soldiers, a natural ability to most, but as with any weapon, there are those who are far more gifted at wielding it.

Halstaer taught Serin and helped his talent flourish. The boy may be at the point where he shoots better than any of the Rendara. His skills with a sword are lacking, which concerns me when it comes to hunting a redtooth-king.

"Do you have an agenda for the day?" I ask with the hope of urging him to consider the finer details of his hunt.

He continues to pluck his quail. "I'm going to eat breakfast."

"And then?"

He shrugs.

"You may want to consider hunting something other than quail."

"I'm considering other things first, like you said I should do. And look." He lifts the quail. "Evoriel answered."

"Could be coincidence."

"I don't think so."

"Either way, I wouldn't count on a king bear falling from the branches."

"Maybe not the *branches*," he mutters.

I say nothing more. He seems to have taken my subtle guidance to heart, although perhaps too literally. I hold my tongue and go about my own morning routine, keeping Serin within sight in case a king bear should aimlessly wander from the trees.

He finishes his breakfast and spends several more hours canvassing the area. He moves the ponies to a different thicket with access to fresh foliage to keep them happy, and then takes some time to complete a series of balancing exercises. Eventually he returns to the tree he claimed as a temporary seat during the night, opposite the mounded ground.

He keeps his sword close but does not care for it as he does his bow. One hand curls around the supple wood, and the forefingers of his other caresses the string. It is constructed of dark vashte wood, made by his own hand.

It is said the vashte were created during the height of Vhanian rule two-thousand years ago. Evoriel planted the trees throughout his lands to protect woodelves who fled enslavement from the Vha. They are said to act as shields much like an Ashacan.

The vashte from which Serin's bow came was found on the border of Rendaran and Nishtari land. The sacred tree fell naturally. If it had been purposely cut, any bow crafted from its wood would be cursed to never bend. As word spread of the opportunity to take the wood, both Rendara and Nishtari swarmed to its location.

I did not care for the fallen tree. Bows not being my favored weapon, I knew I was not amongst the deserving of the fine wood. Still, I went with a group of acans, knowing there would be Nishtari to challenge and brawls to be had. None of us anticipated Serin joining. At the time, he had not yet begun his training, but Halstaer insisted the boy come to distract him from the death of his father.

Serin was shier then. He followed Hastaer like a lost dog and kept his arms crossed over his chest, eyes down. It took us all by surprise when Halstaer led Serin through the bickering group of acans.

A Nishtari girl had just baited me into a fight. *Why are you here?* she demanded of me. *I didn't think your fat Rendaran hands were capable of holding a bow, let alone one made of vashte.*

Halstaer and Serin's appearance is the only thing that stopped me from showing that Nishtari acan exactly what damage my Rendaran hands could do. With Serin trailing close behind, Halstaer parted the tribes, and we momentarily forgot our conflict. He took a moment to examine the fallen vashte and then placed a foot on a narrow branch. None would have thought much of Halstaer claiming a piece, but when Serin began to make his cut, the Nishtari acans fumed.

Halstaer quietly stood as Serin's shield while the Nishtari accosted him. Some tried to grab Serin and shove him away, which incited the Rendara to intervene. I found my place beside Halstaer as Serin's second shield.

Since that day, I have never seen Serin without his vashte bow. Even now, he holds it gingerly, looking down on it rather than the forest he should be scouring for redtooth-kings. In the moment, I ignore what I'm expected to do and act as my father did for me.

"Serin," I curtly say his name.

He calmly lifts his gaze to meet mine. "Yes?"

"Get up and go find your bear."

"With respect, Ashacan, I can't."

"Why not?"

"Because I've already found it."

I glance over my shoulder to make sure one has not crept up on me. The trees are still. "Have you reached the point of delusion?"

"No, I just realized you were right." He gestures with the tip of his bow toward the forest wall. "I don't think I'm meant to climb it. I don't think I'm meant to pass it. This is it, Ashacan. This is exactly where I'm meant to be, and Evoriel has literally placed a wall in my way to tell me so."

"I see no bear."

"It'll come...I think."

"You think?"

He resolutely hugs his bow to his chest. "I know it."

I study the wall, as though I might find an answer there, but I cannot understand what the Gatewood has revealed to Serin's mind.

"All right," I assent, "but you better not be wrong. You're far too talented to not become an acan. You know there will not be another chance."

His eyelids flutter. I cannot tell if he is falling asleep or entering some meditative state. Rather than make my unsettled nerves known, I approach the upraised ground. A latticework of roots compacts the dirt within. Here and there are hovels burrowed by small animals and insects. Spider webs drape over crumbled ground and the moss-covered roots are slick with evening dew. The obstruction stands twice as tall as me, certainly passable, but only with careful effort.

I move back toward Serin. Should I have the privilege of naming him acan, it will be years still before he is considered a seasoned hunter. His skill with a bow foretells a promising future. It pains me to think he might flounder.

"Serin..."

I do not know what I mean to say, but a crunch in the woods behind cuts me off before I can blabber more. I shut my mouth at the noise, and Serin's eyes snap open, wider than I have ever seen them. He shouts something as I turn a moment too late, and a crushing weight descends upon me.

A single paw grinds through my leathers and traps me against the ground. It lingers for an instant before pressing down and shoving away. Two claws dig between my shoulder blades. They puncture armor and skin as they pull away. A guttural roar reverberates through the wood, shaking loose leaves and twigs from the branches above.

The king has no interest in me. Its movements are agile and quick as it launches toward Serin. The moment its weight lifts, I push myself up. Its paw expelled the air from my lungs. I gasp while trying to orient myself, my hatchets drawn.

Serin dives sideways and the king's jaws tear a chunk from the tree he had been leaning against. I'm glad to see his bow still in his hand. He breathlessly gazes upward at the massive bear as it shakes splinters of wood from its mouth.

I have not seen a redtooth-king in many years. Serin's frightful stare is an accurate representation of how I felt when faced with my first true predator—a mixture of terror and awe. The feeling returns to me now, although not nearly as strong. I have mind enough to observe without hindrance of fear. It's imperative I have a clear head should my interference be required.

This king has the look of a normal bear, but its proportions are far larger. Its fur is grey and flecked with hints of red, the same shade as its fangs from which it takes its name. Its lip curls to reveal the fangs' full length.

Serin dodges once more as the bear charges. He missed his brief chance to attack after the bear careened into the tree. I see him thinking quickly. Panic sets in his eyes, but he works to gather himself. Each time he rolls or leaps out of the bear's path, he gains nerve.

The king ignores me and the squealing ponies that pull at their ties. It is a relentless hunter, but Serin is no helpless prey. He'd stand no chance if he were to run. The king bounds across the clearing in two strides, aiming to crush Serin against the wall of root and dirt. He does not dive aside. In the sparse seconds before his body will be clamped in the king's jaws, he stands his ground. The bear lets out another roar as Serin grabs a jutting root above his head and flips himself upward onto the wall. The bear skids to a halt and angles its body to absorb the impact. The entire forest seems to rumble at the tumult. Serin steadies himself atop the mound, unable to nock an arrow without stable footing. The king wastes no time righting itself and scales the wall in one leap.

Serin jumps as the bear takes a swipe. The claws clip his side, tearing his shirt like a leaf. He hits the ground and rolls to his feet, releasing an arrow. The shaft sticks in the bear's side, just beneath a front leg. The beast flinches, causing a ripple to quiver through its silvery fur. It takes pause to look at Serin. The king ignores the arrow in its side and climbs down to level ground. Serin circles with the beast, their eyes locked.

I resist the urge to yell for him to get his sword that he left on the ground. By now it has been trampled several times beneath the king's paws. It's surely bent, if not broken, but it will take more than one arrow to bring down such a massive animal. Still, Serin seems to have forgotten the usefulness of his sword and relies solely on his bow. Keeping his attention on the king, he matches its footwork and pacing, carefully readies a second arrow, and takes aim.

The king invites the attack. The arrow slices air and the bear shrinks close to the ground, letting it whistle overhead. In the next moment, it launches across the clearing and tackles Serin.

I run forward, hatchets ready to strike. A clean hit to the back of its neck would sever its spinal cord. I'd have to jump onto its back to complete the attack, and even then, my hatchet might not be strong enough to cut through its layers of fur and flesh. Its attention won't be drawn, not until its true target is killed. That is something I cannot allow to happen.

I go for the king's neck, curving my hatchet to wedge into its throat and hopefully lift some weight from Serin. It might be enough to startle the bear to rise onto its hind legs and allow me access to the softer skin of its stomach. I curve my hatchet while letting out a warning yell.

I halt mid-swing as the bear's raking claws grow still. Its heavy breaths and muffled growls dissipate in a final huff of air. Its thick head drops downward. The long fangs would pierce Serin's chest had he not been supporting the weight of the king's head upon the crossing shafts of two arrows skewered through its eye sockets.

The wiry muscles of his arms strain to support the weight as he shimmies out from under the bear. One set of the king's claws cuts the side of Serin's arm as he pushes it away. Blood trickles over his hands that pressed firmly against the bear's punctured eyes. Once he extracts himself from the dead king's weight, Serin rips the arrows free.

I lower my hatchet. The boy takes a shaking breath. He pays no mind to the gash down his arm or the seeping claw marks in his side. He finds his bow on the ground half hidden under the king bear but not broken by the ordeal. He brushes the dark wood of dirt and slings it over his shoulder before finally looking at me.

"Did I..." he stammers, "Did I do it?"

I nudge the unmoving bear and release a controlled breath. "I'd say so."

Serin puts his bloody hands to his face and runs them over his head. "I did it. I did it. Right? You didn't save me, did you? Does it count?"

"I didn't touch it," I assure him, "although, I did think you were dead for a moment." I crouch and examine the burst spheres of the king's eyes. "Those arrows went deep. Straight back into its brain. Did you plan that?"

"Not exactly."

"Well, it worked."

"Guess I took inspiration from your caracosh story." He laughs again. "Evoriel's name, I can't believe I just did that..."

"You're not done yet," I remind him. "There will be no ceremony if you return empty handed."

He nods and places a cautious hand between the bear's eyes, not yet claiming the redtooth prize.

"It's not the same as killing a deer," he says.

I say nothing, letting him sift through the odd emotions that accompany the act of claiming a life of Evoriel's finest.

"What will happen to it?" he asks. "Should we take its meat?"

"Not this time. You take only what you must. The Wood will claim the rest."

As he detaches one of the king's red fangs, I remember what it was like to claim the tooth of the echoer at the end of my Long Hunt. Following the hard-won battle, I felt remorse for having killed the creature. With the caracosh, I fought for my life, fought in the names of those who were killed in the weeks of its torment, and in the end, I still felt a pang of guilt.

"I hate to see it destroyed," Serin says while holding up the front red fang of the king. "It'd make a fine necklace, just like yours, Ashacan."

"A heavy necklace," I reply, "and purely a symbol of rank. A good acan does not hunt for trophies."

He pulls his tempted gaze from the king's impressive tooth. "An acan?"

I nod.

"Really?"

"As far as I'm concerned, yes, an acan, but we must survive the trip home before I can declare any rank as official. Remember, this king is not the only hunter in these woods."

The reminder causes him to wince. I can see his adrenaline wearing off and his wounds becoming more painful.

"Sit down and relax," I tell him. "Let me stitch those wounds before you draw something else to us."

Straggler

SERIN HALTS SPECKLES AT the camp's perimeter. I do the same, perplexed by the sight of an uprooted vashte.

Not only uprooted—shattered.

The base of its trunk is lifted and split into three jagged shafts. The rest of the tree lies in splintered pieces. Some shards are larger than others, all scattered widely. Serin lifts a hand high to touch a black fragment lodged in the trunk of another tree, and his eyes meet mine.

"The vashte. They're all…" his words drift, like myself unable to comprehend what could destroy a tree in such a manner.

"I've never seen anything like this," I say, already studying the area for signs of what might have happened. There are no tracks aside from the flattened acan path, nor signs of humans or beasts.

"Where is everyone?" Serin wonders, circling the area. "Someone is usually posted here. And whatever happened to the trees…they would have heard it from camp, right?"

I look toward the camp still hidden beyond a stretch of trees and foliage. Ahead, there is a second obliterated vashte. Then another.

"Wait," I snap as Serin sends Speckles toward them. "Hang back."

He follows my dismount.

"Do you think—"

"Quiet."

He shuts his mouth and I listen for the sounds of camp. No voices cut through the leaves. There is only a soft wind.

"I'm going to look ahead," I say, working to keep my voice an even tone. "Stay with the ponies."

"I want to go with you."

"Not until I know what's happening."

"*Is* something happening?"

"I don't know," I answer too brusquely.

"I'm not staying here if something is wrong."

"You're going to take orders like any other acan. I said stay here. If I'm not back within the hour, ride west. Go to the Elesaan."

His eyes shift in confusion. "Why would I need to leave?" And then, panic. "There is something wrong!"

I drop a heavy hand on his shoulder, quieting him. "Focus. You're an acan now, *sai?* So trust what your Ashacan is telling you. There might be something dangerous ahead, there might not, but right now, you're the only acan I have, so I need you to listen. Got it?"

He faintly nods.

"Whatever did this—" I gesture at the vashte. "—is unfamiliar to us. If it is dangerous, I need you to go get help."

"You want me to just...leave you? Leave the *vashte'rae?* My sister—"

"It's an order."

"Acans don't run."

"Acans do what is best for the vashte'rae."

He scowls.

I squeeze his shoulder. "I will find Sil. And then I will come back here."

I move away with hatchets drawn before he can question more—before he can see my cracking resolve at the sight of our most sacred trees broken into pieces.

I step carefully, yearning for sound through the silence. At the second vashte, I glide a hand over the sundered trunk and balance myself. Take a breath. Pull my hand away. Upon reaching the third, I find blood.

Specks dapple the leaves that grow low to the ground. My father's eyes flash in my mind. I hear his voice. *I don't think this is wise.*

Anxiety flutters in my stomach. I try to keep myself calm and sure-footed, but the longer I hear nothing, the quicker I move until my feet cannot step fast enough. I clumsily fall, skidding against the uneven terrain as though I have never encountered the Gatewood floor before. The thick buildup of forest debris crunches loudly underfoot. My weight pushes into the ground and slows my progress. I stumble over a root. Drop a hatchet. Skin my palm. I claw at the dirt, right myself, and burst into the clearing, hardly drawing air past my lips.

Sunlight warms the area. I will it to reveal camp as I left it, and for a moment, I stand at the treeline, unable to comprehend. Some of the tents still stand, their surrounding areas untouched aside from strewn vashte fragments. Those that were nearest the trees have been leveled. One tent was pinned to a strongwood by several large splinters. With each explosion, the vashte tore into the forest, carving up ground, severing nearby branches and lacerating trees. Where their trunks once stood are swaths of upturned soil and pits of ravaged roots.

Scattered amongst them are my people, each cut and battered like the landscape. Immediately at my feet is a smashed fiddle. Not far from it, Beshtel lays face down, the finest of her golden hairs lifted in the breeze. I stare at her for a long minute before the blood on her back comes into focus. And then one by one, the gruesome details overwhelm my senses. Not only broken trees. Broken bodies.

I try and fail to keep their faces unacknowledged in my periphery. *Eyes forward,* my mother's voice snaps in my head. My body moves, flinching as I go, but the faces demand my attention. Healer Shayv is bent over the body of a child. I turn away before seeing who, and am met by the edge of Giama's colorful skirt peeking out from under a tent flap. Her son Elik is close by. Several crude arrows stick in his back. The deeper I move into camp, the more concentrated the bodies become. I recognize more acans drawn westward from their posts. Lya's body is crushed under a pony, her throat slit and a sword just out of reach. And unrighteously mingled with the Rendara are humans. The likes of which I have never seen.

There are only men, and each possesses strangely inhuman features. Some of their brows are too rigid and thick, their eyes set too deep. Their bodies are disproportionately tall or wide. Many have corded muscles that bulge under fair skin. All have been vividly scarred by various patterned burns.

I lift my gaze to the single strongwood at the center of camp. It guides me toward the main tent in the distance. I step over bodies until I cannot, and then I stop, too terrified to continue.

Then an arrow strikes my leg, tearing above my knee and lodging in the meat of my thigh. I fall against the body of a vaguely human man. His skull is pierced by two Rendaran arrows, one between his eyes and the other through the base of his jaw. On his throat is a knot of skin malformed by a burn.

I wait for a second arrow, but it does not come. Using one of my axes as a crutch, I push myself to my feet, and turn in the direction from whence the arrow came. I keep my axes low, unable to lift them any more than I can make my body move or my brain think. Thoughts of strategy leave me. I see the crude arrow in my leg but have no feeling. I forget what to do next.

A bird startles from the low brambles as a man steps forward. He wears sparse leather armor that appears as neglected as his person. His stature is small with a bald head and dirty face. Eyes sunken in shadow sit beneath a thick brow. He holds a gnarled bow with a second arrow nocked, although he does not take aim. After stepping into the clearing, he waits.

Others reveal themselves. One joins the bowman at the treeline. Another emerges from a distant tent clutching a thick ax with a jagged blade. I glance around and find three more approaching from different directions. One smiles from the distance, showing too many teeth upon an unnaturally wide jaw. Each man is lacerated by an array of fresh cuts, looking as though they were caught in some spray of debris.

I don't realize I'm yelling until the sound of my anguished shout penetrates my shock. My hands take a better grip of my hatchets and I yell again, willing my voice to shatter the remaining trees.

From behind, heavy steps disturb the dead. I turn on my unpunctured leg and swing an ax. A large, bearded man grabs the handle below the head.

"Screamin' won't do no good," he warns, yanking the ax fully from my grip.

I swing the second without thought. It hits his torso but only indents upon his armor of roughened leather. As I pull back, he chuckles and pats the rust-colored tunic.

"Orc skin, little rat. You'll need to hit harder."

I lunge forward again. He swiftly draws a thick sword and catches my attack. The force of his deflection unbalances me for an instant, and in that moment, he strikes me across the face with his free hand. Before I can stand, his fingers burrow into my hair and he lifts me upward, bringing me close to his face.

Hairs pull from my scalp, and his hot breath washes over me. I blink back pain to see two foreign symbols branded into his cheeks. They pucker the skin under his wrinkled eyes. His brow rolls, embedded with pieces of stone, and in his beard, he has woven a variety of teeth.

"Where you been?" he mutters, his coarse accent unfamiliar. He holds me as though I weigh nothing, and then he calls to the rest. "King was right! A straggler!"

The bearded man drops me, and I land upon the corpse of an acan. At their waist is a dagger. I draw it quick, not quite remembering any technique. The man easily kicks it from my grasp.

"Thinks she's a fighter!"

There are seven branded men altogether. I search for another weapon but in scanning the ground within reach, I meet more familiar faces and am unable to think beyond them.

"You want me to put another arrow in her?" the bowman asks, his voice a sharp hiss.

"Not while she's still useful." The bearded leader kicks me soundly in the chest, pinning me beneath his boot. I clasp his ankle but cannot make him budge. He grins down at me, giving hint of a gold tooth. "That it? No wonder why they left you out of the fight."

He bends down, crushing my chest under his bulk and tugs at my necklace.

"Now I like this…"

I spit in his face. He licks it from his lips. Holds the tip of the caracosh claw to my eye.

"Name's Skinner," he says, "but I'm not opposed to takin' eyes."

He presses the claw through the first layer of my skin just as one of his men grunts from the sound of impact.

Skinner drops the claw and steps away, his attention drawn elsewhere. It gives me a moment to gasp for air as they turn toward the direction I came.

Serin stands several paces from the treeline, his bow outstretched. Behind it, his eyes are narrowed in rage, a ferocity I have never seen from him. The bow shakes in his grasp.

The man he shot snaps the arrow from his shoulder and begins to trudge toward him.

Serin attempts to nock a second arrow, but it fumbles in his hand.

"Kill that little shit!" Skinner orders the two men already in pursuit.

Serin forgets his bow and looks to me on the ground. Even at the distance, I see the tears streaking down his face.

"Run!" I yell in Rendaran, my voice garbled. *"Run!"*

Sense seems to register in his mind as the charging men approach with axes prepared to swing. He shoulders his bow and flees just as an ax swipes the air where he stood.

Skinner watches as they disappear into the trees, the branded men running more swiftly than they seem built for. Seeing Serin allows me a moment of clarity, and I lift my eyes from the Rendara around me to the burned man overshadowing their bodies.

I grip a shard of vashte and push off the ground, aiming the sharp end at the side of his neck. The serrated bark skids against his skin as he turns at the sound of my movement. He casts me aside and grabs my throat. I lift my legs and jab my feet into his ribs. He grunts but maintains his hold, tightening his hand around my neck. Spots burst in my vision. With my fading strength, I arc the vashte sideways and run it through his unarmored forearm.

He barks a pained response that distorts into a laugh. Blood trickles along his arm, gushing forth as he strains his grasp once more. A ringing starts in my ears, and I'm on the edge of unconsciousness when he releases me. My lungs expand and I choke on air.

Skinner rips the vashte from his arm. "So," he muses, "there *are* more of you."

He effortlessly pulls my shoulders toward his chest, bending my back at a sharp angle and puts his scraped lips to my ear.

"Let's see who we can draw out," he murmurs, and then he cracks the vashte against my head.

* * *

I wake at dusk with my back to the strongwood and my arms tied tautly around its trunk. My head is heavy, throbbing on the side where I was struck. The center of camp wavers in my view. I try to blink away nausea, but it worsens as I take in the bodies still scattered around me.

I sit upon a portion of the main tent. One corner of hide still hangs from an outstretched branch of the strongwood. The rest of the structure has been laid flat by Frae's body. Blood pools beneath him and has flowed down the creases of the tent. His amber eyes are open, staring at me.

I turn my head and vomit.

My retching calls the attention of the nearby burned men. Some of them are rummaging through the remaining tents. Skinner and another sit upon logs around what was our main cookfire. Their boots are propped on the encircling stones. Between them is the body of Serin's mother, Zanil, a slash of now darkened blood down her back. Her fine hand rests upon a stone, as though she intended to grasp it as a weapon.

Skinner watches me watch her before standing. He steps on her back instead of over it and makes his way to me. There is nothing for me to do but wait. I cannot budge my arms and my left leg is held still by the arrow in my knee. I test my binds as Skinner approaches. They hold tight. My leg burns. The arrow festers with a pulsating ache.

Crouching before me, he pins my good leg with his knee. He fondles his beard in thought, letting the various beaded teeth slip between his dirty fingers. His forearm is poorly bandaged where I stabbed him. Under his brow, I see his eyes are a murky brown. There is an inquisitiveness in them I did not expect.

"You speak Dur, rat?" he inquires. When I say nothing, he makes a contemplative growl at the back of his throat. "Hmm...I 'spect you do. I think you understand me just fine."

"Norveh un diil."

"Norveh?" he tries the word, nodding. "I heard that one a few times the other day. Has a good fuckin' ring to it." He pauses, perhaps waiting for me to say something in the human tongue, but I vow to give him nothing.

"You're a lot like the other one," he continues. "Look like her too—the rat queen of this sad little pack. She didn't want to talk, either."

My heart stops as it did earlier, a new shock pulling it deep toward my stomach. I keep still. Too still.

Skinner holds my jaw, tipping my chin upward to get a better look. "Aye, you do understand."

I forcefully tuck my chin, breaking his loose hold, and then I bite into his hand. The taste of blood and sweat fills my mouth as his flesh tears under my fangs.

Rather than rip away, he digs his fingers into my cheeks and shoves my head against the strongwood, gagging me. I breathe deeply through my nose, inhaling the foul scent of him, the stench of death, my own bile.

"Don't," he snarls, pushing into my jaw hard enough that it threatens to pop. "Don't try. I don't need you. You're only here because you might be useful for a moment, but I don't need you."

He withdraws his hand from my aching jaw. Blood and spit follow it and cling down my chin. A flap of skin hangs from the space between his forefinger and thumb.

"That boy…" he starts. "My men chased him into the woods. They chased him like they chased everyone else. He hid, they told me. Tried to use those *fucking* trees against them. But they found him anyway. They pulled him out. They cut him up. Took that bow and used it for kindling. Not sure why you're fightin' if not for him, but he's dead and you'll be next. The question is, how quickly do you want to be killed?" He leans forward again and with his unbitten hand, he gently wipes my chin. "I have a job to do. Kill whoever's left. As long as you're here, you're gonna help me."

I mean to spit or swear. Instead, I swallow a mouthful of blood and repress a sob against the roof of my mouth. There is nowhere to look for reprieve. I am trapped between Skinner and a field of death. Frae's lifeless eyes continue to bore into me. Others around us do the same. I chose to look at Skinner for fear of finding my mother.

He strokes the claw that still hangs at my neck. "Where are the others?"

I refuse to give him anything, not caring if the truth might better my circumstance. If anyone escaped, the best I can do is buy them time.

"I have to be thorough now," he says, grazing the tip of the claw under my eye. My heart quickens at the memories the sharp provocation evokes. The same claw once punctured my torso and slowly curved under my ribs, similarly holding me to a tree.

I look over Skinner's shoulder, wondering if this is another test and hoping to find my father standing nearby. He could tell me what to do.

"Call them out for me," Skinner demands and without pause, drags the caracosh claw down my left eye.

He cuts through my brow and eyelid as it clenches shut. My voice bursts through gritted teeth and when I bite back my yell, he cuts into my eye.

"Louder!" he shouts back.

The claw hooks on my lower lid and tears down my cheek to jaw. There's no use in holding back my shriek. The moment it's done, I fight to silence myself and instinctively turn my face away from Skinner. My eyes tighten at the excruciating blindness. My arms pull at their restraints, wanting to grasp my face. Blood follows the curve of my eye, spills down my cheek, and drips onto my chest.

Skinner taps the claw against my other cheek. "Best hope someone comes."

He reaches down and wrenches upward on the arrow shaft in my leg. The old wood snaps, leaving half of the arrow in my thigh. A wave of pain steals the sight from my good eye, and I feel my mind lash back into a field of bursting darkness, desperate to slip away.

I force myself to focus and see Skinner motion for his bowman. The comparatively small man steps away from a Rendaran elder's tent. In his hand is a jeweled mirror. He throws it aside.

"Sun's setting," Skinner tells him. "Take up position and watch our rat. If anyone comes for her, shoot them."

"You really think we missed some?" the bowman rasps. "We had 'em surrounded. Did our job. I say we get."

"If none come by morning, I'll finish up with this one and we'll be on our way."

"Could let the arrow kill her."

"That'll take too long. I want to do it myself," he says, examining the torn flesh of his hand.

The bowman studies me before pulling the hood of his black cloak into place. "Should take her tongue, too, so she can't warn 'em."

"They won't get far even if she does. Besides, I like her voice."

Skinner bends down and lifts a hand. I flinch away from it.

"Heh, heh. Get some rest, Norveh."

He pats my cheek and stands, returning to his seat near the cookfire some distance off. I hear the other men ransacking tents, swearing when they find nothing of use. Our most treasured objects are our mirrors. Judging by the sound, they shatter most of them.

The bowman quietly finds a hidden position in the shade of a half-fallen tent. I recognize it to belong to one of the older Rendara. Her name was Kelia. Her favored averlin dyed shoes stick out from beneath the flattened side. The bowman tucks himself behind the tent flap, propping it open just enough for him to aim his bow. Within, I catch the glint of his eyes, and I wonder how he manages to see as night settles.

One of the men lights a fire. Stray flames lick the face of Zanil at Skinner's feet. He does not move from the log. The others take their meals in shifts, tearing into our supplies of dried meat and barking laughter into the night. I count six including the bowman, although there were seven before.

The firelight does not reach me, and I rest my head against the strongwood. The muscles of the sliced half of my face have not relaxed since Skinner severed it. My eyelid strains, as though it could force away the searing pain that lodges deep in my eye. It competes with the burning in my leg where the arrow festers. Based on the bowman's remark, I assume some toxin tipped the arrow. I feel something malignant seeping into my leg. It pushes toward my knee. As I sit, a dozen bruises send pangs across my body. My head throbs from all sides.

I close my eyes and will the toxin to spread. Faces of the Rendara appear in my mind, heralded by those I have yet to find. For a brief moment I wonder if they could be out there, waiting for a time to strike, but my mother would not have left the Rendara, and the Rendara would not have left their chief.

I begin to lose consciousness and let the pain take me.

* * *

I'm woken by the slackening of the ropes. I open my eyes, forgetting the gash in my left and hold back a gasp as torn flesh tries to accommodate my movement. It is still night, and in the distance, the men's fire has burned down to embers. Four of them have fallen asleep. Skinner remains in his same position, staring at the fire, one leg balanced on Serin's mother.

The ropes shift and my arms lower against the strongwood, causing my shoulders to ache. Around the tree's wide trunk and lifted roots, I struggle to see what has loosened my binds. The ropes do not drop entirely, and then they grow still. I glance toward the bowman hidden in the tent. There are a few minutes of stillness. The soft snorts of scavenging rhougls carry through camp. An occasional scuffle of flapping wings and snarls disturbs the night, but neither the bowman nor Skinner stir.

My heart quickens at the loosened ropes, and I resist the temptation to wriggle myself free. I keep an eye on the bowman's hiding place, searching for movement. Then an arrow pierces the night.

The shaft is a blur, whispering close to the strongwood. There is shuffling within the tent, but whether the bowman detects the arrow or not, I hear it strike something solid followed by a low gurgle. The standing portion of Kelia's tent falls sideways as the bowman crumbles against it. Skinner sharply turns his head, first at the racket and then at me. I tug at the ropes, desperate to break free as the burned man stands.

And then a figure leaps over the strongwood's roots.

"Halstaer?" my voice breaks, and I realize the fear within it.

He drops his bow and swiftly cuts the ropes in answer, then he pulls me up and shoves me atop the roots. "Go!" he orders, his voice gruff with pain.

I struggle over the roots, clumsily clawing my way up them with only partial vision. My leg buckles under my weight as the arrow sends blistering toxins through my knee.

Halstaer wraps an arm around my waist and heaves me over the remaining roots. We hit the ground on the other side just as a burned man appears overhead, his ax slamming into the strongwood. Halstaer grabs me again, breathing heavily at my side, and together we run for the stream.

The water slows us, but it numbs my leg enough for me to ignore the burn of each footfall. Halstaer takes my hand and helps me cut through the water. When we reach the opposite side, he throws me up the bank toward the trees.

I roll onto my side, working to catch a breath. I hold out a hand for him to take, and briefly see him under the starlight. His skin is pale and streaked with sweat. Fine lacerations mar his face, and a shallow cut has sliced him from shoulder to abdomen, tearing enough of his shirt for me to notice an arrow wound in his shoulder. It is a knot of black and swollen flesh. From it are branching black lines that delve into his veins.

He takes my hand and pulls himself to my side, this time fighting for air. Across the stream, Skinner pauses on the bank. He points a massive longsword in our direction and shouts as we help each other stand.

"Fuckin' run, you rats! I like a hunt!"

We stumble into the trees as Skinner enters the stream, not caring to expend his energy like his men who splash loudly into the water.

Our pace slows once the Wood envelops us. Brambles and scattered chunks of vashte disrupt our footfalls. Halstaer coughs violently at my side, and I find myself supporting him with my wounded leg.

"Nhu..." he gasps. "Stop..."

Before I can take a step further, he shoves into me, forcing us under the needle laden boughs of a gaea. The pursuing men crash through the trees behind and fan out in the surrounding area. Halstaer pushes us against the gaea's trunk, tucking us away in the dark.

He slumps against me, resting his head on my shoulder. Strings of his bloodied hair stick to my cheek. I lay a hand to his chest and feel his erratic breaths growing shallower as he tries to quiet himself. My fingertips graze the edge of his torn skin and he inhales sharply. His forehead touches mine. I reach for his jaw, feeling it slick with sweat.

"Nhuaela," he weakly whispers.

I mean to hush him but fail to control my own breaths. He puts a hand to my cheek, careful of my sliced skin and gently furls two fingers under my jaw. The heat of him spreads to me—the fierce heat of sickness. So close to me, I feel the muscles of his face tighten in pain. When he speaks, his lips touch mine.

"They ambushed and...the *vashte* reacted..." In place of words he cannot form, he tips forward and kisses me fully. His fangs clip my bottom lip. Tears in his lashes drop onto my cheek, stinging the cut.

He pulls back. "I'm sorry...Ashacan. Go. You need to go."

And then he shoves away from the boughs, the dagger he used to cut the ropes still held in hand.

I want to follow but find myself paralyzed. Halstaer passes beyond the boughs, stepping slow. Three of the burned men do not see him in the dark, and he glides dangerously near as they slash through the undergrowth. The one nearing our gaea senses his presence too late, and Halstaer slits his throat. The man's resounding gags draw the attention of the others, who take guarded stances against the dark—all except for Skinner, who looks to Halstaer's exact position.

They face each other, Halstaer limping and Skinner waiting. A fourth man arrives with a torch, momentarily backlighting Skinner's troll-like physique. As the torchbearer moves to shed light for the others, Skinner lifts his gaze from Halstaer and follows the light beyond the boughs of the gaea directly to me.

I sink back.

He tilts his head and grins. "There she is."

All heads turn toward my hiding place. Skinner steps around Halstaer, who weakly attempts to throw the dagger at his throat. Skinner ducks aside and brings his longsword down in a neat arc midstep. It carves through Halstaer's shoulder and chest with sickening ease, knocking him down in an instant. Skinner lifts the sword, steps over Halstaer, and rushes forward, swinging his blade at the gaea.

I drop to the ground as the blade cracks overhead, sending splintered wood down my back. I dart under the lowest boughs while Skinner hacks away the branches. The torchbearer runs closer with the light, heading me off at the back of the gaea. Weaponless, I yank the caracosh claw from my neck and throw myself against him. He awkwardly twists to cleave into my back with his ax, but the angle causes his blade to glance off my leather armor. I grab the torch and slice the claw through his wrist.

"Fuck!" he yells, his severed hand falling with a spray of blood. His brief distraction gives me a moment to throw the torch backward toward Skinner. I do not look to see if it hits. Already I am running for the dark.

Adrenaline carries me over what was the perimeter path. Skinner shouts orders behind, and I hear the crunching of undergrowth intensify as the men give haphazard pursuit. I do not look back, desperately clinging to the caracosh claw as a deeper darkness of the Gatewood shadows me. I take an eastward turn, hoping they continue north, but my labored footfalls are telling of my course. My leg protests, and I realize the men will catch me soon enough.

My partial blindness and the Gatewood's oppressing dark obscure my vision. Normally, I would have seen precision in the blackened shapes of nearby objects, but now the finer details blur. I hardly see better than what I imagine Skinner sees, perhaps clearer than a normal man, but without the keenness of an acan. Glancing behind, only Skinner has picked up my trail and still he slows with uncertainty.

I wipe the tears from my right eye and take the blunt edge of the caracosh claw between my teeth. I would not outrun the men even if I could. Not while I'm alone and the Rendara are discarded behind.

I reach for a low hanging branch of a tall stilt tree. My left leg is heavy, but my arms are strong, and I pull myself up and over the first branch. With questionable balance, I hold the narrow trunk and ascend to the next branch under a thicket of fat leaves. I shimmy outward as far as the lean but sturdy limbs will support me, then I take the claw from my mouth and focus on evening my breaths. Sitting still, I close my eyes only to see Halstaer be cut down again and again.

I grit my teeth and my breaths quiver with a feeling more violent than grief. I begin to wonder how many others tried to climb upward instead of away, or if I'm the only one weak enough to do so.

Below, Skinner pauses on my trail. He studies the crushed foliage and how the tamped plants suspiciously end.

Shame fatigues me. A child would not have made such a foolish mistake.

Skinner slowly turns. He lifts his gaze.

I push off my branch, left foot slipping as my knee strains, and land atop him before he can lift his thick sword. He twists and roars, using one hand to rip at my back. I grab his beard, gathering a handful of beaded teeth in my palm, and hold myself to him. My other hand flips the claw and drives it into his neck.

The air goes out of him in a short grunt, and I allow him no time to retaliate. I jerk my hand toward myself, carving a semicircle through his neck. Blood drenches us and he falls to the side, using his sword as a crutch. I back away, tripping onto my backside upon the forest floor. Skinner puts a hand to his neck. Blood pulses between his fingers and paints his chest. His sunken eyes bore into me as he loses hold of his sword and slips sideways.

I wait several minutes, ensuring that he does not stand. His blood dries splattered on my face and arm. I flex my hand. My breathing begins to calm.

"Skinner!" another man yells for his leader.

They must have gone back for the torch. I glimpse the bobbing light through the leaves.

With the now crimson claw ready, I hunt them. They stay together under the light. The original torchbearer is not with them, likely remaining behind to staunch his bleeding wrist. I make a note to go back for him.

Instinct takes me. I pick a length of crooked vashte from the ground and move carefully. My leg prevents me from being swift, but there is no need when the remaining men apparently do not share Skinner's sight.

Over their heads, I throw a chunk of debris. It clatters in the branches beside them. When they turn to look, I step forward and crack my vashte crutch into the back of the new torchbearer's head.

He tumbles forward, grabbing at his skull. The second man turns instantly, an ax raised. I catch its head with the vashte, stoop inward, and drive the claw under his jaw. I thrust it upward to break the roof of his mouth. He blinks at me, and his hand futilely pats my shoulder, seeking to dislodge the claw from his head. I tear it free as the second man finds his bearings, and then I spin toward him with the vashte. It connects with his skull a second and third time. I bring the sacred wood downward until the man is on his back and his skull is indistinguishable.

I leave the vashte on the ground beside him. I inhale, feeling the air, but it does not fill my lungs. Upon the exhale, physical pain alights across my body, and I hold my hand over my mouth to stifle my hitching breaths.

I make myself limp back the way I came in search of the last man. I find him resting against a tree, his stump poorly bandaged and held close to his chest. Judging by the blood upon him, and the manner in which he lazily lifts his eyes, I doubt his ability to attack. Even so, I kick away his ax and kneel before him, claw raised.

"Where's the boy?" I demand of him, my voice tearing between my fangs.

His answer is a wheezing sigh.

I put the claw to his throat. "Where is the boy?"

"Dead. Killed one of ours. So, we killed him."

"Who are you?"

He reveals a bloodied grin. "We're the King's *pack*."

"What king?"

He does not answer. I cut into his skin.

"You're gonna...kill me anyway. Fuckin' cut my throat already."

"What did you come for?"

"Won't matter to you. You're gonna...die too."

"Then tell me."

"Go find...your dead boy. Maybe he's next...to your...dead queen."

I slash the claw across his throat. Briefly, it feels too merciful, but such regret vanishes when I lift my eyes to see Halstaer's body over the man's shoulder. He lies on his back, a deep gash halving his chest. From the arrow wound in his shoulder, the black streaks have progressed down his torso and up the side of his cheek.

I brush the hair off his face—try to clean it of blood. Thoughts of what I need to do collide with my panic. Rather than return to camp, I sit beside him, one of his hands held in my lap. And I do not move until dawn.

Roots

GRADUALLY MORNING COMES IN fractured rays of golden light, but it does not warm Halstaer's cold hand. The black threads of toxins appear darker now having bitten into his body. I place his hand upon his chest, lean forward, and kiss his head.

The movement triggers multiple pangs in my head and leg. The skin of my face pulls and seeps. I sit back and using the caracosh claw, cut the seam of my pant leg. My thigh is laced with black.

With my fingertips, I find the broken arrow shaft that pokes from my muscle. The skin around it is swollen and oozes a puslike substance amidst the blackened blood. My grip slips on the splintered shaft. I grind my teeth and inch it outward before tugging it free. There is a slight relief of pressure, but the toxin has already pushed to my knee and reaches toward my hip. It fills the empty space with a sharp pain. I wonder how many days it will take, how long Halstaer waited, or if he meant to wait at all.

I would lay down beside him if not for Serin. Regardless of what the men said, I cannot believe he is dead.

I stand, using another length of *vashte* as a crutch, and retrace my path from the night before. My progress is slow as hunger and fatigue set in, but I continue until I find the stream. The instinct to find Serin keeps me numb. Below, Rendaran faces call my attention. The list of those missing grows shorter with each step.

There is little pattern to the chaos. Many acans fell at the center where the fighting seemed thickest, but they are strewn along all sides of the camp. Rendara who were never inclined to raise swords or draw bows bolstered their protectors, none of them appearing to have fled until they were pushed eastward. Many of the children tried to hide. Small forms are outlined under leveled tents. I flinch and turn away as I recognize Daiva at the base of a tree, an arrow in her back. Her hand is outstretched, as though she meant to climb.

Entangled throughout are dozens of branded men. I focus on them instead, hardly placated by their bodies. Flies and rhougls are drawn to their stench, and at the far edges of camp, brown wolves gather. They yip and snap at each other as they lay claim to the closest burned men. One briefly sniffs along Beshtel's back and nudges at her neck. I take a sudden step in a poor attempt to scare it off, but ignoring me, the wolves leave her. They leave all the Rendara, and looking around, the rhougls and flies avoid them just the same.

Wary of the wolves, I go to Beshtel. I flip her onto her back to see more blood staining the front of her dress. I do my best to brush clean her face. A thread of golden hair catches on her eyelashes. I tuck it behind her ear as I have done countless times before. Then I find her broken fiddle and place it in her arms.

I make myself move away from her, finding it no less difficult than leaving Halstaer. One of the wolves watches me as I return to the path from which I came. Speckles and Lo have vanished from where we left them, but I'm quick to find a trail of tamped grasses and occasional hoofprints in the exposed dirt. They must have been startled by something. I track them southward around the perimeter until I'm at the pony enclosure, or what is left of it.

The rope fence has been cut. It hangs slack between the trees, and the ponies are gone. Some of them were ridden into the fight. One lies dead nearby the enclosure, shot down as though for sport. In the chaos of prints I lose the tracks, but in the center of the pen stands Lo, smacking his lips at a few blades of grass. His saddle has fallen crooked to his side, and his reins have snapped overhead. They drag on the ground beside him. At my approach he lifts his head with ears perked.

He curves his head to smell my back as I lean against him. My leg trembles and he takes my weight. I fish around his saddlebags, first finding a bit of dried deer meat. It goes in my mouth while I pull out bandages and a salve of rosemoss. Shayv never let acans undertake hunts without basic necessities. Rosemoss and a few bandages will do little to cure my state, but they might temper the pain; they might buy me time.

I find my waterskin and wash down the meat with warm water, then I spit to clear my mouth. The salty taste of Skinner's flesh still lingers. While Lo continues to forage, I sit beside him and apply the rosemoss to my face. Shayv lectures me in my head, telling me to clean the wound first, but the extent of the gash is beyond my poor medical knowledge. I'm too frightened to touch my eye. The lightest agitation sends a piercing pain through my socket. For too long I hold my palm against it, fearing what remains might slip from under my lid. It's impossible not to clench my muscles in attempt to flush out the sharpness. Gradually, the rosemoss begins to harden, sealing the long cut and drying to a vibrant red. What remains of the salve dyes my hands. Before it wastes, I smear what's left upon the hole in my thigh. Then I wrap it in bandages.

I have no idea if it's the right thing to do. For a moment I rest my forehead in hand and let my breaths rake my throat. They nearly turn into words, curses, screams. And then I bury everything in the pit of my stomach.

I right Lo's saddle. Take his reins. Together, we find suspicious breaks in the branches and wander until I find a large boot print. The tracks build as I catch more detail in the disturbed Wood, until some distance from the perimeter I find a cluster of uprooted and eviscerated vashte.

Their demise flattened the immediate area. Leaves were shredded and surrounding trees impaled. Speckles and a branded man lie close, thrown from the impact of wooden shards. Their bodies are scathed and battered to pulp. I inspect the fractured root clusters while adjusting to the vision of a single eye. Partially buried in the moist dirt is a piece unlike the jagged shards. I pull at the smoothed wood to uncover half of Serin's bow.

I carefully set it down, afraid of whatever power splintered the sacred wood. *The vashte reacted*, Halstaer said. Even if such force came from within the Gatewood—from Evoriel himself—it is none I have ever seen or heard tell.

"Serin!" I shout, seeing no sign of him.

The Gatewood returns no voice. I circle the area, scouring for tracks and finding none. Just then, a fiery sensation spikes through my leg. I grab Lo's mane to keep myself upright as the toxin constricts. Peeking at my bandages, I notice the lacework of black carve a finger's length down my shin. The pulsing heat fades to a dull throb as the toxins pause. It steals my breath. I hold tighter to Lo, realizing my time is limited just like Halstaer's.

I recall the heat of him, the strained rise and fall of his chest under my hand. *Go. You need to go.*

I wonder what things he could not say. What he would think of me abandoning Serin, of abandoning them.

But there is no time to linger on such thoughts. I heave myself upward onto Lo's back, hooking my good leg overtop and pulling myself into the saddle. It hurts to turn Lo in the direction of camp, but if I do not, no one will. The roots would not be called, and I will have failed the Rendara even in death.

On our return, the scavenging animals are snout deep in their meals, rooting through torn flesh and plucking eyes from the burned men. The smell of death ripens under the rising sun.

I dismount, ashamed to ride above my kin, but still too cowardly to look at their faces. They have no trouble staring back. It is a meadow of condemning amber eyes.

Lo shoulders my weight until we reach the center of camp, and then I leave him stand as I pick through my parents' tent. Like the others in the vicinity, it has fallen and appears to have been pilfered, although there was nothing within that might have tempted the men. They seemed to have realized that upon entry.

I shift the hide to find the interior largely untouched. My father's favorite fur blanket remains upon their bedroll. My mother's wooden brush is beside her pillow. What little clothing they owned has been toppled from a wicker basket. The only personal item they did not carry was my mother's mirror. It was a gift from my father, centuries ago. She always kept it carefully wrapped and tucked away.

Someone found it. Its back is bent, as though they tried to pry away the green and gold dragon scales before smashing it on the ground. Sparkling glass bursts outward from beneath.

I leave it. My eyes land on Frae's body as I turn. This time, I do not look away. I take in the sight, accepting his presence, and then I look to the next. Lo steadies me as I acknowledge them, count and memorize their faces. I pull Zanil from the firepit and allow her to face the sun instead. Unable to do more, I move more hurriedly as I near the eastern edge of camp, beyond the thick of battle.

My tent stood at the eastern edge overlooked by a grove of vashte my father adored. The grove is now no more than a few broken stumps. Vashte scattered violently across the area and leveled my tent. Surrounding the fractured trees are the corpses of eight men, each large and armored in reddish orc skin. Their faces are gradients of blood and dirt picked clean of their eyes. Longswords and crude axes litter the ground and slumped in the center of it all is my mother.

I rush forward without Lo. The sharpness in my leg grips me and I fall, landing hard beside her.

She is tied to the remains of a vashte, her chin tucked to her chest. All of her is limp against the ropes that strain to keep her upright. I lift her head between my hands.

Her face is badly bruised, her nose broken and right eye swollen shut in a black mass. Familiar dark tendrils climb her throat and span upward from her chin. Like Halstaer, she has paled and is cold to the touch.

Cuts and bruises mottle her bare arms. The skin on her knuckles is scraped to the bone, and her many rings are missing. Splotches of blood dampen her shirt in various places where a blade pierced the hide.

Her chieftain necklace of dweller bone is gone, and it is one of Halstaer's arrows that mercifully pierces her heart.

My hands shake, making my grip unstable as I try to cut her free. Eventually the ropes give, and her weight falls against me. I wrap my arms around her as the shaking spreads until it racks my body from head to toe.

Of course, she would be at the edge. The burned men did not come from the heart of camp. They came in ambush, from the east. Had she not been here—had they not overwhelmed her first—they would not have succeeded.

I raise my head, searching for comfort at the sight of dead men. Their twisted necks and bent limbs are the result of my mother being pushed to violence. She may have supplanted physical strikes with weapons she snagged from the men—that would explain their discarded appearances, not beside their wielders but carelessly thrown. It was her style to be versatile and precise. She could channel agony into any jab and incapacitate an opponent with only her fists. I'm not surprised by the amount of dead men. I am surprised that she is alone.

My hand slowly pauses in its stroking of her hair. She *is* alone, without acans at the brunt of the attack.

It isn't right. She would not be so senseless. She would have rallied the acans. They would have followed. And yet the nearest acan is a distance away at the first row of tents.

"Why are you out here?" I ask against her temple.

Somehow, they wore her down. Somehow, they restrained her, and the acans were unable to help aside from an eventual arrow to her heart. I shake my head, realizing anyone would have helped. My father was no fighter, but he never would have left my mother to suffer. Not unless he was already—

I did not think it possible for a deeper sense of dread to overcome me. He often meditated in this grove, at the very spot my mother was tied.

But he is not here. He was not anywhere within the camp, and he is not here, the one place he would be—at my mother's side.

Something drove her here. Madly in desperation. In my absence, there was only one who she would abandon the tribe to protect.

And he is not here.

I lay her down to let her rest. Then I stab the caracosh claw into the vashte above. It lodges in the bark, a red-stained arc of white slicing through the black.

"Evoriel!" I shout, my voice echoing across the camp. A few rhougls take off into the air. *"Evoriel!"*

The ground shifts. From the depth of the Gatewood, the forest sighs. A strong wind blows and branches groan. Out of the underbrush, roots rise.

They come forth in a quiet rumble, snaking over the carnage like reaching fingers. The wolves dart into the trees as the roots sluice over-top the burned men in favor of the Rendara. Each body is delicately retrieved, caged in the care of Evoriel's grasp.

Soon the roots come to slither around me. They furl around my mother, lifting her arms across her chest and supporting her head. Finer threads weave over her face until they have stolen the last glimpse of her from me. They snap the arrow from her chest. I move to grip the roots, suddenly terrified to be left alone. One of the tendrils lashes around my wrist and holds me back. I pull against it, enraged.

"Where the *fuck* were you?" I scream at the roots, uncaring that they are only Evoriel's tools. "Where were you!"

They do not answer, and the grip on my wrist tightens as I struggle to follow my mother.

"Where's my father? Don't touch him! Don't—"

A second root grabs my ankle and rips my leg out from under me. My back slams into the ground, and the forceful tuber drags me farther into what remains of the vashte grove. Upon its release, my body reminds me of my aching wounds.

By the time I sit up, the last of the roots are retreating into the undergrowth with the remnants of my people. The dead men remain, and just as quickly as they left, the animals return to descend upon their feast.

I compose myself as well as I can and discern why the root brought me here. In the past I have seen them called to reclaim the dead. Oftentimes, it was a peaceful ritual, but never before have they shown aggression. Looking about myself, I half expect to find my father tied to the backside of the vashte, but there is no sign of him, not even a hair.

All that is left are two distinct imprints amongst the overlapping footsteps and marred ground. They are two shallow dishes where my father used to kneel and listen to the Gatewood. Crawling forward, I place my knees upon them. The left protests, seething at my weight. I bite my cheek and do it anyway. Angling my head, I adjust to the absence of my left periphery and try to see what he saw.

Aside from the typical hints of large bodies charging through the forest, nothing gives tell of what happened. My father may have been here. My mother might have been with him, and upon her return to camp, she may have heard an ambush. Or maybe my father is a few paces forward, dead in the underbrush.

I consider limping to the perimeter in search of his fair face, but if he was present the roots would have taken him. The toxins in my leg surge, reminding me there is no point. I will be dead in a number of hours or days, not enough time to learn anything of use.

But perhaps enough time to complete the only task left to me as Ashacan. The Damicus must know the Gatewood has been attacked, and I am deserving of their judgement should I make it that far. If not, then it only seems appropriate that I should die alone in the woods.

Lo follows me as I pick through the weapons of burned men, choosing two cruel war axes to wield as protection. They are ugly and heavy with heads of rippling metal, but they promise ferocity in every swing—appropriate should I encounter more men.

Lastly, I go to Skinner. He has not moved from where he fell, although apparent marks along his skin indicate an array of recent carrion creatures. Something dug hungrily into his throat, making it remarkably easy to fully detach his head. His eyes were chewed away. Flies gather in the pulpy sockets, but the brands in his cheeks are still noticeable beneath the dry blood.

"As long as you're here, you're going to help me," I say to him.

I tie the head to Lo's saddle and make for Daerva'Tor.

Onduris

THE JOURNEY TO DAERVA'TOR takes seven days. It should have taken five. Neither Lo nor I could handle a faster pace. I pity the old gelding that has faithfully carried me. I've not been able to move since I mounted him the day before when the pressure in my thigh amounted to an unbearable throb that could not support my weight. Each sway of Lo's belly threatens to burst the rotting tissue. A sludgelike substance blackens the leg of my doeskin pants. The threads of poison send stabbing pangs throughout my ribs as the toxins near my heart. Fever fires through my veins and makes me sweat the dried blood off my skin. Before entering onto the main path, I lean over Lo's neck and vomit. Then I right myself, wipe my chin, and try to keep my head high.

Lo takes his time plodding to the gate. He looks no better than I. His hair is matted and scruffed by sweat and dirt. The stench of Skinner's rotting head encompasses us, although I'm sure part of it is my own.

The border of Daerva'Tor appears suddenly. Blending with the forest, the gate stands between two massive strongwoods whose tops are unseen in the heights. The doors are gilded and reinforced with shimmering dragon scales. The remainder of the border wall delves deep into the woods as tall as the trees themselves. I halt Lo at a safe distance and wait, acting as I had seen my mother do in the past.

The grand doors open just enough to let two armored guards out. They are not as pristine as many Daervish fairborn. Their armor is a dull gray, well-worn, and their cloaks are tattered from exposure. They do not wear their hair in any elaborate style but in single braids of conformity. Each carries a fine sword at their hip. Upon seeing the extent of my wounds, they keep their distance. Shock brightens their white eyes.

"I..." The sound of my voice is strange after so many days. I realize just how much it is like my mother's. A more broken version of her, but the tone is there. I swallow, not wanting to break down in front of the guards. My dry throat nearly keeps me from forming my request.

"I need...the Damicus."

The guards quickly confer before one goes running back to the gate. The remaining one motions me forward. Seeing the command, Lo obeys.

"What happened to you?" the guard asks, first observing my weapons and then my ugly pony. When his eyes land on Skinner's rotting head, he slightly pulls back.

My Rendaran elvish is heavier than his Daerv. It grows thicker with my uneven breaths. "The Rendara. There was an attack."

"You are one of them?"

I give a shallow nod, exhausted by the movement. "Their Ashacan."

Mentioning the rank has the intended effect. The guard's caution is swiftly replaced with expediency. Even here they know an Ashacan without a *vashte'rae* is a harbinger of something ill.

"You better come in," the guard decides.

Lo tiredly follows him through the high gate onto the rolling fields surrounding Daerva'Tor. I'm met with piercing sunlight as the dense canopy abruptly falls away. Vast fields of gold and green grow toward the base of a single mountain that juts from the heart of the Gatewood. Spanning the length of its base is an upraised wall of rock—a small mountain in itself—within which are carved several archways. From previous visits I know there are hundreds of buildings in the valley beyond them, mainly the cramped homes of the base-born. Peeking above the ridge wall is the first tiered landing of sturdy shops and lodgings for visiting merchants. Curving roads and a series of bridges lead to the mid and high sectors far above that are separated by heavy gates. They consist of the oldest and wealthiest fairborn families, often those related to elders of the Damicus, diplomats, and city officials. Atop it all is the Damicus Hall. From the distance, the structure is hardly a speck at the mountaintop.

Three roads meet at the hub of the Base district. One winds beneath me, stretching from the southern guard outpost to dip over fields before inclining up a modest foothill. Two more roads connect the west and eastern gates. The west road is commonly traversed by dwarves from Surroc; the east is a human road from which few have permission to enter. Unseen from common view behind the mountain is a steep cliffside, nearly a sheer drop descending into a battered landscape now occupied by training grounds for the Undecayed. From there, a worn road heads north to a reinforced gate more menacing than the rest. There, only soldiers venture through to the road leading far north to Fort Se'lae and the Shadowed Threshold.

Inside the outer wall, two mounted guards meet me, disrupting my view. Their horses tower over Lo. Far ahead on the path, I notice a third rider galloping toward the city.

"We will accompany you to the base," one of the mounted guards says with an air of authority. She fails to mention what happens next.

Lo sighs at the miles ahead but bravely walks on. I am limp in the saddle, unable to cling with my left leg or sit tall. I knot my hand in Lo's mane and keep my eyes forward. *You must reach the city. Enter and you will have succeeded in one thing.*

The sun swelters my fever. I squint my right eye, and the left moves with it, feeling as though a rock is shoved under my lid. Every minute movement irritates whatever remains under the plastered rosemoss.

There are several homes upon the fieldland. They are tall and regal to save space for crops and storage. Many have fencing for herds of livestock: brown clipers, flocks of brill, and lumbering cordstock. As we near the mountain, base-born laborers pause in their work to watch us pass. To the east, a large stable and pasture stretches along the road. Spirited horses lift their heads. Some near the fence to investigate Lo's intruding scent. Still, my pony walks on, slowly closing the distance to the city.

At our pace it takes us an hour if not more. Lo walked far longer than he should have, longer than I should have asked, and I do not blame him when he stumbles outside the Base district ridge. The movement jerks me forward against his neck. I grip his mane as he catches himself. The toxin flares in my veins. It strikes upward into my chest and steals my breath.

The lead guard anxiously glances back, her braid sweeping over her shoulder. "Stay on your pony," she warns, as though falling is a crime. "Once we—"

A firm voice calls out from behind the guard, cutting her off. "What's going on?"

The guards shift their horses, revealing the Ashan standing under the Base district archway, a mounted guard beside him. Two more guards posted outside the wall suddenly straighten. Nearby, laborers carrying baskets or pulling cartloads of crops from the fields pause and look. Behind the Ashan, a group of base-born peers outward, keeping their distance. My escorts pull their horses back several paces, seeming equally stunned by his sudden presence.

I squint, thinking him a hallucination, but as he nears, the horror in his eyes is too apparent to be false. His gaze urgently flickers about Lo and me before settling on my blood caked face.

"Nhuaela," he carefully says, "you need a healer."

It sounds strange to hear my name from him, but it momentarily brings me some clarity to reorient my thoughts.

I had planned a formal greeting, one that was level-headed and collected, but the fever makes me dizzy. I open my mouth to speak and instead slip from the saddle.

The ground collides with my body. Another swell of toxin fires up my throat. I convulse, my lungs seeking air as heat builds in my veins, seeming to split them open from the inside.

The Ashan gestures at the guards with some command that is muffled behind a sharp ringing in my ears. The horses dance nervously, their hooves shaking the ground and upsetting the calm sky. Darkness gathers at the edges of my vision, and as the Ashan appears above me, it closes in and snuffs out the light.

* * *

I wake beside my father in the woods. Together we sit in the dark, a small fire crackling before us. I do not recognize the area, not even the trees. They are not the ancient and moss-covered giants of the Gatewood. These are gathered close, almost like vashte with shades of black and purple, glistening with bark like razors.

My father appears as he did the day I left him, but his expression is softly contorted in anger. I see it in the halos beneath his eyes, the slight curl in his upper lip to show the hint of a dark fang. He stares into the flames, the orange light lost in his black gaze.

"You should not be here, my acan," he says without looking at me. "But perhaps it is better that you are, if only for a moment." There is malice in his tone. It keeps me at a distance.

"Where is here?"

He does not answer my question. "It was only supposed to be me."

"What do you mean?"

"I trusted wrong. It wouldn't be the first time."

"You mistrusted me," I correct him. "You all did."

"No. You took care of them."

"I failed."

"You have done nothing of the sort. Now you have responsibilities, Ashacan. See to them."

* * *

My right eye slowly focuses to see the interlaced vines of a steepled roof. The left does not open. A ridge swells from my forehead to chin held firm by fine thread, a sliver weaving through my skin to suture the lid.

I lift my head to see coarse brown blankets covering me from the waist down. The clothes I remember wearing have vanished altogether. In their place, I wear a long linen shirt, likely pulled over my head by whoever gave me a bath, leaving me smelling faintly of soap instead of death.

The room reminds me of a healer Shayv's tent, although with more space to scatter countless ingredients: the roots and stems of woody plants, multicolored flowers, ugly weeds, and jars brimming with strange liquids. A long table is cluttered by herbs, bowls, knives, and bloody lengths of bandages. Two wicker chairs sit before a squat stone chimney that holds a small cauldron above simmering coals. There is a single window on the far wall, but it is shuttered against seeking rays of sunlight.

My head pounds. A deep ache spreads throughout my body followed by a wave of nausea. I try to lift my hands and find that they've been tied down. A leather strip traps my wrists to either side of the cot. I tug at the restraints and frantically shimmy the blanket from my chest. I kick it off the cot, as though it might make it easier to escape.

"No, no. Don't do that."

I freeze and search for the intruder. Standing in the doorway of the hut is an onduris. The small creature stands no taller than the table, like a wizened tree stump come to life. A braided, mossy beard hides most of his body and shaggy hair covers his head. He wears a green tunic and leather slippers. His dark skin is gnarled like centuries old bark from deep in the Wood. Inlaid below his protruding brow are two green eyes. One is narrower than the other, as though he squinted too many times and caused the look of scrutiny to stick. I wonder why he is in the city at all.

"Wait a moment and I'll untie you," he says while stepping into the hut. His voice manifests the low groan of a swaying branch. He bolts the wooden door behind him and sighs before turning toward the room. Then moving to the table, he stands on his toes and slams a tangle of wittleweed upon it. It knocks over a stone cup. He ignores it rolling in the dirt, picks up a wooden stool, and drags it to the bedside.

He takes a careful step onto the stool, grunting as he does so. "I had to pin your wrists," he explains "You kept thrashing. Made it damn near impossible to tend to your wounds. Now, can you promise to be still?" he asks, fixing me with his wide eye. Up close, I notice the peaks of his cheekbones and bridge of his nose are overlaid by bark that grows from his dark skin. "No running. That won't do us any good."

I nod.

He pulls the leather binds and they release. After a moment, when I have yet to run and he has made no threatening advances, his gaze softens.

"I'm Halen," he says, "resident healer to the base-born. Although now my services apparently extend to nomadic passerbys."

"...Nhuaela," I hesitantly reply.

"Yes, Nhuaela Elendira. I know exactly who you are. Seems every time I try to retire, Rolan kicks my door off its hinges. Now here I am with Selejor's daughter in my bed. *Tied* to my bed. As if I don't already have the entire Base peeping through my window."

At my father's name, I turn away. I wish there was an open window to look out or something to make the sharp turn of my head appear natural, not like I've just taken a hit to the jaw.

Halen lays a knotty palm on my forearm. "Whatever happened, child, know that I am very sorry."

I close my eyes but am met with the image of Skinner's leering face and my mother's battered body.

"You need not say anything," the onduris continues. "Your wounds have told me enough."

"Did they tell you it was kind to let me live?"

He withdraws his hand. "I am a healer. It is not my job to perform kindness. Just to heal."

"It would have been better to let me die."

"Would it have?" he poses. "Perhaps I should have thrown you in the street. Or the prison. Those are more suitable places for self-loathing."

I glare at him.

He continues drily. "I should have known there would be no use in saving the near-corpse Rolan brought to my door." He measures me with his gaze. "Is that what you want me to say?"

"Yes."

He sharply flicks my knuckle with a stony nail, leaving a sting. "Your time is not over yet. That is a fact you must accept."

You have responsibilities, Ashacan. See to them.

I have no energy to say more. I let the onduris work at my wounds. He plucks at the stitching in my face and closely examines my eye.

"You get to keep your eye," he informs me, "but not your vision."

The fact does not strike me in any particular way. It's insignificant compared to everything else.

"I'll remove the stitching in a few days. It's better to let the body heal itself where it can than force magic upon it."

He moves to the side of my cot and draws the remaining blanket aside. Beneath it, my previously poisoned thigh is wrapped in bandages. The swelling has gone down. I'm surprised at its lack of feeling. As Halen unravels the bandages to prod the wound, it feels thick with stiffness. The black infection has withdrawn from my veins as though it was never there. A dark knot of flesh remains where the arrow pierced me.

Halen speaks as he examines its progress. "I expended most of my energy on your leg. Nearly had to bleed you dry to siphon the toxin. Have you any idea what it was?"

"No."

"Hmm. I extracted a sample for inquiry. It's very cruel, whatever it is, and foreign to the Wood. The good news is you'll heal. You'll walk. There'll be a limp, but you'll strengthen yourself again."

It's entirely wrong that I'm here now, alive and well, listening to an ondurian healer remind me of my luck.

"You should eat," he tells me.

"I'm not hungry."

"I did not ask if you were."

He moves onto a bench near the table and roots around the piles of herbs. I notice the furniture of his hut is standard in size and perhaps meant to accommodate patients rather than himself. When he returns to me, he tosses a clump of wittleweed into my lap.

"Start by chewing that. Your breath is rancid."

The weed makes me think of Sil. I never found her body. I never looked, despite what I promised Serin. I couldn't bring myself to do it. I put a hand to my eye as though to rub my head. *You abandoned him. A child. Your charge.*

"I do hope you like soup," Halen gently interrupts my thoughts. With the curve of his hand, he casts a wave of orange sparks into the coals of his cookfire. The dim embers sputter and then flames flare upward to hug the bottom of the pot. "This is one of my own recipes using roots from my garden. I know elves of the vashte'rae maintain quite a unique taste for tubers…"

I couldn't care less about his soup. My brain remains caught on his casual display of magic. "You're not only a healer?" I ask.

"Certainly not. I consider myself well versed in many areas. But anymore it seems my only use is to heal."

I have seen few types of magic aside from healing. It is rare for an elf to possess anything but non-restorative magic. There have only been a handful who could wield more volatile powers, but an onduris is not an elf.

"What else can you do?"

"Other than pull you back from the brink of death?" he poses. "I think my cooking abilities are of quality."

The ache of freshly tended wounds coaxes me back onto the soft pillow of the cot. Already, fatigue threatens to take me. Then there is a knock on the door.

Halen rigidly ceases his soup stirring. Upon meeting my eyes, he puts a finger to his lips and gestures for me to remain where I am. When he opens the door, it shields the cot from sight.

"What do you want?" he cantankerously demands of the unseen visitor.

A curt voice responds. "What is the state of the Rendara?"

Halen maintains a firm grip on the door. "She's not awake yet."

"It's been five days."

"And I'm bloody well aware of the time, but five days is hardly enough to gain back consciousness when you've met the edge of death. Not that you'd know that. I don't suppose they teach such sense to city guards."

"Do not test me, *onduris*."

"Aye? What're you going to do?"

"I will report your insolence."

"Ha! To who? I'm retired."

"The Damicus demands to see the Ashacan. You were meant to give daily reports on her state, and you've given none."

"She's asleep. She's been asleep. Now get out of my yard. Your boots are crushing my clovers, you clumsy *rihar*."

At that, he slams the door.

* * *

Time passes without more than a smattering of words shared between the onduris and me. Halen does not press for further details of the Rendara, and I cannot find the strength to express them. Despite my initial hurry to find help, I know the dead do not require immediacy, and I'm too cowardly to make sense of what happened. Halen asks for no explanation and has the courtesy to ignore my uncontrollable outbursts of grief. My despair is enough to convey what I cannot manage to say.

Each day, another guard knocks on the door, and every time, Halen sends them away.

I spend much of my time asleep or pretending to be. Every few hours, Halen makes me eat and drink. At the beginning and end of each day, he examines my wounds. He gives an occasional nod or shake of his head, fidgets with his beard, or raises both of his leafy brows in concern. He gives short commands of *hold still* and *don't do that*. When I've regained the strength to stand, he begins to give me chores, such as dusting his high shelves.

He does not trap me within the hut. It's my choice that I do not step outside. Several times, he leaves the door ajar as though to tempt me, but the urge does not exist. The tasks he gives me are mindless. My existence is mindless. Even our occasional conversations are without meaning.

How many days has it been? Seven.

Is it raining? A drizzle, I think.

What are you cooking? Fried roots.

On the eighth day of my wakefulness, Halen gives a new order. "Go outside and gather me some of those yellow flowers. A cluster will do."

"Why?"

"Because a walk will do you good."

The day I began to move from the cot to the table, the onduris thought it proper to find me a suitable pair of pants rather than leave me in the short tunic. I did not mind the quantity of my bare skin, but Halen opposed my perspective.

"Please remember I am not as tall as you," he said while shielding his eyes with a curved arm. "I've no desire to see everything Evoriel gave you. Not unless you require medical attention, which you no longer do."

Since then, I have worn the thin pants he scrounged from a corner chest. Like the shirt, they are a poor fit. I miss the tailored skins of nomadic attire, but when I asked after my clothes, he gave a cheery reply. "I burned them."

Everything I arrived with was confiscated, according to Halen. Including Lo, who he said was last seen being led away by a guard. I've been too afraid to ask further details about my pony, thinking it likely he eventually collapsed from exhaustion. I've been afraid to speak of anything. When I try, the fear overwhelms, and the resulting guilt sends me spiraling.

Some of it lifts when I step outside. The expanse of the Base stretches out before me—*below* me, as Halen's hut sits a secluded tier above, not quite in line with the shops nor welcome amongst the shacks of the base-born. The bulk of the homes span between the ridge wall and mountain base without view of the fieldland, but Halen's small plot of scratchy mountain grasses gives sight to the miles of pastures and crops. Dozens of plants that should not thrive on the mountain blanket his crooked yard. The hut is bordered by a vegetable garden. There seems to be no organization to the rest of the flora. Plants tangle over one another. Flowers are scattered in an array of colors, some of which I have never seen in the Gatewood. A narrow stream of mountain water trickles through the plot, feeding the lush space. The high rocks of the mountain cast many of the elven huts in shadow below, but Halen's is a burst of life precariously watching over them.

The base-born shacks are constructed of old and twisted branches packed with stone, sections of metal, or stray shingles that may have blown off the nicer homes far above. Barrels and crates that are not small enough to fit within the shacks are placed around barren fire-pits, their flames marking gathering places for miles in either direction. A narrow path leads downward from the hut into the nearest bunch of homes. There, a wiry woman sits on one of the crates. She wears linen pants and a taut strip of material around her breasts, leaving much of her skin bare. Dust and sweat smudges her brow as she focuses on the dead rabbit in her lap. Another piece of fabric is tied around her head to keep the hair from her face. Several braids reach far down her backside, each entwined with brown cord. Perhaps sensing my gaze, she lifts her eyes to me. I'm surprised to see they are dark. Not black like my father's or amber like my mother's, but a light shade of silver, similar to the Ashan's. And then they narrow slightly, the woman understandably annoyed by my presence. Glaring, she rips the remaining skin clean off the rabbit's legs. Then she turns away and moves toward one of the barrel fires. I wonder which shack is hers, if she has a family, if I'm wearing her clothes.

My fingers itch to clench my claw necklace. An ax. My father's shoulder.

A shoe pads softly upon the bed of clover behind me.

"Do you help them?" I quietly ask, still watching the woman.

"The base-born are self-sufficient," Halen replies, "but I do what I can when it is asked of me."

I turn toward him. "And why are you helping me?"

"Because I'm a healer."

"I don't mean physically. You keep lying to the guards—to the Damicus."

"Well, do you want to talk to them? You won't even talk to me."

I look up the mountain and am unable to see the top. When there was no time, I wanted to see them. I know I still must, but I haven't been able to relay recent events to Halen. Each time I consider it, panic grips me. It's not a feeling an Ashacan can show before the council.

"Come inside," Halen tells me, ignoring my lack of response. "I need to take a look at your stitches."

"What about the flowers?"

"Forget them. I just wanted to make you breathe some fresh air."

* * *

Halen holds his face a few inches from my own and scrutinizes my stitched eye. He gingerly prods the lid with two careful fingers. I feel my left eye move with my right, but there is nothing to see. The blindness is frustrating, and I reflexively attempt to turn my head to look with my good eye.

"Stop that," the onduris chastises, tilting my head back to its original position.

"Sorry."

"You'll adjust in time."

"You can't fix it?"

"It is fixed."

"My vision, I mean."

"I know what you mean. And no. You're lucky I was able to save your eye."

It was a stupid question. No manner of healing magic can restore what is not there. I recall Shayv lecturing me as a child when I cut my finger with a hunting knife. *Be careful, child. You only get ten fingers in a lifetime.*

"You know your body, how it moves, and you still have ears. Soon enough, you'll not remember you're half blind. I'm going to remove the stitches from your lid."

He rummages around the hut. When he returns to his stool it is with a fine silver blade in hand.

"Don't turn your head this time," he warns and raises the knife to my face.

My hand shoots up, grabbing him by the wrist.

He does not flinch at my reaction. After a moment's pause he slowly flips the knife between his fingers and angles it away.

"Suppose you lie down?" he calmly suggests. "I'll bring you something for the nerves."

I let him go. Once he turns his back to me, I release a held breath and feel my heart punch the back of my ribs.

Halen returns with a small cup in hand. "Drink this."

A fermented scent wafts from the clear contents of the cup. I take a sip and swallow before it bites my tongue too hard, and then I take another. By the third swig, I start to appreciate the sharpness.

I grimace following the last drink. "That's worse than lickthorn."

"It's more effective than lickthorn. Lie down."

I do as he says, already feeling the potency of the liquor. He leans over my face. "The one who did this to you…" he gently inquires, "were they an onduris like myself?"

"No."

"Then you have nothing to fear from me."

"You're holding a knife to my eye."

"I have steady hands."

He plucks the stitching below my brow and teases the fine thread from my skin, leaving two other segments in my forehead and cheek.

There remains a ridge of scarred skin through my upper and lower lids. It's tender to the touch, and I'm hesitant to move it.

"Can you blink?" he asks.

I sluggishly open my eye.

"What about movement?"

I shift my gaze.

"Good, good. Be gentle with it to start."

"What does it look like?"

"Sit up."

I swing my legs over the side of the cot and prop my chin on my hand.

"Look at me like you mean it."

I'm unsure what exactly he wants. I look at him evenly, tiredly.

He shakes his head and turns away, disgruntled.

"What is it?"

"Nothing. Well, no. It looks like you took a blade to your eye, but it's not too bad, considering."

"Then what's wrong?"

He drops his gaze. "You have your father's eyes. Not perfectly the same. They're certainly not black, but he's there in their depths. And you look so much like Lizana that—" he pauses. "I'm sorry. You likely don't wish to hear any of this."

"You think I have his eyes?"

Hesitantly, Halen turns back to me. "Unfortunately, yes."

The response jars me in the slightest. "What do you mean by that?"

"Well..." he ponders, seeming to regret the comment under my darkening gaze. "Understand that I held great respect for your father, but I did not like him."

"Maybe that's why he never mentioned you."

He shrugs. "I'm an old acquaintance in a far-off city. I'm sure he had no need to mention me. Unless it was advantageous to him."

"Then why do you care if I have his eyes?"

He grumbles awkwardly. "It seemed like something that might comfort you is all."

I studiously cock my head at him, quietly angry.

"That's it," Halen observes, gesturing at my face. "That's precisely the look he would always give me when my suggestions were perfectly reasonable—"

"How did you know him?" I cut him off.

"Old colleagues."

"You're a healer not a diplomat," I note.

"We crossed paths long before he was…" he chuckles to himself, "…a diplomat."

"What are you laughing about?"

"I apologize. I should not have said anything."

"No," I insist, "I want to know what you know about him. You might know something that…that could help me find him."

Halen's mildly amused look hardens. "Find him?"

"I don't think he's dead."

Halen's brow creaks in thought, first empathetically and then in consideration. "I assumed you would not be here if any Rendara were still alive to protect."

Now I regret having pushed for more. I look down, unsure of how to justify my actions. "There weren't any left," I manage, "but my father was not there."

"Was he missing before the attack?"

"I don't know. I wasn't—" I swallow, forcing my heart back down my throat. "I wasn't there. Not when it mattered. And then I forgot how to do anything."

"I see." Halen takes a heavy seat on his stool, this time seeming to speak with a genuine desire to comfort. "Well, soldiers react in all sorts of ways when faced with threat."

"Not Ashacans. Not having been there in the first place is…" I grasp for the correct word, but none harsh enough seems to exist.

"Based on your wounds, it does not seem that you were *never* there," Halen points out. "If I may be blunt, you obviously seemed to have faced something head on."

"I was captured."

"And what are the rules regarding an Ashacan being captured?"

"None as long as I'm the one in danger and the vashte'rae is not. But that's not what happened."

Halen waits, saying nothing. I take a timid breath.

"There were men," I begin, "burned men."

Awakening

I TELL HIM EVERYTHING. The details come slowly. Some take me longer to recount. A few times I pause to find my breath or wipe my eyes. Halen lets me ramble, take tangents, and break for long moments of nothing while I stare at the winking fire. I thought I might have been able to speak clearly with an amount of stoicism, but I quickly crumble under the recent memory. It disorients me to think the slaughter happened only days ago, that weeks before, I was overseeing Serin's hunt. Now it seems that I never truly took part in that life, and the one I'm living is not real.

For a long time after I conclude the events, Halen is quiet. He stares into the dying fire, one hand twisting the tresses of his beard. Then he stands from his chair, goes to a small keg in the hut's corner, and refills my cup along with one for himself. On his way back to his stool, he wordlessly passes the drink to me.

"And so you never found Selejor," he finally says.

"No. I found everyone else but not him." *Not Serin. You abandoned him.*

"It's possible he fell elsewhere. However, it also strikes me that Evoriel was trying to tell you something. It is curious that the roots would interact with you."

"He would not have left. Not willingly."

"In that, I think you are quite right."

"He wouldn't have left my mother," I continue, as though Halen needed more convincing.

"No," he solemnly agrees. "He would never have left her."

"Which means he was taken."

"We should not assume—"

"But what would those...*men* want with him?"

A knock rattles the door. We both ignore it, but then it persists.

"*Iesh...*" Halen mutters, descending from his seat. He opens the door a crack and gives his usual send off. "She's sleep—"

Before he can finish his sentence, a fair hand grips the edge of the door and shoves it inward. Halen stumbles backward, cursing as the Ashan steps into the hut.

"Sleeping?" he questions, his inquisitive eyes glancing over me. "She's rather alert for a sleeping patient."

Halen aggressively straightens his mossy beard and shuts the door to the hut. "Have you no respect for healer-patient confidentiality?"

The Ashan ignores the disgruntled onduris. "I need to have a word with you, Ashacan."

"No." Halen interjects, placing himself between us. "None of that. Not now."

"This conversation is long overdue," the Ashan answers Halen while still looking at me.

Halen steps close to the Ashan's leg and lowers his voice, seeming to forget my ears were not injured. "Rolan," he reasons, "she's only just gotten comfortable."

"I wouldn't call it comfortable," I say.

The healer turns his wide eye on me.

"It's okay. I just told you everything, didn't I? May as well say more."

My words are perhaps too bitter, but they cause Halen to back down. The Ashan shifts his cloak aside, giving a glimpse of his rather casual attire save for his dwellish bracers. He reaches behind himself and repositions a wicker chair to face the cot. The movement appears familiar to him, as though he has taken a seat there a thousand times before. There is an exhausted look to his eyes as he naturally settles into the chair. He leans forward and rests his elbows on his knees. A few of his white braids fall around him. I half expect him to lower his mask like one might cast aside an unnecessary layer of clothing after a long day, but he does not.

After a moment of thought, he speaks. "The state in which you arrived made clear that there was an attack of some kind. We have already begun to investigate what occurred, but it would help to know your account of what happened. I know it is difficult to discuss, but this is a matter of defense."

"I brought you a head," I say, unsure of how else to start again. To be more thorough I add, "It was on my pony's saddle."

The Ashan nods slowly, as though too quick a movement might startle me. "I saw, but one rotted head does little good without further explanation."

"It was burned men," Halen interjects. "A pack."

"Have you heard of them?" I ask the Ashan.

"I have," he says reluctantly, "but I have never encountered them before. They have no business this far north."

"What are they?"

"Not men, from what I gather. They hail from the south, beyond the Everwatch's border. They are a people who were banished from Durast centuries ago and crossed bloodlines with inhabitants of the Burned Lands. They're more beast, if anything."

I recall Skinner's reflective eyes through the trees.

"Nhuaela," the Ashan redraws my attention as the memory creeps up. "I need facts like any other report. The basics, *sai?*"

His framing it as a report is a minor comfort, but having just told Halen, I'm numb to the idea. I down the ondurian liquor and without pause, tell him what I can.

"We were on a Long Hunt—an acan and myself. It was about two weeks after you and Elder Tolorian had left, and we spent two weeks out. When we returned, we found the camp destroyed. Everyone was..." I pause, take a quiet breath, remember the facts. "I was ambushed. There were seven burned men left behind. More of them were dead. They said something about picking off stragglers. The acan—Serin—I ordered him to run. They chased him and captured me."

The Ashan taps his cheek just below his eye, mirroring me. "They did this, I presume?"

I can't help but angle the left side of my face away from him. Knowing I have the freedom to do so reassures me. There are no ropes here. "Skinner," I recall, and then looking back to the Ashan I say, "the rotting head. He was their leader, of sorts. But he wasn't the leader. There was a King, he said. And that they got what they came for—"

I break off and share a look of realization with Halen.

"Norveh," I curse. "Do you think...?"

"It is possible," the onduris agrees.

"They took something?" the Ashan presses.

My heart races, and the warmth of the hut begins to fade. The walls crack and deteriorate like pieces of vashte in the dirt where my father knelt.

"Ashacan," the Ashan abruptly brings me back. "What did they take?"

"My father."

He waits intently for a moment more before accepting my answer. Then his gaze gradually falls. It drops all the way to the floor, and then his forehead follows straight into his hand.

"*Iesh.*"

Halen reaches up to pat his shoulder. "And that is what we were discussing when you barged in."

He shrugs off the healer's hand.

Halen persists. "It might not be as bad as we think."

"What part of *any* of this sounds good to you?"

"I didn't say good."

The Ashan sits up, ridding himself of apparent concern, and asks more. "This isn't a useful line of thought. Do you have an estimate of how many men attacked? What direction did they go?"

I bristle. "Hang on. Why would anyone take my father?"

Neither the Ashan nor Halen speaks.

"I can be silent too," I warn them.

Halen makes to respond, but the Ashan cuts him off.

"How much do you know about your father?" he asks.

"Is that a serious question?"

"Entirely."

"I know he had no business with burned men."

"Perhaps not, but he was magically inclined. It is the only thing that might have made him a target."

I laugh with a nervous timbre. The contrastingly careless sound unsettles the room. "My father is good with words, but he's no mage."

"He did have magic, even if he didn't tell you."

"Why would he not tell me?"

"Magic is dangerous. I imagine he wanted to protect you."

"And yet you know?"

"I know where every magic wielder is posted along our borders."

"He isn't one of your soldiers," I say cuttingly.

"He was a friend."

"Then you're quick to think your friend is dead."

"You're quick to assume my thoughts."

"You don't know anything about my father."

"Not your father, no."

"Alright," Halen intercedes "Rolan, move on. Nhuaela, have another drink."

I refuse to touch my empty cup.

The Ashan continues, unperturbed. "So, seven men, including this Skinner, but there were more?"

"It was a pack like Halen said," I reply tersely, now irritated. "I'm not sure how many. Enough to take losses. Enough to kill—" I'm unable to finish the sentence as grief stings my eyes.

"Do you know what direction they fled?"

I shake my head. "I saw no signs of their movement north, nor did they appear to venture west, but I don't know for sure. The whole perimeter was affected."

"What do you mean by that?"

Haunted, I reiterate Halstaer's words. "The vashte reacted."

"They reacted?"

"They exploded."

The Ashan looks to Halen. "Have you heard of this before?"

Halen's posture slumps upon his exhale. His reply is tired. "Not in ages."

"But you have heard of it," I say.

"Most think it a myth."

"It's not a myth I'm familiar with," the Ashan admits.

"It's one of the more hidden facets of the Vhanian Reign," Halen explains. "Not many have memory of it. I only know because of my Giver."

I recognize the phrase in passing, although it takes me a moment to recall its meaning as applied to the onduris.

Halen continues, seeming to ponder the memory of his mother tree. "In my creation, she instilled the stories of *her* creation. But that was centuries ago, and I have not heard mention of it since."

"How many centuries?" I ask.

"Roughly the helm of the Mortal Age."

I glance at the Ashan, hoping to find a similar disbelief in his eyes, but he appears indifferent to the admission, seeming to have heard it before.

"That was three-thousand years ago," I say, incredulous.

"I told you. I'm old." Halen returns.

"Is that normal for an onduris?"

"We require a long lifespan in order to educate elves."

"Then please educate us on exploding vashte," the Ashan presses.

"How well do you know your history?" Halen asks of me.

"Which part?" I challenge. "The crafting of Uunshyl? The Sibling's Watch? Or do you mean something more recent, like the Silence of Edgewood?"

"Well," he nestles into his seat. "One of those is of particular interest, but we'll get to that later. You know the vashte are sacred, but do you know why?"

"Evoriel created them," I supply, not favoring his questioning approach.

"Evoriel created all trees, all nature. Why do vashte matter, specifically?"

The Ashan and I share a look of uncertainty.

Halen chuckles. "You've accepted them without question."

"Iesh." I try again. "They're strong."

"All trees are strong."

"Vashte are connected," the Ashan says. "They respond."

"That's why they make good bows," I add. "Humans steal them because they think they know their use, but vashte will never answer to them."

"There you have it," Halen interrupts. "Vashte are Evoriel's answer. Vashte are his direct line to you. They assist you. They help in times of need."

"As a defense," the Ashan remarks, both of us realizing our ignorance at once.

I mimic my mother's words, wondering if she knew. "They're tactical."

Halen nods, pleased. "They were protecting the Rendara. As much as they could."

After a moment, I shake my head. "That sounds like mythical horseshit. We've been in danger before, and the trees have never reacted."

"But have you ever been desperate? Truly desperate?"

"So now we must be desperate in order for Evoriel to answer?" I retort, offended.

"Gods cannot always answer how they might wish."

"If that was his answer, then all he did was help level our camp. His answer likely killed Ser—" I stop myself, not wanting to pour my hatred into Serin's name. "It would have been better if he did not answer at all."

"I know you are angry, but there is more going on here. This is very old magic, Nhuaela, and we must be cautious about its awakening."

"No, she's right," the Ashan says. "There are vashte in the north, and we have had many moments of desperation. Yet they have never reacted."

Halen sinks lower in his seat. "I have no explanation for it. I don't even know if there is an explanation. All I can tell you is that the last time this happened, your ancestors were running and hiding from the Vha. The vashte were Evoriel's only means of assistance. He was too weak for anything else. Which is why I'm concerned about their defensive nature resurfacing. I fear it reflects a similar distress in our god."

"I only care about the distress of my people," the Ashan replies bitterly. "There's enough to consider without thought of distraught gods." He looks at me. "I will take your account to the Damicus. They need to hear it, and then you will have your audience."

"I hardly think it's necessary that she stand before the Damicus," Halen says.

"It is." The Ashan stands and returns the wicker chair to its original place by the fire, signaling an end to our conversation. "While I do not doubt you, Ashacan, the Damicus is less likely to trust your word until we have further evidence to support it. Until then, I'm sorry to say you must stand trial for abandoning the Rendara."

Halen jerks forward. "What utter nonsense. You come in here to pick her brain only to accuse her!"

The Ashan lifts a calming hand to the onduris, which Halen immediately dismisses.

"She brought you the bloody fucking head of a burned man!"

"*Halen,*" he says, exasperated.

The onduris glares.

"This is not *my* accusation." The Ashan meets my blank gaze, his silver eyes two clear slashes in a darkening space. "I am on your side, Ashacan."

Halen scoffs. "If you were on her side, you wouldn't put her before the Damicus."

"She will end up before them whether I tell them or not."

"Can't you send her north with the rest of the troubled cases?"

"Those troubled cases are sent north by decision of the Damicus."

Halen grumbles under his breath in the ondurian tongue.

"I deserve to stand trial," I finally manage. "I failed my people, and that needs to be answered for."

"Ridiculous," Halen scoffs.

The Ashan addresses me around Halen's displeasure. "The Damicus gathers tomorrow at midday. I will send an escort to lead you to the Hall. And *you*," he points to Halen, "you are not to interfere."

Halen takes a steady drink. "A bit late for that."

The Ashan is sure to slam the door on his way out.

* * *

"Here." Halen passes me his half empty cup.

Consecutively reopening the wounds has ruptured my resolve. I was exhausted after describing the Rendaran slaughter to Halen. Explaining to the Ashan has left a wider hollow in the pit of my stomach. It is one thing for my healer to see me completely vulnerable. It is another for my superior to glimpse my failure.

The liquor has left me dizzy. I close my eyes but cannot face the memories within. My heart races, and the frail composure I've mustered over my conscious days betrays me.

There is nothing to keep me present within the hut. Its vine walls wither under the crushing grasp of slithering roots. The world outside is a field littered with cleaved tents caught in a strong wind. The burned men rise from the dirt, chunks of vashte tumbling from their backs. Skinner reaches for me, and then Halstaer is there, jumping in front of me to take the hit from Skinner's sword.

When the vision releases me, there is a sharp pain in my leg. The burn intensifies until the walls of the hut are solid once more. I jerk my leg from the pressure of Halen's thumb where he digs it into my tender knee.

"*Rihar!*" I growl.

"Some thanks would be nice."

"Why?"

"You're back, are you not?"

I hold my leg to my chest.

"Pain is an easy way to ground yourself," the onduris says. "Remember that when you're standing before the Damicus."

"I'll be fine."

"They're going to pick you apart like a flock of rhougls. You'll have to stand your ground. Don't let them blame you."

"I am to blame."

"Did you send the burned men? Did you kill your own?"

"I was not there to protect them."

"If you were there, what more could you have done?"

The strength and conviction in his words pulls the light of the room inward. The flames of the fire whip.

"It doesn't matter," I say weakly, having lost the will to yell. "I wasn't there, and I should have been, if only to die beside them."

"Selejor once said something very similar."

I tilt my stone cup. The liquor climbs to the edge. I debate swallowing it in one gulp.

Halen shakes his head, exasperated by my silence. "You really have no idea. No idea at all."

"Stop telling me what I don't know."

"It's important that—"

"My family is dead! And this King who did it is still out there. The only thing I *want* to know is what direction he is in, so I may hunt him down and put an ax in his skull. Can you help me with that?"

Halen scowls. "Rolan might not want to tell you, but *magically inclined* is an understatement about your father."

I recall my dream of him, the malice in his eyes, the stark unfamiliarity of his demeanor, and lean toward Halen.

"I know my father," I say, "and he is all I need to know."

"This is no time to stick your head in a tree hollow."

I finish what's left of the liquor, and following the Ashan's lead, rattle the door hinges on my way out.

I lie upon a bed of Halen's precious clover with my face toward the distant Wood. What dew collects on the lush clover cools through my borrowed clothes and soothes stiff muscles. A gentle wind breathes down the mountainside and rolls through the valley. It ripples across the fieldland where flecks of silver starlight shimmer in the grasses.

For a time, I close my right eye and will vision to return to my left, but there is nothing to penetrate the darkness. When I close them both, I search for silence beyond the muffled sounds of Daerva'Tor and pretend I am back at camp.

I'm reminded of cool nights from before I was Ashacan. Nights after arduous hunts or long watches when Halstaer and I would inevitably make our way to each other—not that we were ever far. We always worked close, intuition telling us when we were moving near one another. It's what made us excellent partners in everything. The hunter's language of subtle gestures and sharp whistles was fluid between us. At a glance we could read each other's frustrations and know how to handle them. I only ever felt a similar connection to Beshtel, who we separately turned to when we could not turn to each other. Without her comfort, the rift of rank might have deepened, but in many ways, she kept us close, kept us talking until we adjusted.

I wish she were here, too, if only to refuse sleeping on the rough ground of Uunshyl or to steal away the blankets and nudge me from her space. It was Halstaer who preferred the open air.

I touch my stomach in search of his hand. Most often he would sling his arm over my waist and fall asleep with his face pressed into my braids. Many nights I held him closer. Many nights I never coveted a blanket.

I grasp my borrowed shirt, knotting my hand in the scratchy linen. Beneath are two scarred lesions under my ribs where the caracosh nearly killed me. *What a difference it would have made.*

Eventually, I fall asleep, cold against Halen's hut.

The Long Walk

I WAKE TO THE patter of rain. It sprinkles my face, and I pull my blanket over my cheek, resting a moment longer before remembering no blanket accompanied me outside the night before. I sit up in the grey dawn and wrap the blanket around myself. The rain continues in a steady rhythm. I burrow my toes into the clover, attempting to alleviate a slight headache until the sun crests behind clouds, backlighting them with a dull yellow.

I'm streaked with water by the time I reenter the hut with the blanket draped around my shoulders. Damp dirt clings to my feet. I pluck a clover leaf from my cheek.

Halen sits at his table with a cup furling with steam. "You sleep better outside," he remarks before taking a sip. "Or maybe it's just the liquor."

I shrug off the wet blanket and close the door—gently this time.

"Get yourself a cup from that cupboard," Halen instructs. "I've just heated tea. Sunleaf. It'll wake you up."

Having studied his hut during my days of bedrest, I know exactly where the cups are kept. Each is painted with flowers. I choose one adorned with yellow lacelets. Beshtel used to press them to her wrists to leave a sweet scent.

Halen fills my cup. "You'll need a bath. They won't let you into the Damicus Hall looking like that."

I sip the bitter tea still in a daze from the revelations of the night before. "Does Elder Tolorian know?"

"I'm sure Rolan has mentioned the details to him by now. I suspect he would have been first to know the moment you were stabilized."

"I thought he might have come down."

"The Elders do not come down here unless it's to pass through."

"I suppose there's no reason for him to come," I realize, gripping my cup. "He must be so ashamed."

"I doubt that is the case. Let me have a look at your stitches."

He perches on the tabletop to examine the remaining threads through my forehead and cheek.

"These can come out," he decides. "Another day wouldn't hurt, but Elder Creeva is liable to turn you away at the door if you arrive with stitches in your face."

"But the scar won't offend her?"

"I'm afraid everything offends her."

I have not met her but know to dislike her by name. She is partial to the Nishtari, and our few visits to Daerva'Tor always resulted in argument between my mother and her—arguments I never witnessed but over the decades gathered their context.

"She disagreed with my mother being chief," I say, already honing a bitterness toward the Elder.

Halen extracts the thread from my forehead and brow. "Elder Creeva will instigate you. It's her method of control. Lizana never stood for it, and that is why they locked horns. I expect nothing less from you, of course, but you mustn't let her provoke you. Not now."

"I won't stand quietly if she speaks ill of my mother. Or any Rendara."

"I would expect nothing less, but they are going to be looking for anger. Hostility." He holds my gaze. "Anything that might implicate a lone Ashacan or speak to perceived faults."

"They can think what they want about me, but not about my mother."

"Just try to be tactful."

He steps down from the table and proceeds to exit the hut, leaving me to finish my tea. A few minutes later he returns. He dries his wet hands on the front of his robe.

"I filled the bath around back when you're ready."

"Filled the bath? You were only out there for a minute."

"It's been raining all morning."

"It hasn't rained that much."

"No," he says impatiently. "But across the entirety of the fieldlands it has."

I give him a confused look over my cup.

"Depths, child. *Magic.*"

"You can control water?"

"It's too early for this. Go make yourself presentable."

"What about the crops?"

"It's still raining. They'll be fine."

Halen's bath is a wooden tub large enough for an elf. A canvas blind shades it from view of the base-sector. It provides more privacy than I have ever known. Nudity meant little to the Rendara, and while there were some days when I wished for privacy, I'd give anything to have my vashte'rae with me again; for my mother to help me brush through snarls in my wet hair; for Beshtel to teasingly flick water at my face, or Lya to glare at me whilst Halstaer tactlessly stole a glance in my direction.

The bath water laps against my bent legs. I rest my head on my knees and let the rain pelt my back. Eventually, I wash away the mustiness of the hut and familiarize myself with my bare wounds. A bar of soap leaves me smelling like the sharpness of a gaea. I work my fingers through my hair in attempt to untangle my matted braid, but it is no use. I pull the knots downward before they refuse to budge at the top of my shoulders.

Frustrated, I leave it and dry myself. I pull the long tunic over my head before slipping back into the hut.

Halen flicks his hand toward a stack of folded silks. "Put those on. They should be a proper fit. There's a brush, too. Do something about that rat's nest."

I discard the linen tunic without care.

"Iesh," Halen gasps, averting his gaze.

"Surely you've seen naked elves before," I say while pulling on the clothes.

"I've seen everything. And I don't wish to see any more."

I dislike the grey fabrics, but they fit my stature better than the oversized linens, and it's nice to have a pair of shoes once more. I'm thankful they are not a more lavish material, or the elaborate lengths of robes worn by highborn fair. The fitted, simplistic style reminds me of something my father might have worn for a visit to the city, but I do not fit the part. The clothes are silly when paired with my ugly scars and matted hair.

I doubtfully look at the brush. My hair has been tangled before. Badly tangled. I might be able to straighten it given enough time, but the prospect tires me. Exhausts me. All of it does.

Taking a knife from the table, I saw away my braid just above my shoulders.

"Gods and dragons, girl!" Halen exclaims.

I throw the length of my clumped braid into the fire and shake the shortened strands out around my face.

"May as well take your clothes off too," he tells me.

"Turn around."

Halen gives me privacy while I brush through what remains. I divide it into sections and thread two braids along my skull behind my ears. There's hardly enough for them to meet at the nape of my neck where I twist them into a tight knot.

"Are you decent?" he asks.

"Sai."

He cautiously peers over his shoulder to scrutinize my appearance. "It'll do."

We partake in a small breakfast until the arrival of my escort. They come before midday, likely allocating enough time for me to limp up the mountain road.

Halen and I wait a moment before answering the impatient knock, each of us taking one last sip of tea. He grabs a walking stick from the corner and pulls an overcoat about himself. Then he offers me a hand.

"Ready?"

I accept, fitting only three fingers upon his palm. He squeezes my hand instead of physically tugging me forward, but the encouragement helps me get to my feet. I rub the soreness from my thigh before opening the door to four Daervish guards.

Each of them is pristine, unblemished by dirt or scars. Their white braids are identically woven and they all carry a sword at their belts. Their fine plated armor catches the dull light of the dreary morning. They look less than pleased with their orders. The man closest to me grimaces as he looks at my face.

"By order of the Damicus, you are to follow us to the Hall," he says, hardening his voice in accordance with my glare.

Halen taps his stick against my calf, nudging his way across the hut's threshold. He addresses the guards. "Yes, yes, let's get on with it then. Come along."

"You are not to venture forth, onduris," the lead guard warns. "The Damicus has not requested your presence in this matter."

"I'm not going to the Damicus, you *rihar*. I'm just going for a walk alongside my patient. To make sure she is seen safely to the Hall."

"Your assistance is not requested."

"No?" Halen retorts. "And if she passes out halfway up, are you going to fetch her a glass of water? If her leg buckles, will you massage her muscles? Perhaps let her lean on your shoulder?"

I curiously raise my brow at the guard. All four of them remain silent.

Halen assuredly steps forward. "That's what I thought."

The man turns on his heel and takes the lead before Halen. The other three flank us, ushering us through the Base-sector, unable to maintain a hurried pace due to Halen's short strides. I'm grateful for it. We're hardly out of sight of the hut when my knee begins to protest at the steady incline. Halen pats my leg, and a numbing sensation sinks through my knee.

"That should get you there," he mutters upward. "Just keep pace with me."

It takes us some time to make our way through the final homes of the base-born. They are strange lodgings, cramped between the nooks of sharp rocks. They possess no grandeur, no detailed engravings or inlaid scales. There are doorways of hide or fabric, frail roofs, and deteriorating frames, but I find familiarity in their practicality. Between them are strung lines upon which are various garments and faded sheets. An occasional mountain flower bursts through the muddied ground, persisting despite the strengthening wind. Cats lounge in window sills and glare from tight alleys. They eye us indifferently, caring more for the darting bugs stirred up by the warm rains.

The few base-born who do not labor in the fields or serve the high families watch as we pass by. They give me single glances, curious but preoccupied by their daily work. Scrawny children scamper furtively across the narrow streets, pausing in their games to whisper to each other. A pregnant woman turns her head while scattering feed to a group of clipers. Upon seeing her, they leap over the rocks, their round eyes expectant. Other base-born make their descent to the valley, their plain clothes already dampened for a day of fieldwork. They move to the other side of the narrow street when crossing our path, pretending to not see me.

The streets of the mountainside are vine-like in their way. Some climb the stone in steep shortcuts for those brave enough to risk them. The main road is wide and flat, carved into the mountain where necessary so that horses and carts can safely pass. At the height of the first tier, we encounter a smattering of sturdy shops and lodgings crafted of dark strongwood. Men and women bustle around market stalls to bid on cheap cuts of meat, overripe vegetables, and hardening breads. The lowest base-born are not present here, and the plain clothes for hard labor brighten with an array of soft colors, finer leathers, or simply embroidered garments. The unique lengths of string threaded in their braids become shades of green, purple, yellow, and red. Guards stand posted at certain intervals. They lean against buildings or are caught in casual conversation. Judging by their clean armor, I doubt they have seen much action within the confines of the city. I imagine it is a coveted position compared to guarding in the north.

As we near Paths district, we pass a stout tavern asymmetrically built into the slanted mountain. Under an overhang outside, three dwarves smoke, keeping their long pipes dry from the light rain. They wear fine, tailored jackets and have braided their beards in the tidiest of plaits adorned with jeweled beads. Even their boots are polished and intricately laced. They scrutinize the milling streets from behind swirls of smoke as an unkempt Daervish boy hitches two impeccably groomed oxen to their large cart. When I pass, one of the dwarves adjusts his gold framed spectacles, flashing multiple rings as he does so, and studies me close.

One of the guards at my back pushes me forward. "Move," he instructs.

The dwarf makes an unheard comment to his companions as I'm ushered to the Paths gate. Between the mountain landings are short crevasses to catch any falling rocks and prevent them from smashing down the mountainside. At least that is what Halen tells me as we pass through the thick gate and across the stone bridge that links each sector.

"They have their strategic purposes as well," Halen mentions, "although those purposes have not been needed since the Siege."

I glance over the bridge to the shallow canyon below. A small brown dragon slinks between the hunks of stone. It appears to be hunting some creature, likely a rodent. It pauses to shake its scales of rain and briefly spread its wings, but upon seeing us on the bridge, it shimmies into a burrow beneath the rocks.

One of the guards spits over the bridge toward it. "Pests," he mutters.

"In the Wood, they'll kill you," I say, feeling antagonistic. In truth, such a little dragon is of no threat regardless of its whereabouts. Something along the lines of a root dragon would be of greater concern, but I don't expect a city guard to know that.

"We're not in the Wood, *Ashacan*." He spits the rank as he spat at the dragon. I imagine by now rumors have spread. Enough people saw me arrive, after all. At the very least they know I'm alone, far from my vashte'rae. I'm sure they are glad to see me headed to trial.

Paths is less populated and largely comprised of finer homes and specialized shops. The dirt road is replaced by flagged stone. Manicured flowers hang outside windows or wind between alleys, creating quiet sitting areas. Those who we encounter on the streets walk with purpose, lifting their robes from the wet stone. Harsh glances are cast my way. Outside a bookshop, a dwarven woman pauses in conversation with a fairborn man. They initially look confused and then offended by my presence. The dwarf puts a thoughtful hand to the red scruff on her chin, her blue eyes narrowing with intrigue.

The wind whips us along the path until we reach a secret entrance to the Peaks, the highest district in Daerva'Tor. By now, the rain has strung my flyaway hairs to my temples and neck. The grey silks of my fitted clothes are peppered with dark stains. My knee aches when we pause for the silver scaled gates to pull back, granting us entrance to the highest tier.

The highborn fair whose homes stand in proximity to the main road wait upon their balconies on pillowed chairs to judge my arrival. Their long robes fan outward and pool around their feet. Each is made of rich materials and embroidered with patterns of flowers, water, or mountains. Their white braids fall in long tresses entwined in cords of silver, gold, and icy blue. The women weave theirs into complex styles atop their heads. Despite their scrutiny, it is impossible to say they are not beautiful. An ethereal glow emanates from them. They are so perfectly cut they could be statues with eyes of starlight.

As we enter the courtyard of the Damicus Hall, I look back. Over spired roofs of the highborn, the fieldlands are glossy patches veiled with a grey rain. Beyond them, the outer wall of Daerva'Tor is an inky line. It barricades the Gatewood that seems to consume the entire world as it fades into the horizon.

And somewhere deep within is the leveled camp of the Rendara. Somewhere, a hundred bloodstained vashte are shattered in the rain, and far beyond that is a pack of wild men, pleased with their spoils, perhaps dragging my father through the dirt.

"Nhuaela," Halen tugs my pantleg. "We're here."

I turn my attention to the Damicus Hall. My chest tightens. The peaks of the Hall's sloped roof are lost in the clouds. High spires in the shape of upturned claws stretch into the sky. Between them, the roof dips like the webbing of wings. It sits at the edge of a sheer cliff that descends to a deep ravine and overlooks the Undecayed encampment. The dark wood of its siding flakes. Its shingles furl with the strong winds. The grand stairs that curve toward its reinforced door are worn with age and dangerously smoothed from exposure. Growing between them is a thicket of vashte trees. The clouds briefly break, allowing for a ray of sunlight to glimmer against the dampened wood. Hues of deep purple mingle with the black and then the clouds shift, stifling the shimmer of the jagged bark.

I take a moment to catch my breath under the gaze of the Hall. I shift my weight to my good leg and rub the knot of tissue above my left knee.

A guard rudely shoves his way between Halen and I. The onduris jumps backward with a swear.

"You are to remain here," the guard reminds Halen. "The Ashacan enters alone."

My obstinate companion works his walking stick into the crook of two stones and leans against it. "Fine by me. Use your head, Nhuaela, and I don't mean as a hammer."

I nod at Halen, clinging to any advice he could possibly give as the guard wordlessly leads me to the stairs. He pauses at the bottom and jerks his chin upward, signaling for me to continue alone.

If it were not for Halen, I would not have been able to traverse Daerva'Tor let alone climb the stairs to the Damicus Hall. Each bend of my knee tugs the strings of muscle that were severed by the burned man's arrow. I'm glad to be facing away from the guards so they cannot see the slight winces that twitch upon my face. At the top, I bite the inside of my cheeks, forcing an expression of control as I approach the large double doors guarded by two *vatanukro* soldiers.

They are unlike the other city guards and have noticeably served in the north. The double swords crossed on their backs tell of their rank, but their scars express it more. The woman on the left embraces a row of puncture-like divots along her neck and jaw, as though something bit her, and the man bears an ugly gash along his skull. Their armor is not the plate of city guards, but a make similar to that of the Ashan's. It is light yet defensive, meant for quick movements just like their swords. I know their kind. They are like my mother, like Halstaer, or Frae—soldiers who have no need for layers of metal and chain. Their eyes remain forward and their bodies motionless, but I know better than to think they have not already made note of every detail upon my person—that they would not be ready if I were to move recklessly.

Carefully, I place my palm against the engraved door. The heavy wood swings inward, and I enter a sparse antechamber.

The constant whisper of mountain wind and rain are silenced as the door closes solidly behind me. I'm glad to find myself alone in the space. Grey light seeps in from narrow windows that crown the entrance wall. The rays light the room in a dim glow. The air is warm and carries the unexpected scents of the Gatewood. Old wood. Ancient bark and sharp stone. Damp soil. Dewy vines. I've no idea how they've captured such a scent, or why it surprises me that the heart of Evoriel's land reflects the forest that encircles it.

It does not comfort me as it once did. If existing in Daerva'Tor has provided me with one thing, it is the distance needed to bind the unspeakable grief and bury it deep within myself. But suddenly it seems I'm not in the city at all and am stranded in the Gatewood surrounded by terrible things.

There are paintings on the walls. Every inch of the antechamber is adorned with black ink upon pale wood.

The strokes are quick as though the artist dashed their brush wildly across the wall. While the lines are vague, they are defined enough for my mind to connect their overall portrayal of the Creation of Uunshyl and the Sibling's Watch, Andapura's Rise and the Vhanian Reign. It follows the long wall, beginning with a vague depiction of Andapura settling on the surface of Uunshyl. From his outstretched arms fall five children: Evoriel, Ixis, Duporr, Tekna, and Lelendelus. Then Andapura's form sinks into Uunshyl, leaving his children to overlook the land as he falls to the Deep. In their watch, they are shown creating the mortal races. Evoriel breathing life into the leaves of the trees to create the elves. Ixis scattering magic rays upon her humans. Duporr crafting dwarves from stone. Tekna shielding the orcs with a white light. And Lelendelus pulling fire and shadow into the hearts of the Glim.

Then, Andapura returns, rising from his Depths to find Uunshyl overtaken and his children sharing love and gifts with mortals. In response, there is an image of Andapura's wrath. He steals the best qualities from each race except the Glim, who Lelendelus hid in shadow. And in the reaches of the desolate north, Andapura withdrew to create the Vha.

The mural drastically darkens, overtaking the wall with images of enslaved mortals being whipped into submission, constructing cities, and fleeing toward their creator gods who faded to near nothingness as mortal faith was eradicated.

Following the period of darkness is the fall. Evoriel, the oldest of the Five, stole into Vhania and vanquished the Vha. In their destruction, Andapura was banished to the Deep, trapped there by the Five.

The elaborate painting concludes with the Siege of Daerva'Tor. It occurred after the Vhanian Reign ended nearly one thousand years ago. It was then, at the height of Kallish rule, that the first human empire clashed with elves.

In the heat of battle, each soldier is faceless aside from white or black marks denoting the eyes of fairborn or vashte'rae elves. I step closer to the most impressive moment. A warrior wields a dagger against the gaping jaws of a deepdweller on a blotchy field of dead. The elf's form is fluid and graceful, cast larger than the rest, and I'm caught in the gaze of their black eyes.

The door at the end of the room opens. In my periphery, I notice the Ashan enter, but still, I cannot pull my eyes from the wall. My hand seeks to trace the lines.

The Ashan loudly clears his throat to put a stop to my hand's advance. I withdraw my arm and angle away from the mural. He has changed from last I saw him. Instead of casual linens, he is back to wearing the practical vestment of an elite soldier—layers of dark greys and icy silvers interspersed with straps and patches of leather at his forearms, shoulders, and legs. A belt wraps closely around his waist, containing a sheathed sword. A thicker strap cuts diagonally over his chest to hug a second sword to his back. He crosses his arms. The bracers of dark dweller bone flex with his movements, and above the seam of his mask, his eyes shift between me and the painting.

"Do you need a moment?" he asks.

The question lands lightly on my ears. The gentle words go against his appearance. They chisel a crack in my composure.

Of course, I need a moment, I want to scream, but instead I step away from the painting, pretending it holds no meaning. Then far too late, I perform the half-step bow. In my current attire, it feels ridiculous, and then I worry he might think me mocking.

"It's alright, Ashacan," he says. Crooking two fingers, he urges me to step forward. "There will be enough formalities inside, do not worry about them out here."

He rests a hand on the door to the inner chamber. Closer now, I notice dark halos of exhaustion under his eyes.

"Elder Tolorian will greet you," he informs me. "Bow to him and then he will proceed with introductions."

"And then?"

"And then they will discuss your circumstance. Ready?"

I nod. "Let me be done with this."

He parts the doors.

A Sensible Thought

BEYOND THE DOORS, A long hall spans forward. Ornately carved strongwood columns line the bare walls to a raised dais at the room's end. There, five Damicus members sit upon high backed chairs. They are difficult to see. I recognize Elder Tolorian by his radiance, but each member is overtaken by a glare of grey light that envelops them from behind. At their backs is a highly steepled open wall leading to a wide balcony. It stretches into an abyss of coalescing clouds. Considering the Hall's place at the sheer side of the Daerva'Tor's crown, I'm sure the balcony overlooks the north and Undecayed base. I wonder if this is where the Damicus safely watched the Siege a thousand years ago.

A brisk wind enters the room. It chills the sweat on my brow. At the base of the dais and in a line leading to the council are open beds of hot coals. They are kept in dishes of sand to prevent fire to the ancient Hall. Occasionally, a low flame licks upward with the wind.

The Ashan moves confidently ahead of me. His long braids sway against his back. I notice they are interwoven with black thread. The thinnest strands catch in the breeze around him as he glides forward. I wish I could carry myself the same. The limp in my leg becomes more prominent with each step, and the rest of me is tightly wound.

The wind dies when the Ashan stops before the council. He bows swiftly, and then steps aside to take his place against one of the strongwood columns, leaving me stranded and bare to the Elders' colorless eyes.

I mean to look at them directly, but I'm drawn to the coals lying at the foot of their dais. The flames grow unruly against the hollows of a large skull. From within, a pulsing orange light highlights a rocky brow. Even without his skin and hair, Skinner's likeness remains.

"Nhuaela," Elder Tolorian speaks first. The edges of his words crackle in a soothing key, drawing my eyes upward.

The brilliant old elf rises, stooped but still powerfully present and outstretches a hand. If I were nearer, I know he would take my palm or perhaps squeeze my arm.

"Although the circumstances are dire, I am pleased to see you safe," he says. "While I am very sorry for what has transpired, you understand I must remain impartial until we have concluded our meeting today. Welcome to our Hall."

I follow the Ashan's instructions and bow in response.

After a moment, Elder Tolorian releases me. "Rise now, acan. There is much to discuss."

Tolorian retakes his seat and continues in a less formal tone. "The Ashan has relayed your story to us. Since then, a great grief has weighed on my heart." He pauses a moment. A wetness glitters in his eyes. "I have tried to refrain from believing anything just yet. I would first like to inquire about the details of your predicament, as would the rest of the Damicus. Before we begin, however, allow me to introduce you to the full council."

Each Damicus Elder is fairborn. Following the row of chairs beside himself, Tolorian begins with the Elder on his right, an aged but muscular man whose hair has long since grown into corded lengths of unmanageable locks. His unwelcoming expression is weathered by small scars that I imagine descend beneath his dark robes. His hands are bound in black binds, as though he means to spar following the trial.

"This is Elder Drynn, Voice of the Undecayed. Beside him is Elder Creeva, our Head of External Relations."

Being the only woman on the council, I recognized her the moment I entered the room. Like many highborn fair, she possesses a condescending countenance. Her purple stained lips are naturally pinched, drawing the gaunt skin of her cheeks sharply toward her chin. Her silvery eyes fiercely study my scarred face and short braids. The only indication of her age are several pristine lines at the corner of her eyes. Her white hair is woven with gold and pulled into an intricately braided bun at the top of her head. Dark purple robes the same color as her lips drape around her feet and off the dais like a waterfall. A deeply cut neckline reveals the hollows of her collarbone and sternum upon which a golden pendant rests.

"Next is Elder Jerus, the Grand Judge."

His robes are a deep green embroidered with gold leaves. There is an off-putting richness to him, and his title is far from my concern as a member of the vashte'rae. The Grand Judge is to preside over city matters, not tribal. Like Elder Creeva, he tilts his chin for the sole purpose of having a higher place to look down from, although his gaze must first pass the length of his hooked nose.

"And lastly there is Elder Tan, the Overseer of Trade, who still has many years to grow into his title."

"You flatter me," Elder Tan replies before nodding to me in greeting.

His sharp face maintains a boyish youth. The corner of his mouth is held in a constant smirk and his braids have an almost golden tint. He appears far more charming than the others but there remains a coldness in his perfectly pale eyes. Like Tolorian, he wears an immaculately tailored white robe, the only difference being a subtly embroidered blue dragon that winds up one sleeve.

"And of course, there is the Ashan," Tolorian remembers, motioning toward him against the column. I'm glad he took a position to my right where I can still see him in my periphery. "Who, while not a member of the Damicus, is directly involved in terms of the Gatewood's defense and as your superior, he too is welcome to question or provide insight as he sees fit. Now, Nhuaela Elendira, presently known as Ashacan of the Rendara, do you hereby swear to speak the truth under Evoriel's watch?"

I sigh. "Yes."

"And we, the Damicus, shall judge accordingly as Evoriel guides us. Elder Tan, will you present Nhuaela's charge?"

The young elder's smirk flattens, and his eyes pierce me as he recites my crime. "As Ashacan, you have failed to protect your vashte'rae, the Rendara of the southern territory. You effectively abandoned them on several points, including the loss of an acan under your watch and the abandonment of any others who may have survived. You fled, leaving your enemy at large and your lands undefended. For someone of your rank, this is an unforgivable crime against your kin."

Despite my preparation, the accusation withers me. My heart shrivels downward into my stomach. I remain still, hoping to give no tell of my shame.

Elder Tan continues on. "We are here to determine the extent of your offense, whether or not you had prior knowledge or motives involving these burned..." he momentarily hesitates, his eyes darting to Skinner's skull in the fire. "...shall we call them *men?* Humans? They do not sound like any human I have met."

"If humans did this then the Ashacan truly has no excuse for such failure," Elder Drynn roughly remarks.

"They were not human," I say too firmly.

Elder Drynn glares.

"Call them men for now," Elder Tolorian advises. "They may not be human, but they are still men."

"A pity to be associated with," Tan says. "Anyhow, Ashacan, we have several clarifying questions for you. You will answer them, and we will decide the best course of action based on those answers. Quite simple, really. And then we will be on our way."

"You have somewhere to be?" Drynn demands.

Tan's smirk returns. "I always have somewhere to be."

"This is a serious matter," Tolorian chastises. "I will not abide carelessness for the sake of frivolous engagements."

"The utmost importance," Elder Creeva speaks for the first time, emphasizing Tolorian's point. Her voice is deeper than I expected. It fills the room as she leans forward in her chair to look closer at me. "You take after your mother."

"Why is that relevant?" I ask, my anger suddenly clouding whatever anxiety I felt a moment before.

"Lizana had a penchant for upheaval. If you inherited it...well, I'm not surprised something unfortunate has finally befallen the Rendara."

"And what do you mean by that?" I press, wanting her to go further.

"It's what you are doing right now. Instigating. Asking for a fight."

"My mother is dead, and you would blame her?"

"Not entirely. You are the one before us."

"Then don't speak of her. I know she doesn't care to hear your voice."

There is a momentary silence as the council anticipates Creeva's response. I wait too, hoping she gives reason for me to say more. Instead, she settles back with predatory patience.

"If we could please move on, I for one would very much like to know why you were not present when your tribe was attacked," Elder Jerus says to me.

I swallow what little saliva wets my tongue. "I was on a Long Hunt," I begin.

"A hunt?" Jerus questions.

"A *Long* Hunt."

"What in Evoriel's name is a long hunt?" Creeva demands.

I do not immediately answer, baffled by their ignorance. "It is sacred," I say, "a trial to test the skills of aspiring acans."

Only Tolorian and Drynn follow me. The others share skeptical looks. From the corner of my eye, I glance at the Ashan, but he is unreadable.

Elder Jerus humors me. "So, you were out hunting when this attack occurred. Why did you not return?"

"Why did you leave in the first place if there was trouble afoot?" Creeva adds.

"There was no trouble," I answer. "Aside from the humans to the south, there was nothing."

"Hang on," Drynn interjects. "There were humans infiltrating our borders and you chose to ignore them?"

"We weren't ignoring them. They just weren't an immediate threat."

"Neither were burned men," Elder Jerus remarks, "and you seemed to ignore them, too. Tell me, as Ashacan, is it not your responsibility to deal with any and all threats when they arise and no later? You appear to have taken a leisurely approach to your position."

"And without symbol of rank, how are we to know you were fit to be Ashacan at all?" Creeva wonders.

Save for Tolorian and the Ashan, the others nod in agreement, eyeing my bare neck suspiciously.

The broken vashte in which I left the caracosh claw flashes in my mind. Still, I do not regret leaving it. I let my gaze drop to the floor, unsure of how to explain its absence.

Elder Tolorian gently asserts himself. "Nhuaela, where is your necklace? I am sure I saw it upon my visit."

"As did I," the Ashan corroborates. "There was no doubt it was legitimate."

"Then where has it gone?" Creeva insists, unsatiated.

"I left it," I say.

"That's it?"

"Do I need a better reason?"

"If I may," says Tolorian, "it *is* quite an important relic, Nhuaela. If you did not have our word to confirm its existence, your position would be far more precarious."

"But I do have your word." I look back to Creeva. "I didn't feel like keeping it after it was used to blind me."

She scoffs. "Was it not sacred?"

"The Rendara were sacred."

"And yet you left them," Jerus questions. "In favor of a hunt."

Irritation creeps back into my voice. "I did not leave them defenseless, and it was not a simple hunt."

The Ashan speaks up. "There is no reason for an Ashacan to be permanently tethered to their vashte'rae, particularly when they are seeing to their responsibilities."

Again, I glance his way, recognizing the words from our first meeting. He returns a pointed look.

"May I ask why there need be an Ashacan at all if they contribute nothing of note?" Tan questions.

"Why do you have an Ashan?" the Ashan rebukes. "Would you say I contribute nothing of note?"

Tan narrows his eyes at him.

Elder Tolorian clears his throat. "Ashacans are leaders. Leaders intended to fight or defend against specific threats. They unite their people. They possess an inherent intuition regarding defense. And," his twinkling eyes land on me, "they are profoundly skilled in the nature of combat. That does not sound useless to me. As to *why* they exist we cannot know until their threat is faced."

"Were these burned men her threat, then?" Tan asks.

Tolorian thoughtfully puts a hand to his mouth. We all await a reply.

"I cannot say," he finally answers. "Nhuaela, what do you think?"

A droplet of sweat rolls between my breasts. I shake my head, knowing if I open my mouth to speak only a cry will escape. I ball my hand into a fist and dig a nail into my palm.

"Time will tell," Tolorian graciously detracts their attention from me. "As of now, we should return to our initial questions. Our Ashacan was on a Long Hunt. For those unfamiliar, this is not a trial that can be disrupted, nor is it freely decided by the Ashacan alone, am I correct in that, Nhuaela?"

I nod.

"Evoriel initiates it," the Ashan mentions.

"You mean he speaks to the Ashacan?" Jerus asks.

I find my voice. "It's difficult to explain. It's a gut feeling. And once it's acknowledged it must move forth."

"I see," he says, unconvinced.

"In other words, a Long Hunt is a justifiable reason for her absence," Tolorian surmises. "What concerns me more is that Evoriel would incite it whilst enemies were on the horizon."

"He can't know everything," Drynn says.

"I see no sense in spending time questioning Evoriel when his chosen leader is the one who failed to protect in his name," Creeva remarks. "She was not there. And perhaps we know why she was not there, but that does not excuse her actions. You had a companion with you, I am told. A child, correct?"

My heart races at the mention of Serin. "A young acan."

"And he was not caught in the initial attack?"

"No."

"So, you could not even protect *one* Rendara under your direct watch."

I stare toward the balcony, wishing the sun to rise from behind the clouds, to warm my face so I might feel something other than hollow.

"No response?" Creeva pushes.

I exhale, despising myself for ever mentioning Serin's name to anyone. "I told him to run. It was my fault for expecting him to listen. He...he wanted to help."

Elder Tolorian stirs uncomfortably in his chair.

"I don't know what happened to him," I admit. "After I was ambushed, I never saw him again. They said they killed him but—"

"You allowed yourself to be ambushed?" Elder Drynn sharply accuses. "Depths, girl, were you even trained as an acan?"

It's as though he slapped me. For a moment I struggle for a response, but then my mother is there in my head, unapologetically speaking through me.

"Forgive me for not being trained to walk through a camp of my murdered kin," I snap at him. "Walk over the bodies of your slaughtered family and you won't notice an ambush either."

They mull my retort in silence, Elder Drynn cracks his knuckles beneath his chin.

Tan lightly chuckles. "I'd say her ability to escape is a mark in her favor," he poses to the room. "Without her, who knows how long it might have taken us to realize something was amiss."

"And who knows what lies she tells?" Creeva returns. "I'm uncomfortable with the lack of witnesses."

"Who needs witnesses when you have the head of the attacker?" Tan asks, gesturing at Skinner's skull. "It's not as though we have *no* evidence."

"We are still lacking too many details for me to comfortably absolve her of anything."

Drynn nods in agreement. "I'm also curious to hear how you managed to escape when you couldn't avoid being caught in the first place, acan."

I was careless to give them Serin. I refuse to give them Halsater. "I got free of my ropes," I tell them.

Creeva taps a ringed finger against her jaw. "Is that all, dear? I'm beginning to think they may have let you go, or perhaps they never captured you at all."

In my periphery, the Ashan takes a step away from his shadowed column. He speaks toward Creeva before I can question her insinuation.

"I'll not listen while you suggest she plotted this," he warns her.

"Oh?" she smiles at him. "Have you evidence to support her innocence?"

"The fact she is an Ashacan at all."

Her smile thins.

"Evoriel wouldn't grant the rank to someone who would betray their own."

Jerus leans toward Creeva and they share hushed words. Drynn stirs uncomfortably at the unexpected defense. The Ashan steps forward to the low fire along the dais. The embers glow in his shadow.

"None of you saw her arrive," he continues, planting his boot upon Skinner's head. He tilts it side to side in examination. "There was so much blood and rosemoss on her face I almost couldn't tell who she was. Then there was the fever. Convulsions. Blackened blood. Not even Halen was familiar with whatever toxin was in her veins." He rights the skull. "And then she died."

"What?" I mean to be demanding, but my question is hardly a whisper dampened by shock. The Elders' mirror my horror. The Ashan disregards us all.

"The burned men slaughtered the Rendara, and then they killed the Ashacan. Slowly. Cruelly. Yet you want to believe she had a hand in this. For what?" He crushes the skull underfoot. Flames dance across his boot, but he does not seem to care. "You're wasting time blaming her while the real enemy is on the run."

"And who is the real enemy?" Elder Jerus cautiously asks.

"Burned men," the Ashan replies while taking a few steps back. "Or dwellers in the north. Take your pick. They are both far greater threats than her."

"But what conflict did these men have with the Rendara in the first place?" Tolorian presses. He looks around the Ashan to me. "Do not mistake my inquiry for accusation, Nhuaela. But we must consider *why* they attacked. As far as I know, your vashte'rae had no qualms with anyone aside from the occasional human."

"Any conflict we ever had with humans was resolved without violence," I assure them.

"Because of your father, I presume?" Creeva asks. "Your mother always advocated for more aggressive tactics."

"You don't know a damn thing about my mother."

"She was shortsighted. She always chose for the good of herself, tearing apart the Nishtari because she couldn't just listen—"

"Enough!" Tolorian hisses in her direction. "We are not here to discuss Lizana or the Nishtari, and I will not hear any more of your vile comments."

Creeva's fingers clutch the arm of her chair so tightly that I hear her nails scrape, but she says nothing more.

Tolorian sinks into his chair with a delicateness akin to leaning into water that's slightly too hot. He tiredly puts a hand to his eyes. "The fact of the matter is we know nothing yet. Not truly. Burned men were present, that is clear. I suspect our Ashacan is telling the truth. If she was not, if she had ill intent, why would she have come to us? A wise fiend would keep their distance, and that appears to be the case. If we are to take action, we must garner more answers first."

"That's all well and good," Drynn says, "but there is still the matter of punishment. Innocent or not, she still failed as Ashacan."

"He is right. We cannot let her wander about without consequence. We have sent people north for less," Jerus says.

Creeva speaks in an insidious tone. "So, we are to forgive her for tragically failing her people? Fine. I will allow you that. But there is no excuse for her failure to protect one child, acan or not. If she is not part of the problem, she is at least unqualified to handle it, and therefore, I would see her stripped of rank."

"What place will she have without rank?" Tan asks.

"None, as far as I'm concerned."

The Ashan interjects once more. "The rank of Ashacan is not within any of our rights to assign or revoke."

"Not officially," Drynn concedes, "but without her vashte'rae, no one will acknowledge her."

"Then send her north," Tan suggests.

Drynn shakes his head. "We need reliable soldiers in the north."

"Then send me south," I say.

"South?"

I look to the Ashan. "Didn't you say the burned men were from the south?"

His answer is reluctant. "I...did."

Creeva lifts an intrigued brow. "Now *there's* a sensible thought."

"Sense?" Tolorian questions, aghast.

"You can keep my rank, too, if it pleases you," I decide. "I don't want it. I just want to find whoever did this, and I want to find my father. So, send me south."

A muttering ensues. I easily overhear their traded concerns and in Creeva's case, excitement. The Ashan tilts an ear. He crosses his arms, and despite his hidden face, I swear his expression is uncertain. A slight pinch between his brows alights his eyes in a distinctly concerned way. It is the same look he gave when I first mentioned my missing father.

So I find it strange when none of the Elders respond to the detail. They ignore the issue of my father entirely.

Tolorian is first to pull me back into the discussion. "Nhuaela, have you any leads as to where these men might have gone?"

"No, but I imagine a pack of burned men in Imperium territory can't be hard to track."

"Yet they made it this far."

"And do not make the mistake of thinking you can idly pass through the Imperium," Tan warns me. "The human Everwatch has never trusted us."

Tolorian frowns. "I fear more for your well-being, Nhuaela. Should you make it beyond the border..." he shakes his head. "You will not make it. Not alone."

"If I die, it will be no trouble to you."

He pulls back, hurt. A small part of me regrets the abrasive statement. He's the last one I mean to snap at. If I still wore my necklace, I might've fiddled with it, but for the first time since waking, I feel a sense of purpose.

"It is a rather tidy solution," Jerus says. "However, I dislike the idea that she should simply disappear on her own terms. Such an exit is lacking consequence."

"The sheer danger of the task is consequence enough," Tolorian replies.

"Gods and dragons," Creeva sighs. "*Banish* her. She has no place anyway. And if she wishes to return, her acceptance will be contingent on the kind of information she brings."

Tan gives a thoughtful nod. "I must agree with you. There is no reason to think this threat has subsided, but we need to know more if we are to react in any way. Ashacan, you could learn for us without drawing unnecessary attention or a need to divert any forces. At least not until we know exactly who is behind this and why the attack occurred."

"It's settled then," Creeva says.

The elders look down their row to Tolorian. The old man slumps his shoulders. "Before we finalize this decision, Nhuaela, have you any final words? Typically, we would allow for a final plea against punishment, but rarely does the individual in question determine let alone *agree* with our decisions."

For an instant I consider asking about my father, but their obvious avoidance of him disturbs me. I fear anything they say will solidify what Halen and the Ashan have already said. Any hope that there was no reason my father was targeted will be dashed.

Carefully, I look at them all, feeling my frustrations well up inside me, and yet there is also relief. Aside from Tolorian, their clear impatience at my pause motivates me.

"If I'm to leave," I say, "I need to know, where is my pony?"

Elder Creeva leans forward with a critically raised brow. "Your...pony?"

"Yes, that faithful creature who carried me here. Some call them ponies." I glance at the Ashan. "Did he die too?"

He blinks at me, bemused for the briefest moment.

"Best if it did," Creeva snaps. "We have no use for those grungy beasts."

"And yet, there's still use for you."

The old woman stands sharply from her chair, casting a hand outward. A shock of yellow light carves toward me, but before I can flinch, it is intercepted by a wall of white. The two spells collide, discounting each other and ricocheting to the far corners of the room. A stray spark of yellow lashes my cheek before dissipating. Left in its place is a fierce burn.

Clutching my face, I lift my gaze to see the Ashan standing beside me, his arm outstretched. He and Creeva glare at one another, and their hands steadily lower simultaneously.

"Get. *Out!*" she spits at me, and then to the Ashan says, "I want her out by nightfall, or I will take both your heads!"

Elder Tan chuckles. "I would pay ten thousand gold scales to see you lug a sword."

Creeva throws her glare at him. "I would not use a sword."

The Ashan grabs my upper arm and nearly drags me from the base of the dais before I can hear more. I briefly trip with my bad leg. He catches my weight and pulls me upright, continuing on until the doors shut firmly behind us.

Favors Done

ONCE IN THE ANTECHAMBER, the Ashan withdraws his grip. "That was foolish," he admonishes. "You just sabotaged what was an amicable end."

I gingerly touch the lash in my cheek. "Amicable? None of that felt amicable."

"Considering your position and some of their hostilities, I thought it would turn out worse."

I lower my hand, pretending there is no bite to the fresh burn. "I was being serious. What happened to my pony?"

"That's quite a menial question for your Ashan."

"As far as I know, you're the last one who saw him," I remind him, and then seeing the sudden intensity in his eyes, I lower my gaze. "I'm sorry. He was my father's horse."

A moment passes before he replies. "The pony is fine. Halen made sure of it."

I nod, my emotions welling up within me. The surrounding paintings disorient me. I imagine the flat brush strokes dancing to life and black-eyed fair stepping from the wall.

Then the inner chamber door opens, and Elder Tolorian enters the room. He nods to the Ashan before turning sympathetic eyes toward me. There is an odd warmth to their crystalline depths, like the angles of a fractured gem in the sun. With long fingers clasped before him, he glides to my side, his white robes silent against the smooth floor.

"I hoped to catch you before you ran out," he tells me, offering a hand. I take it properly, but before I can complete the gesture, he places his other hand atop mine and squeezes it gently. In his moment of silence, he pats my hand several times, seeming to contemplate what to say.

"I'm sorry," he quietly begins. "You do not deserve to carry such weight, nor the insults of a bitter old woman. If it was my decision alone, I would do better for you. And this banishment to the south, it's..." he thinks. "Well, I know you would go even if I had the final say. So, I will not stop you."

"I need to find him," I say, my voice sharing in his meekness.

"I understand."

"You never asked about him," I accuse. "Did the Ashan not tell you?"

"He told us."

"Doesn't it concern you?"

"It concerns us greatly."

I wait for him to elaborate, to somehow allay my fears or corroborate the Ashan and Halen's claims.

"We cannot assume Selejor is alive," he says, "but for all our sake, I pray that he is. And if there is anyone capable of finding him, it is you, Nhuaela."

He lowers my hand and finally releases it, as though his sympathy is answer enough, but I do not push for more.

He continues. "To aid in the likelihood of your success, we have agreed to equip you for this journey. The Ashan will provide you with any weapons or provisions you require, and you will take my horse. He will be of service to you."

"A horse in the south will not fare well," the Ashan mentions over his shoulder, allowing us the illusion of privacy.

"Mournstar will do just fine," Tolorian assures me. "Daervish horses are bred for adversity."

Do they catch arrows? I want to ask, the dead ponies of the Rendara flashing in my mind. Instead, I force a brief smile. "Thank you."

"Evoriel guide you." He moves away and returns to the inner chamber.

Once alone, I look at the Ashan. He looks back, expectant. I take a thoughtful moment to debate whether I truly want to know anything beyond what is manageable. Finally, I speak.

"How long was I dead?"

"At least an hour."

I wish he were the type to jest. His words might have convinced me to laugh. Instead, I stare blankly while trying to rationalize the timeframe. The notion is absurd; the Ashan's even expression is not.

I look away, poorly hiding an inward panic. "Halen didn't tell me."

"He didn't know what to make of it."

"And you?"

He ponders the question for a moment. "I've seen many soldiers die. I've never seen one come back."

"I thought I was dreaming—about my father." A creeping realization sends my blood rushing. "If I was dead and he was there..."

I lose myself behind my heart pulsing in my ears.

"Ashacan?"

Slowly, I face the outer doors, one hand to my burned cheek, my breath caught in my throat. On the exhale, I flee, bursting from the Hall with enough force that the guards startle. I hear them draw swords, only to pause upon seeing me crumple against the stairway banister. I lean upon it, one arm working to keep myself upright. The rain falls steady, coating every surface in a dark sheen. Various guards are stationed around the courtyard. I feel their eyes upon me. I search the area around them until I see Halen.

He moved from his defiant place in the center of the courtyard, choosing instead to rest upon a stone bench along the path. His stick leans beside him. Rain dampens his coarse hair like dew on moss. As I come near, he curiously raises a brow at my burned cheek.

"I warned you to be tactful," he says.

"Why didn't you tell me I died?"

The collected control of his posture stiffens, and then his gaze sweeps past me without focus. "I thought it'd be safer."

"An hour!"

"Sixty-five minutes and twenty-seven seconds."

"I shouldn't be alive."

"No," he calmly agrees. "Not based on the state you left us in. You were dead and getting cold, far beyond the aid of magic. I was debating calling an Agent of Allay for your sorry soul when you suddenly took a breath. I've never been so startled in my life. Dropped my favorite teacup."

He removes a flask from his robe while I stand, incredulous. He shakes it at me after taking a swig. Wordlessly, I accept it.

"I still don't know what to make of it," he confesses. "For a moment, I wondered if I had somehow drawn a Vhanian remnant from the Wood, but after three-thousand years, I think I know the extent of my capabilities."

"So, you had nothing to do with it."

"It'd be a ruddy shame if I'm only just discovering an aptness for Vhanian frames."

"What?"

He waves away my confusion. "You came back on your own. Seemingly without damage. Still don't understand it." He takes another sip. "Don't know if I want to."

I have to agree, unsure of how to handle anything beyond the simplicities of a hunt. I quietly lock the foreboding thoughts at the back of my mind.

"How did it go?" Halen asks. "Or am I better off not knowing?"

"They banished me. I'm going south to hunt the rest of the burned men."

He nods, as though it is a revelation he entirely expected. "You'll need some better clothes then."

"I must leave by nightfall."

"Will you feel ready by then?"

"I'm ready now."

"Well," he tilts his head toward the stairs. "I'm sure Rolan can scrounge up some spare weapons for you."

I look behind myself to see the Ashan descending the stairs of the Hall. He takes long strides through the rain. Each guard he passes executes an elegant half-step back despite his disregard.

"Gods, he only ever looks wretched anymore," Halen remarks.

The Ashan narrows his eyes in approach, and I wonder if he heard Halen's comment. If so, he makes no mention of it and switches his gaze from the onduris to myself. The guards nearby straighten at their posts. They subtly tip their heads to listen.

I do not bow again. I'm not sure if the formality applies when I've been banished.

"Follow me and we will gather what you need," he says to me. "There's only a few hours until sundown, and do not assume Creeva will forgo her word."

"You best go with him, Nhuaela," Halen advises. "You won't get far in the world without proper weapons."

I look down at my healer, surprised by his compliance. "Will I see you before I go?"

"You'll see me when you get *back*." He removes his flask from his pocket. "Here. Take this. Just don't drink it all at once."

He tosses it to me before I can refuse. I stare at the leather-bound metal and tighten my grasp as my hand begins to tremble.

"Go on, now. Neither burned men nor dwellers will wait."

* * *

I follow the Ashan down a discreet path through the Peaks. Those who notice us are reluctant to say a word. The servants of high-born fair quickly duck around corners to avoid our path. Guards stop in their tracks and press their backs stiffly against the sides of buildings. The Ashan periodically looks over his shoulder at me. When he does, I notice the way his mask fits to his cheekbones and follows the line of his scars from the corner of his finely angled eye. Droplets of rain darken the grey fabric with dashes of black. The mask dips down and around the nape of his neck. It is hidden under layers of his darkly threaded braids that have been disheveled by the wind and rain.

We emerge along the side of the mountain on a narrow trail. It is well traveled but merely a footpath. Outside of the city tiers, it snakes steeply down the mountain and branches between districts, a path of hidden roads in itself. As I look over the edge to the sectors below, I notice guards dotted here and there, walking the trail on patrol. My knee aches at the slope but compared to the busy city streets and pressing air of the Hall, I feel more at ease.

The Ashan leads me wordlessly until we reach the Base at the eastern ridge wall. The carved archway to the Imperium road looms over us like an open mouth. With many of the base-born still at work in the fields, the streets are relatively empty. Those we do encounter seem less taken aback by the Ashan. A few even lift a hand in greeting but turn away upon seeing me.

Separated from the homes of the base-born is a row of barracks. Their structures are worn but well-kept and identical in appearance, looking like humble homes hewn of wood and stone. Unarmed and armorless guards mill about the yard, uncaring of the rain. All activities pause as we walk by. I refuse to shrink against their stares and hold tight to Halen's flask, keeping my eyes ahead.

The main guardhouse stands tall above the barracks. From the second story, a diamond shaped window looks down on the sparring yard. The Ashan leads me up the stairs and through the door.

Inside, he takes a set of stairs to the upper level. An old door blocks whatever room waits. He puts his shoulder against the metal plated wood and budges it inward. Once inside, he pushes the stiff door back in place and bolts it shut.

The new room is rather modest, formed of dark wood and a steepled ceiling. There is warmth to the air. Chairs are pushed along the walls, at the ready. On the main wall, rain patters against the diamond window. Grey light casts itself down a long table in the center of the room. Its surface is blanketed in countless parchments and unraveled scrolls. Smaller scraps have hastily scrawled messages in Daervish script. The words are fragmented by crumpled lines, likely from being carried in the pocket of a cloak or saddlebag. There are maps of the Gatewood, maps of the city, maps of places unfamiliar to me. I'm drawn to a detailed rendition of the border in the north and Fort Se'lae.

Thrown atop the haphazard parchments are two familiar war-axes still stained with the shadows of blood. Engraved in the metal are the symbols of burned men.

I lift my eyes to the Ashan. He moves soundlessly to the table's head, drawing a hand overtop the various papers.

"What is this place?" I ask.

"An unorganized stockpile of things I've no idea what to do with." He rifles through the parchments, picks one up, rips it in half and casts the pieces aside. "An office, of sorts."

"You kept the axes."

"I wanted to study them, and then I thought you might want them back. You favor them, do you not?"

"I favored *my* axes."

"You carried them all this way."

"For protection. And proof."

"Well, if you want them, take them."

"You don't have any others?"

"Aside from a woodcutter's ax? No. They are not supplied for the Undecayed."

At my hesitance, he picks one of the war-axes off the table and holds it outright, eyeing its hold. "These are crude. Heavy. Inefficient, if you ask me." He drops it back on the table with a solid thud. "And I realize they are of no comfort, but unless you'd rather have a sword, I suggest you take them. You know how to wield them. What power they offer will serve you well the farther south you go."

I stare down at the war-axes that crush the bed of parchment. The single sided heads hook downward to sharp points, perfect for snagging bones and tearing muscle. A flash of mangled bodies in my mind reminds me of that.

Tucking away Halen's flask, I take one from the table and let its weight sink into my grip. The handle is worn smooth and bound in leather. I slink my hand upward, holding it higher than a burned man might. Doing so allows a better grip. The tired muscles of my arm tense under the ax's heft, but it is a satisfying heat. I'm tempted to give them each a practice swing, crashing them down upon the cluttered table with all the strength of contained rage.

"There will be plenty for you to hit once you are out of the city," the Ashan warns, seeming to notice my radiating anger. He glances expectantly between the ax and table. "There's no rush. I'd like a word."

Slowly, I set it down, questioning, "Aside from what's already been said?" The burn in my cheek stings along with my words, striking the impatience within me.

"I wanted to speak to you without the Damicus looming overhead."

"I've been honest."

"I don't doubt you, but I disagree with this idea of banishment. It's reckless."

"The Damicus decided it."

"You suggested it, and I'm tempted to order you otherwise."

"Am I to take orders when I have no rank?"

"You have a rank, Ashacan." The bite in his tone abruptly puts an end to any discussion of the matter, and the sudden abrasiveness in his glare makes me flinch. "Even if you don't want it, you still have it, and therefore will follow orders."

"I agreed to leave."

"You agreed to a thoughtless punishment that *you* presented. I'll admit there is purpose in it. Some punishment must be tied to the actions of a compromised Ashacan but not a thinly veiled death sentence." He pins me with a knowing look. "I know you don't intend to come back."

I bite my cheek.

"You cannot throw yourself away like that."

"Why not?"

"Because there are bigger conflicts than your own vendettas."

"Then someone better than me can handle them."

"I have plenty of soldiers keeping back the evils of this world. They all have their own plight. Many of them think themselves insignificant, but the Gatewood needs every last one of them. Durast needs them, whether the Everwatch realizes it or not. You are no different."

"And how many of your soldiers have gotten their vashte'rae killed? I have no reason to come back."

He reprimands my petulance with a glare. "I don't think you've thought deeply enough about that statement. Deny the vast amount of reasons, if you want. I'll give you a clearcut one; I'm ordering you to come back."

"That's rid—"

"Come. Back. Learn anything pertinent, of course, but mainly, you are to return."

I shake my head, some of my grief alleviated by his bluntness. "And what if I don't?"

"Then I'll know you disobeyed orders."

"That's not fair."

"I'm not asking for your feedback. Fail to come back after too long, and I'll have to tell the Damicus that you've shirked your duty. Is that understood, Ashacan?"

The suggested consequence stings. I'm sure he knows it. Reluctantly acknowledging the order stings more. "*Sai,*" I force.

"Good," he concludes and begins to pace along his side of the table. "You should know Rendaran lands will be protected while you are away.

I've sent a regiment to stand watch as well as investigate the area of your camp without disturbance. The Elesaan, too, have been diverted from their position in the west. Our relations with the dwarves are strong enough, and chief Atel insisted on safeguarding the border while the grounds are allayed."

"I already called for the roots. They came."

The Ashan nods solemnly. "Even so. You are not trained in the frame. Chief Atel will want to be sure. And he'd like to pay his respects."

I blink a few times, shifting my focus to the rain on the window. "Has he encountered any Rendara?"

"Not since we last spoke."

"Does he know about me?"

"He knows you were badly injured."

Not for the first time, my heart stutters within my chest, ashamed that Chief Atel should know of my failure. I want to drop the topic, but I force myself continue. "If you speak to him again, can you ask him to keep a lookout for any Rendara? In case anyone escaped. Especially my acan, Serin."

"I'm sure he is already searching, but I will tell him."

"Thank you."

"Is there a chance this Serin is alive?"

"Maybe. I couldn't find him. But he was hurt."

"How do you know that?"

"I found his bow."

The Ashan waits, and I realize what is an obvious explanation likely means nothing to him.

"He wouldn't have left it if he were okay," I say, remembering Speckles' pulpy corpse nearby the shattered vashte, the burned man, the blood.

I dab a tear from my cheek. The burn slashed across my skin flares when I touch it.

"*Iesh!*" I curse, withdrawing my hand. "Old *rihar*!"

The Ashan raises a brow.

"Creeva," I clarify. "And I won't apologize for that."

"She does not warrant apologies," he replies. "Would you like me to heal it?"

"Heal it?"

From across the table, he casually lifts a hand.

The burn seems to intensify the longer I hesitate.

"There's no reason you need another wound," he reasons.

"I didn't know you could heal."

"I am not Halen, but I can manage a burn."

Curious, I step around the table to his waiting hand. It's widely known that he possesses magic aside from the restorative. Such capabilities seem to be a necessity for an Ashan. His shielding of Creeva's attack was proof of them if there was any doubt in my mind.

He places his fingertips along the length of the burn. I resist the urge to pull away from the reactive sting and watch his eyes fall to focus on my cheek. An instant heat emanates from his touch and is followed by a sinking chill. My skin pinches and pulls as threads of energy accelerate the healing, uncomfortably forcing a minor reconstruction of tissue. And then it fades.

The Ashan winces and lowers his hand. I feel where the mark was a moment before and find my skin numb. The act of being healed is not unfamiliar to me. Healer Shayv had done the same on numerous occasions, although he often used runes rather than take on the pain himself. What perplexes me is the Ashan's willingness to do so.

"Why are you helping me?" I ask of him, my hand still held to my cheek.

He takes a step away to reestablish an appropriate distance and flexes a soreness from his fingers.

"You're a soldier under my command," he says.

"I'm not the only soldier."

"No, but you were the one being accused. I had to vouch for you, as I would have vouched for anyone else I knew was innocent."

"You didn't have to shield me. Or heal me."

"As a favor to your father, I do."

There is a depth in his eyes that is amiss in the other fair, and I do not understand the reason for it. "You owed him a favor?"

"As a friend. He was there for me at a time when no one else could have been. He spoke for me when I quite literally could not. And he reminded me of my rank when I did not want it. I think he might curse me if I do not do the same for you."

"My father wouldn't curse a fly."

"If that fly let his daughter run toward certain death without aid, he would."

I say nothing more, not wanting him to think me ungrateful, but inwardly, a sense of frustration irks me. He leans against the table head, pressing his palms atop several unlucky scraps and meets my eyes.

"You have put so much blame on yourself you seem to forget that protection of the Gatewood is *my* charge. My focus on the north left your people abandoned. Burned men slipped past *my* watch, not yours. For that, I am sorry."

I cannot find the words to reply.

"Let me help you," he implores. "Give me time and I can lend you more than two axes and an old horse. You need not sentence yourself because of an oversight I made."

My voice returns to me. "With respect, Ashan, you could give me an army, and I would still go alone. No curse will befall you because of my decision."

"I'm not so sure."

I fiddle with an edge of parchment, searching for the confidence I felt when sentencing myself. "It's just a few burned men."

"It will not be as simple as a few burned men."

"Right now, it is that simple. Some men and their king." I pick up an ax. "I'll find them."

"And then?"

I take up the second ax. "Then I find my father."

"Ashacan."

I look up.

"I am giving you those axes in good faith. In three weeks' time, I do not want to hear rumors of a rogue Rendara terrorizing the Imperium in search of burned men. If I do, I will track you down myself and drag you back here for an entirely different trial in which I will *not* speak for you. *Sai?*"

I lower the axes. "Do you also think me shortsighted with a penchant for upheaval?"

"You're angry. And when you're driven by anger, you're less likely to think, and when you don't think, people get hurt, including yourself."

The axes suddenly feel a bit heavier as we lock eyes. I struggle for an appropriate response.

"Or," he suggests, "I could give you a bread knife until I feel confident of your mental faculties."

You have no idea what I could do with a breadknife. I bite my tongue and lower my eyes. "I appreciate your concern, Ashan."

"I don't want your appreciation. Acknowledge the order."

I pull my shoulders back. "*Sai, Ashan.*"

"Alright. Let's find you some armor."

* * *

I sit alone in a barrack room before a mirror I have yet to look in. After some hushed words with one of his soldiers, the Ashan scrounged up a set of light armor meant for travel. The leather is a deep brown that flexes easily. To my liking, it does not weigh me down and smells like the musty forest floor. A dark green cloak and soft boots were offered as well. I dressed quickly enough but froze at the mirror.

Earlier, I avoided the glimpse of my scars reflected in my bath water. The extent of their ugliness showed in the startled expressions of gawking fair as I ascended the city, and I am afraid to see the vestiges of my parents looking back at me.

You have your father's eyes.

And how am I to face them?

...Lizana is there, too.

What likeness I gained from my mother has been stricken. Her boldness and warmth have left me. I've no idea how to feel anything but cold and hollow.

I lift my gaze.

The scar down my face is an upraised and lumpy thing. It has healed in a crooked line that bulges my eyelid and severs my brow, causing the color to ripple. The corner of my mouth is tugged downward. The darkness within my burnt amber eyes swirls mockingly. A distorted creature looks back at me, and it has no place.

I turn away from the mirror and quickly rebraid my hair, my fingers continuing to familiarize themselves with the shortened locks. The jagged cut above my shoulders is difficult to manage, but I soon find a rhythm. I create a neater pattern than what I accomplished in Halen's hut and bring the plaits together at the base of my neck. Then I gather the axes.

Unlike my hatchets, they do not suitably fit in a belt at my hip. It is awkward to carry them so, and unconducive to riding long distances. Instead, the Ashan provided a chest crossing scabbard similar to his own—a garment of the vatanukro. Rather than two swords, it has been altered to fit the heavy axe heads down against my lower back. I drape the cloak over them, but it does little to hide their sinister presence.

When I step outside, I meet the stares of the few fairborn guards on break from their duties. Pausing on the barrack steps, I take a sip from Halen's flask, hoping the liquor will blur the images of their faces.

The Ashan reappears beyond them. I'm not sure where he went while I readied myself, but his return startles the soldiers into breaking their stares. I cap the flask.

As is his tendency, he moves without explanation. I follow, not needing to be told his purposeful steps are an implied order. We move through the remainder of the Base and beneath the cavernous ridge to the fieldland. The main stable stretches along the edge of pasture containing dozens of stalls. Stablehands lead tall horses in and out of their stalls as younger base-born sweep the aisles of hay. The horses wicker at our arrival and peer at us from between the slats in their stalls.

The Ashan extends an arm to the first stall on the right. "This one is yours. Mournstar."

I recognize the sturdy beast. Elder Tolorian rode it south. The large bay hangs his head over the stall door and perks his ears in my direction.

"Elder Tolorian is generous," I remark.

The Ashan gains the attention of a poorly hidden stable girl tucked within a nearby stall. She peeks her head out as he calls to her. In rushed Daerv, he asks for Mournstar's tack.

"And have my horse readied as well," he adds as she hastily nods and trips from the stall.

I approach Mournstar's gate with a wary hand, in awe of his powerful frame. He willfully bobs his muzzle into my palm and inhales. Then I slip into the stall to trace my hand along the warm muscles of his thick neck, his bulging chest and shoulders. A white patch of hair stands out in a burst of specks at the crook of his shoulder. I lay a hand upon it, and his muscles twitch in response.

I consider asking for Lo, if just to see him, but forgo the idea. He has earned his rest, and saying goodbye to him would only hurt.

Soon, the girl returns laden with tack and provisions. The Ashan takes it from her arms, and she scurries away. Wordlessly, he passes the saddle over the stall door for me to fit on Mournstar's back.

"Are you to escort me?" I ask while taking the bridle.

"Just to ensure you are given no trouble at the gate."

I slide my thumb into the corner of Mournstar's mouth and part his jaw. He gladly takes the bit.

"There's one more thing," the Ashan says as I tighten the girth and double check the given provisions. They went so far as to allow me a short bow and quiver of arrows with the saddle. Rather than ride with it beside my leg, I swing it over my shoulders with the axes.

Turning back to the stall door, he tosses me a purse of coins. Heavy, Imperium coin.

"Is this another favor?" I ask.

"It's what Halen paid for your pony."

I blink, baffled. "He bought Lo?"

"To keep him safe, he said. Technically, the creature was not ours to give, so the payment belongs to you."

Not feeling obliged to refuse, I secure the purse to my belt. He opens the stall for me, and in the yard, retrieves his own horse. Lo's belly required a certain finesse to hug with my legs. I'm unaccustomed to the bulk of a warhorse. It takes me a moment to adjust as I urge Mournstar to follow the Ashan toward the south road. My hips sway in a rounded pattern to accommodate Mournstar's forward moving steps, and I can feel my seat more solidly beneath me. The road is long enough for me to experiment with his gait and familiarize myself with his movements. My weakened knee strains at the impact of his broad strides, but by the time we reach the outer wall of the fieldland, the sharpness has ebbed.

The guards greet the Ashan less formally than those within the city. They nod to him, and he lifts a hand in return. He loosens his reins and brings his horse alongside Mournstar.

"This is where we part," he tells me. "Send word, if you can do so safely—to Elder Tolorian. Or Halen. I will be north by then."

I tip my head, knowing I will not write. "I don't think myself lucky, but I suppose I was lucky to arrive while you were still here."

"Call it luck."

The guards part the tall gate, revealing the darkening Gatewood beyond. I tighten my reins, although Mournstar is not eager to leave.

"Thank you, Ashan," I say. "You have been kind."

"*Zashtavah, Ashacan.* Remember your orders."

With a laden heart, I enter the Wood and do not look back.

Forestfall

FOR SIX DAYS, THE grey clouds coil overhead. The rains follow me through the Gatewood, dampening every surface that might have made for a dry bed or warm fire. My cloak is allowed no time to dry between onslaughts of rain. The water seeps between the gaps in my armor and the threads of my underclothes until it chafes in a clammy layer against my skin. Mournstar hangs his head low. Thin rivulets drip off his muzzle and eyelashes. It is with an aching chill we enter upon the east road.

The moment Daerva'Tor's gates shut behind me, I could not urge Mournstar one step toward Rendaran land. Traveling east across Nishtari territory seemed more bearable, but for nearly a week, I've been haunted into exhaustion as visions of my people keep me from sleep.

They are hundreds of barbs hooked under my skin, each tethered to the south by an invisible string. With each passing day, another snaps, ripping away what is left of me. I am scattered through the forest, smothered under the rain and names of those I lost. They will not rest, and the barbs dig deep.

Mournstar's hooves slosh against the muddy road. The path does not venture far into the Gatewood. It abruptly ends to prevent unwanted visitors from reaching Daerva'Tor. I follow the stretch of road until the trees part. The slippery path dips downward and winds unevenly through rolling grasses and the last lonely trees. In the near distance is the rain darkened village of Forestfall. Beyond it, fields for harvest and an occasional sturdy oak stand as shadows on the horizon.

To my knowledge, it is the only village wherein the humans are familiar with elves, and I feel assured my presence will not entirely startle them. The few merchants and farmers who trade with Daerva'Tor often stay here while the Nishtari or fairborn come to them. On rare occasions, a human is permitted to travel the length of the Wood, albeit accompanied by Nishtari who no doubt test their nerves. I've only visited the village a handful of times, the last of which was roughly fifty years ago.

In the distance, the solid walls of the inn promise a dry night and perhaps an innkeeper willing to refill Halen's flask. Mournstar walks with a new vigor, excited for a similar promise, but we've only just entered the village when the sounds of malcontent reach my ears. Lured by terse voices, I slow Mournstar as we pass between thatched roof homes to the village center.

A cluster of humans gather outside the inn. They stand defensively with a leader at their front. He is a large man—tall and broad, with thick hands to jab in emphasis of his loud words. They are directed at a fairborn soldier who stands opposite him.

"That's enough!" the big man shouts. "You've had your look, but I won't have you stickin' your fine fuckin' noses where they don't belong."

The fairborn is rather small for a soldier of elite standing, but he does not flinch at the overpowering man. He glares, catlike and calm, offering no more reply than casually placing a hand upon the pommel of his sword. Flanking him, an amused group of fairborn chuckle.

"Daerva'Tor protects this village, so my *fine fucking nose*—thank you, by the way—has every right to search your buildings."

"Horse shit."

"The security of the Wood is not horse shit."

"You accusin' us of harboring burned men is horse shit."

"Burned men?" I interject. My speech shifts slowly to Dur, sounding heavier than it does in elvish. It is thickened by my Rendaran accent and draws the attention of humans and elves alike.

Our differences are striking. The humans' faces are round and flat, their noses wide and eyes searching. I see the slight twinges in their plain expressions—the wrinkling of nostrils and shifting jaws. They are dirtied from the day's labor. The rain leaves streaks of dirt down their clenched hands and chapped lips. I can almost see them aging before my eyes.

As for the fairborn, they are not all elite – only their lithe leader. Those that stand away from the humans keep hold of quick looking horses. Their smirks disappear as their eyes fall on me. The leader is last to move. He angles his head a fraction in my direction, highlighting his contrasting elven features in the setting light of the grey dusk. The contour of his cheekbones draws a line from his temple to chin. His white eyes appear pulled up and back, aligning with the curving ears that arc into harsh points along the side of his head. Taut braids accentuate the sternness of his eyes, the tresses woven with gold threads of a highborn family.

I've forgotten how drastically we stand out when not within our own borders—that I share in his harsh features, only mine are not nearly so flawless.

"You are the Rendara," he notes, putting a hand to his chin.

I ignore his observation. "Have you seen the burned men?"

"No. Partly because these humans refuse to cooperate."

"Say that one more time, little elf, and we'll not allow one bit of trade into your woods," the big man warns.

I glance around the village center. The old homes are weather-beaten, but not in a state of disarray. There are no marks of pillaging, no children with arrows through their throats.

"Burned men have not touched this place," I inform the fairborn. "I don't think they left this way at all."

The small elf steps toward me, momentarily forgetting the humans, and eloquently changes from Dur to Daerv.

"You're more intact than the rumors led me to believe," he says, circling Mournstar with a scrutinizing eye. "I should think you were half-dead at the hands of some healer, or better yet, kept within a guarded cell, not escaped from Daerva'Tor with a stolen horse."

"Who are you?" I ask, also switching back to elvish.

"Telian. Front Rider of the mounted guard. I've been charged with the investigation of any breaches in our borders." He places a gentle hand between Mournstar's eyes, and the horse responsively lowers his head. "This is Elder Tolorian's horse," he remarks. "How did you manage to steal him?"

In place of answer, I dismount. I'm careful to land with a purposeful hardness. My armor flexes and the axes jangle. Over the fairborn's shoulder, the humans watch intently, seeming to forget their own quarrel. The amused expressions of the fairborn riders fade. They nudge their tall horses nearer.

Telian lifts a hand, and the guard ceases their advance.

"I am no thief," I say.

He looks up at me with all the condescension of a downward glare. I stand almost a head taller than him, but I'm no fool to think his armor and swords of the *vatanukro* were not rightly earned. I pull Mournstar with me as I edge around him.

He grabs my arm, halting my advance. "You overstep, Rendara."

I refrain from breaking free of his grasp as he continues.

"Those savages infiltrated the Wood on your watch, and now we are the ones diverted to address your mistake," he chastises. "Have you any idea what kind of strain we are already under without your carelessness?"

I turn my head and speak in his ear. "*I* am addressing my mistake. Stick to your patrol, Front Rider, and let me handle the burned men."

"You had your chance to handle them."

I roughly knock my shoulder against his as I tug free and lead Mournstar to the humans. I study the crowd, more daunted than I'd like to admit. The mob moves as one, an uncoordinated, shambling creature. They stiffen at my approach, and the big man steps forward, standing his ground. His eyes are a bright blue pinpricked by two dark centers that lock onto me. I'm both anchored and unsettled by their precise hold. They flicker between myself and the fairborn, distrusting of us all.

"You're not with them," he comments, nodding at Telian and his gathered riders. "You're one of them border elves. Like the Nishtari."

"Not Nishtari," I clarify, speaking in Dur once more, "and I'm only passing through. Give me a bed for the night, and I'll make sure these fairborn leave."

He consults with those closest to him. Behind me, the mounted guard stirs. Their unruly horses snort and spin, channeling the discontent of their riders. Telian takes hold of a dancing dappled mare and swings gracefully onto her back. His next words are biting.

"Hunt your burned men, but do not presume to reenter the Wood unless you'd like to find yourself at the end of my sword."

"*Norveh un diil.*"

He flashes his fangs at me, hissing as he does so. He pulls his horse back into a rear and for an instant I think he might charge, and then he tugs her mouth in the direction of the Gatewood. His riders follow him up the muddy slope to the east road. They gallop close, causing the humans to leap back and stumble over one another. Splashing hooves splatter us in mud. Once the fair vanish within the distant trees, the man wipes his face.

"Depths…" he grumbles and brushes the front of his shirt, smearing the mud against the fabric. "I suppose you've made them leave then."

"Who owns the inn?"

"That'd be me. Name's Shod."

I flip him a silver cet from my purse. He reflexively catches it, and looking at the shining silver, his eyes go wide.

"Is that a *cet?*" an old woman prods him, peering close.

Shod quickly hides it in his grasp. "Stable's over there, just 'round back of the inn."

* * *

The inn faces Forestfall's heart. I follow a path around back as Shod said. The wet ground gives underfoot. A few chickens peck amongst the dustings of hay for lack of scratch. A cow for milking stands in a small pen, unperturbed by the rain. The stable is hardly a shed with an overhanging roof. There are four stalls; all are empty.

"Take whichever you please."

The firm words startle me as a stout girl slides around Mournstar and enters the stable ahead of us. She wears an old but clean dress, and her light hair tied in an imperfect bun. Rather decisively for a child, she throws open one of the old stall doors.

"Put him here. I'll get him some hay and feed. Can brush him down too, if you like." All of this she says before granting me one look. When she does look, it's with the same assertive, blue eyes as the innkeeper. She holds out a hand. "But first, that'll be three bits."

I reach for my purse.

"You got a name?" she asks. "Da never asked."

"Nhuaela."

"Well, Nhuaela, shouldn't open your purse so obviously, or keep all your coin in one spot. 'Specially when you've got as much as you do."

I tie the purse shut and drop the three copper bits into her palm. "What's your name?"

"Love."

Love, pronounced in the same cadence as *clove*.

I take my flask and purse from the saddle then hand her the reins. "This is Mournstar."

She coaxes the horse forward, expertly turns him, and ushers him into the stall. "Where you from?" she asks. "Clearly you didn't come with the fair."

"I'm from the south."

"Don't think we've ever had anyone come from the south. Not elves, anyway."

I do not tell her we simply had not been in her lifetime. "How long were the fair here before I showed up?"

She removes Mournstar's bridle. "Not terribly long. I came out to hunt eggs and saw them poking around the barn, so I called for Da. Next thing I know, they're shouting in the street. Apparently, they were searching other barns as well. They could've just asked instead of raking through our stuff, but the fair aren't as polite as the Nishtari."

"No?" I ask, baffled by the idea of polite Nishtari.

"They watch over us. Sometimes they trade. Haven't ever fought with Da. Do your people do the same in the south?"

"Sometimes," I make myself say, knowing it would be inappropriate to tell her Forestfall maintains an entirely unique relationship with the Wood. I'm unable to stop myself from thinking further on the question, and I begin to step away as memories flood my mind. My father, calmly speaking Dur with humans while my mother loomed behind, ready to intervene at a moment's notice.

I'm sure that is how she died.

"Thank you for the stall," I quickly tell Love.

With Mournstar looking content, and the evening growing dark, I return to the front of the inn. The sounds of jovial voices press through its walls. An inviting glow pulses from a fire within. Above the door, a painted sign reads *The Baited Brill.*

I stop outside and consider returning to the stall.

"Elf!"

I jump at the barking voice reminiscent of Skinner's. Coming from the well, Shod carries a bucket of fresh water. Its contents slosh over the rim as he walks to the inn. I subtly edge away from him, maintaining a distance.

"Come inside," he invites. "Have a drink. You've more than paid for it."

I hesitate at the offer, distrusting his kindness. It's unlike any I have ever met in a human. When he reaches the door, the glow of the inn warms his expression, and I relax to his presence.

"There's hot stew," he further entices me. "We'll see Chella. She's got the strongest swill in all of Durast."

I quickly fan my cloak over my axes, knowing it does little to hide them. The fabric catches on the crossed handles, and they make a muffled clank as I walk. Shod doesn't seem to mind. Not waiting for my answer, he shoves open the door and ushers me inside.

Light and noise greet me at once. The main floor seems to be packed with every villager in Forestfall. A long bar wraps around one end and a fire burns in a hearth at the other. A monstrously fat brillbird is strung

above the bar with its wings permanently outstretched. The few tables
and chairs are filled by raucous farmers and children running between
legs. A small boy toddles too close to the hearth. An old man sitting
beside it outstretches his leg, barring the little one from falling into the
hard stone. The child shrieks excitedly and stretches his stubby arms
toward the flames. A worried woman scoops him up from behind, props
him on her hip, and speaks sternly in his ear.

There are those who look over the rims of their mugs. It takes some a
moment longer to notice the elf in their midst, but I do not break their
mood. The atmosphere stays warm. The voices continue to hum. No
one tells me to drop my axes at the door.

"Chella!" Shod makes use of his strong voice.

A bustling woman behind the bar looks up at our approach. Curling
black hair tumbles over her shoulders and atop the dirty apron fastened
snugly around her waist. She glances up with a smile as she laughs with
her patrons.

The bar is full, but the innkeeper shoves his way between two young
men, drapes his arms over their shoulders, and has a brief conversation
that results in them deserting their stools. They look forlornly back at
Chella.

He motions for me to follow. "Come sit!"

I'm not fond of the closeness of the crowded bar. My shoulders rub
with Shod and a woman to my left. She scoots her stool away from me as
she turns her back. I take the opportunity to distance myself from Shod,
whose wide movements threaten to knock over the mug that Chella
places before me.

"Welcome to the Brill," she says kindly. "First ale's on me. Or Shod.
He owns the place. I just care for the customers. Hungry? I saw you

send that little fairborn running. I imagine that'd work up an appetite in anyone."

"Give 'er a meal and a shot a honey," Shod orders, setting the water bucket behind the bar.

She looks at me with mischievous eyes. "So, you want some honey, honey?"

Her inviting demeanor leaves me grasping for a reply.

She flashes a teasing grin. "It'll have you calling everyone honey within the hour." She ducks below the bar and emerges a moment later with a modest glass filled with an amber liquid.

She winks at me. "Won't go down like honey, I promise you that."

"You'll want some stew first," Shod warns. "No one should drink Chel's brew on an empty stomach."

I lift the glimmering shot. It smells like honey, although there is an undertone of something wicked beneath the sweet surface. Shod and Chella watch me intently, causing the others around the bar to look as well.

I remember the hauntings I endured on the journey through the Gatewood, and the tugging barbs in my back. I feel the ache in my thigh, the chill of unnatural rains, and Skinner digging the caracosh claw into my eye. The honey, while hot and cutting, fails to numb. It does not beat back the hollow ache or mollify the knotted ball of grief that is lodged between my ribs. It does not blind me to the constant specters that drift in my periphery.

Those around me are quiet when I set the empty glass on the bar. The honey coats my throat and stomach with a sensation hardly comparable to the heat of blood fever. I slide my flask toward Chella.

"Fill this."

Stunned, she takes Halen's flask, and ducks below the bar once more. Shod breaks the silence by slamming a bowl of stew in front of me. I sip the mug of ale. It tastes like water following the honey.

Chella carefully returns my flask. She leans against the bar and lowers her voice. "That'll be two bits. *Or,* you can tell me the story behind that scar."

"It's not polite to go asking after unpleasant wounds," Shod warns her. "Dredge up memories, you will."

Chella sighs in disappointment, appearing to have heard Shod's warning many times before. I slide her the coins, and a group of men call her to the other end of the bar, giving Shod a moment to pry.

"Really, though," he wonders, "what ill-fated thing happened to you?"

I take a drink to avoid answering.

"Alright," he catches on. "At least tell me what you're doing here other than passing through. In my experience, your folk don't pass through."

"I'm hunting."

He snorts into his mug. "Aye, because the best game lies *outside* of that enchanted forest of yours. Next, you're gonna tell me this has nothing to do with burned men, either." He pauses for another drink. "I've never heard of those heathens north of the Ridgeguard, let alone near our humble home, and suddenly there's a legion of fairborn on my doorstep, actin' as though I'm one of them savages. Now, why is that?"

"If I give you another cet, will you leave me alone?"

"I let you into my inn with two war-axes on your back and gave you a hot meal. I think I have a right to ask such a question."

I pick at my stew, debating my answer. "Burned men invaded our lands not long ago. I suspect they returned south. Others continue to look for their trace."

Shod nods. "I wonder if that's why the Marked have been lurking around here as well."

I try not to drop my spoon into my bowl at their mention. "What do you mean by that?"

"About a month back, some of the farmers saw a few on horseback. Now, that's not a common sight out here. They stick close to the cities, unless it's a time of war—and to the best of my knowledge, we ain't in a time of a war. Then, only a few days ago, we saw them again. This time closer. Not in Forestfall, but around it. I counted two riding along the Gatewood, but then they disappeared. There've been rumors from nearby villages, too. As far north as Nurgos and down to Waylay. But if they're here to stand between us and burned men, I'm glad."

Their proximity ignites a territorial instinct within me. "The Everwatch should keep their mages away from our borders."

"Like I said, they were along the Wood, not in it."

"You think they knew of the burned men?"

"Seems likely. A pack would have to cross half of Durast before reaching the Wood. I doubt they went unnoticed."

"Is it just as likely the Marked were outsmarted by burned men?" *Just as you were outsmarted, rihar?*

He glances knowingly at my scar. "I think we've all been outsmarted by burned men."

He sets his mug firmly on the bar and leaves me to join a new conversation. Those seated beside me abandon their stools, leaving me to eat alone. Threads of their words reach my ears unbeknownst to them. They question Shod about his sanity in letting me inside. They wonder who I am and why I'm here. *You think she can hear us with those ears?* one whispers. *From across the room?* answers another. '*Course not. They're long, not magic.*

Still, the possibility of my hearing ability drives out their gossip. The inn begins to empty. Shod bids his patrons good night while Chella and Love tidy the tables. When Shod returns to my side, I cannot neglect the question that hangs in the air before me.

"Did anyone speak to the Marked?"

"They're not the type you want to talk to. *When the marked arms show, it's time to go,*" he recites.

"Go where?"

"To wherever they bloody tell us. The Tungisel. The Ridgeguard. Some unlucky bastards are sent north. I dislike going to Nurgos well enough. Can't imagine going all the way to the Waterwatch. I've heard stories of what twisted creatures walk through the Dwellwater."

I recognize the names. The Dwellwater stretches across northern Durast, separating the Everwatch from what was once Vhania. The north of the Gatewood touches it. That is where Fort Se'lae stands guard, keeping dwellers from the Wood.

"I've done my service," Shod continues. "Not fond of being sent one way or the other anymore. So, I keep my distance from any mage in blue."

"As will I."

"You should keep your distance from most folk once you're out of here," he advises.

"I would have avoided Forestfall if my horse didn't deserve a stall for the evening."

"Was it that your horse needed a stall, or you needed a drink?"

I finish the last sip of ale and stand. "Where am I to sleep?"

"I can show you," Love eagerly pipes up as she swipes my empty mug.

I look down at her, perhaps more tensely than intended.

"You look like you need a rest," she observes, unflinching.

"Help Chella with the dishes," Shod tells her. "I'll show her."

"She doesn't scare me, Da."

He shoots her a warning glare. *"Dishes."*

I make no comment, understanding why he doesn't trust me. I would not trust him if he wandered into camp.

Shod takes a candle from the bar to guide the way up a rickety set of stairs. I watch the large innkeeper warily just as he casts a guarded glance at me. He seems a good man, but as we meet the dark of the second floor, I lose sight of his assuring expression. With his back to me, Shod the Innkeeper no longer exists. His broad frame, darkly outlined in the faint light of the bobbing candle, appears menacing. The wrinkles on the back of his bald head contort in the darkness. They morph into the shape of brands. His shoulders seem to hunch, and in the opening of a bedroom door, I see glinting eyes in the dark.

"Nev!" I gasp, my hand jumping to my chest as though to shield a poisoned arrow. The man in the dark jumps and stumbles into the door-frame. The candle wavers and the likeness of Skinner vanishes amidst the trembling shadow.

Shod's startled eyes meet mine. I freeze in an advance I did not realize I took. Half shrunk against the wall, the innkeeper lifts a negotiating hand.

"Easy there," he says, "how's about you lower that ax?"

I do not recall the exact moment I drew the weapon, but I hold it in the air beside me now, ready to swing.

Horrified, I let it fall to the floor with an awful thud. After a moment, Chella's voice calls up the stairs. "Shod? What was that?"

"It's alright!" he replies. "Just tripped in the dark!"

"We heard a shout."

"I almost dropped the candle, that's all."

I hear her grumble to Love. "He's so clumsy..."

Meanwhile, the flickering flame calms. Shod straightens and releases a tense breath. "You almost got me, there," he nervously chuckles. "What was that you said? *Nev?* What is Nev?"

"I'm sorry," I stammer. "I don't know why I did that."

"Most of us don't."

"Don't what?"

"Don't know what comes over us sometimes." He crouches down and holds his candle to my dropped ax. He studies the crude weapon briefly before looking up at me. "You got an ax of a burned man, you're askin' about burned men, and if I had to guess..." he gestures at my face.

I say nothing, my heart still in my throat.

"You aren't huntin' brillbirds."

"*Nev.*"

"You know," he confesses as he slowly stands, "I spent four years stationed at Piesamur. At the Ridgeguard. I've stood upon the Skirt before the Burned Lands. I've been met with burned men. Got the scars from them. Just like you." He lifts the hem of his shirt, revealing a knotted wound in his torso, now long healed and distorted by a healthy gut, but brutal all the same.

"The moment my service was done, I got out," he continues, concealing the scar. "Told myself I'd never raise my girl so near to the Burned Lands. I chose Forestfall because it's safe. It's quiet. And if any enemy were to come here, I knew I'd have elves protecting us. You can be a difficult lot, but I know you keep terrible things at bay. Or at the very least, attempt to chase them down," he says with a pointed look.

"Even so, I still have memories of my time at the Ridgeguard. I still suffer unpleasant dreams. See monsters where they don't exist." His expression softens with his voice. "If you want those memories to lessen, then you have to take yourself away from them. You have to stop."

I lift my ax off the floor, taking care to hold it loosely and low. "I haven't started yet. I won't stop until their king is dead."

"A *king?*" he questions. "Which king?"

"Is there more than one?"

He shakes his head, baffled. "Burned men got lots of kings. They all war with each other when they aren't warring with the High Mage Surasis."

"I'm looking for the one who made it past the High Mage then."

"The fact they got past Surasis means they'll cut you down in the blink of an eye."

His phrasing reminds me of how quickly Halstaer fell. I hide my flinch with a scowl.

"You'll only get away from them with your life once," he says.

Not once.

"They took something I have to get back," I tell him. "Even if I die trying." *Again.*

He sighs. "Do you have to do it alone?"

"It's my duty."

He extends the candle to me. "Well, at least you'll have a night's rest first. Take this. Just be sure to put it out before you fall asleep. I don't need the only walls I've got burnin' down around me in the night."

I have trouble forming a reply. Part of me wants to follow him back down the stairs to question him about the Burned Lands and his own memories, but at the moment, I don't trust myself to be around anyone else.

"I'll have Love draw you a bath in the morning. There'll be breakfast, too," he says. "Try to get some rest."

I check the shadows of the small room before sending Shod away with a parting word. *"Ai'shtanu,"* I say.

"Ai—what now?"

"Ai'shtanu. Good night."

"Ah, well, ai'shtanu."

He steps away from me, knowing his way through the dark hall. I listen for his weighty footfalls to descend the stairs. As his presence fades to the lower level of the inn, so too do his words, and I find that there are no walls that can keep my memories at bay.

Waylay

IN THE DAYS FOLLOWING my departure, the dense life of Evoriel's forest gradually ends to mingle with the woods of the Everwatch. All that is lush and imbued with ancient magic does not grow here, and my mind wanders with the passing time until a stilted river town appears shadowed by the distance.

Waylay looms over a fork in the river, intercepting the waters at a narrow point where a barge is situated. A contraption of thick ropes helps the boat to cut across the river's flow. I watch it slowly pull along, carrying a few travelers to Waylay's entrance. The vessel crosses at a decent pace and eventually drops the passengers on the opposite bank where a stone road leads them upward to the town's gate.

I watch the bargemen work into the evening from a hidden position upriver. Mournstar blends well and rests quietly in the trees, and the few riverfolk do not notice me at the distance. If I were closer, their eyes might find my figure pressed up against a tree, but I doubt it. The bargemen appear harmless. Two guards dressed in the light blue raiments of the Everwatch are stationed on either side of the river. I was wary of them at first, but they've been welcoming enough to travelers. *Human travelers.*

Before making my approach, I take two cets and a few bits from my purse and slip them into a pocket, knowing they will be a generous bribe if necessary. With Love's clever advice in my head, I consider hiding the rest of my money. If only I could also hide my face. Forestfall's acceptance of elves does not apply elsewhere in the Imperium. Humans have not favored us in the best of times, and we certainly have not favored them in return. We do not cross each other's territory unless it is mutually discussed. There are no laws against it, but it is not done. If an armed human were to enter the Wood without explanation, I would not let them take a step out of my sight let alone continue on their journey unquestioned. After the burned men, I do not know if I'd even offer them a chance to speak.

Humans have felt similarly toward elves ever since the devastation of Edgewood. The city's ancient ruins stand silhouetted to the north near the original border of the Wood. The fractured outline of once sturdy walls juts outward at a turn in the river, seemingly meek from the distance. Waylay looks on the wretched city every day—one of the few disastrous incidents that has not faded to time.

I pull up my hood to cast my face in shadow, knowing I will not be welcomed in the shadow of Edgewood. Next, I fan out my cloak to conceal my axes as best I can. With my shoulders hunched, there is a small chance my impression of a tired hunter will trick anyone into overlooking my face beneath my hood.

I lead Mournstar at my side as we walk to meet the barge. It slugs across the river, the current lapping against its wooden hull. The stamping of boots on deck carries on the wind as the workers on board attend to their duties. On the dock, an old man guides the vessel with the crook of a hand, nodding until it drifts into position. As the barge gently knocks against the dock, the two posted guards move in, relaxing as two others exit the barge in a change of shift.

I focus on keeping a calm hold on Mournstar's reins and let my shoulders drop despite the tension running through them.

One of the arriving guards notices me first. She pauses on the dock and lifts her chin as though it helps her vision cut through the fog.

I consider turning away. Surely there is a narrow place in the Uduro where I could coax Mournstar across. But before I can decide, the female guard calls out.

"Step forward if you are here for passage, traveler."

In the fog, my performance as a tired hunter goes unquestioned. Even Mournstar passes as a stock horse in the mist, but as we emerge, something about my figure sets the guards on edge. The woman's hand drifts to her sword while the other scrutinizes my figure, and I realize I'm still carrying myself too lightly, too quietly as I step one foot before the other, nearly soundless upon the forest floor. Had I made myself heavy it would not have mattered. I'm still too tall for a typical human.

I see the guard's throat bob as she swallows hard. The others on the dock stiffen as their eyes fall on me one by one. I stop as well.

Then the woman clears her throat. The guttural sound reanimates the bargemen. "I said, step forward," she repeats to me, her tone forceful. "You are looking to cross, Recluse, are you not?"

I continue forward, allowing my body to straighten at her slur.

"Pip," she barks at the old man. "Help them board."

The old man looks frightfully at the guard and then snaps shut his agape mouth. "R...right," he stammers while carefully descending the dock to me. "Apologies, uh, miss? We...we don't get many Rec— I mean *elves*—coming through here. Startled us is all. If you'll please come this way."

He gestures for me to lead Mournstar up a ramp to the barge. I glance at the guards who watch me closely. Mournstar huffs against my shoulder, calmer than I. His hooves grind heavily upon the path. Other than the flowing Uduro, it is the only sound that perforates the fog.

Their impact ascends to a fierce clap as I lead him onto the barge's deck. A deckhand holds the low gate aside so we may board. His gaze darts between my hooded face and the warhorse at my side. For too long after I pass, he remains frozen in place.

The guards leaving their shift stare at me from the opposite side of the barge. The moment I'm on board, Pip hurries to them. They exchange the briefest of words, so succinctly that I do not catch what is said before the old man flees the deck. I keep Mournstar between myself and the rest of the barge, feeling a bit of nausea roll through me.

Mournstar does not fear the river or strange sway of the barge, but the movement is odd to me. I've forgotten the last time I was aboard any kind of boat. The crossing is just long enough to addle my stomach. I grip Mournstar's mane and concentrate on standing as Waylay becomes more defined beyond the fog.

Much of the town is walled. I determine the stilted homes outside likely belong to fisher and bargemen, based on the upturned boats that rest in their shade and the nets that hang from upper porch rails. The structures are old and strong, seeming to have withstood many floods. In the blanket of fog, their stilt supports appear like sinister fingers shooting upward from the Deep.

I shrink deeper into my hood as the boat docks on Waylay's bank. It would bring me greater comfort to hold the axes, but the humans are already too frightened—too quiet and clumsy as they hurry to dock. The moment we are still, the guards disembark. Over the barge's side, I watch them head toward Waylay's gate.

With Mournstar in tow, I exit just as quickly, ignoring how the remaining bargemen hastily step away from me. It is discomforting to be so exposed at the foot of the town, particularly a town located several days from Aleauna, the heart of the Everwatch's rule.

The plan was always to subvert Waylay with as little human inter-action as possible. Crossing the Uduro was necessary, and the humans' panicked responses were anticipated, but I will take no risks regarding their paranoia. After all, I never left encroaching humans alone in the Gatewood. If they are the same, better that I disappear before they can bring me to question.

The barge creeks as it pushes off from Waylay's bank, leaving me alone in the settling darkness. I wait a moment, searching between the crooked legs of the exterior homes as I tighten Mournstar's girth. All is still. There are no traces of guards or inhabitants. The only light comes from two distant sconces on either side of the town's gate, the only movement from the flames within.

"Our business is not with them anyway," I mumble to Mournstar as I mount.

He chews his bit in response.

I guide him off the road around Waylay as soon as the trees grow suit-ably thick and glance behind to ensure the guards did not find courage in their retreat. The empty road behind reassures me that the humans are content within their walls. My nerves calm once covered in a more complete darkness.

Mournstar trusts me to navigate his path. Although his Daervish bred bloodline gives him clearer sight than any Imperium mount, he still shies at the disturbed animals in the shadows. I let him walk to maintain his footing and together we find bearing on our surroundings.

Our surroundings are not what I'd call a proper wood. The trees are standoffish of each other, making for a sparse canopy through which the faint moonlight filters. The undergrowth does not grow thicker as we press on. The roots do not rise. I have no reverence for them, only pity that they should grow so weak.

My mind drifts, thinking of everything and nothing at once while we walk. I miss the acans I used to hunt and travel with. Halstaer is always at the forefront. I allow space for him, knowing he is all I can manage. Thinking of all the Rendara is too painful. I've not yet been able to recall them as they were before the attack without the overlapping memory of Skinner and his men. My father missing, my mother beaten, Beshtel silenced, Serin abandoned...only Halstaer has begun to return as comfort. I can see him without the blood or poison. Sometimes the memories end before Skinner's sword. Perhaps because he let me go. Told me to go.

Mournstar suddenly sidesteps, jostling me from my thoughts. His head jerks right, alerted by something unseen.

An arrow hisses through the dark.

I twist with its impact as it pierces my shoulder. Mournstar rears, catching a second arrow in the meat of his shoulder. He squeals and stumbles on his hind legs, throwing me from his back. My axes pinch my shoulders when I hit the ground. With the air knocked out of me, I roll for cover behind the closest tree. Mournstar flees in the opposite direction from which the arrows came. I let him run, knowing an attempt to stop him will only get me run over or shot again.

I grit my teeth and yank the arrow from my shoulder. Peeking around the narrow tree trunk gives me view of two approaching archers. They creep hurriedly through the brush, long bows held at the ready as they use streaks of moonlight as their guide.

A twig snaps at my front. I curse the blindness in my periphery and snap my gaze back to see three more figures pushing through the dark. They abandon all pretense of stealth and quicken their movements upon realizing my attention. The center figure—a man wielding a tangle of rope—rushes forward as though to lash it around my wrists.

"Norveh!" I curse, enraged by yet another man intent on binding me. His armor is sparse, and I notice none of them are dressed for a prolonged fight. I pull a small hunting knife from my belt and whip it at the rope man.

He grunts as the blade lodges beneath his collarbone, pausing to clutch the wound as the two swordsmen lunge forward. I shove to my feet and draw my axes, my arms moving quicker than their legs. With the archers at my back, I know it foolish to step away from my tree, but the idea of being pinned to yet another trunk forces me away. Two more arrows are released my way. I angle out of their path and pinpoint where the archers have taken position in order to muddy their aim amidst the foliage. The swordsmen close in, but three humans in the dark are easier evaded than confronted. Dodging around them and chasing after Mournstar is a simpler strategy. But then the flames go up.

They appear from nowhere, flaring from the forest floor without spark or tinder. I leap backward as the writhing fire threatens to caress my face, and through the flame notice another figure, their arms held aloft in control of the fire. The edge of their dark outline wavers beyond the light, and as they bow their head, a crown of tangled horns appears.

For an instant my heart palpitates, startled by the menacing figure. My attackers are not nearly so surprised. They use my confusion to advance, the first slicing toward my middle with a sword. I swing downward, meeting him with both axes.

In anticipation of a deflection instead of a strike, he underestimates the strength behind my attack. The blade, not poised for such force, slips from his grasp, and I retaliate with an upward arc to his jaw. The ax head cracks beneath his chin, sending him backward with a spray of blood into the flames.

I assume an offensive stance and face the other two with the flames at my back. The archers maneuver in the distance, seeking clearer aim while their companions step forward to meet me. In the light, they appear as common bandits, wearing patchwork armor without loyalty, but the way they fight is regimented. I dance with them, catching and dodging their blows in a series of agile motions as they try to make contact. They are not sloppy and balance each other's movements as a trained pair. The archers restrain themselves, loosing arrows only when they have a clear shot. I avoid several more with a few simple turns. Some graze the surface of my leather armor, none seeking any vital areas. The wound in my shoulder burns with every movement, but it is nothing I can't momentarily ignore at the hands of humans.

They tire quicker than me. I wait for their attacks to become unbalanced and then strike fast. I curve one ax at the second swordsman's arm. As he deflects, I send an ax low into the side of his knee. He falls with a cry of pain. I recoil to swing the ax downward when his female companion gives a vicious shout from behind. I dive forward over the man, rolling to my feet in time to see the woman stab downward. Rather than hit me, she shoves her blade deep into her companion's chest.

She snarls and withdraws her sword, indifferent toward the man as she furiously swings at me again. An arrow penetrates my bicep the moment I block her blade. The fresh pain weakens my hold, and the woman hooks her blade under my ax head. She pulls me toward her hard and punches me across the jaw. I stagger backward, dropping the ax from my arrow riddled arm. The woman closes the distance, determined not to let me go. Rather than run, I jump and roll over her shoulder, throwing my second ax as I land on the ground behind her.

The ax carves the air and slams into the archer's chest who moved nearer after seeing their companions fall. Without pause, I grab the dead man's sword from the ground and spin back to finish the woman.

The blade is thrown from my grasp by a bolt of white energy. My hand thrums with a vibrating pain. The woman and remaining archer hold their attacks and follow my gaze toward the wall of flame. The whipping fire rises briefly and then furls away, allowing a gap to the shadowed woods through which a man steps.

He wears a long coat that trails the ground. Peeking from beneath either sleeve are steel bracers adorning his arms. The plate continues across his chest, each piece of it engraved in jagged runes. He is perfectly immaculate aside from an even stubble that shades his cheeks and jaw. His hair is the color of honey and seems to have once been cut in a military style before growing unruly at the front. In his hand, an orange glow pulses. He holds it idly, studying me with a curious look. Behind him, the figure darkly outlined beyond the wall of flame waits in a wash of bright fire.

The Everwatch mage takes a step closer, rotating the orange orb in hand as he does so. The remaining archer and swordswoman back off. I stay still, unknowing of what magic he holds.

"So," he says, looking down at me, "not a mage then. Just a Recluse escaped from its hovel."

Quicker than any human should be able to match, I reach for my dropped ax, intending to leap up and drive it into his chest. In the same instant, he extends a hand, and a bolt of orange light bursts from his palm.

Scraps

I WAKE AGAINST OLD stone. I can feel its age pressed close to my cheek, a smooth dusting of past time and exposure. There is comfort in knowing I'm still outside. A soft wind keeps the stone cool. The sweet scent of dew dampened woods is nearby and the crackling voice of a fire. Flames waver against my eyelids, invading my own darkness.

My arms and legs are bound. There is no strain of rope or metal vices, yet I cannot budge my limbs from one another. Even my hands are balled and caged. The restriction of movement reminds me of Skinner's rope crushing my ribs to the tree at my back. My pulse quickens, and I struggle to keep my breaths contained. In a different time, I might have had an ability to keep still from detection, but now I pull fiercely at my binds, desperate to be free.

A sudden jolt rattles through my body. It begins in my extremities and ricochets between muscle and bone. I convulse sharply. The shock is the first new pain I've felt since waking, and it sends my eyelids upwards.

The Marked watches me bow to the shock. After a moment, the pain passes, and I can study him more clearly. He sits on what looks to be a fallen pillar, elbows resting on his thighs and hazel eyes looking down at me. Beside him, the wall of an old stone tower partially encircles us. Vines and branches creep through cracks in careful reclamation. A similar stone floor spreads outward before sinking beneath dirt and moss. Firelight pushes at my periphery, but I fear turning my head will incite more pain.

In his relaxed position, I see the extent of the fine plated armor that shields his chest, legs, and arms. The blue robe falls around him, its Everwatch sigil half-hidden in its folds. He maintains a soft smile that hardly wrinkles his cheeks as he glances at my restraints.

Following his gaze, I see my binds will not be easily broken, if at all. Fiery orange cords wreath around my limbs, locking them together.

The Marked continues to watch me, perhaps waiting for me to writhe some more. Anger and instinct scream for me to fight, despite knowing there will be pain. It takes all my self-control to remain still and weigh my lack of options. *Halstaer won't save you now.*

The Marked gestures at the magic vices. "This is a binding spell," he calmly says. "You won't break it, although you're welcome to try. Just know that I've seen men kill themselves trying to withstand the shocks in favor of freedom."

"Nesh tar unveh."

"Come now. I know you Recluses can speak Dur. Don't hold back."

I hold him with my glare, heart palpitating. "You men and your fucking binds."

"A precaution."

"I'm not here to be a threat," I insist too desperately and quick. Ashamed, I force my tone to strengthen, my tongue slowing with the heavy Dur. "I have no business with the Everwatch. You're just in the way. Let me go."

"You have not been permitted to enter Everwatch lands. On that account, I must detain you. Oh, and you murdered three of my men in the dark of night, so I think I'll keep you right where you are for now."

I grit my teeth, holding back what I know would be a useless defense. In my stillness, new sensations awaken, and the details of my surroundings clarify. I recognize a soreness in my shoulder and bicep where the two arrows struck. The raw pain of the wounds has since been numbed by restorative magic. I distrustfully curl my lip at the given aid and the mage before me.

"You are one of the Marked," I say.

He casually glances at his robed and plated arms. "That I am."

At the back of one hand, I see the faint line of an inked rune like those carved in his armor. Their complexity irks me. Had I any affinity for magic, I might know how to face him as I know how to adjust to an opponent's weapon.

But I know nothing beyond recognition of the intricate lines. They are, in fact, runes. Runes as I have seen them scattered throughout my life: harmlessly cut into healer Shayv's implements, reinforcing the walls of Daerva'Tor, or in the blades of the *vatanukro*. I know them, but only enough to realize my own ignorance.

Even if I were free, I would not know how to fight the Marked. The practiced smirk he gives tells me he is quite aware of his advantage. I slowly sit up without tugging on my binds. The compliant movement staves off shock, and I feel safe enough to carefully turn my head.

Under the crumbling wall of an old watchtower, the Marked's remaining companions rest for the night. I notice the surviving swordswoman and archer. They sit apart from one another, each claiming their own throne of stone debris. The archer fiddles with a scrap of dinner, uncaring of our conversation while the swordswoman watches intently. She holds her sword in her lap, prepared to use it at a moment's notice. But if the moment is to occur, neither she nor the archer worry me. It is the third companion who rouses my fear.

They were the one behind the flame. Even now, the large form sits hunched dangerously close to the too large fire in the basin of the tower. The wild flames nearly lick the horned figure's bent legs. They are in the light, but it does not penetrate the shade that envelops them. They make no acknowledgement of my prying eye and continue to be entranced by the flames.

I return to the Marked who has been observing me observe the others. "What do you want?" I ask.

"A conversation."

"Attacking me is a poor way to compel conversation."

"I thought you'd find it more compelling than if I were to execute you outright."

"You were going to execute me?"

"I am going to execute you."

Again, the memory of Skinner holding his knife to my eye resurges. My heart drops at the Marked's words, and I work to maintain composure within my restraints. *Eyes forward*, my mother chides from the back of my mind.

"I know, you must be confused," he goes on, "but there's no reason to worry. I'm not a burned man, you see. I'm not going to waste time by carving pictures into your face. Just cooperate, and it'll be over quick."

"How do you–"

"After all you've been through, I should think you'd like to rest, but I need some information first."

I blink away the momentary fog of emotion and find my words. A heat grows between my shoulders as they tighten to prevent me from pulling at the magic binds. "How do you know about the burned men?"

He leans forward. "Because I'm cleaning up after them."

I pretend Halstaer is with me, pressing a hand to my back as he once did to temper my anger.

"They're fond of leaving scraps," the Marked continues. "We don't often see them here, but along the Ridgewall, they sometimes sneak through. They'll raid what they can where they can and leave a trail of scraps. Broken buildings. Broken bodies. Whatever they didn't particularly need but wanted to destroy. That's what you are—a lucky scrap. Hardly worth my talents, yet I've been ordered to track and kill you, which leads me to believe you are not a scrap at all."

My chest pushes against the magic tethers at the force of my breath, and they respond with a sudden thrum of shock. The Marked slightly raises his voice above the blood rushing in my ears.

"The way I see it, if you *were* just a scrap, the Everwatch wouldn't care about your loose fucking tongue. After all, who would trust a rogue rat? We let you go long enough, some drunk peasant with the slightest proclivity for destructive frames will put you in the ground for us. Instead, my superiors have spent a great deal of coin and time to ensure you are silenced immediately by someone who won't leave a trail for anyone to find. Why is that?"

The fragments of information begin to shift together. I mean to speak vehemently, but my words come out weak and confused. "You...you know."

"*Depths*," he sighs, exasperated.

"You knew a pack was here."

"And currently they no longer are. By now, things are nearly back to normal except for a few lingering details that *you* are going to help clarify."

"You did this!"

"No. I did my job. I am still doing my job. What upsets you was the cruelty of a ravenous pack."

"A pack that was allowed entry by the Everwatch."

"Yes."

His blunt answer gives me pause. In my startled silence, he continues to speak.

"In short, it came to our knowledge that a southern rabble of elves was harboring a fugitive of the Everwatch—a fugitive we have searched for decades to bring to justice. Since the Everwatch cannot freely enter the Gatewood, it was determined necessary that we employ a third party to assist us in attaining said fugitive."

What words I had preemptively chosen for response are overcome by several waves of confusion and fear. Rather than allow them to come forth, I slightly tug my arm and intentionally incite a shock to steel myself. Energy crackles up my forearms. I brace against it, refusing to fear a human mage as I feared Skinner.

The Marked watches, intrigued, and then he bends forward to trace a pattern on the stone. As he completes the symbol, various marks darken on the stone around me.

"The Everwatch has its goals," he tells me, brushing the dirt from his hands. "I trust the Command, and I have done many things to ensure the safety of my home. However, recent events have involved cruelty uncharacteristic of Everwatch strategy, and it seems the precise details of my orders differed from the burned men. A mistake, I'm sure, but a mistake I believed cost unnecessary life." He meets my eyes. "So, to prevent further loss going forward, I need you to answer my questions honestly."

I mean to curse him or to say nothing at all, but his cajoling tone draws my words up and out.

"All right," I say, the consent not coming from myself. As the runes pulse faintly around me, my body relaxes in its tethers.

"Now," the Marked continues, slowly blinking in an enchanting manner. "What was the name of your tribe?"

"My *vashte'rae*," I correct, unwillingly. "We are the Rendara."

"Rendara," he repeats with a nod. "*Were* the Rendara. Was your tribe in conflict with the Everwatch?"

"No, just the humans to the south."

"What humans?"

"A small village. They were..." I try to resist, "...trespassing. Taking our trees."

"A typical dispute."

"We would have negotiated, not fought."

"Of course. No need for excess violence when humans fear your kind enough."

"We don't kill without reason. Not like you."

"Of course, you do, and it's never without reason. I'm trying to determine that reason right now."

"Norveh un diil."

"What was that?"

"Fuck off."

He smiles diplomatically. "Back to your tribe. Why were you Rendara harboring a war criminal?"

"I don't know what you're talking about."

"The fairborn amongst you."

The runes seem to deepen into the stone as I hold back any reply. The Marked frowns at my reticence. A brief anger flutters across his eyes.

"The fairborn," he prompts. "Do you know of whom I speak?"

"...Yes."

The magic binds seem to tighten as the Marked scrutinizes my expression. He passes over the heavy scarring on my left eye and focuses on the intact portion of my face, leaning nearer.

"Who was he to you?" he asks.

I bite into my tongue.

The Marked taps his boot atop his drawn rune. "*Who* was he?"

"My father."

The truth comes out of me as a gag. I lurch against the binds, and they retaliate with an intense jolt down my spine.

The mage sits up, victorious. "And so, you are not just a scrap. Tell me, how long have you been a soldier?"

"What did you do to him?" I press.

He ignores me, tapping his foot once more. "How. Long."

"One hundred years."

"What skills do you possess beyond what you've already showcased in killing my men?"

"I'm..." I try to resist and fail, "...an *acan*."

"What does that mean?"

"Hunter," I spit.

"Share any of your father's talents?"

"Only my mother's."

"Oh? And what was her specialty?"

"Beating the shit out of men like you."

He blinks, unflinching. "No magic?"

"Not your kind of magic."

"And yet you think you'll manage to...what, exactly? What are you doing so far from home, acan?"

"Hunting."

"Burned men?"

"Yes."

"I regret to inform you that they've long since been sent back to the Burned Lands."

"I'll find them. Once I kill you."

He gives a musical laugh. "I retrieve Bharien Liadon of the Fractured Night, without a scratch to my armor and you think you'll kill me? Break free of those binds first and then you can amuse me, acan."

Any wrath I might have had for his retort is muffled when he speaks Bharien's name. It echoes through me and prickles the back of my neck. For once, I'm perfectly still in my binds as I stare up at the Marked.

"What did you call him?"

"You know the name."

"No. That's not his name. That's not who he is."

The anger returns to the Marked's eyes. It sharpens his pupils like a hawk. "I am at odds with the events that have transpired, but it is not because we had the wrong individual."

"Bharien Liadon has been dead for centuries."

"Dead or hidden?"

"We're not immortal, *rihar*."

"And we," he says, gesturing to his companions, "are not as forgetful as you think. The atrocities committed at Edgewood will be answered for."

"My father is not Bharien Liadon. Let him go. Wherever you've taken him, whatever you've done, let him go. Please."

He holds my pleading gaze a moment before scraping his boot along the rune, marring its image. "A Recluse does not leave its hovel as a defensive tactic. It does so because it is hungry. The Everwatch can't afford to have Bharien and his equally violent daughter loose in the world." He stands from his pillar and adjusts his sleeve. "No one who shares his blood deserves a quick death, but I have dignity."

"All the dignity of a man who would follow burned men."

He swiftly pulls one arm back, as though to dash an invisible object atop my head, but as he tries to complete the movement, his arm resists.

He yanks against the air, seemingly restrained by nothing. He growls a curse at his frozen arm and looks over his shoulder. There at the fire, the dwellish silhouette continues to watch, one clawed hand held aloft, talon-like fingers crooked.

"Lumin!" the Marked calls to the figure, infuriated. "For such a wise man you are making a remarkably stupid mistake."

The figure stands behind the flame. He towers over the tall fire, claws precisely held as he takes his time stepping within speaking distance. A long black cloak hangs around him, giving momentary view of the dark plate beneath. Despite his height and weight of armor, he steps almost silently upon the crumbled stone strewn about, and when he pauses at a careful distance, I notice his clawed hand is merely that—claws absent of armor.

He shifts his burning orange gaze between the Marked and myself. Like his dark attire, his skin is a grey slate, and his features appear as though they were harshly cut from stone. His skin melds into his tangle of horns that twist back like a cluster of intermingling roots.

"Let me go, and I'll forget this insubordination," the Marked tells him evenly.

Lumin replies in the gravelly voice of Uunshyl's deepest stone. "Stay your hand; we are not done with her yet."

The Marked lifts a conceding brow.

Lumin flattens his claws and the Marked's strained arm releases. He steps forward, his entire body relaxing as he shakes his arm loose. Then without pause, he swiftly angles himself, and slams the back of his hand against my cheek. The impact throws me sideways and the binds react to my movement, sending another rippling shock throughout my body.

"Pray tell, why are we not done with her?" the Marked casually asks while rubbing his hand. "Have you glimpsed something of import?"

"Nhuaela."

I shakily lift my head, my body still thrumming with energy. The looming figure stares down at me, and I realize he is no dweller.

"What was that?" the Marked demands.

"*Her*," Lumin says. "The name."

"You know her name?"

"I have known."

"You mean you've seen her?"

"Yes."

The Marked watches him skeptically. His hand tightens. "Why have you not mentioned this before now?"

"It was of no import to you. Still, it is not." In the cradle of his claws, I notice two pulsing red mists.

The Marked instantly drops his eyes to the simmering glow. "What do you think you're doing?"

"It is time I leave you, and I require her."

"*Leave* us? You are bound to service. You do not get to leave at your will."

Lumin stares back at the Marked.

"I'm afraid I can't let you take her," the Marked decides. "We cannot run the risk of her being free. I'll figure out the rest of my questions another way."

"I advise you to return to your Command, Boon."

Boon, the Marked, shakes his head, coming to some realization. "Another warning not heeded, that we should trust a fucking *glim* as well as burned men."

His loud assessment draws the attention of the two soldiers. The woman stands with her sword. The archer nocks an arrow but upon seeing Marked and glim at odds, he backs into the trees.

"You never trusted me," Lumin remarks, "but I trust you well enough to let you go."

"I have orders, Seer."

"...very well."

At once the mages sling their hands forward in a clash of bright light.

Glim

LUMIN SLICES HIS ARMS through the air. For a brief moment, an intricate glyph appears on his palms. They permeate his gathered mists, turning the dull red to a vibrant scarlet, and at the flick of his wrists, the haze sharpens and arcs forward in a cutting wave.

Boon reacts instantly, swooping his arm upward in a streak of white light. Lumin's red wave collides with the white barrier and separates around Boon. The severed wave splits in two more directions and fans outward. It rumbles like distant thunder until it crashes into the upper branches of several trees. Limbs crack and splinter. I fall sideways as a fragment of red careens over my head and shatters the crumbled stone wall I leaned against. The vice of magic bites deep into my skin, releasing excruciating waves of its own. Around me, the stone walls explode in a cloud of pulverized rock and dirt. Sharp granules slice my skin. Heavy branches crush into the ground below, bringing a shower of bark, twigs and leaves with them.

The swordswoman yelps as a wave cuts through her, rippling on impact. Several smaller waves branch across her body and carve through her armor with ease. She screams before falling limp and apart. Her arms slip from her shoulders. Her head tumbles to the side. There is no blood, only cauterized flesh.

The waves diminish rather than continue on across Durast, and all sound dies in their parting. The trees and stones settle. Somewhere downhill, a horse snorts in fright as I exhale with an equal shakiness.

It is a brief chaos. The stillness of my body and quickness of my heart remind me of my helplessness.

Lumin has hardly moved. He glances in the direction Boon last stood, and then cocks his head as if to listen more intently. After a moment, he lowers his guard. Pulling his robe snugly around himself, he takes a careful step in my direction. He stops a few paces from me so that his plated boots are level with my eyes. Their metal is a dull shade of black and scraped by wear. Silent, he sits upon the piled stone Boon occupied minutes before. It seems easier to stay quiet and let him proceed with whatever it is he intends, although in his stillness, I wonder if he intends to do anything. The longer he allows the silence to linger, the more impatient I become.

"Did you kill him?" I finally ask, glancing toward the place Boon previously occupied.

His voice is drawn and low. "No."

"Did you mean to?"

"Yes."

"What about her?"

He follows my gaze to the fallen swordswoman, contemplates, and then decisively replies, "A casualty but not unjustified, much like those you killed."

Not knowing how to reply, I move on, unnerved. "You know my name?"

"My god revealed it to me."

"Lelendelus."

"The Eye of Light and Lid of Shadow," he confirms. "You know of my kind, then."

"The glim, yes." I recall Boon's words. *I have orders, Seer.* "But you are not just a glim."

Lumin settles and his shadow draws back. Once more, he scans the darkened woods around the battered camp, not deigning to respond.

"What is a glimseer doing so far from Scerk?" I try. "And why are you working alongside the Marked?"

"...I was looking for you. You came to my mind when my god spoke his will into image. An *acan*," he recalls, briefly pausing after the elvish word. "A wretched elf with a face marred by torture. One not to be trusted, but as for your place in my path..." he drifts and grimaces. "It remains clouded."

His introspection is unmistakable. Weary, his claws clench within his lap, as though he is waiting for instruction that will not be given.

"He's silent, isn't he?"

The question oversteps some unknown line. The stoic glim glares, and orange light pushes against the crooks of his claws.

I make to raise my hands defensively, forgetting they are pinned to my sides. The movement incites the magic cage, and an angry shock burns through my armor. The fine tendrils flare along my skin while they stab through my veins, jolting my heart against my ribs.

Lumin kneels and places a hand of splayed claws flat to my chest. His arm stiffens as though to absorb the impact of magic current and the pain recedes. I'm acutely aware of the sharp ends of his claws so near the base of my throat. He stares down at me as I catch my breath, and I'm sure he knows he could kill me one way or another.

But not without the word of Lelendelus.

He curls a claw under a thread of the magic tethers and plucks the first like a string. One by one, his claw breaks the magic threads. They snap into frayed sparks and dissipate into the air. When they have all vanished, I rest my head against the ground and stretch my aching muscles. I would not run from the glim even if I were in a fit state. He'd likely quarter me with fire before I could reach the nearest tree.

"Are you here to kill me as well?" I ask, debating if I should settle on relief or fear.

"I do not yet know."

"But you *require* me. Dead or alive?"

He nods. "Though either state offers its own implications."

I sit up. The large fire that halos Lumin's form is too grand a signal for anyone or anything that might linger nearby. I want nothing more than to be away from it, hidden in the seclusion and dark of the woods.

"What do you mean to do with me?"

"I do not—"

"—Not what your god wants. What do *you* mean to do with me?"

He thoughtfully considers my demand, and when he answers, each word is nearly a sentence of its own. "I have traveled too far and too long to find you. I will not lose sight of you now. Not until the Eye sheds light on my path."

"And when there is light, what then?"

"Then I follow what the glimpses convey."

Slowly, I stand. He mimics my movement. Within arm's reach, my eyes are level with his plated chest. I lift them upward. He looks down.

"Do you serve the Everwatch?" I quietly ask, finding it oddly difficult to strengthen my tone.

"I serve my god."

"Through aligning with the Everwatch."

"All to find you."

I pointedly look him over, studying every aspect of his person as though I might find a reason to trust him. Unconvinced, I let out a strained breath, hoping to drive the lingering shocks from my body.

"I'll believe you aren't loyal to the Marked—for now. So, what have you done with my things? My axes. My horse." Feeling a sudden grip of anxiety, I spin, glancing around the immediate area. "Where's my horse? One arrow wouldn't have killed a Daervish breed."

Lumin lights a brilliant flame in his palm and lifts it toward a precise break in the trees. I look pointedly at his flaming claws. Then, without another word, I march into the darkened trees indicated by the fire. After a moment, his steps rustle the path behind me, his flame disrupting the night.

"I will accompany you," he says to my perturbed look.

I bite back the feeling of discomfort toward his looming presence, choosing instead to see the advantage in the following mage. Still, I wish I had an ax to combat his hand-turned brazier. I feel unsteady without the weight of my own weapon.

"Then put your light out," I tell him. "I don't need it."

He clutches the flame near his chest, as though offended. "I do not wander the dark unguided."

"I do."

"That is unwise."

"You've already made a spectacle of us. If Boon is out there, he'll know exactly how to find us with that beacon of yours."

"Boon has fled."

"You don't know that."

"It is his way. He will not fight a battle he knows he cannot win."

I edge away from the ring of light. "Just stay here. You're going to scare my horse."

Despite my warning, he trails me, keeping me just out of the throw of firelight. I do my best to ignore my bright shadow and instead listen for Mournstar. The horse may have been bred for war, but I doubt he has experienced any battle. Having witnessed the powers of magic, the poor creature might have realized he is not fond of his intended occupation. Searching for him is perhaps a waste of time in itself, but a tight worry for the frightened animal prevents me from leaving.

Lumin's red wave broke and charred everything it touched. The fallen branches leave trails of splinter-shaped embers. Close by the area where the horses were tied, I find their tack. Counting three saddles, I exhale in relief. Although dumped in a pile, my things are unharmed and accounted for. In one of the saddlebags, my hand locates Halen's flask. The feel of its worn leather relaxes me, and I take a quick drink.

Lumin watches me as I sling my axes onto my back. His held flame flickers, but he does not protest. A survey of the ground reveals a mottling of hoofprints and flattened brush. The horses likely ran together. I find the largest hoofprint and most impressively snapped twigs, then continue to follow their haphazard trail.

We walk for some time, first one way and then the next as the trail winds through the trees. It turns sharply and begins to circle back before I hear heavy breaths rooting in the underbrush.

Remembering a trick horse-master Egen taught me, I allow the tune of the Rendara to sound in the back of my throat. Its melody weaves into a clear hum as I step nearer the horses. Both animals lift their heads and prick their ears at the sound, but they do not startle. The hum builds, and I let it roll back to its initial gentleness when I lay either hand upon the wary beasts. In the muscle of Mournstar's shoulder is a healed knot of skin where the arrow struck. I draw my fingertip around it and watch him twitch his skin near the tender mark.

I tease Mournstar's head upward and then the other's, leading them into Lumin's warm light. The unfamiliar horse is a shade of chestnut, tall and strong, but not quite so bulky as Mournstar. It seems to recognize Lumin's scent and pokes his nose toward him.

"There were two others," he notes, in turn offering his claws to the curious horse. "This was the woman's horse."

"Boon and his archer may still be close. I don't trust it. Here." I reluctantly offer Mournstar's lead.

He hesitantly studies my outstretched hand.

"Take him. Before I change my mind and make you walk."

"I did not anticipate your cooperation in my following, let alone an offer of your horse."

"Are you going to follow me regardless of my consent?"

He drops his eyes to his fire, seeming troubled.

"*Norveh*, take the horse," I insist. "Mournstar can carry you better than this Aleaunan, and I need to move, which means *you* need to move."

He carefully takes the warhorse's lead. "Where are we to go?"

"Away from here."

As I ready the horses, shifting my personal belongings from Mournstar's saddle to the Aleaunan's, Lumin familiarizes himself with Mournstar. The horse side-eyes me skeptically, also distrustful of his new rider.

I do not want to lend him. I've grown fond of the large animal's delicate strength and the way he gently presses his muzzle to my shoulder when walking beside me. My relief upon seeing him alive is a gamble because the Ashan was right. A horse will not fare well on the path I take.

I doubt he will do any better on Lumin's.

"Does this one have a name?" I ask the glim as the Aleaunan nervously shifts under my touch.

"I do not know."

Of course not. With a quick glance at the gelding's red coat, I choose a fitting elvish term. *"Norrl."*

"Norrl?" Lumin repeats with perfect inflection.

"Rust."

I mount the horse before he can move aside and quickly catch the bit in his mouth. He responds well to a firm hold, clearly calmed by the presence of a rider.

Lumin watches, perhaps waiting for me to flee.

"You have my horse," I remind him. "And what use is there in running from a seer?"

Seeming unconvinced by the effectiveness of his collateral, he too mounts. Prior to stepping into Mournstar's stirrup, he transfers the flames in his hands to his horns where they flicker, leaving the rest of his face streaked in dancing shadows. Mournstar stands well enough, his head warily angled as the flame-crowned glim climbs onto his back. Lumin ruffles his mane, appeasing the warhorse for the moment. Then he gestures for me to lead on.

I keep Norrl still and guardedly look at the glim's flaming horns. Atop Mournstar, he appears menacing, not a man nor mage I'd like to have at my back in the night.

"Ride with me," I say, gesturing to my right. "Let's talk."

"I have not quite formulated my thoughts."

"Then formulate them beside me, not behind."

"There is no threat should we rest here."

"Just because you think Boon fled doesn't mean he won't be back."

"You would run rather than face him?"

"I'm not running," I snap. "I'm...*formulating*."

He sighs in a low grumble but concedes with a nudge to Mournstar's belly. With him in my periphery, I send Norrl forward more comfortably. I first try to locate the road downhill. If the ruin we sat in was that of a watchtower, a path should be nearby.

"The Kallish road will take us as far as Piesamur if we stay our course," Lumin suggests, "but we should not remain upon it lest we draw attention."

"I know that."

"Apologies. It struck me that you know very little."

I bristle. "At least I know how to make a decision."

"But you do not know if your decisions are correct."

"And you do?"

"My god does not lead me astray."

"Half a world away from your home and you don't think it's astray?"

"No. I have found my quarry."

"And have no idea what to do with it."

"Perhaps not, but that does not mean I do not know what to do at all."

For a long while after, we do not speak. The only sound is that of hooves on the soft ground. It is a soothing sound, the sound of distance being laid, of time bought so I may pull together my unraveling thoughts, and while I dislike the glim's shadowy presence, he is not the harrowing thing on my mind.

A war criminal...the fairborn amongst you.

The barbs in my back tug more fiercely in protest of the thought.

The Fractured Night.

With shaking hands, I fish Halen's flask from my belt and bring it to my lips, his words taunting me as I do so: *You really have no idea. No idea at all.*

When the tepid liquor flares over my tongue I realize my thirst and drink a bit more, tapping the last drops from the bottom. The ruin of Edgewood occurred a thousand years ago—somewhat fresh in elven history, but far too long for humans to maintain a grudge or for Boon's suggestion to align with my father's age. Or anything about him.

Bharien Liadon was merciless. He eviscerated Edgewood enough to haunt human history. My father could not haunt a human if he tried. Every time we ever negotiated with them, they gravitated toward him with a rare extension of trust.

I wipe my scarred eye with the back of my hand, feeling a wetness welling within it. My core trembles at the notion of my father being wrongly accused—at my absence and failure to defend him. Thinking of him crumbles my resolve. One by one, the Rendara creep to the forefront of my mind until I begin to see their shadows in the cast of Lumin's light, the glim now the least of my worries.

I pull Norrl toward a thicket in the wood.

"We've not gone but an hour," Lumin remarks at my sudden stop.

"It's far enough," I say, dismounting.

I hear the rattle of armor as the glim dismounts. For a moment I stare at Norrl's side, gathering myself. After a few calming breaths, I lift my head. And see Halstaer leaning against a tree.

I jump at his bloodied chest. He cocks his head.

"What are we doing, Nhu?"

He asked such a question on many hunts, often letting me take the lead. *Where to next? What's the plan?*

I find no words to answer before Lumin speaks, and at the sound of his voice, Halstaer vanishes.

"Nhuaela?" the glim says, as though in repetition.

I turn my head, not liking his use of my name.

He studiously narrows his eyes. "You are not of sound mind."

"Having worked with the Marked, you should know that."

"Of you, I know only what the Eye revealed."

"And what is that?"

"Both a great deal and very little."

"The fairborn," I simplify for him, gripping Norrl's saddle for support. "The..." I cannot make myself say it.

"War criminal?" Lumin gathers.

"What has become of him?"

"Aside from what was overheard from Boon, I have no notion of whom you speak, nor what fate awaits them."

I glare at him askance through his flame. "Were you there?"

"Where?"

"You know where."

"I do not."

The words strain through my teeth. "The slaughter of my people."

He ponders the idea, as though it is an insignificant memory to recall. "Were your people burned?"

The image of camp is flawless in my mind. Every detail of it remains as it was, never to return to the home it was before, but there was no ash.

"No."

Lumin splays his claws, his flames crackling in innocence as he takes a seat at the base of a tree. "You do not need to trust me as I do not trust you. However, you are of importance to me, and I am of value to you.

Rather than speak in circles of skepticism and distrust, sit, *acan*, and let us strike an accord before we travel one more step."

I continue to stand. "I don't need to make a deal with a stranger who may kill me at a moment's notice."

"Such strangers are precisely the reason treaties are made. I have encountered your ilk before. I will share no knowledge until an agreement is made."

"My ilk?"

"Those not of sound mind," he explains. "Unhinged tyrants and mad warlords. Grieving parents. The frightened and vengeful. You are all dangerous without boundaries."

"I had boundaries before the burned men breached them."

"Running unchecked will not help you restore them. Have you a plan?"

"Yes, and it doesn't involve a glim."

"That is unfortunate, because my plans involve a stubborn elf."

"I don't have time to wait for your silent god to speak."

An intensity flares in his eyes like the waver of a flame. "What light is shed is for my eyes alone. Your part is simply to move, and I will follow."

"So, I'm to await a firebolt in my back?"

"If I am to kill you, it will not be without warning."

"Your magic against my axes is not fair regardless of warning."

"Have you not lived long enough to understand that existence is rarely fair?"

"I've lived longer than you, seer."

"And have not experienced half of what I have, which is why I do not believe I was sent to kill you. That would be a waste."

"I've messed up enough for it not to be a waste."

He glares. "Not a waste of your life. Of mine. Quite like Boon argued, a basic assassination is not worth my talents. Any halfwit with a modicum of framework could kill you."

"It wouldn't be that easy."

"Then a hungry wolf." He waves a claw vaguely upward at the trees. "Or a weak limb. But perhaps I have somehow disappointed my god and this is my penance…"

"You would prefer to help me than kill me?"

"It would certainly give me greater purpose to *follow* you."

"I'm going nowhere safe, and I'm not planning to return."

"As Evoriel once said to Lelendelus."

Mention of Evoriel strikes a chord of anger. "Your god is silent. Mine abandoned my people. Let's not compare ourselves to them."

"Abandoned them?" he asks. "The gods do not abandon us."

"Evoriel did."

"To burned men?"

"And now to the Everwatch." Saying as much sends a sinking feeling from the base of my throat to my stomach, and finally, I sit. I look side to side in the dark, from the rough direction of Aleauna to Piesamur in the south. "What do you know about their dealings?"

"I should need to know your story before I can be of assistance."

"And what about your story?" I counter.

He lowers his hand, sending the ball of flame rolling upon the ground. Rather than consume the undergrowth, it appears to feed off itself. The horses warily angle their heads toward it. Lumin lays his hands on his bent knees and patiently leans back against his tree.

"Once you have explained yourself, I will tell you whatever you wish to know within my knowledge. Please, speak."

I'm silent for several minutes, not because I don't know how to begin, but because beginning has become familiar. As with the Ashan, I give only the necessary details and keep the rest to myself.

When I finish, Lumin thinks for as long as it took me to speak. All the while he stares into the fire, eventually asking, "Until now, you have pursued this pack?"

"Yes."

"Boon's interference has changed your plans."

"He has my father."

"The Everwatch has your father."

"And how in Evoriel's useless name am I to fight the Everwatch?"

"You do not."

"I will not abandon my father again."

"It does not sound to me like you abandoned him at all."

"He's gone, isn't he? Taken under my protection."

In the softest attempt his voice can manage, Lumin asks, "Have you any lead on his exact whereabouts?"

"Not exactly, no."

"And his physical state?"

"No," I say more pointedly.

"Let us assume he is kept in Aleauna. Perhaps alive, perhaps not. Either way, how do you intend to infiltrate the capital of the Everwatch or attain the scale of revenge I suspect you desire?"

I consider the advantages he could bring me, knowing none of them are enough. "You could help," I say anyway.

"You and I alone cannot discreetly enter there. We will be found. We will be caught and bound by the magics of the Everwatch. And then—" he abruptly stops himself, looking down. "No. We cannot achieve your goals without more force behind us."

"We have a chance."

"We do not. You are desperate and therefore foolish."

I surreptitiously dig my nails into my palm. The barbs tug me one way, my guilt welling up, but sense and orders pull me southward. *There are bigger conflicts than your own vendettas,* the Ashan's voice reminds me, his warning clear. *In three weeks' time, I do not want to hear rumors of a rogue Rendara terrorizing the Imperium in search of burned men.*

Lumin speaks almost in conjunction with the Ashan. "Unless you have a hidden army, I encourage you to think about where we are to go."

"I might have had an army," I mutter, recalling the offer of more help had I waited.

"What you might have had is irrelevant."

"What I did have is not."

"But the memory does not serve you now."

"I'm only out here for my people."

"You are here because it is where anger has taken you. At this rate, you will die for that anger, not your people."

"Why do you care what I die for?"

"Because I myself am much more likely to survive one scenario over the other. At the very least, I still have a purpose to fulfill, and you are seemingly part of that purpose."

The barbs burrow deep at the mention of purpose. I recall the dream I had prior to waking in Halen's hut, of my father beside the fire and his furious countenance. *You have responsibilities, Ashacan.*

My muscles ache as I stand, and I realize my stomach is empty. "Let's go," I decide, exhausted.

The glim waves his hand, and the flames jump to it. "What path?"

"I start with the King," I force myself to say. "My duty is to the vashte'rae, not just my father. He knew that." *Knew that I needed to hear it.*

Lumin bows his head in agreement. I quickly gather myself and mount Norrl before impulsivity changes my mind.

"You are adamant that your father is not the criminal Boon accused him of being," Lumin mentions, "but was he talented?"

"Absolutely talented, but he is no fighter."

"That does not make him weak."

"It doesn't mean I'm right to leave him either."

"Well..." he sighs. "In my experience, when an enemy goes to such lengths to abscond with an object of desire, it is not to simply be rid of it."

Knowing the Everwatch thinks they have a reason to abduct my father makes me nauseous. If anyone knew of such a reason, it should have been me. Or my mother. She clearly knew nothing more than I.

"It's your turn," I change the topic while turning Norrl southward.

"Where would you like me to begin?"

"With your first glimpse of me."

The Taken Path

OUT OF SIGHT IN the Old Wood, we loosely follow the path of the Kallish Road, a relic saved from the empire that fell a thousand years ago. The Everwatch fondly maintained the road across Durast—I suspect not only for practical purposes. Many humans still consider the Kallish reign to be the height of their power, but the Gatewood does well enough to remember the atrocities of the human and Vhanian alliance.

I grip Norrl's reins. *Traitors to the Five. Puppets of the Vha. And now patrons of burned men.*

"...and after the ship was set aflame, the surviving crew and myself took rest on the shores of the Burned Lands, just south of the Skirt. We had to swim to shore...and despite the entire ordeal, I found that to be the most unpleasant part. If not for the orcs, we would have never made it to the Ridgeguard." Lumin pauses in his long-winded telling of his journey from Scerk. "Nhuaela."

"What?"

"I have lost your interest."

"I was thinking."

He quietly looks away with a frown.

"Bone-cutters," I pick up where he left off, feeling rude despite myself. "They attacked your ship. And not one of the glim saw it coming."

His burning glare turns back. "My god shows me what I would not discover on my own, not every conflict. You, I could not have known without his vision. Adversaries at sea were something I'd cross regardless of sight."

"Did you see what would happen to my vashte'rae?"

"I do not glimpse the ends of all. I see only what happens to *me* and whoever happens to be in my path. I saw the moment in which we would meet, with you bound and scarred in the shadow of a blue-robed mage because that was also my fate."

"That's all it took for you to sail here? One vision?"

"Yes."

"How did you know where to find me?"

"The context of the glimpse. You were clearly one of Evoriel's beings, and the mage in blue was notably from the Durastian Everwatch."

I turn my attention back to the dense foliage ahead, embarrassed by the lack of forethought in my question.

"It is a common misconception that my kind know all," Lumin grants, allaying my stupidity. "Glimpses are not detailed plans. They are moments of crucial decision that will determine an end."

"And I was the end?"

"You are an obstacle in my path. What kind of obstacle remains to be seen."

"Which is why you have not killed me yet."

"And why, I believe, you have not killed me."

I do not disagree. "You swam to shore," I return to his tale. "Orcs helped you to the Ridgeguard. Then what? How did you fall in with the Marked?"

"First..." he replies in his slow manner, "*First*, I fell in with Piesamur. I have noticed my kin are uncommon in Durast, so the Ridgeguard were initially distrustful of the remaining crew and myself. They were inclined to deny us entry to the Everwatch. Glim were too unpredictable, they said."

"Did you attack them with fire as well?"

"Do not project your violent solutions onto me," he admonishes, remaining silent for a moment too long before continuing. "No, I explained to them our predicament, and they agreed to escort the crew to port where they might find passage to the Tungisel and from there, home."

"What about you?"

"I read their fortunes, and they let me pass."

"I thought you couldn't see the fates of others."

"I cannot, but an educated guess may find its mark. They permitted me to enter the city. It was not long before word began to spread. Humans are fascinated by their lack of time. Many came to me seeking answers for various plights they could not resolve. I amused them while waiting for my god to speak, and in that time, I eventually drew the attention of the High Mage Surasis."

"Iesh," I scoff in disbelief. "The High Mage?"

"They are not one to overlook an ally. You are not the only one locked in conflict with burned men. Surasis was wise to call me for counsel, and for two years I advised them on the defense of the Skirt, assisted soldiers when ambushed by roving packs, and created an occasional glimpse of hope."

"For two years?"

"I was learning."

"You had to have known I wasn't in Piesamur."

"You were not the only individual on my path. I had a purpose alongside the High Mage. That purpose was more imminent than our meeting, and it led to my place with the Marked."

"Whom you are no longer with," I say, searching for reassurance.

"I was never one of them. My reputation as the High Mage's counsel preceded me and as with Surasis, I caught the Marked's attention."

"So, you did not volunteer?"

"I...*cooperated* upon recognizing Boon from my glimpse."

"It required your cooperation?"

For several steps, he is contemplative. I dig a strip of tough meat from my bag and chew it in the saddle until he finds his voice.

"Surasis was reprimanded for enlisting my help," he shares, his layered tone confessing some regret. "They were not favored by the High Command prior to my assistance and certainly were punished for *keeping an asset secret*, as the Marked put it."

"An asset?"

"I am a glimseer."

"Did they want you to tell them their future?"

"Quite."

"Just like the Ridgeguard."

"But without the thread of amusement. They told me that so long as I was within the Everwatch, I would be working for the good of the Everwatch, and so I was given the choice to cooperate with their request or be cast onto the Skirt for delvers and bone-cutters. Little did they know I needed to go with them."

"Was it Boon who recruited you?"

"He was amongst them, yes."

"And what did he say to you about the Gatewood?"

"Nothing, for four years."

"You've been here for six years?"

"I have been here for seven. All that time you lingered in my thoughts, but my god did not reveal you until now."

Seven years is hardly any time at all, but since I trudged through the Gatewood with poison in my veins, time has slowed. Every minute seems to be priceless now, as every minute spent traveling and waiting is another minute the elusive King and his pack slip away, and my father's fate remains unknown.

"What were you doing all that time?" I ask.

"Lying. Telling vague futures. Sharing false glimpses."

"About what?"

"Many things. Rarely would I be given explanation behind a request. I was simply told to consult my god about a location, an object, or unfamiliar term and recount what was seen.

"Why ask Lelendelus and not Ixis? She gave humans magic in the first place."

"She also revoked their frames of Sight almost *immediately* after creating them—for the exact reason woodelves lack destructive frames."

I nod curtly, taking his meaning.

"When mortals dabble in frames outside of their own, it upsets the balance of the gods. That is why there are few glimseers. Only those of us who are capable of guiding others are born with the Eye."

"You guided humans with a magic their own god did not give them access to."

"I guided them both toward and away from whatever it is they seek, but having heard your plight, I fear they have subverted my deception."

I pull Norrl to a halt and look squarely at the glim. "What are they trying to achieve?"

"I fear a great many things."

I continue to stare at him, impatient.

"Of which I only know scattered details," he concedes. "And I do not yet know what I should reveal to you."

"If you know anything about my people, you'll tell me now."

"I know what you have shared with me."

"Is that a lie too?"

"It is not. Over the last year, the Marked and the High Command became more secretive. Boon, particularly, was distrustful of me. He began to see through my misdirection, which is why he insisted I work at his side at all times."

"And so, you were with him when he attacked me."

Lumin nods in affirmation. "It was time. Any longer in their midst and I'm sure the Marked would ensure my usefulness came to an end."

"You're welcome," I say dryly.

"In some way, you saved me as well, Nhuaela Elendira." He nudges Mournstar onward, putting me at his back. "And if I must kill you...it will be a shame."

* * *

As we take rest the following evening, Lumin lays his flames within a dip in the ground. They roll from his palm onto the leaves without losing their brightness. He lifts his claws, and in response, the fire grows. Over our brief time together, he has never let his flames go out after dusk, and the trading of fire from horns to hand and then the ground between us has become a ritual to light our conversations.

Tonight, he maintains a dim glow upon his horns as well as the ground. I find it interesting to track the manner in which he wears his flames. Some nights he insists on being brighter than others.

I lean forward, closer to the light, and catch his burnt gaze. "Are you afraid of the dark?"

"Very much so."

"Why?"

"Because I cannot see within it."

"I can."

"You are half blind."

"*Half.*"

He shakes his head, lambent horns flickering. "All mortal vision is limited."

I search the area around us as I have done every hour since we left Boon behind. There has been no trace of the Marked or any other threat. Even now, the Old Wood is silent aside from the faint rustling of creatures in the undergrowth.

"There's nothing out there," I say.

"Nothing within your sight."

"You can't be afraid of everything out of sight."

"Being a conduit for the Eye, I have learned to fear what my god cannot show. And I have been blind for some time now." He momentarily looks beyond me in thought. "The Everwatch is not to be underestimated, particularly not the Marked."

"If I underestimated them, we'd be in Aleauna by now."

"Boon's absence worries me."

"You're the one who drove him off," I remind him.

"With the anticipation that he would soon follow. He has not."

"My goal was to lose him. Perhaps we have."

"If he were an ordinary mage, perhaps."

"Elves have survived this long because humans cannot follow our tracks, ordinary or not."

"Need I remind you that your tribe was located easily enough?"

His words bite and another barb pulls, snagging a deep sensation of ignorance from me.

"No," I deny. "I don't know how they found us, but it wasn't due to a human's ability to track."

He tilts his head, unconvinced. "How then?"

"Norveh un diil."

"You have neglected important questions," he chides, ignoring my crude remark. "Burned men are clever, but their aggression overshadows tact. The Everwatch employed them to complete a task, so it stands to reason they were led by humans—by Boon, specifically, who was charged with finding your father."

I shake my head despite his logic, unable to believe my vashte'rae was ambushed so effortlessly by anyone.

"The Marked are an ancient sect," Lumin explains, "trained and retrained to accommodate the current needs of the time. As I understand it, there has always been an active rift between elves and humans. Therefore, elves are what the Marked have specialized in handling."

"Humans haven't had to *handle us* in centuries and even during the Blight War they could not."

"Is it not true they nearly destroyed the Gatewood?"

"Daerva'Tor," I correct him bitterly. "And that was not because of human ingenuity."

"Regardless, Boon being able to track us is not far-fetched. It is what he was trained to do."

"You think he's avoiding us deliberately?"

"Potentially."

"If he does so long enough for us to enter the Burned Lands, so be it."

Lumin makes a noise that sounds like a snort. I half expect flames to flare from his nostrils. "Surasis does not permit anyone upon their Skirt without permission. They would obliterate you from the high tower before you could take a step toward the Burned Lands."

"I doubt it."

"Again, foolish."

"The Skirt spans hundreds of miles. They can't see all of it."

He lifts a claw. "Ah, but there is only *one* point of passage from the Skirt to the Burned Lands. That lies within sight of Piesamur and is therefore under Surasis's watch."

"A constant watch?"

"Presumably."

"Then I'm sure they noticed a king and his pack entering Durast and did nothing to stop it."

Lumin considers my assessment, opens his mouth to refute it, and then closes it, conflicted.

"I enter the Burned Lands my way," I tell him. "Not by leave of a mage who is complicit in the Everwatch's crimes."

"And then what?"

"I hunt." As I say it, my hands itch to wield their axes, needing to make up for when I could not act.

"Surasis can help us more easily than you can subvert the Ridgeguard, and my contacts in the city can assist us."

"I have no intention of entering Piesamur."

"We will need provisions. And what of the horses? We cannot bring them onto the Skirt. Delvers will swallow them within minutes."

"Then we leave the horses behind. Better yet, why don't you watch over them, and I'll cross the Skirt alone."

"Ah, a lone death on the Skirt. Such a fate is reserved for those far worse than you."

"No, it's not."

He takes what appears to be a calming breath and moves on. "How do you plan to enter upon it?"

"I'll pass over the Ridgewall."

"The Ridge is heavily patrolled."

"I'll find a gap."

"The Ridge itself was constructed to be nearly insurmountable without use of the correct paths—paths which are, as I said, heavily patrolled. This must mean you intend to climb. What climbing skills have you?"

"Rocks aren't so different from trees."

"I disagree. Even so, say you reach the far side of the Ridge beyond the Ridgeguard. The descent will be treacherous without a clear path. If you do not slip and fall, and somehow manage to touch down on the Skirt without Surasis knowing, the delvers will likely swallow you."

"I'll move fast."

He passively nods at the simplicity of my answer. "And the chasm?"

"What chasm?"

"The chasm that divides the Skirt from the Burned Lands? It spans the continent; cleaved by Tekna herself. She wanted to isolate the purity of her creations from the corruption of the world. And so, the world sent their corruption to her." He lowers his gaze to the dish of fire. "A single bridge allows passage over the chasm. It is a bridge Surasis long since crumbled, leaving only a few stones upheld by magic should they need to reach the Burned Lands themselves. The bridge tempts the kings and their packs, making them believe it is crossable at the loss of the clumsiest amongst them. As an elf, you might fare better...but you will not last for long."

"But with you, I'll survive?" I question, disliking his desired reliance.

He lifts his eyes to me. "With the aid of *others*, you will survive."

I consider him for a moment, some part of me hearing the sense in his advice. It is the same part of me that heard sense in the Ashan's advice—that woman who became Ashacan, who could have been a shield.

"No one failed my people but me," I tell him. "I have one purpose now, and survival isn't part of it."

I turn away from him, signaling an end to the conversation, and move for the darkness outside of his light. He watches me until I find a comfortable place in the night-washed roots. I do not put my back to him, and while he allows me space, he does not entirely look away—thus is our ritual during the weeks ahead.

Piesamur

WE FIRST GLIMPSE THE city from a crest on the Kallish Road. Several leagues in the distance, the impressive Vha architecture strikes upward from the horizon. The single tower of the far wall appears as a black rift cutting through the blood orange sky. The Skirt and lands beyond are barred behind a tumultuous ridge of rock that blends into the city wall.

Norrl snorts heavily to clear his nose of the bitter dust that swirls in the dry air. Heat scrapes my face on the tails of a near constant breeze, dust and sand wafting in its wake. The comfortable weather of the Old Wood shifted days ago, when the trees fell away to sparse patches of thorny brambles. Thick forest growth thinned to long grasses until soil crumbled to sand and stone, the soft air of northern Durast unable to beat back this harsh heat that tastes of metal.

I turn my head and spit from the saddle. Lumin halts Mournstar alongside me. The big horse pushes his nose against my knee almost in a comforting manner as my eyes drift over the daunting sight in the distance. Stemming from the smooth walls of Piesamur are the jagged heights of the Ridge wall, far higher and treacherous than I imagined. Before the city and Ridge spans another obstacle of shadowed forms, the nearest edge of which gradually shifts like a mirage. Specks of firelight dot the undefined mass that disperses amidst dips in the rocky landscape, encircling the city as a second wall under those of Piesamur itself.

"What is *that*?" I ask the glim.

"The encampment of the Ridgeguard."

"All of it?"

He squints. "It has grown since I was last here."

"That's as large as the entire Daervish army," I return, as though to refute the thing before us.

"And it is just a portion of the Everwatch's forces."

I fidget with my reins, hopelessly scanning for a discreet path around or a weakness in their fortified encampment. It seems possible, eventually, if we travel several miles east or west, but then there is the Ridge to face.

"Please," Lumin gestures me onward with a claw, "You were going to find a way through, correct?"

"Is there a gate?"

"Into the city, yes. Three."

"I meant to the Skirt."

"It also lies within the city built into the far wall at the base of the prison, which can only be reached by entering the prison, and therefore, the city."

"There are none built into the Ridge?"

"That would be foolish."

"And building a gate directly into the city from the Skirt is not foolish?"

He patiently crosses his claws over the pommel of Mournstar's saddle. "Piesamur was built for one purpose, and that is to stand as a stronghold against the Burned Lands. The gate that is constructed into its walls was very deliberately placed, not as a weak point, but as a strategy for defense and accessibility. When it exists as the only gate, then it is the only place one must watch."

"*Iesh.* How then," I inquire, slightly turning Norrl toward him, "did a pack of burned men manage to enter Durast if the one entrance is watched? Did someone answer their knock?"

He thinks, something I'm beginning to realize he does far too much. "I suppose a pack could have found a way to traverse the Ridge, but it is unlikely they could cross the Skirt without someone spotting them first. If they did, however, they would be at a disadvantage so long as the Ridgeguard held a higher position in anticipation of such a breach. In either case, it is impossible that Surasis was unaware in all capacities. And so, it is a point of inquiry I intend to pursue."

"If you speak to the High Mage neither of us will have a purpose anymore because we'll be detained by the fucking Everwatch."

"Surasis would never betray Piesamur," Lumin snaps with a flame in his eyes. "Nor me."

"And what about me? You tell a human's false future and they trust you unendingly, but I'm still an elf. There's no lie I could tell that would convince them I'm not a Recluse here to kill them all."

As Lumin thinks about my point, I notice the acceleration in my heart, and a sudden fear of the thousands of humans ahead. Seeing them easily outnumber the forces of the Gatewood makes me remember why we ever struggled against them. It was not magic that nearly defeated us, but their ability to overwhelm.

The idea of being in an enclosed space amongst them keeps me from sending Norrl forward. *How easily they could force me to the ground, pin me, bind me up and use me as bait...*

"I see," Lumin mutters, no longer looking toward Piesamur, but at me now several paces away from him. I loosen my hands on Norrl's reins, realizing I have pulled him back.

I clear my throat to drive away the shakiness in my tone. "I can't go in there."

"When Evoriel sought to enter Vhania, he did not balk at being outnumbered by Andapura's creations. He simply relied on the talents of a friend."

As he says his last sentence, Lumin lifts his claws and slowly rotates them toward himself, as though to draw an invisible tether away from me. I look down to see the remnants of evening light shed off my skin. In its place, shadow washes over me, cloaking me in an act of subterfuge. I flip my hand and watch the shadows shift with me, concealing my appearance in black.

"A friend?" I question, privately mesmerized by the shadows I cannot shake.

"...acquaintances."

"Is this not more obvious?" I move on.

"You see shade where others will see features distorted just enough to convince them you are only human under your darkened hood."

"You couldn't have suggested this earlier?"

"I did not register your elvenness as a complication until now."

"Right," I say, absentmindedly staring at my hand. "Will it stay?"

"As I will it, yes."

Fully reliant. I lower my hand and pretend to be unphased by my acquaintance. "And what do you see?"

"You."

"Because you cast it?"

"Because I know you, and so I cannot be deceived. Will you consider speaking to Surasis now?"

"No. And you're not going to, either. Who's to say Boon isn't already here, waiting for us alongside your High Mage?"

Another halfhearted snort. "Surasis does not identify as one of the Marked."

"They're still an Everwatch mage."

He brushes my worry away. "Politics. Although, I do not trust that Boon is not a step ahead of us."

Out of habit, I glance behind—not that the Marked would follow so closely. I see nothing as I have seen nothing for weeks. "We should keep moving."

"I agree, but in what direction have you settled?"

I carefully study the far encampment, feeling safer as the sun goes down. Lumin, at least, has the good sense to keep his flaming horns dim.

"You will still be wanted," I remind him. "No matter how many futures you tell."

"I am known here."

"Which means you will be easy to catch."

"With Surasis in power, I will remain untouched."

"Your confidence in this person unsettles me."

"A discomfort you must adapt to."

"Or a discomfort I need not face at all," I retort, casting him a sharp look. "I don't care what frames you possess. If I did not see advantage in your knowledge, I would have ended this arrangement weeks ago. *You* are following me. *You* adapt to my path."

The intensity of my words is sudden, driven up by frustration in the depths of myself. Lumin tilts his head in a manner I have learned to be a sign of mild surprise. The flames on his horns stir with intrigue as one might raise a brow. "Is that an order?"

The question conveys the curiosity of his flames. My father often used the same tone when posing difficult questions. Rather than find

an answer, I recall the last time I used such a commanding voice and see
Serin running through my mind.

"Norveh," I curse and send Norrl beyond Lumin before he can see
the brunt of my grief welling up. Serin's face appears with perfect clarity.
Perfect fear. The brief reprisal of authority fades back down my throat to
nestle into a knot of anxiety in my stomach. All the while, I see my acan's
face, the shattered vashte, blood without a body. Me, leaving.

I halt Norrl only a few steps away and study the human mirage again.
Lumin rides alongside me.

"It is only a city," he says, "and we are entering from the correct side."

"It's the only way," I reply, hoping to convince myself.

Lumin nods.

I take a second look at my shaded hands still distrusting of the thin
veil. Even so, I straighten in the saddle. "Alright."

"You are sure?"

"No rabble of humans is going to make me turn back now."

Steadying myself, I push on, following Halstaer who limps before me,
his blackened blood leaving a trail. He limps to meet Skinner's sword,
limps toward Piesamur, showing me the way.

* * *

Lumin leisurely rides Mournstar toward the human encampment,
one set of claws hanging loosely at his side. Despite the various cookfires,
the glim sends flames climbing up his horns the moment the sun sets. I
follow closely behind with my hood up and axes hidden. Under cover of
night and Lumin's shade, it seems impossible that a human could see my
face at all, yet a darkened figure seems no less trustworthy.

To them, far more trustworthy than an elf, I remind myself.

We are quickly spotted. Still, Lumin rides on, not allowing the gawking soldiers to interrupt our casual pace. The humans present no hos-

tility, merely curiosity and recognition of the horned glim. I brace for aggressive shouts or drawn swords as their eyes pass over me, but after a few seconds of scrutiny, they turn their attention elsewhere, undisturbed by whatever it is they see.

It is clear the encampment is their home. Many take rest in various states of undress, partaking in their evening meals or games of cards. There is laughter and curses, casual conversation and talk of defense. Men and women alike gather around cookfires, sharpen their swords, or emerge from tents, properly adorned in armor for their nightly patrol. Most do not immediately care to turn our way, and when they do, it is with a look of wariness without fear. I look back at some and wonder what it is they see—wonder what wariness would give way to fear if they knew.

Roughly halfway to the distant gate of Piesamur, a soldier finally steps in our path. He is older but seemingly no less formidable than the others. Shirtless, dust and grime cling to his chest as he leaps up from a seat outside a tent. He pushes back locks of greyed hair and firmly crosses his arms.

"Seer," he greets Lumin curtly.

Lumin gently pulls Mournstar to a stop and tilts his head toward the man. "Rojer. How is your leg?"

"Fuckin' busted."

"Yet you are not retired."

"I was. Then a pack of burned men came over the damn Ridge. Figured I'd come back since the whole damn Ridgeguard falls apart without me."

"Of course."

"What brings you back? Read the right fortune and the Marked let you go?"

Lumin's claws flex at his side. "I saw your troubles regarding this pack, and I figured the Ridgeguard, in fact, falls apart without me."

Rojer barks a laugh that quickly fades. Nearby soldiers draw closer upon hearing the conversation. The old man grows serious. "Maybe so," he solemnly says. "Don't know what curse has gotten into our High Mage, but things have been different as of late. I suspect they've taken ill. No pack would ever get past 'em otherwise, yet here we are, burned men finding cracks in our armor, ridgers fleeing down from the Veins, and a seer at our doorstep ready with good fortune...and a friend, I see," he says, searching beneath my hood.

"An associate," Lumin speaks before Rojer can say more. "She will be of great assistance in resolving this issue of roving packs. We need only enter the city first."

"Saw everything except the gates, did you?"

Those listening chuckle at Rojer's remark. Together, Lumin and I look more closely at the nearest gate—the only one on this portion of the wall. Closer now, it is obviously barred shut.

"No one goes in. No one goes out," another soldier shouts.

"Why is that?" Lumin inquires, still studying the gate.

"Don't know. Command don't tell us nish. All we seen is a notice from Surasis themself stating the city is to be closed until the end of an ongoing investigation."

"Surasis ordered this?"

"Yeah," Rojer scoffs. "Starve their own people in favor of an investigation. Leave their soldiers abandoned on the porch without explanation. That sound like our lovely mage to you?"

I sense the stony grimace on the glim's face. From the slight downward tilt of his horns, I know it is there.

"Perhaps we can help," he suggests.

"Can't allow that," Rojer says. "Don't know what's going on, but none of us are ready to break orders yet."

A small, growing audience of listeners grumbles in agreement.

"How long since this closure was instated?" Lumin asks.

"About a week."

"No one will be starving yet."

"No. Just getting unruly."

"And you will not let us in?"

"Afraid not."

"Not even for fortune?"

Rojer shakes his head. "One fortune don't erase five years gone, Seer. And no offense, but we don't know your associate." He turns his attention to me. "Where you from?"

"The Tungisel," Lumin answers for me, "and she is not entirely familiar with Dur."

A few looks of skepticism are shared between the surrounding soldiers. They narrow their eyes in my direction, as though to search for a certain quality indicative of the archipelago.

"A pirate on a horse," Rojer states, disbelieving. "Well, that don't help your case much. Not about to let a fuckin' pirate in when we can't hardly let merchants pass. I suggest you stable those horses before the ridgers can steal 'em. Or go back to wherever you came from. The Tungisel..." he chuckles, "depths..."

Rojer moves away to join a group of soldiers gathered around a fire. Those who drew near to the conversation steadily back away, returning to their evening activities although none entirely avert their stares.

Lumin turns Mournstar toward me. I cock my head, worried my voice will betray my identity.

"To the stables then?" he asks of me.

I nod and follow, gathering my thoughts in the time it takes us to cut through the encampment to what buildings stand outside Piesamur's formidable walls. The entrance to the city sits deep in the wall some distance away, yet it remains a looming presence. I imagine the other gates are no more inviting. Two guards stand outside it, leaning against the smooth slab that seems to have grown polished from the ground of Uunshyl. The towering walls travel outward in either direction, only curving toward the southern Ridge when they are nearly out of sight. It is architecture no human could construct unlike the ragged stable outside. When Lumin dismounts, I do the same and tow Norrl closer to the glim.

"What now?" I whisper.

"We stable our horses."

"I meant about the city."

"We stable our horses," he repeats, leading Mournstar toward the aged stable before I can protest. My heart thuds anxiously at the base of my throat as he leaves me standing alone. Fearing his concealing shroud will fade from my skin should he step too far from me, I quickly move to catch up.

The stable is old but well cared for, almost appearing as an after-thought beside the massive city walls. It is hardly a stable large enough for several horses let alone an encampment's worth, but it quickly becomes clear the humans of Piesamur do not rely on them. Considering the treacherous Ridgewall and dry landscape, I realize such refined animals would not thrive in this space. The stable, I gather, is of no use to the soldiers at all—more likely visitors. And with the city closed, the stable is rather barren.

Lumin's flames give light to the darkened aisle. Either end of the structure is open. Dust and stray bits of hay swirl as a draft cuts through. Thick webs cling to the rafters. In the first stall, an old mule hangs its head, only perking up to glance at Mournstar and Norrl. At the end of the aisle, a figure appears shadowed by the night. They lift a lantern, giving light to the tanned face of a middle-aged man.

"Lumin?" he gently inquires as though there might be a different glim before his eyes.

Lumin opens his claws in answer. "Criv."

"Put those damn flames out in my barn."

He douses his flames but only as the man with the lantern moves near enough to cast us in light. I edge away from the warm glow, but the man is not interested in me. Instead, he lifts the lantern and studies Mournstar's physique. Carefully, he touches the warhorse's neck, pats it twice, and steps back.

"Stunning," he mutters, gazing up at Mournstar. "Absolutely stunning."

"He carries me quite well," Lumin agrees.

"Aye, you found the one fucking horse in Durast that could manage that feat, my friend. But tell me, how'd you come by him?"

At that, Lumin motions toward me. Criv studies me with equal scrutiny, nodding with a taut expression.

"Lucky you came south, not east," the stablemaster continues. "Closer to Aleauna, a trained eye would know a Daervish draft in an instant." His green eyes soften in my direction, although he keeps a cautious separation between us. *"Ai'shtanu."*

For a moment, I do not move, stunned into inaction. I look down, thinking Lumin's magic has faded, but the shadow remains.

"There's no cause to panic," Criv hastens to say. "Whatever deceptive magic you're wearing is working just fine. But a horse? A horse is harder to hide."

"Criv is a friend," Lumin says to me, "and he has spent time in the north."

"The Waterwatch," he explains. "I'm retired now. Didn't expect to ever meet an elf again."

"Again?" I speak up too forcefully, my Rendaran accent shockingly prominent beside his Dur.

A corner of his cracked lips upturns in recognition. "There's no space for rivalry at the Dwellwater. I used to fight alongside your people. Even had the pleasure of seeing some drafts in action," he says, glancing fondly at Mournstar. "Just never thought I'd see any of you standing in my humble barn."

"You spoke Daerv."

"Sai. You pick up a thing or two when there's a need for communication."

I shake my head, hoping to recall knowledge around a sense of intense ignorance. "You defended alongside *elves*?"

"For ten years."

"There are..." I stop myself from revealing my lack of understanding. Criv still picks up on my thoughts.

"It's not well known," he assures me. "But we have a common enemy coming out of those cursed waters. After a while, it becomes counterproductive to fight your neighbor when they're dwellers bearing down on everyone."

My hand reaches toward my neck—to the necklace I no longer wear—and I fidget with my cloak instead.

He clears his throat. "Anywho. Depths are you doing here, Lumin? With a damn elf, no less?"

"Nhuaela," I sharply correct.

He tips his head in acknowledgement. "Apologies, Nhuaela."

"We need entrance to the city," Lumin replies.

"City's shut down."

"Precisely why we need entry."

"For what purpose?"

"...Assistance."

Criv lifts a scarred brow. "Listen, I'll watch your horses, but it's been five years, Lumin, and last I heard, you were taking up with the Marked. And no offense, *Nhuaela*, but I never fought alongside *you*."

"We are not—" Lumin begins.

"Remove this magic," I say.

Lumin and Criv both stare.

"Take it off," I repeat. "Now."

With a skeptical look toward the stable's entrance, Lumin lifts a hand and opens his claws wide as though to push the shadow from me. A stray piece of my hair blows back, and the dust stirs around me. As the shadow disperses, Criv's stoic look gives way to a fiercely controlled surprise. His eyes shift as whatever features he first saw become my own. I step into the lantern light.

"Do you need to fight alongside me to know I did not drag a blade through my own eye?"

"I've seen elves do some interesting things," he remarks.

"I'm not here for humans. I'm here for burned men."

"Fair enough, but there aren't any burned men in the city. The Ridgeguard chased them back across the Skirt months ago."

"We need provisions," Lumin remarks. "And entry to the Skirt itself. Both of which are located within."

"What then? You two going to take on the Burned Lands alone?"

"Ideally, no."

"Yes," I say in unison with him.

Criv slowly nods and gestures between Lumin and I. "Might want to sort that out first."

"I can pay you," I offer.

"Dragon scales don't transfer so well down here."

I pull a cet from my purse and drop it at his feet.

He stoops and rubs the coin between forefinger and thumb, confirming its worth. "Tekna's tits..."

"Will that translate?"

"That'll cover your board."

"I have more."

He thinks, still looking at the coin. "I'd say a cet has earned you some information. There's a woman." He slides his gaze to Lumin. "One of Mindy's."

"She is still in business?"

"Whores never go out of business, and as soon as the city shut down, she had her doves moving a day later."

"Doves?" I question.

"Messengers," Criv answers. "Soldiers and ridgers have wants and needs. Mindy's doves help supply them. And I don't just mean whores."

"Can they get us inside?"

"I'm sure if you've got another cet, then they'll have a way."

I weigh the heavy purse in my palm and glance at Lumin.

"Put that magic back in place first, though," Criv advises "and keep your flames low, Lumin. Mindy's doves won't know you like she does."

"Where might we find one of these doves?"

"Lately, she's been sending one by the name of Jeanne. She wanders between the soldiers and ridgers. It's where her talents are needed most, I suppose."

"After only a week?" Lumin asks, surprised.

"An inconvenience now, sure. But what about two weeks? A month? Who knows how long things will be locked up. Mindy's starting business early, establishing a path."

"Surasis would not allow their city to be closed for so long."

"Won't they?" Criv challenges. "Burned men cross the High Mage's unpassable Skirt, their insurmountable Ridge, after years of no issue and an unending watch. So, what changed if not our overseeing mage?"

"You have always supported Surasis," Lumin counters.

"That was before a pack slipped through in the night and caused havoc along the Ridge. Before your friend here encountered them. There's no reason our High Mage Surasis should have let them get out of sight let alone as far as the Gatewood. And yet..."

Lumin shakes his head, a few stray sparks blinking upward. "There is much we do not know."

"We know we need inside," I tell him and then pass Norrl's reins to Criv. Cautiously, he takes them, and I begin removing my necessary belongings from the saddle. Lumin stares at the ground, seeming to grapple with some thought.

"Lumin," I say.

He lifts his head.

"Eyes forward."

After a moment, he furls his claws toward his palm, and shrouds me once more in shadow.

In the Bottom of the Well

A SERIES OF WELL-PLACED questions by Lumin eventually leads us to the western edge of the encampment. I stay close to the glim, deeply distrustful of the shade that tricks human eyes. Few are inclined to speak to me, and when they do, Lumin interjects before I need speak. I begin to wonder if humans would know my accent at all. No others appear to be as keen as Criv. They are more interested in asking prying questions of Lumin rather than me. And so, I keep myself quiet as the glim makes small talk and spins vague fortunes.

"Is that her?" Lumin asks of me, trying to see beyond the modest flames in his hand.

I follow his gaze along the barren space defining the end of the encampment and beginning of the ridger's refuge. It is not a large gap. The two camps could easily shout to one another, but they do not seem inclined to mix. Lying along the partition is an occasional, powerfully muscled dog to defend the gap.

I lower Lumin's arm as a distant figure emerges from the ridger's camp. In the dark, I see only a shadowed outline. The person seems to compose themselves, adjusting a bag around their torso and digging something from it. They step toward the nearest dog. The animal raises its head, but before it can act, the person tosses something its way.

Preoccupied with a treat, the figure easily passes the dog, traverses the brambly gap, and reaches the encampment.

"I'd say so," I answer Lumin, already moving to head her off.

The late hour assures for a relatively quiet camp as we discreetly make our way toward the messenger, but I soon lose sight of her amongst the tents. I pause a moment, holding up a hand to signal to Lumin and listen closely as I would for a rabbit in the brush. But there is no stirring or movement. No quick shadow darting away.

"Who are you to pursue a woman in the night?" an indignant voice suddenly demands.

Lumin and I turn to see the same figure step from the shadow of a tent. Her plain clothes are too large for her small figure, and a roughspun scarf bunches around her neck. Between it and the tangles of black hair that frame her pale face, she is drowning in her own attire. But she does not give the impression of being intimidated. She firmly crosses her arms and tucks her chin into her scarf, her darkly haloed eyes piercing us like daggers.

"You're that glim I've heard men talking 'bout," she accuses Lumin. "Word of wisdom—if you want to follow someone, put your light out."

"I do not wander the dark unguided."

"You will if you want my help. That's what you're stalking me for, aye?"

Lumin looks at me, seemingly at a loss for words.

"And you." Her eyes rake over me. "What's your aim? Some say you're a pirate."

"A hunter," I reply, not bothering to hide my voice.

She tilts her head, and while she does not show concern, she seeks to study me more closely. My pulse quickens under her gaze, and just as I begin to think she has seen beyond Lumin's magic, she nods.

"You want into the city, I presume?"

"Yes," I say.

"Why?"

"It is not the job of Mindy's doves to ask questions," Lumin interjects.

Jeanne's indignation refocuses on him. "That was before burned men came through. Before the city shut down. We don't take chances no more. Not on merchants. Not on whores. And certainly not on glim and their mysterious hunter friends. Now, you here to bring harm or no?"

"If we were, why would we tell you?" I pose.

"I'm not short on business, aye? Answer the question or I leave you outside."

"We are not here to cause harm," Lumin answers while I hold back my tongue. "Quite the opposite, in fact. I intend to seek lodging with your Lady. You may accompany us to her if you would like and see that we are not foes."

"You're not one of her usuals."

"I have not been in Piesamur for some time."

Jeanne searches each of us once more, her frustration ebbing slightly as we await her approval. In turn, I study her, noticing the signs of a hard life. Her fair skin is discolored on her cheekbones, worn by sunlight and dust. Her nose is crooked—unevenly healed, and her bottom lip is engraved by a nasty scar. She has a habit of dipping her chin downward in order to glare more effectively upward, but when doing so, she hides her mouth and takes refuge behind her large scarf.

"Alright," she finally nods, lifting her chin. "Let's call it twenty eversilvers each. Ten to get inside. Ten for me to not ask more questions."

Not having twenty eversilvers, I offer a cet instead; carefully, between my knuckles.

She eyes it distrustfully. "Rather rich for a simple hunter."

"Not simple."

"Well, I suppose I won't ask why," she says, reaching to take the coin.

I pull my hand back the moment she pinches the cet, hoping to avoid her touch through Lumin's magic. He never explained what happens when someone else interferes with it, but her fingertips brush mine despite my efforts. For the first time, she looks at me without a glare. Lumin's firelight catches in her dark blue eyes, and I take comfort in knowing her gaze is far too uncaring to have seen me beyond the magic.

"I revise my deal. A cet from you," she remarks, "but I want a fortune from the seer."

"Will that be all?" Lumin inquires.

"One fortune and no flames."

"And you will ask no questions?" I add.

"And I will ask no questions."

Lumin grimaces at the idea. "Telling a fortune takes time."

"So long as these soldiers hold the gate, I've got all the time in the world."

"We will need a quiet place to sit."

She tilts her head slightly in thought. "Tell you what. Why don't you ponder my fortune while I lead you inside. We'll all go to Mindy. You can prove your good intentions, and then I get my fortune. And, yes, I mean my *fortune*. Not that other shit the whores get up to in the back room. Deal?"

I feel a need to interject, to question Mindy and her establishment of whores and doves, but I lost such control of things when I allowed Lumin to cloak me in Lelendelus's shroud. Instead of protesting at all, I nod my head.

Lumin waves his claws toward the city, as though he is the one inviting Jeanne inside. "Please, lead on."

* * *

Piesamur's portcullis sits deep in a large archway carved within the outer wall. The heavy gate is lowered, emanating the impossibility of entrance without invitation. Its crosshatched bars are layered upon each other until there is no space to see beyond, and they project an odd chill. Four torches line either wall leading the gridlocked bars. Their light is just enough to reveal a narrow door adjacent to the main entrance.

One of the outer guards puts his back to us as he fumbles with lock and key. After a moment, he pushes it inward, producing a high-pitched whine from its hinges. He turns back to us, his eyes falling expectantly on Jeanne.

Without word, she passes him a handful of coins. He grips her wrist before she can retract her hand.

"Two persons costs extra," he tells her.

She pulls back. "Since when?"

"Since your guests stopped being whores."

She casts a glare toward Lumin and I. "Who says they aren't whores?"

"I recognize that seer."

"And you've no idea what he does in his personal life."

"One cet," the guard demands, craning over her. "It'll be my hide on the Skirt if the Marked find out I let you in, so *one cet*."

She rummages within her baggy shirt beneath her hanging scarf and slaps the coin into his hand. "A lot of fuckin' good that'll do you on the Skirt," she snarls.

"Maybe it'll pay off some burned men."

"As if they care about coin," she mutters, deftly moving around him. "C'mon, whores," she calls back to us before gliding through the door.

We enter a cramped passage within the wall. The guard shuts and locks the door behind us. Jeanne immediately turns close to me in the tight space, her voice low.

"You owe me another cet," she snaps. "And you," she accuses Lumin, "that fortune better be good."

The low flame in his claws flickers in an uncertain manner.

"A cet," she insists, stepping close enough to me that she forces my back against the stone wall. She bares her palm.

Carefully, I fish another from my purse but withhold it. "Are there Marked here?"

Her brow furrows. "Aye. Who d'you think is investigating?"

I share a look with Lumin while placing the coin in her palm.

"How many of these have you hidden in that purse?" she asks.

I hand her another, letting my hand hover over hers for an instant. "No questions," I remind her.

The coin placates her, and she allows me space once more. "Fine. Keep quiet and act like you belong. You still headed to Lady's Way?"

"Yes," Lumin answers, understanding the phrase.

"Good. I need a drink."

She continues down the narrow hall which curves sharply for several paces. I gather its path directs us around the external portcullis. At the opposite end, there is an identical door to the last constructed of solid metal. Jeanne pauses, and Lumin brightens his flame.

She glances warily over her shoulder, her eyes meeting Lumin's light. "That fire won't do on the other side."

"We are not on the other side yet," he says.

She shakes her head and returns to the door. She knocks loudly twice followed by two more succinct taps then waits.

"So," she says, "what shall I call you?"

"Lumin," Lumin immediately replies.

Her gaze turns to me.

"We agreed no questions," I repeat.

"Depths, I asked for a name, not for your entire life story."

I briefly bite into my cheek. "Nhuaela."

"Nhuaela," she tries. "Doesn't sound like it's from Touge. Pretty, though."

The rattling of keys in the door puts an end to further questions. I place my hand upon Lumin's forearm, my downward glance silently asking him to lower his light—a futile attempt to conceal ourselves from the guard's view as the door swings open. My hand tightens around his plated arm as the guard eyes us closely.

He nods at Jeanne and steps aside. With torchlight filtering through the door, Lumin extinguishes his flame and pats my hand twice.

"One who belongs," he reminds me.

I abashedly detach my hand and keep my eyes forward, resisting the urge to glance down every dark alley for Boon. My acan instincts heighten in the close quarters of the city. It's not the same as Daerva'Tor. The sky is too far away and cut by rooftops, making me feel as though I've fallen to the bottom of a well. Looking around, I find there are only walls of cold stone and structures of rock and metal. The towering walls are entrapping; the compact buildings overlooking cobbled streets will not bend and shift should I need to flee; the humans will not move, their slow senses yet another barrier thick as sludge. Every line is rigid yet curved to cut off the light and create pockets of constant shade. It was a design favored by the Vha and adopted by the humans when they moved into their cities. A disorienting design to separate them from the external forces of the world and lead me deeper into an impossible maze of endless threats.

"Hey, Nhu—Nhuaela? Tits, what was it? Nhu!"

Nhu.

I snap my head toward the sound of my name, hearing nothing but Halstaer's voice.

Instead, I see Jeanne and Lumin some paces ahead, staring back. Jeanne cocks her head, her black hair falling across her face.

"Problem with pirates," she calls, "is they spend too much time on their ships. Forget what a city looks like."

I hurry to catch up, hoping Lumin's shade hides any chagrin that creeps onto my face.

"I won't hold your hand, so stay close, aye?" Jeanne suggests as I approach. "You draw attention, I disappear."

"Understood," Lumin answers for me, and when Jeanne continues on, he chastises me with a narrowing of his eyes.

Feeling no wiser than a child on their first hunt, I duck into my hood and follow close enough to avoid contact with passersby but far enough to not appear reliant on her or Lumin. In fact, I feel no less panicky than a deer that briefly catches the scent of a wolf.

The humans we pass are like the soldiers outside. None seem to recognize me beyond Lumin's shade. They are far more distracted by the glim, but he continues forward as though he belongs, and eventually the humans look elsewhere. I try to look ahead as he does. Confident, as I would be on a hunt, but the deeper we delve into the maze, the more uncertainty I feel. Like Serin before he found his kingbear.

Before the king found him.

I steady my breaths and make myself study the city around me as I taught Serin to study the Wood.

The main gate opens onto a wide cobbled street that moves forward into the expanse of crooked buildings. Orange lights bobble along the main road, idly casting a magic glow without flame. An occasional human passes underneath, weaving away from the light, seeming to value the lateness of the hour. They wear hooded cloaks, patchwork armor, tattered tunics, and scarves bunched around their necks ready for first light. I imagine anyone possessing finer attire keeps inside or far away—an ilk of human who would not choose to live in the lower reaches of Piesamur.

Jeanne quickly leads us off the main road, guiding us westward through branching alleys. Lumin mulls a dull flame in his palm as the glowlights blink out and our pathway becomes uneven, tilting downward as we skirt the outer wall. A foul scent creeps from the base of the smooth stone where a narrow grate fills with refuse. The buildings appear less stable, more sharp-edged and liable to collapse under a stiff breeze. The few inhabitants who ignore Lumin's presence lie slumped in the dark recesses of the Vha architecture. I notice one stir—an old man who angles his gaunt face toward the glim's flame, showing deep purple splotches mottling his skin.

"Leechers," Lumin mutters to me. "Keep out of their reach."

As he tells me this, a purpled hand grasps from underneath a stoop. It weakly grips at Jeanne's boot. She swiftly kicks it aside with a curse.

"What's wrong with them?" I ask Lumin.

"They are desperate."

He continues on before I can ask more. The small form of a child scurries across our path. Jeanne pauses and glares sharply, making sure they continue into the shadows. Groups of roughened individuals gather in the tight cruxes of streets. Jeanne largely guides us around them, careful to leave a buffer of buildings between us and them. Once, they look our way, but when Lumin intentionally brightens his fire to flare upon his horns, the group hastily diverts their course. We continue, gradually winding our way through the constricted dark, dodging individuals, avoiding leechers and urchins, and working to breathe shallowly to keep the putrid air from our lungs until we enter upon a wider road marked as *Lady's Way*.

The street expands, leaving a large berth between a length of buildings and the outer wall. As we follow the street, I have to crane my neck to see a hint of the top that curves slightly inward like a frozen black wave. At its base, a series of pulsing glowlights reveal the arch of another small door locked behind heavy bars. Nothing stands outside it, and it seems quaint under the massive wall, but its distance from all else tells of something sinister within.

I pull my gaze from it, becoming acutely aware of my desire to be hidden instead of standing in the road. As though sensing my distress, Jeanne pauses at a large wooden building. Its dilapidated neighbors lean on the two-story whorehouse for support. The shutters of the upper floor hang open, and embellished moans seep forth. A long porch of sagging planks stretches along the front. Broken bottles lie discarded beneath it. Carved into the frame above the door are the words *Midnight Singer*, under which someone has incorrectly scraped the word *Screemer*.

Jeanne turns back at us as she reaches the top of the porch stairs. "Alright, Mindy don't sleep much, but don't go running off to her before giving me my fortune. Board's not free. Drinks aren't free. And no touching unless someone's touched you first, aye?"

"Is that free?" I ask.

"For you?" She quickly looks me up and down. "No. This is a place of business."

Lumin glances down at me from the corner of his eye.

"Let's get inside," I urge, regretting the joke.

Jeanne enters and I follow, Lumin hesitating a moment before snuff-ing his flame and ducking through the door.

The interior is thick with contained warmth inside a city of heat. The air swirls with dust and the scent of dried herbs. Much of it looks no different than the inside of a tavern, and I'm reminded of *The Baited Brill* in Forestfall, but with more color.

Fabrics adorn the wooden walls and long tables. All are worn and faded, yet spotless in a space where stains seem inevitable. Strings of beads drape from the rafters, glimmering in the faint glowlights. The space is wide and along the side wall is a curved bar behind which shelves of dark bottles wait to be uncorked. Three men sit at a table in the center of the room, engrossed in conversation with a flirtatious woman. In one corner is a fine-featured man, shirtless with curly brown hair, leaning suggestively toward a guard. At the bar are three other whores, all dressed in thin robes that reveal their bare legs and cling to their various shapes.

Jeanne moves familiarly to the back. "You're with me, Seer," she tells Lumin. "I want privacy."

Her demanding words draw the curious attention of the patrons, and then their eyes grow wide at the sight of Lumin. The few whores glance his direction before rolling their eyes or giving excited waves of recognition.

Lumin lifts one hand, splaying his claw in acknowledgment. Then he turns to me, lowering his head closer to mine.

"We will be safe here," he informs me. "Mindy will give us lodging."

"Which one is Mindy?"

"I do not see her."

I chew my cheek, sensing multiple eyes on us. "Go tell her fortune. I'll be at the bar."

"That is wise."

Lumin follows Jeanne to a curtained alcove at the back of the room. I take a seat at the empty bar as near to the glim as I can remain, somewhat hating what familiarity I've attached to him. Still, I leave a respectful distance between myself and him as he spins Jeanne's fortune. Having heard him concoct several clever fortunes for multiple soldiers in our search for Jeanne, I've stopped caring what false truths he tells. Perhaps they are not false, but they all regard such human problems that eavesdropping no longer interests me.

Instead, I sidle up to the nearest wall, ensuring no patron or whore is at my back and that Lumin remains in my only useful periphery. It leaves the bar hidden by my blind eye, but my hearing takes over, telling me there is only a whore idly swirling their own drink as they wait for paying patrons. It seems a slow time between evening and the deep night, when customers have either moved behind closed doors or returned to their own homes. Or the street. I try not to listen too intently to the muffled—and sometimes not muffled—sounds of the Singer, although they serve as a needed distraction from the taut anxieties in my mind.

The whores occasionally look my way, but when I do not return their inquiring gazes, they lose interest. I ignore them and tighten my fingers around Halen's flask. It has been empty for weeks now, but the liquor itself was never what comforted me. It reminds me of the onduris and his emerald eyes, his healing hands. If I had any sort of magic, I'd use it to send myself back to his hut and hide away.

"Need a fill?" a gentle voice asks me.

I heard her approach—her, based on her songful voice. Her robe caresses the floor sounding like sand on the wind, and a conglomeration of beaded necklaces clacks around her neck.

I angle in my seat, for the moment trusting Lumin at my back, and face the cajoling voice. The woman is unlike the others I have seen.

Her robe is elaborate, albeit old. Once colorful threads have faded, their flower patterns now washed out by sunlight and wear. The necklaces around her throat jangle as she leans forward. Her sun-bleached red hair is piled in a bun atop her head. One curl falls loose toward her green eyes. She smiles, showing wisdom in the creases beside her lips.

She gestures at my flask. "You've not had a sip," she observes. "Must mean there's nothing left."

Hesitantly, I slide her the flask. She ducks below the bar and emerges with a dark bottle. "Swill an' ale's all we got here. Swill's all anyone needs. Burn the lies right out of your fuckin' mouth."

My eyes dart to her defensively.

Her smile turns to a smirk as she pours. "Don't worry, love. No need to lie here. Unless it's on your back. Can tell us anything and we won't share."

"I don't have anything to tell."

"No? That accent sounds like it's got a lot to tell. Where you from?"

I accept my flask as she offers it. "The Tungisel."

"Must be quite a traveler to come from so far."

I nod and take a sip of swill to avoid further conversation.

She is not dissuaded and leans upon the bar. "I saw you come in with Lumin. Gods, I love that seer, but I also know where he's been for the last five years, so forgive me but..." she lowers her voice to a whisper, *"...I don't believe you're from the Tungisel."*

I'm careful not to avert my gaze.

She narrows hers, their pinprick centers dilating. "I trust Lumin. I trust Jeanne to only conduct my business with respectable folk, but there's been some strangers here lately, so I'm giving you fair warning. Don't cause *fucking trouble* in my house."

"Do you not specialize in fucking trouble?"

Her glare sharpens at my impulsive remark, and I fear I've not bitten my tongue when I should have. Then she laughs. It is surprisingly raucous compared to her voice.

"Aye," she agrees. "You interested?"

Her casual offer takes me off guard.

"Mm, I know that look," she says.

"What look?"

"You've got someone."

Her words subtly pierce my heart. Beneath it. Like a needle drawing a steady sting.

"Oh. I'm sorry," she says after a moment.

"Had someone," I find myself replying, realizing why she so easily draws answers from me. Her hair catches the light like Beshtel's. Her carefree approach is so like Halstaer. The fact she even came over here reminds me of my mother. "Had many."

"Well," she sighs with a punctuating exhale. "Drinks on me then." She raises her bottle of swill. "To the Many."

I lift Halen's flask in answer, and we both drink.

It is not long after that Lumin returns from the backroom. The woman lifts her eyes from her bottle. "Lumin."

"Good evening, Mindy," he says over my shoulder. "It has been some time."

"Taking my doves into the backroom, I see."

"For fortune."

"If you were anyone else, I'd say that's horse shit."

I sense his hesitant expression behind me, unsure of how to respond.

Mindy chuckles. "Oh, Lu. Jeanne doesn't take clients in that manner."

"Just finishing up some business," Jeanne answers for herself, running a hand down the length of the bar before slouching against it several paces from all of us. By her indifferent expression, I cannot tell if she was pleased with her fortune. She slides a cet toward Mindy. "Here's your cut. Can'I've an ale?"

Mindy smirks at the coin and looks for a mug. Sensing a familiarity closing about the room, a surge of discomfort returns to my veins. Lumin must notice me searching for an escape.

He clears his throat, grinding stone. "Mindy, is my room still available?"

"Five years," she tersely reminds him.

He waits.

Mindy rolls her eyes. "Depths. I've used the space for storage, but I suppose your bed is still up there, crammed amidst the mess."

"Would you permit us to stay?"

She eyes him closely. "No open flames."

"Then I shall require a lantern."

"Jeanne, go find him a damn nightlight."

Jeanne sighs into her mug.

"You," Mindy says, her eyes darting to me. "What're your intentions here?"

"Passing through."

"You good with those axes you carry?"

I sit a little straighter.

"Please, love. I take note of every weapon that comes through my door. Now, you know how to use them or not?"

"Why wouldn't I?"

She shrugs. "Plenty of patrons like to pretend. Show off more than they've got."

"Yes, I know how to use them."

"Good. You stay, you protect my place. That's your board."

"Certainly," Lumin accepts her terms before I can question further.

"And if either one of you brings trouble here, you'll only wish your fate was the Skirt."

Jeanne, who had briefly disappeared, punctuates Mindy's threat by pushing an old lantern toward Lumin. He hooks it in his claws.

"Thank you."

She leaves without reply.

Lumin lifts the lantern, gesturing me in an unknown direction. "Shall we?"

I pull Halen's flask close to my chest and stand. The room wavers slightly. Lumin catches me by the elbow and directs me toward a wall behind the backroom. Finding my balance, I try not to move too quickly toward refuge, as though a hidden Marked might notice my retreat. I feel Mindy's curious gaze follow us from the room, and regret what trust I inadvertently placed in her. I risk a glance back only to see Lumin patiently following with his lantern.

"It is the attic room," he discreetly tells me, misreading my look.

We continue up the dark stairs to the second floor where a hallway of uniquely decorated doors reflect the whores that claim them. Carved in the wood are simple flowers, thorns, or birds. In the space of one doorway hangs a green curtain. Behind another comes a gruff snore.

"End of the hall," Lumin instructs, casting his now lit lantern toward a dusty ladder that nearly vanishes against the wall.

"You've stayed here?"

"When in need of privacy."

"A hideout?"

"In some ways."

"No one would search a whore's attic."

"They are often more interested in the basement."

I lift a brow before climbing the ladder, which proves somewhat difficult under my slightly shifting vision. Lumin gives me space to do so, likely in case I should fall. At the top of the ladder is a hatch. I shove my palm against it several times before it stiffly opens. After pulling myself through, I lower a hand for the lantern, which Lumin offers before following me up.

The weak flame of the lantern hardly reveals the immediate space. Old chests, stacked chairs, and crates of empty bottles clutter the room. The roof steeples in the center with cobwebs dangling from the rafters. A small, shuttered window rests in the peak. If it were open, I imagine Piesamur would shed no light from the slum.

Not far from the window is the frame of a narrow bed. I weave my way through the refuse to grimace at the dust covered mattress more closely.

"You fit on this?" I ask, seeing Lumin can only stand his full height if he remains in the crest of the roof. Even there, his horns would surely light the place on fire if they were lit. The bed is only the length of a man. *One* man. "There's not much room."

"You may take the bed."

"I don't know if I want it."

"You need rest."

"So do you."

"I will retire below."

"And risk letting me out of sight?"

"You will not venture far."

There is assuredness to his words. An inquisitive glow flickers in his orange eyes, and somehow, I do not trust that I will ever truly be out of his sight. I clasp Halen's flask tightly to my chest, feeling very exposed in the attic of the slum in a city infiltrated by Marked.

The barbs in my back pull. The weight of the axes makes me question if I do know what I'm doing.

I thrust the lantern toward the glim.

He gently hooks a claw through its ring, eyes still on me.

"Ai'shtanu," I snap.

He bows his head, and as he is swallowed by the tavern below, I finish what swill is left in the flask.

Interference

A SOFT WHISTLE MOMENTARILY cuts through my racing thoughts. I glance toward my tent's entrance to see the flap sway aside. A familiar figure crouches through.

"Nhu?" Halstaer whispers.

"What are you doing?"

"Making sure you're okay."

"You are aware my mother is likely watching this tent," I reply.

He tosses himself alongside me on my bed of furs. "I know. She told me to check on you."

"She *what*?"

"Doesn't think you'll sleep," he mutters, shimmying closer to me. "I'm here to help you sleep."

"I'm supposed to be alone."

"Do you want to be alone?"

I say nothing.

"We're not gonna let you be alone, Nhu. Let that happen earlier, and none of us enjoyed it."

He pulls me close to his chest and puts his lips to my brow. I wrap my arms around him, having overlooked his own terrors while succumbing to my own. He relaxes against me, letting one arm hang heavily around my waist. Admittedly, its weight calms my nerves. I shrink beneath it, wanting to be small for a moment.

"How's your leg?"

"Shayv healed it."

"Good. You're gonna need it."

I exhale, exhausted by the idea. My breath tells Halstaer enough. He learned to read its various cadences long ago.

"Everything's okay right now," he assures me.

"Right now."

"Nothing outside this tent matters."

"But it does."

Now, he sighs.

"It should be you, you know," I say.

"*Iesh*, if it was meant to be me, then it would be me, but it's not."

"I'm not ready."

"If you weren't ready, you wouldn't have come back."

I suddenly want to push him away in frustration. Instead, I find myself forcing my head beneath his chin as the recent memory of the caracosh viscerally flashes in my mind. I jerk my leg as the sensation of its long claws returns. He reflexively shifts his ankle over mine to still the anxious twitch.

"I might not come back again," I say.

"You will."

"I'm afraid of it."

"Yeah? I'm terrified of it. Honestly, I wouldn't have been able to shoot it."

"Don't lie."

"I'm not lying. We've both seen that thing tear people apart. I'd rather fight a dweller. I'd rather fight your *mother*."

A strained laugh creeps its way into my uneven breaths.

"As if it has the audacity to test you again," he says, lazily brushing my mussed hair from my forehead. "Truth is, I'm not here to comfort you. *I* couldn't sleep."

His quick pulse affirms his words. I put my hand to his heart, for once unable to refute him.

"It doesn't stand a chance," he insists.

"Feels like it has a decent chance."

"Not against you." His voice begins to drift with sleep as he settles beside me. "Not against Nhu..."

*　*　*

Heat wakes me, but it is not the warmth of Halstaer at my side. The attic room of the Midnight Singer is thick with rising air. Morning light filters through the slats in the shuttered window. Caught in its rays are specks of dust. I close my eyes again, searching for my dream, but the warmth and noise of the slum below have chased it away.

I lie still for a while, not wanting to move, not wanting to be awake. The thrum of a headache pushes behind my left eye, and my mouth tastes of stale liquor. I sit up, trying to gauge the time of day when a tapping comes at the hatch. It is thrown upward before I can answer. In a sudden panic, I look to my hands for Lumin's shade and find it still shifting upon my skin.

My heart slowing, I watch as a woman's hand grasps the floor for purchase. Jeanne heaves herself through the hatch, her tangled hair and scarf briefly consuming her.

Her eyes meet mine. Their hue is more noticeably blue when caught in the thin rays of daylight. She sits beside the hatch, arms draped over her bent knees.

"Thought you might've been dead up here," she says. "It's nearly noon."

I clear my throat, searching for my ragged voice. Instinctively, I reach for the flask on the bed beside me, but dejectedly recall its dryness.

"Gods," Jeanne comments. "Swill, first thing?"

"I'd rather water."

"I'd say. A whole fucking bath of it."

I stare at her, too tired to retort.

"Didn't notice what a mess you were last night. Look like a leecher crawled out from under the porch." She hesitates. "No, not the porch. Can't place it."

"Our deal is done," I remind her.

"Aye, but I'm between runs, and Mindy asked me to check on you."

"Why?"

"'Cause she likes you. But sure as depths doesn't trust you."

I push the pad of my thumb beneath my brow, feeling my scarred skin through the shade. "*Is* there a bath?"

The amused tightness at the corner of her lip softens. "We'ave a basin. I can show you."

I straighten my armor, my body stiff from having slept in it. I considered removing it before dreams took me but thought better of it.

Better?

There were occasions on our journey when Lumin and I would rest, and I would bathe in the nearest stream or puddle. They were the only times he would turn his back to me. But it has been some time since I've felt more than rainwater on my skin, and beneath my armor, I'm suddenly acutely aware of how awful I likely smell. Armor or not, not even Halstaer would have approached me in this state.

Jeanne interrupts my thoughts, some part of her tone taking a timid note. "You're not the worst patron I've seen. C'mon. It's downstairs."

She shows me the room with the green curtained door which serves as their washroom. A wardrobe furnishes the far wall, and a cracked mirror hangs above a cabinet on which a wide basin is placed. Beside it is a pitcher, soap, and brush. Towels hang on hooks along the wall, some appearing more used than others.

"Water should be clean, mostly," Jeanne tells me. "I'm looking forward to seeing what you really look like under that grime."

She leaves before I need answer. The heavy curtain falls closed, allowing me to collect myself before looking in the mirror. I'm startled to see my own face seemingly unchanged by Lumin's magic. An occasional flicker of shadow rolls over my features, but I see no difference in them. My scarred eye remains an ugly, crooked line from brow to jaw, permanently brightened by upturned flesh. The longer I look, the more I become aware of my blindness. I lower my head and splash myself before thinking further.

I hear Jeanne's footsteps before she bats at the curtain. When I give no response, she pulls it aside anyway. "Brought you some water and mint. Can wash that taste from your tongue."

I lift my face from the towel, mildly disturbed by my true reflection juxtaposed with her unknowing presence.

"What?" she teases, setting the cup beside the basin. "Haven't seen a clean face in a long time?"

Her grin is missing a tooth along the side. I find it disarming in an endearing way, and for a brief moment, I forget my anxieties. Seeming to remember the detail, she angles away and steps back toward the door.

"Thank you," I say after her.

Shyly, she turns back. "Aye. Just looks like it's been some time since you've taken care of yourself."

I drink in place of answering and set the cup down more forcefully than intended.

"Guess I should've brought two up," she remarks.

"Is there more?"

"I'll find some."

I rummage for another cet and extend it to her.

She shakes her head. "Keep your coin. I'm no whore."

"You don't need to help me either."

"Maybe I want to."

"You seemed ready to be rid of us last night."

"'Cause you were rid of me."

"And now?"

"Well, the deal is still done, but you're rather unsure. You *and* the seer. Don't think he could tell his own fortune let alone mine, and here you are, don't know how to wake up or get water. Probably don't know which way's north in this city. And I mean no offense, just that you...you need help."

"I assume most of your patrons need help."

"Aye, but you show up with a seer, have a pocket full of more coin than I've ever seen, and some obvious secret."

Her bluntness mollifies the stress that was building from her observations.

"I've never wanted to question someone more," she says. "And I won't, of course, but that doesn't change that you're clearly lost."

"And you want to help me find my way?"

"I want to buy you a drink."

I carefully set the dirty towel beside the basin and take a bite of the mint leaf, my fears briefly held aside in favor of thought.

"How about more water," I suggest, "and then you can tell me which way is north. Or south."

"South?"

"It's where I'm headed."

"There's nothing worthwhile south."

"Not worthwhile. Necessary."

I return to the attic room to collect my axes and cloak before meeting Jeanne at the bar. The *Singer* is appropriately empty for a whorehouse at midday, and the bar allows us enough privacy. I don't yet look for Lumin, not entirely wanting him to join our conversation. Jeanne pushes the fresh water toward me along with a plate of hard bread and dried meat.

"So," she starts, "how far south?"

"Beyond the Skirt."

She gives me an almost reprimanding look. "Do you have any idea what's beyond the city walls?"

"I'm aware."

She releases a long breath at the notion. "I'm not sure you are."

I don't argue the point and instead take a bite of meat.

"Can't just walk onto the Skirt. Can't do much of anything right now. Not with the city locked down."

"And the Marked around?"

She nods with a frown.

"Have you seen them?"

"From a distance. They don't care about the slum."

"But they're interested in the High Mage?"

"That's the rumor. Ever since..." She briefly closes her eyes and opens them with more assuredness. "Ever since the pack came through."

I resist the urge to close my own eyes.

"Didn't see them or nothing," she continues. "They of course didn't come through the city itself, but I heard things from the encampment. Some stories from the guards. And the ridgers." She looks back to me, her gaze cold. "Burned men do terrible things."

"I know."

She studies me, unblinking. "*That's* your secret."

"Roughly."

"I knew you weren't no damn pirate."

"I told you. A hunter."

"And the pack...?"

"Crossed my path."

"Gods. No wonder."

"No wonder what?"

"You're such a mess. How'd you survive?"

I shake my head, having misjudged my ability to guide such a conversation.

"Sorry. Too many questions," she realizes.

"I need to find them."

"I assumed the Ridgeguard finished them off."

"No," I answer, recalling Boon's revelations.

"Look, I can help you *in* the city. Won't go near the Skirt."

"I just need a way through."

"I think the seer is working on that part. If you're of the same mind, that is."

"What do you mean?"

"Didn't he tell you? He left last night. Said he was making inquiries."

"Last night?"

"After you turned in."

"*Norveh.*"

"What?"

"Fuck," I correct, now cursing myself for the slip up.

"Something wrong with him making inquiries?"

"He's going to—" *draw attention. Get caught.* "Where did he go?"

She casually chews a bite of bread, making me wait for her to swallow the old brick before answering. "He didn't say, but a grown glim can handle himself."

"He has too much confidence in this place."

"Nothing more dangerous than a confident glim."

Her words give me pause as I'm about to stand from the bar. I realize a truth to them, what danger he possesses whether he means to or not. Lelendelus's shade creeps over my hand. By Lumin's command, I could be revealed, and he need not even recall the shade, only speak the truth, tell Surasis, return to the Marked, and an entire city of humans will close in as the burned men did to my vashte'rae.

"How did you meet him?" Jeanne interrupts my racing thoughts. "Glim are rare in Durast."

"...We have a deal."

"And who's working for whom?"

"It's a mutual agreement."

"It's never mutual."

I say nothing, knowing she is right.

"Should get out of any deal as soon as you can," she goes on, "even if you think it's worth it."

I make to reply but stop myself, finding it difficult to give a simple answer. "I think it's a lot of things."

She nods in silent agreement. "Well, like I said, a grown glim can take care of himself, aye? Maybe you should rest rather than run after him. Especially when you don't even know where you're running to."

"That's what makes me nervous. He knows this place."

"And I bet I know it better than him." She touches her fingertips to my forearm. "How about you wait. Just an hour. See what happens. And if he's not back, then I'll help you find him."

I study her hand. Her fingers unknowingly push through the magic. They send three pulses of warmth through me, and I realize how long it's been since I've felt such simple care. Not since—

Wood shatters from the wall beside the Singer's door. Splinters burst into the room, scattering across the floor and pelting a lounging whore nearby. She cries out and turns away from the burst wood, one hand grasping her sliced thigh.

Jeanne retracts her hand in fright and grips the bar instead, as though it could be ripped from the floor as a shield.

"What in the *fuck* was that?" Mindy demands, rushing from the back room with her robes gathered in one hand for ease of movement. Her whores retreat behind her as she nears the broken wall, her expression hardening with recognition.

"Deflected impact," she determines, then glancing back, instructs her whores. "Go to your rooms. Stay low until I come get you."

They flee to the back stairs except for Jeanne, who flickers her eyes between Mindy and the wall.

"C'mon," Mindy gestures to us both, "not the first time this has happened. Best take cover until it's over."

I disregard her entirely and approach the impact. Jeanne breaks away from the bar and follows.

"Get back!" Mindy demands, lowering her voice to a whisper as though whatever is outside intends to sneak in. "Both of you are gonna end up with an eyeful of splinters!"

Jeanne gingerly maneuvers around the splinters on the floor, shadowing my own steps. Outside, I hear the commotion of people hastily moving, gasping, shouting. Dust stirs upward from the street. Jeanne edges around the crack in the wall. I take the other side, and together, we peer out.

Standing before the *Singer* is Lumin, his back to us, one hand held aloft and behind, the same stance he took when previously deflecting a bolt of Boon's magic. Opposite and adjacent to him are three mages cloaked in the light blue shade of the Everwatch. City guards accompany them but keep their distance, well aware of their uselessness in a standoff between mage and glim. Anyone who was present on *Lady's Way* has since retreated like the whores, a few risking positions close by, tucked in alleys or far toward the outer wall, as though any stray magic might dissipate before reaching them.

"Lumin of Scerk," the lead Marked calls across the street. His clipped words clatter off the *Singer's* walls. "Glimseer of Lelendelus and former consult to the Mortal Everwatch, you are hereby under arrest for desertion under contract and interference with diplomatic Imperium relations."

Lumin's claws clench toward his palm.

The Marked continues, "We advise you to cooperate in this matter or we will forcibly detain you."

The claws soften, seemingly in thought.

"And should you cast one flame, this slum will burn to the ground."

"I am not so careless," Lumin replies, lowering his arm nonetheless.

The lead Marked steps forward, briefly letting flame weave around his inked hand. "As I said, this slum *will* burn whether you are careless or not."

Jeanne pulls back from the cracked wall, shrinking into her scarf.

Lumin and the Marked stand frozen in opposition for a long minute, neither moving in the heartbeats that follow. Jeanne keeps herself flat to the wall, breathing more rapidly as the flames continue to flicker around the Marked's hand. Onlookers of the slum intently gauge the mage's flame. My hand twitches for an ax, but what function my weapons would have at the wrong end of a spell seems obsolete.

At last, Lumin's frame appears to relax. He tilts his head enough for me to see the corner of his eye, but he does not glance toward the *Singer*. The accompanying guards step closer.

"By whose order do you relay the charge?" Lumin inquires.

"The *Everwatch*," the Marked snarkily repeats.

"Yet you have brought guards to subdue me. Guards of Piesamur, and therefore, guards of the High Mage, Surasis."

"Doesn't matter who fucking ordered it. The warrant still stands."

"But it does," Lumin counters. "You cannot issue Piesamur guards to arrest me if Surasis did not give leave."

The mage smiles flatly. "The Marked have jurisdiction here, not your corrupt, shameless mage. We have authority to issue whoever we like to do whatever we like. Now, present. Your. Arms."

Lumin slowly lifts his arms forward. The lead Marked nods at his two followers, who cautiously step nearer. I chew my cheek, uncomfortable with the fragile calm that falsely floats in the street. My thoughts race for a solution. If he were closer, I could risk stepping out and grabbing Lumin by the arm. We could rush back inside with some time to reevaluate, but he is too far out of reach, standing just beyond the steps of the whorehouse. If I possessed any knowledge of frames, the solution would be easier. I clench one ax, frustrated by my limitations and knowing any form of attack on my part would be useless.

If it were only me in the *Singer*, I might risk it, but looking between Mindy, who mutters a soft prayer to Tekna from behind the bar, and Jeanne, who looks worriedly at me rather than the wall, I can't bring myself to be so careless.

And then, the shackles fall. They rattle as one of the Marked draws them forth from their cloak. Lumin's head instantly jerks toward the sound, and an array of magic ricochets between the four mages.

Lumin swiftly arcs his left arm toward the shackle-wielding mage, and a flash of white flares in their direction. The mage instinctively ducks and lifts their own arm, forming a shell of shimmering energy around themselves as Lumin's attack breaks upon impact. The fractured magic pelts the walls of nearby buildings and draws several yelps of pain as they hurl into the gathered crowd. One slams into a man's chest, the white streaks of energy fading under a spray of blood.

With Lumin's backside vulnerable, the second Marked releases their orange light. Lumin angles, lifting his right arm to take the brunt of the spell. The impact pushes him back several paces, but he remains on his feet as orange tethers begin to weave around his plated arm like fire to dry leaves. Without hesitation, he drags the claws of his free hand through the progressing binds before they can spread beyond his arm. The tethers snap and dissipate into the air as he slashes through them, but he is not quick enough to fully shield a secondary spell from the shackle-wielding mage. The glim partially manages to deflect, but the latter half of the attack strikes him in the chest. He is thrown backward just as the deflected portion careens toward the front door of the *Singer*.

I grab Jeanne's arm and throw us both toward the edge of the room as the door shatters inward. The wild crack of snapping wood deafens us. Sharp fragments bombard our backs and fly further into the room where Mindy fully vanishes behind the bar. Several more impacts pepper the *Singer*, raining splinters upon us from all angles before they cease.

Jeanne gasps for a steady breath. Pieces of the whorehouse fall from the crevasses in my armor as I move back to the broken wall in time to see Lumin brought to his knees before the Marked.

The glim cradles one arm in his lap as though it was broken by one of the various impacts. The lead Marked now holds the metal vices as he looks down at Lumin, his fellow mages surrounding the glim with new magics prepared in their hands. The guards establish a perimeter around the scene, some shoving back slum dwellers who have grown angry at the sudden attack. Their voices rise in a chorus of cutting accusations and fright.

I pull an ax from the sheath on my back but stay still behind the wall, unsure of how to insert myself between Lumin and the Marked.

The lead Marked sighs, much like Boon in his mannerisms, but his face is not the same. There is a lack of thought, a carelessness in response to the people.

"Lumin of Scerk," he repeats, ignoring the riled slum. "We advised you to cooperate."

"I cast no flames," Lumin replies, his words sounding muddled by blood.

"And so, we will remain civil." At that, the lead Marked reaches for Lumin's cradled arm, and jerks it outward toward the shackles. Lumin grunts at the action but keeps any other vocalization within himself as his arms and claws are completely locked into the vices.

"Get up and walk," the Marked orders. "Step one foot out of line and I'll have your horns staked outside the front gate."

Lumin complies, hanging his head tiredly, and in doing so, glances directly at me. He makes no move to communicate, only meets my gaze through the crack in the wall, and then follows the Marked at the end of the chain.

I move toward the broken doorway.

Jeanne, back on her feet, deftly grabs my wrist. "What are you doing?"

"I—" I hesitate, a hectic energy urging me to go forward and out, presumably after Lumin. *But then what?* "I need him."

"Tell me why, and I'll let you go."

I look at my wrist, knowing I could easily break her hold, but her request gives me pause. Something about her continuously gives me pause.

"Why?" she presses. "Weren't you just telling me you don't exactly trust him? Now look. Seems to'ave proved your point."

"Lumin is a friend," Mindy firmly interjects, finally creeping out from the protection of the bar.

"Aye, and even you've mentioned not trusting him," Jeanne retorts. She returns her attention to me. "You say you need him. You need him enough to get blasted into a hundred bloody pieces? 'Cause that's what the Marked'll do if you take off after them."

"I owe him."

"Then at least be smart about it."

I jerk my wrist from her grasp. Her warning echoes that of nearly everyone else to cross my path, and suddenly it's not just a bold human reminding me to think, but a glimseer preaching wisdom, the Ashan giving order, an onduris sighing heavily. Then there's my father, eyes dark like Jeanne's, speaking through them, imploring me with a single, sympathetic look.

And like my mother, I'm tempted to challenge it.

"He'll eventually find me again," I insist, knowing Lumin will not stop so long as his god commands him, and he is alive to do so. "I may as well find him first."

"Then let us help. We know this city. We got you both in. Can get you both out."

"I'd like to see him safe, too," Mindy adds. "No matter what it is they claim he did."

"He helped me," I say, realizing the adrenaline is not only due to an imminent fight but a fear of loss as Marked and glim vanish beyond sight. "I need him," I repeat. "He's...useful."

"He is a friend," Mindy corrects.

"Gods," Jeanne mutters under a breath. "If I were crossing into the Burned Lands, I'd want a fuckin' glim with me too. Necessity isn't friendship. *Mutual agreements* are not binding."

Mindy frowns at her.

"But he *is* useful." Jeanne says to me, her sympathetic expression not matching her tone. "So, let's find him."

Underneath

I TURN OVER MY hand. Lumin's magic shroud persistently shifts overtop my skin, and I take it as a sign that, despite his altercation, he is not yet in a dire state. The shadows flutter. I wonder if they have always fluttered, seeming frail like the wings of a moth.

"What do you think?" Jeanne asks me, her voice kept under her breath.

I look to the fortress imbued in the outer wall. It is not as tall as the wall but constructed of the same Vhanian architecture. Its edges swoop and curve to deflect light and maintain an overbearing shadow across the ground. It stands about half as high as the wall, semicircle in shape with its ends bleeding into the outer wall, no doubt internally connecting. Its entrance is rather small compared to its size—a single, heavily armored door. For half the evening, Jeanne and I watched the guards patrol from a hidden vantage point up the gutter of a nearby roof. Their regular disappearance around the side of the fortress betrays a secondary, inconspicuous entrance. At any given moment there have been five guards pacing the fortress's yard, two posted at the main gate, and two wielding crossbows at the top of the wall. Promptly at nightfall, they left their posts and the yard unattended.

"They know we're here," I observe.

"Aye."

"You're sure Lumin will be in there?"

"If he is alive, he'll be there."

Again, I glance at my shadowed hands. *As I will it*. Still, willing it.

"Are you coming with me?" I ask.

"Into a trap?"

"I could use a guide."

"I told you I'm not going near the Skirt."

"Not onto the Skirt. Just to Lumin."

Her eyes sharpen defensively. "What makes you think I know a fucking thing about the inside of that place?"

The narrowness of our hiding place has forced us close together, and looking at her face, I recognize the various little scars, her crookedly healed nose, her general dislike for confrontation.

"You specialize in sneaking around," I answer, not saying what I truly think.

She tucks her mouth into her scarf and averts her gaze. "I'll do it if you tell me why they'd lay a trap."

"They want me dead."

"Why?"

"Because—" I stop myself, unable to explain their mistake of my father's identity and instead recall Boon's justification. "Because I'm a scrap."

I expect her to press for more, but she does not. "Scraps have their purpose. Guards 'ave rooms where...where they take what they need from us scraps, and they're in that fortress."

"You know where?"

"...aye."

"I'll lead. You direct."

"Gonna protect me?"

For an instant, the barbs dig deep, and I answer her passive question with a quiet ferocity. "Yes."

She nods with a careful bit of relief. "Then what's the plan?"

"We get inside."

"Just walk in?"

"Seems like an open invitation."

"Right into whatever they're planning."

"I don't see another option."

"There could be Marked in there."

"I'll take care of them."

"Like you took care of them earlier?"

"I have more advantage in close quarters."

She doubtfully grimaces.

"Ready?"

She gestures to the edge of our roof where a latticework allowed us to climb up. "You first."

In the alley below, I wait for Jeanne to climb down. She moves efficiently, this clearly not being the first building she has scaled. About a foot from the ground, she drops herself, landing lightly with only a stirring from her scarf. She quickly readjusts it before turning toward me.

"The courtyard gate is on the side. It should be locked."

We walk with our faces down, working to appear inconspicuous in a corner of a district we do not belong. Unlike the slum, there are few people milling about, standing on porches and corners, or waiting in the dark. A patrol passes at a distance, but they pay us no mind as we briefly flatten ourselves against the wall of a fletcher before turning toward the empty space between the prison and city.

The fortress itself has a gated yard, which appears to have no function other than to withhold space from the people. Peering through the metal stakes of fencing, there is nothing in the empty space. It would make for a nice area to spar, but the neat ground attests to little activity other than the pacing of a guard. The walls are higher now, and as we brazenly approach the gate, I feel as though every eye in the city is on me.

"Alright," Jeanne breaths nervously, sidling as close as she can to the outer gate. Beyond it, the fortress looms. It casts a deeper darkness than the natural hue of night. Two torches burn at the main entrance. Another lights the less obvious door on the side. Like the guards' door into Piesamur, their entrance to the fortress is far simpler.

"It's unlocked," Jeanne recalls my focus. She presses her palm against the metal, jostling it. "It's fucking unlocked."

Instinctively, I glance behind us, half expecting the trap to have already been sprung by the anxious warning in Jeanne's tone, but the quiet street remains empty.

I put a hand on her shoulder. "It's fine."

"Depths, they're gonna be waiting right inside."

"Do you want to leave?"

She exhales sharply. "No. But I won't do much good in a fight."

I maintain her gaze. "Whatever happens, you will get out of here. I promise you that."

She blinks, seemingly confused for an instant, and then finds her voice. "Once inside, you'll want to take the hall forward. If it's still the same, that is. I can't be certain nothing's changed. It'll put you into a larger room. There's another door there that leads deeper into the fort. To the rooms where...where they take what they need before sending a prisoner to the prison or Skirt. It should be locked down tight, but at this rate it'll be wide fucking open."

I squeeze her shoulder, putting a stop to her rambling. "Good. Once we get there, tell me more. Until then, stay low."

I push open the gate, finding it easier to go against the human city than hide within it, even if it does mean walking into a trap. As I step into the yard, I don't mind the invisible eyes on me. I take strength in knowing this is the last obstacle. As we reach the fortress's gate, I draw both axes. Jeanne's eyes widen upon them.

"Are those...?"

I jostle the door, not so stealthily shoving it inward before I need explain my weapon of choice. She creeps in behind me and gently closes the door before it can slam against the metal frame.

Inside, we stand in a dark and narrow hall. It curves slightly, and at its end, a larger room casts a warm light into the pitch. We wait a moment, both of us listening for the rush of boots on stone or voices hissing orders prior to our approach.

When there is nothing, Jeanne nudges my arm in an urging manner.

I turn toward her. The glint of light from the next room gives me plenty to see by. Jeanne squints forward, her eyes finding refuge in the meek light, her body tensed with the intention to help without knowing how. I take her hand and guide her forward. Her fingers respond by clutching mine, but her eyes continue to shift aimlessly in the dark, not seeing me as I see her.

I lean forward, placing my voice close to her ear. "Stay close but keep out of the way."

Her gathered scarf brushes my jaw as she silently nods. "There will be guards ahead."

I keep her hand. She does not protest as I help her along the dark hall toward the dim light. The stone floor allows for an undetectable approach. Unlike the forest, there is no need to cautiously determine proper footing or avoid dry sticks and leaves. I add a slight roll to my step, assuring complete silence. Jeanne, practiced in quick and quiet movements, creates no disturbance at my back. My breaths fall evenly to my core, and rather than uncertainty, a sense of calm washes over me. My muscles relax under the weight of the axes, my jaw unclenches at the idea of a single fortress—a single hall—separating me from the expanse of Burned Lands.

Before the hallway's end, Jeanne's grasp tightens. I pause, feeling her heightened pulse through her palm. Carefully, I angle toward her, and gently push her back to the stone wall. If she were an elf, it would be easier to say something without detection from whatever force waits in the next room, but her human ears would not catch my secretive pitch. We would have to speak loudly; still a miscommunication as I would not know what to say, and she would be unable to reply.

Instead, I hold her hand one moment longer before teasing my grasp from hers. I step away, into the length of light that pools in the archway to the next room and risk peering around the edge.

The adjoining room is not nearly as large as I anticipated. It is well lit because of its modest size. Two glowlights pulse in the center of the stone ceiling, bobbing over the heads of two guards. They sit across from each other at a small table. Between them, some game of cards takes their focus. The first, older guard fidgets with his hand, his roughened fingers hovering over a specific card before nimbly switching to another, drawing it, and placing it flat toward his opponent. The other guard, a much younger man, chews his bottom lip at the play and shifts in his seat. The glowlights above rotate indifferently, far more intent on their duty of lighting the barred door on the far side of the room than the men's game. The door's heavy fortification of sliding bars appear to fit into rungs embedded in the stone wall. The sturdy mechanism might excuse the guards' carelessness if the door was actually locked.

As Jeanne predicted, the bars have been left unbolted. The door itself stands slightly ajar, and the guards continue their game, their swords leaning against their table, ready to be drawn.

I lean back and flatten myself behind the archway, my sense of confidence somewhat shaken by the simplicity of our path. I risk another glance, searching for a hidden door from which more guards might spring, but the only door is the one leading deeper into the fortress—left open for ease of access.

The cards in the younger man's hand tremble slightly. The older guard leans forward, seeking a more comfortable seat in his patchwork armor, and his hand drops closer to his sword hilt.

It's with the softest intake of breath that I retreat once more, realizing where I have seen their nonconforming leathers; in the woods, being ambushed by Boon.

The instant his name appears in my mind, the door from the hall behind grinds open. The sound echoes forward, proceeded only by Jeanne, who swiftly joins my side. She grips my forearm, pulling my attention away from the posted guards. In the course of a moment, I hear the steps of heavy boots on stone, feel Jeanne's nails digging deep into my arm, sense the posted guards rising from their seats to cut off the hallway and trap us between them.

I lunge into the light of the next room, making myself the biggest target apart from Jeanne, who in shock, shrinks down against the wall and floor. As adrenaline fires through my veins, the humans' reactions grow sluggish as they reach for their swords. I spin, seeing the old guard first, his sword unsheathed before the younger man has shut his gaping mouth. Without hesitation, the old man jumps toward me, throwing his full weight into the arc of his sword. I catch his blade under the head of one ax. He pushes down upon it, seeking to throw me to the ground rather than recoil and strike again. My muscles fiercely tense under the weight of the man before me. I meet his brown eyes, noticing them narrow with a fearful understanding that my hold will not break as a human's.

Their companion moves around to my backside, taking aim with their own sword. Without withdrawing my first ax from its locked position, I angle, swinging my second ax upward and back.

The metal bites into the young soldier's neck. They stumble back into the wall, blood gushing forth from their hand as they grab their torn throat. The old man yells ferociously, brokenly, and withdraws for a second strike. I quickly turn back and carve my ax under his arm, burying it deep in his side.

The incoming soldiers rush in as the old man falls to his knees. They stumble in their steps, briefly startled by the scene before them. The woman soldier quickly lays her blade flat across the chest of her companion, stopping him in his tracks as he tries to engage.

"Find the Marked," she commands.

"But—"

She shoves him back down the hall. "Now!"

The man backs away, teeth gritted, eyes locked on me before disappearing in retreat. The fear in his eyes and the echo of the old man's cry bring a sudden nausea to my stomach.

My heart climbs my throat as I realize the approaching woman wears the burnt orange of Piesamur, not inconspicuous leathers. She swiftly curves her sword, moving efficiently to not betray her tactic. My arms fatigue too early as my mind clouds with flashes of remembrance. The demolished camp. The dead, cut down as quickly and thoughtlessly as the guards at my feet. Serin, running, scrambling to the Wood as the guard fled the hall.

And I cut the woman down as Skinner struck me. I don't follow my movements, but I have no choice but to end the close skirmish as my body tires and her strikes become fiercer. I feel outside of myself, breathless as the woman falls beside the rest. I gasp for a deep breath, but my airways constrict with my rising heart. The barbs bite so deeply into my back that they hook around each vertebra, each rib.

"Nhu? Hey."

Jeanne tugs at my arm, her body bent above mine as she tries to pull me to my feet. I don't remember falling onto my hands.

"C'mon. We need to go. We *have* to go."

Ashacan. Go. Halstaer says after her. *You need to go.*

I meet her eyes and grasp at her. Her hand finds mine. My hand, which no longer stirs with the shadow of Lelendelus. I think the loss of shadow signatory of Lumin's state, but Jeanne does not react. For a moment she averts her eyes, seeming to be disturbed or ashamed, perhaps both. But she helps me up anyway and then cautiously moves for the ajar door. A door from which no backup came.

"You and the glim need to get out of here," she reminds me, her voice far stronger than what I expected of the shocked woman who huddled on the floor minutes ago. "So, we need to keep moving."

I nod, still fighting through memory to focus on our task. Jeanne takes my hand, and with her other palm on the wall, slowly leads me further into the fort. All the while, my mind swims as though thrust into the Deep where waters of slaughtered Rendara, lost ranks, and fragments of bone crash like the tide. The barbs snag as the caracosh reaches through the torrent, pulling my leg, dragging me downward through the dark to a fate unknown.

I rip away from the claws, rip away from Jeanne in whatever dark hall we are in. I hear her gasp at my unexpected recoil.

"We're almost there," she tells me, speaking softly in what sounds like an attempt to calm. "We need to hurry before more guards come."

"You can see me."

Occasional glowlights have lit our curving path through the fort. One hangs several paces ahead, casting enough light for her to know.

She stares at me as though caught in a lie. "Aye."

"Then why are you still here?"

"Because you need help. And at this point, so do I."

"I'm an elf."

"And I'm a ridger. An elf is new alright, but it isn't the worst thing." After saying as much, her eyes stop flitting to the comfort of anything other than my face. Finally, they rest there. She uncrosses her stiff arms. Lifts her chin from her scarf. "You've known I'm human this whole time and haven't hurt me. You know who has hurt me? Hurt *us*? Guards. Burned men. And none of them are gonna stop because we feel guilt."

The conviction in her voice does its part to strengthen my resolve, dusting a portion of my panicked thoughts from the edges.

"Let's go," she urges, coming near. Bravely, she touches my arm and tilts her head upward to see my face, the proximity not frightening her in the least. The dark centers of her eyes expand, bleeding into the blue. I find some comfort in their solidity as she searches my face. Her scarred lips part, revealing the gap in her teeth, but then she firmly presses them shut and steps away.

She clears her throat. "Did the seer put that magic on you? Whatever hid you?"

"Yes."

"Seeing that it's gone, we should hurry, aye?"

The shade was my only indication of Lumin's safety, assuring me he was at least well enough to maintain his magic. It hardly flickered when he faced the Marked in the street and held strong when he was struck with pain.

The implications of his vanished shadow cuts through my ill-timed self-doubt. I grip my axes and continue forward, passing Jeanne impatiently. The winding hall curves toward an open cavern. There, a protruding wall of natural stone arcs some hundred feet before curving out of sight. At its center is a gap, like a wedge in a cutting block hewn by the force of a god—the Ridgewall.

A hint of light tinges the jagged rock orange. Jeanne and I step from smooth stone to the grit of natural ground. The air is chill so far within. The light draws me forward, similar to the hue of Lumin's fire.

I turn the corner of the wall. Like the guard post, the space is too narrow and well-lit to bother with stealth. Much of me would not care to go undetected if the space allowed such an approach, but upon stepping into the light, I stop so suddenly that I would have drawn all attention regardless.

Another massive door stands pushed into the wall; its edges crimped by crooked stone like a festering wound. Before it is a waiting, blue robed mage. He appears more roughened by exhaustion than last we met, but when he pushes away from the door, it is with a restored energy.

Boon looks at me evenly, magic alighting his lifted hand. My body tenses in preparation to jump left or right, whichever way his spell denies, but he does not reciprocate with an attack. The shimmering tethers around his hand are withheld as his gaze passes over me.

"Jeanne, take her weapons."

In his next breath, the spell releases. And my body, stiff with new dread, falls like a guard beneath the weight of an ax.

Breathless

FAMILIAR MAGIC ENTRAPS ME before I can consider if there is a way out. Orange tethers snap around my body. Their impact brings dizzying black spots to my eye as they knock me flat. It is only desperation that keeps me conscious.

I grit my teeth through the pain of feeling bludgeoned, almost grateful for the inability to move. The magic shocks might otherwise kill me before I have a chance to reach Boon.

Or Jeanne.

She timidly steps around me. My axes dropped where I stood seconds before. Without looking at me, she picks them up. The handles are too thick for her grasp. The weight of the heads drag her shoulders downward.

Boon watches her closely as she approaches. He reserves a glare for her that I would have expected to land on me. It gives her pause halfway to him. Keeping her distance, she presses herself to the Ridgewall and tucks the axes behind a jutting stone.

Boon eases his glare at her submissive stance, seemingly pleased. "You've been far more useful than I want to give you credit for. Once I open this gate, lead them out, and our deal will be done."

She nods, her eyes gleaming darkly over her scarf.

"And I encourage you not to forget my face. I certainly will not be forgetting yours."

He angles away from her and faces the gate. It is wrinkled like the stonework of the wall. Intricate vines of rock lace overtop the barred doors. They seem to grow outward from the Ridgewall itself, apart from the embedded metal behind. The construction should be immovable while entirely locked by ancient stone.

Boon places a hand upon the nearest vine. A soft glow emanates from the space beneath his palm, and then runes alight across the rock. The orange markings appear faintly at first before gradually blooming into a deep red. Their designs are unfamiliar to me, certainly not of elvish or Dur.

When the runes become so bright I can no longer distinguish their shapes, the light blinks out, and the immovable lacework of stone fades, leaving the metal door laid bare. Boon takes a step back, and commanded by some unseen force, the tall doors begin to open.

It is a slow movement preceded by a deep grind of metal on rock, and when the doors stand apart, there is a sudden quiet. A soft breeze drifts through, bringing with it the scent of open air unhindered by walls. Wisps of sand dust across the ground. With them comes the sharpness of a fouler scent.

The tunnel beyond hollows the width of Piesamur's thickest wall. At its end, the path crests the top of an ascent from the barren Skirt. Beyond, the flatland extends for miles out of sight. For a moment, I mistake its nightly tinge for that of water, but its ripples are too still and unnaturally strained. Several silent minutes pass before the first pair of reflective eyes glint under the glowlights in the cavern where I lay.

The animalistic trait resides in the face of a branded man, one who could be Skinner brought back from the dead. And behind him, more follow.

Boon does not move for them. Four men fan out, partially encircling him in the narrow chamber. Like their eyes, many display bestial traits: wild, matted hair; white skin ravaged by sun, sand, and self-infliction; inhuman cords of muscle, disproportionate limbs, scavenged leathers and chains; cruel weapons fashioned to hurt rather than kill. They simply *are* beasts appearing as men.

If I were not bound, I do not know if I would run or fight. My heart races at the sight of them—only the beginnings of a pack. Shame creeps up after my fear, and I steel myself. At least bound, I need not decide how to react. If only briefly, I can let what fear lingers beneath my anger rise as they encroach.

They could overwhelm Boon in an instant with their numbers and clear strength, and yet they do not. Not as haphazardly as I expect, they take positions around the Marked, and then one steps through.

He is neither the largest nor most wild. In fact, he seems almost human, and I would not have thought him to be the King if not for the way the others defer to his passing. His fair skin is rough with age and riddled by what appears to be infection. A black beard hangs overtop his chest with the center cut close to his chin, revealing a brand burned into his throat. Amidst the strands of either side are woven beads. The knotted design of his brand edges down his exposed collarbone and presumably farther beneath his dirty linen shirt. Across his chest is a simple leather strap affixing a pauldron to his shoulder. On the same arm, he wears a gauntlet and sleeve of scaled leather. Upon the knuckles of his gauntleted hand are three long black claws overreaching his fingers. I recognize their distinct shape and follow their curve to where the King's own hand rests on the pommel of a black dagger.

Any doubt for his identity vanishes as my fear sharpens to something more refined.

The King steps close to Boon, his glim-clawed hand not budging from my father's dagger and my eyes not moving from him. He is surprisingly shorter than the Marked, yet proceeds to lean close in challenge. Boon looks down and does not give away his space.

"All gates are opened," he informs the King. "You may proceed as discussed."

"All of it?" the King asks, his voice hardly a rasp.

"The entire city. Take it as you please."

The King smiles. "An' resistance?"

"Enough to ensure there is no association between us. So, if it is a fight you are asking for, yes, you will get one."

"Aye..." disenchanted by the conversation, the King glides around Boon. Having received no signal to move, his waiting men stand still as he examines the cavern. He smiles upward at the sleeping city through the passages above, and then his gaze falls on Jeanne, instinctively seeming to know exactly where she lurks.

His grin fades. "Come 'way from that wall, little spider."

She does as told but not without lugging the axes with her. The King meets her halfway, moving suddenly in a manner that causes Jeanne to flinchingly stop. He forces a hand along her jaw, turns her head in examination.

"Don't drop those axes," he warns. "You carry 'em. All the way up. Not one fuckin' scratch on my floors, aye?"

She could not nod had she wanted to. He holds her jaw firm for a moment longer, and then shoves her, causing her to stumble back.

"Lead the men out," he orders, then waving toward the burned men within the room, gives order. "Our spider knows the way out of this hovel! Follow 'er up! Lay claim to our city!"

The men within range cheer raucously, and their exuberance spreads backward through the gateway. Their guttural voices mingle like the roar of some creature, spilling downward to the Skirt and forward into the tunnels. The voice of hundreds.

Jeanne separates herself from the sound. She slips along the wall and without a second glance at me, continues back the way we came. The men follow except for the King who steps out of line toward me.

He looks down at me curiously, head cocked to the side. His eyes are a similar blue shade to Jeanne's, but their lids are rotted. Flecks of his skin peel back. His flesh deteriorates along his flat cheekbones and down the side of his nose, but I have no care for whatever plagues him.

I glare upward, not having seen his face until now, yet feeling as though I have known it forever. Everything I anticipated and more stands over me, infuriatingly human, uniquely disgusting. For a moment, I feel only confusion about how such a man could overtake the Rendara. The longer I look at him, the more enraged I become. He should not have managed it. He could not have managed it, and if not for Boon's magic, I could certainly kill him now.

He crouches next to me, seemingly unaware of the rot in his eyes, and observes my face. "You look like her."

As he leans near, I notice the beads in his beard are not beads at all. They are fangs.

"What?" he prods. "Thought you were gonna kill me? She thought that too. Stubborn bitch."

The mention of my mother glides from his festering lips and between the tresses of Rendaran fangs, all stained in blood. My voice is beyond me, stifled under both the impact from Boon's magic and the piercing barbs that burrow through my throat to hook my words, yank them back, and keep me shamefully silent. I want nothing more than to drop my eyes, but my mother chastises me. *Eyes forward. Eyes up and ready, acan.*

The King takes my chin in a rough hand, much like he grabbed Jeanne. With the other, he draws my father's dagger and presses its edge to my lips. The corruption around his eyes seeps.

"Difference is," he muses, "ain't no one goin' to grant you silence. No rats here to take my kill."

I could spit or bite. Shake my head away despite the shock. Do something. But his grip is firm, and my will to protect myself vanished with the entangled bodies of my kin. My thoughts are far away, thinking of my mother and the Rendaran arrow in her chest.

Boon's voice cuts through the chamber toward the King. "She belongs to the Everwatch, and as such, you will not damage her."

The King looks back at him. "Don't need her teeth now, do ya?"

As he taunts the Marked, his arm stiffens, and the blade does not budge. I feel it frozen upon my lips. Its green streaks wink up at me against the black metal. The King strains against an unseen force, still trying to drive the strength of his arm down through the blade and my jaw. Blood and pus pools in the corner of his narrowed glare as he futilely pushes against the spell. Under the stalemate, I shift my gaze sideways and see Boon gently holding his hand aloft. His hazel eyes gauge the King. Burned men continue to stream in behind him, boots confidently stamping toward their prey. None notice as Boon restrains their King by an invisible tether.

Vitriol separates the mage's words into their own sentences. "Go use your filthy fucking hands to lay siege before I *cut them off.*"

The King makes a guttural sound at the back of his throat but cannot speak. One of the fangs brushes against my cheek.

Boon splays his hand and shoves the King back several feet. The blade nicks my lip at the pushback, but the King maintains his grip on the hilt even as he is thrown into the line of burned men. Boon's hold severs. The King catches himself upon the shoulders of his pack and forces them toward the ground to maintain his own footing. Boon takes a step in my direction, his swiftness anticipating a fight. The King seeks to return, wielding my father's dagger as though it has the length of a sword or heft of an ax. Rather than summon a defense, Boon wonders at the dagger.

"What is that blade?" he demands.

The question abruptly halts the King's approach. His fearsome posture changes, instantly shrinking back in a protective stance as he lowers the dagger to his side.

"That is not a weapon of the Burned Lands," Boon observes.

The King bares his teeth and steps back toward his pack. The men bow around him, and using them as a barrier between himself and Boon, the King allows himself to be swept away in the procession.

Boon watches after him, watches after each burned man hulking through the gate and down the cavern.

"Fucking *animals*," he eventually mutters. Then, almost as a second thought, he bends down, and unaffected by his own magic binds, throws me over his shoulder. He stoops briefly under my weight before righting himself, seemingly unhindered although I am equal to him in size.

I experimentally push against my binds. They respond with a jolt that stiffens my body once more. Boon sighs as he walks efficiently, surpassing the line of jostling burned men.

"I won't feel it," he tells me. "But keep trying. Perhaps you'll have less shame while unconscious."

I consider it, but ultimately keep still with fangs bared as my head bobs against his back and try to reason with him. "This pack will slaughter your people at your will, and you seek to tell me about shame?"

He does not answer.

"You questioned why my vashte'rae needed to suffer and still unleash these packs on your own city."

"This is not my city."

"And the Rendara were not your people!"

I thrash over his shoulder, still able to throw my weight even while bound. The resulting current causes me to cry out. My voice echoes down the hall to the delight of the nearby men. They push around us as my motion successfully breaks me from Boon's hold. My body topples off his shoulder, hits the ground. The burned men snarl and surge, some wanting to rush for the city above, the rest tempted to linger. Before I can consider my next move beyond a slight inconvenience, Boon straddles my stomach, and clamps his palm over my mouth. He forces my head back against the ground, grinding the back of my skull in the dirt, and the pack roars.

I try to sink my teeth into his hand, but already the sensation of working magic locks my jaw shut. My teeth are forced together as a prickling energy weaves between them and down my throat. I breathe sharply through my nose, panicked by my inability to fight the silencing magic. Still with his hand clasped over my mouth, Boon speaks.

"The Everwatch has no use for your voice, acan. Now, be quiet."

He maintains his grip a moment longer, allowing me time to memorize the rough scars of runes in his palm. Then he gathers me over his shoulder and hoists me upward. I work to control my erratic intake of air through my nostrils.

"That's better," the Marked says at my stunted breaths and carries me out.

* * *

Chaos unfolds upside down. I cannot lift my head while strewn over Boon's shoulder. Even turning it to witness the attack stuns my body into stillness, and I'm left held in place, unable to intervene. Boon weaves through the throngs of burned men untouched. His steps separate us from their ranks, placing us apart from them or anyone else as battle ensues around us.

I make myself look at what befell the Rendara and realize that one pack overwhelming a vashte'rae is little compared to thousands overturning a city.

And there must be thousands, far more than the single pack whose numbers surely dwindled following their ambush in the Gatewood. The men rise through Piesamur's cracks like ants. They burst not only from the fortress but the base of the outer wall itself, clawing their way through the intermittent doors with weapons brandished before they barrel into the streets. They are distinguishable in traits. Just as I recognize differences between the vashte'rae, so too there are qualities setting sects of burned men apart from the others. Discrepancies in armor, tactic, brands, and general willingness to follow certain leaders creates disorganization in their attack.

Not that it matters. No one is expecting it. Not the Rendara. Certainly not the fortified city.

Boon turns down a narrow side street, cutting off my view before I can hope for an end to their numbers. Their assault raises sounds that seem amplified in the absence of my breath. The wave of realization gradually spreads ahead of us. Citizens occupy the streets, occupy the shadowy spaces under stoops. I hear them hide, slamming doors or scrabbling for safety in the recesses of their homes, but their attempts to hide do not fool the burned men whose eyes cut through the dark. They gleefully break the barriers, kicking and smashing their way through locked doors and shuttered windows. The slum, hardly standing as it is, meekly crumbles under their heavy steps as the grass flattened in the Gatewood. And the humans, familiar in their territory as the Rendara knew the Wood, are suddenly unsure of their escape. Some choose the openness of the street to the cramped spaces in their homes. A brave few wield common items as weapons, their hands flexing uncertainly as they crane their necks to make sense of the snarling breaths that whisper through the alleys.

Following the barks of men, a fear grows. Like fire alighting, screams ignite. They give voice to the silence in my memories.

Despite Boon's winding path and quick steps, the pack surmounts us. I sense the grit in his teeth as ambush disrupts his retreat through the city. Citizens cloud the streets and mingle with the pack—darting rabbits unaware of the agility in a wolf. Some are lucky enough to reach the next street, the next building, the backside of a paralyzed guard who takes the hit for them. Too few are soldiers, and the soldiers are not prepared. Boon abruptly halts as a man is cleaved in two steps in front of us. The assailing burned man notices the Marked and offers a wicked grin. In answer, Boon diverts his path, nearly colliding with a woman sprinting by. Blood streams down her back. He angles away just as a child bolts from beneath a porch and is struck by a wayward blade. On the backswing, it cuts up his chest and knocks his frail jaw upward, his head sharply back.

I try to break the magic hold from my mouth, but my body does not respond. Somewhere in my throat, my rising voice catches and falls back as the child's body tumbles under an arc of blood.

And Boon carries me onward. We receive a glance or two, but the horror in the citizens' eyes is already established, merely confused upon seeing an elf in addition to burned men. They see me over the shoulder of a Marked and assume he is on their side, but he deftly avoids their desperate hands and pleading eyes.

Boon hastily turns a corner when a wave of Piesamur soldiers breaks through the next street over. Whatever ranks that were on patrol seem to have rallied at last. They part for those who flee before closing their ranks to meet a slew of rushing burned men. I hear the clash of metal and flesh, more shouts of orders and pain, and overtop it all, the first strike of magic descending upon the battle.

It comes from the open length of Piesamur's main road. From my view, the yellow burst curves upward. Its brightness fades as it arcs through the early morning sky. All noise seems drawn to it and is dampened by its tail as it carries above the rooftops. Somewhere in the street, it lands, rumbles outward forcefully enough to shake the frames of every structure and born of it, a translucent wall fans outward.

Boon pauses just long enough to recognize some meaning unknown to me. In the quiet, his breath catches. "Gods."

Doubling down on his grip, he sprints forward.

The wall ripples through the buildings behind us, shaking dust from the rooftops and drawing a piercing shriek from their structures. The reverberating force catches Boon's heels and throws us forward with a flash of blinding light. I feel my body hit the ground once, twice, and then my shoulder skids into the cobbles. Instinctively, I tuck my chin to my chest and try to bring my limbs to my abdomen. The jolt I receive straightens my spine, causing me to arch upon the ground with arms and legs strained under their tethers. Ears ringing, eyes wide but blind with shifting light, I gasp for a breath that does not come.

"Breathe through your nose."

Above me, my father's figure forms in the light. His angular, black eyes solidify, the rest of his sharp face taking shape around them to drive back the white-hot magic. A pressure upon my chest takes away the uncontrolled current that overworks my heart. I try to lift my hand in search of his, wondering how he could be so close.

"Stay still now."

I make to speak only for my words to lodge in my throat, muffled by Boon's spell. Frustrated tears dampen my eyes. The pressure of my father's hand moves away from my heart. I think it glides along my cheek, but the feel is like that of a warm breeze, nothing more.

"You almost have it."

As his touch vanishes, so does he, and I'm suddenly aware of myself. Vision returns to my right eye. My heart finds a steady rhythm as air makes its way to my lungs.

"That's it," a new voice says. "C'mon. Find your breath."

The sounds of battle come rushing back, and at the new voice, I nearly lunge off the ground, but my body does not respond how I intend, and Jeanne's firm hand keeps me on my back.

She stares down at me, her black hair tumbling around her shoulders as my father's silver braids did moments before. Her dark eyes take the place of his. They briefly glance aside in an apologetic way before returning again.

"Fine that you don't trust me, but you have to for a moment," she says, out of breath herself. "I'm going to cut you free. Keep still, aye?"

I take an even breath through my nose and wait. Her hand disappears in the folds of her scarf and reemerges with the characteristic claw of a glim. As Lumin did when freeing me from Boon, she draws the claw overtop the magic threads like a knife. They snap and fade, allowing my blood to rush beneath my constricted skin.

My arm shoots upward, and I grab her by the throat. She easily folds under me as I pin her to the ground. My eyes flicker between her face and the glim claw held tightly in her hand. The ringing in my ears diminishes, but the sounds of assault continue around us, echoing down the many nooks in the surrounding structures. Several steps away, I see Boon lying flat on his stomach. His cloak is disheveled and singed by the impact of magic, his armor scraped. One of his hands pathetically scratches at the cobbles. The rest of him is not conscious enough to follow. Not far from us, burned men pace behind the translucent barrier of magic. Its shine begins to dull. The pack eyes us through it, both hungry and curious but unable to pass. I lower my gaze to Jeanne. Her hands are free, but she does not fight my grip. She has no need to under my lack of pressure.

"I can take you to him," she imparts. The frail bones of her throat caress my palm. "The King. I know where he is."

I want to ask why. She seems to understand that I cannot.

"You can kill him."

I lean forward a bit, conveying my unspoken question with the slightest pressure of my hand.

Her hand climbs mine, hardly afraid. She simply links her fingers around my wrist.

"I had to," she whispers.

Boon manages to push himself onto his hands and knees. Looking between him and the branded men, I abruptly release my hold on Jeanne, ashamed.

Without so much as rubbing her throat, she tiredly rests her gaze. "My only way to escape was this."

I roll off her, the ache of my body spreading deep in my mind. Before I can process a reply, the magic barrier dissipates.

Had I not been under Boon's cursed spell, I still would have no time to breathe. The burned men run forward, and the moment of stillness breaks.

"Axes!" Jeanne coughs, lurching upright. She points to the war-axes left on the ground nearby. I gather them in an instant, angle toward the pack, and deflect the first man to meet us.

Jeanne darts around me as I catch the ax of the burned man. Unlike the guards, he wastes no time bearing down with his weight and instead brings a secondary ax toward my side. Recognizing the move, I easily block his second blow and break the first. Two more men come to aid him, one curving a blade toward the back of my knee, the other, my neck.

And then they are engulfed in flame.

Each drops their weapons at the summoned fire. They flail and fall, writhing as their skin boils. The fire comes close but dances over me without threat of heat.

For a moment, the endless wave of burned men hesitates, not daring to step toward me. They look beyond me, a fear in their glinting eyes. Then a dozen soldiers flood forward from behind. I'm swallowed by their advance.

They jump over the three charred bodies and take advantage of the pack's brief uncertainty. To my right, Boon stands, similarly attempting to shake the magic blast from his senses. The soldiers of Piesamur break around him, uncaring of the Marked in their midst. He dumbly spins, searching.

His eyes land on me. He parts his arms and contorts his fingers in my direction.

A claw grips my shoulder and yanks me from his line of sight.

Lumin steps around me. He tucks me at his back and takes the brunt of whatever magic Boon releases under a conjured shield. White light sparks around his plated shoulders. As it passes, he quickly glances back.

A line of blood cuts across his rigid brow and a mottling of purple bruises discolors his jaw. The fire in his eyes has never been brighter.

"To the wall," he orders. "We cannot hold."

I turn, glad for an order in the fight, and collide with Jeanne. She boldly grabs my arms as though to keep my axes parted.

"The King," she reminds me.

Another spell explodes around us. Burned men and soldiers blend together under the fragments of light and clash of steel.

I hastily nod at Jeanne.

*　*　*

We weave against a tide of fleeing people. They run toward the outer wall rather than the eastern sectors that have yet to be infiltrated by burned men. Many evacuate from the direction of the slum. The rest come from the city center where the brunt of the packs push back the weakening line of Piesamur's guard.

Under the night sky, intermittent bursts of magic cast light on the battle. Somewhere west, from the far edge of the slum, a fire pulses above rooftops. Flashes of magic color the sky in the direction of Piesamur's encampment. Smoke wafts through the streets and high overhead, the crackle of flames a coming threat beneath the howls of burned men. Wood snaps under the force of the moving pack as men break through doors, stamp upon floorboards, and shatter glass. Muffled screams slip through the cracks from those who do not escape. Louder voices course through the streets from those who are uncertain of their fate. Soldiers shout commands. Burned men bark theirs in an unfamiliar language of disjunct growls. Battlemages take their own paths, some standing strong behind lines of soldiers to cast shields or volleys of spells. Others dart through the burned men, their fingers contorting and runes alighting on their armor as they slice magic at those who do not fall to blades.

At some point, Jeanne took me by the arm. At first it was to guide me through the streets, but soon she leans close to my side. The men begin to notice us running toward them rather than away, and they divert their attention to our path.

I continue to move as they meet us. Jeanne adeptly avoids the swing of blades as I raise my axes to whatever beasts throw themselves in our way. They favor exposed brands upon their necks and chests. Some are entirely shirtless, and I slash toward flesh whenever I see it. A few men fall, but many simply stumble, snarl, swear. I keep moving under the spray of blood, trusting Jeanne to keep her hold on my arm as I carve a path down the main street. Finding the frontline is easy enough, and I know it is where he will be. Instinct draws me there. A distinct shade of yellow magic dominates the street—a smaller version of the wall that briefly staved off attack. Soldiers move beneath it, but they fall one by one with each step I take. The shield is pushed back as its caster is forced to retreat their line.

The High Mage turns their head to shout toward what soldiers remain. I cannot hear the order, but the men break off. They refocus on the closest buildings, the nearest alleys. They shout within. One man vanishes down a side street and reemerges with a frightened woman. He grips her by the arm and shoves her in the direction of the wall. I do not need to hear the command he mouths at her.

Run.

Eyes wild, the soldiers frown at the remaining structures and the streets they cannot reach. Then they, too, run.

They glance at me and Jeanne, but upon noticing me, they startle. Flinching mid-step, bewilderment seems to mix with their fear, but they do not stop.

The bright shield falters. One of the men manages to swipe through and slash the side of the remaining caster.

I break from Jeanne's grasp and join the person who I only assume is the High Mage Surasis. Another burned man jabs his arm through the shield toward the High Mage. I reflexively grab his wrist before his blade can sever Surasis's arm and twist it sideways. Beneath his skin, bones shift and snap. The man cries out. Surasis strengthens their stance, and their shield fortifies once more.

In the moment of reprieve, they meet my gaze, their brown eyes cutting overtop their shoulder. Yellow light reflects in them. Sweat drips down their shaved head, leaving clear lines through layers of grime. On their tanned cheeks, tears do the same.

And they nod.

They thrust their hands forward through the shield, and the shimmering wall vibrates outward. It jolts through the pack. Energy thunders through them, knocking many of them flat and throwing others into the walls of nearby buildings. I flinch, expecting to be pushed one way or another, but the High Mage angles a hand, and guides the magic around us both. Their bones press sharply against the back of their hands as they control the breaking shield, then an invisible hold seems to snap. Their hands soften as the magic ripples away, but Surasis wastes no time. They switch their grip to my arm and pull me backward several steps.

The minor retreat steals us a moment to breathe and allows me to take my own stance alongside Surasis. They gracefully lift their hands in a defensive position. I do the same with my axes and scour the crowd for the King as a second wave of burned men runs forward.

Surasis's hands glow, and with the elegance painfully reminiscent of Halstaer's movements, they deftly glide through the men. Their magic cracks like a whip as it burns through armor and deflects an onslaught of blows.

A stray few come at me. We entangle briefly, but the burned men veer away almost as soon as they approach. One skids to a stop, teeth bared, and hastily refocuses on the high mage.

I turn to follow the burned man's gaze. Too late, I think to listen beyond the sounds of battle. The deliberate exhale of a breath reveals itself in my ear.

Claws pierce through my back; three distinct punctures just beneath my ribs. My gasp of air knots in my throat. The muscles of my lower back tense as the claws push deeper and curve upward. Like the caracosh, they pause against my ribs, knowing of their power.

The King tugs back, yanking me to his chest. His putrid breath roils hotly under my nose as he hisses in my face. "I'll take those fangs now, rat."

The claws retract as cleanly as they entered. I feel for my grip on the axes, and try to turn swiftly despite the searing pain, but the King moves quicker, and shoves his knuckles into the wound.

Another cry is strangled by my constricted airways. He grabs the collar of my armor and flings me sideways.

I'm surprised by his strength as I hurtle through the air. My focus returns to more immediate concerns as I collide with the crossed frame of the nearest shop window. Remaining shards of previously shattered glass snap along with the woodwork as my body slams through it.

Inside the building, I scatter the objects just within the window display before striking the hard edges of a row of shelves. From somewhere above, several books and scrolls rain upon me. As I lift my arm to protect my face, I realize how little sense I have used in the past months. As the books pelt me, I nearly see my father casually perusing the shelves.

Not an ounce of sense, he remarks, his back to me.

In my mind, my mother's critique follows. *No tact, acan.*

I shove the books away just as the King bursts through the shop's door. Above him, a bell rings. I throw the nearest book toward him. He bats it away. I clumsily get to my feet. At first, I stumble, my palms scraping the floor as the muscles pull in my back. The punctures from the King's claws are deep. I feel them etched beneath my ribs, protesting with sharper pangs under every heartbeat. The sensation forces me to breathe shallowly through my nose. In my struggle to stand, I realize the King is waiting. He cocks his head, observing me with a restrained eagerness.

"Didn't think I'd find an elf weaker than that chief of yours, but I'm not surprised seeing that you never fought in the first place."

I stand up, the binding of a heavy tome clasped in hand.

"You gon' kill me with them pages?" he taunts.

I roll my shoulders back against the shelves and find a balance with the book's weight. Then I lift my eyes. What remains of my vision cuts perfectly through the dark store. No firelight pushes beyond the windowsill or open door. With his predatory eyes, I'm sure the King also sees through the dark, but that is where his advantages end.

Rather than rush forward, I step back and let the darkness of the long aisles consume me.

He pursues the moment I slip away, but the path is narrowed by cluttered books. Like roots in the Wood, they branch outward from their shelves to catch the feet of those careless enough to blindly rush forward. I agilely step around them, swiping more from the shelves as I go before silently angling down the next aisle. Somewhere behind, the King loudly trips. His hand grips a shelf, inciting a creak from the wood. I continue to weave away from him.

The shop is not large, and so as to not corner myself in the back, I return to the front and press myself to the backside of shelves on which he caught himself.

Through the shelves, I hear his garbled breaths, as though blood or rot chokes his throat. The wood beneath his nails peels back as his grip steadies, and sensibly, he listens.

At the backside of the bookshelf, I still myself. Holding my breath is made easy by Boon's spell. The throbbing punctures in my back distract me from any fear. I count their replies to my heartbeats, each louder than the next.

His shoulder thuds as he shoves into the shelves, and with a strained creak, the case at my back leans into me. Books and bottles topple from the upper shelves, nearly scraping my back as I duck around the falling structure. The King, expecting me, turns to shove my father's dagger into my neck. I lift my book to shield from the blow. The impossibly sharp blade glides through the bound pages, stopping short of my cheek. Before he can recoil, I twist the book sideways and cast the knife to the floor.

We briefly pause, both searching for the thrown blade amidst the strewn books, but when it is not immediately noticeable, I quickly angle and slam the punctured tome against the King's face. His jaw pitches to the side and his body stiffens, already moving to counter me as I swing the book again. He grabs my wrist and brings his other fist toward my face. I lean back to avoid the strike, breaking my held wrist free as I do so. He reaches forward to grapple me. I slip from his attempt and send my elbow to crack against his brow. The force causes him to stumble, but rather than fall, he jabs upward, and shoves the glim claws beneath my ribs.

They strike exactly as the caracosh did, carving my scars anew. A cry of pain lodges against the roof of my still locked mouth. Not withdrawing, the King backhands me with his free hand, then shoves the claws deeper until I am backed against one of the still standing shelves. He grabs my throat and pins my neck at the edge of a shelf.

My eyes glide over the quivering Rendaran fangs threaded in his beard to look beyond. I search for my father, expecting him to be watching as he did when the caracosh sought to kill me. I expect he would do the same now. The part of him I never knew would surely be disappointed in my inability to kill a single man.

But my father is not there. None of the Rendara are, and instead, the broken shop window fills with the slinking form of Jeanne. The edges of her figure blurs as my remaining vision becomes splotched with black. Spiderlike, she crawls through the frame and delicately lands amidst shattered glass and scattered books. Without hesitation, she lifts something to her mouth, and a powerful exhale jolts her torso.

A short dart pierces the King's forearm. Then another sticks his neck. His flesh twitches under the puncturing barbs, and his eyes slowly shift away from my face to glare at them knowingly. Furious, he leans into me, claws shoving deeper, wild eyes watering behind the rot, and reluctant, he wrenches his hand away from my throat.

I nearly crumple beside the bookshelf but steady myself with a sharp breath through my nose. Leaning into my new wound, I hurriedly search the floor for my father's dagger.

The King roars. His enraged voice fills the space as he angles toward Jeanne, her darts still lodged in his skin. He hulks toward her, seeming to have forgotten about me altogether. Still fighting for a deep enough breath, it's all I can do to outstretch my leg as the King lunges for Jeanne.

He trips over my ankle. Jeanne shrinks out of his reach, scrabbling atop the table under the window. Uselessly clutching my side, I get to my feet, surprised to see the King hardly moving faster than me. He pushes against the floor, skidding books and parchments as he does so. In their shifting, a brief sheen draws my eye. Like the black bark of a vashte, I notice the subtle glint even when immersed in darkness.

I reach for the blade beneath the books. Seeming to recall the dagger, the King whips around to meet me. I spin the blade and angle my strike to undercut his grasp. He lifts his arm to block my returning arc and slams a fist into my ribs. I fight the urge to furl inward at the rush of pain, only partially resisting as my body contracts. The King grabs my wrist, yanks me upward. He drives his thumb against the base of my own. It bends back, beginning to break hold of the hilt. I feel for the muscles of my legs or free arm, thinking I might finesse my way free, but exhausted, I simply draw a breath through my nose as the King shoves me into the shelves once more. His fingers find hold on the dagger's hilt, and he parts his yellow teeth to snarl in my face.

A black line carves upward from beneath his beard. The King himself no longer matters as I follow the thread. It climbs the crook of his nose to rest at his tear duct, meeting the rot around his eyes. Over his shoulder, Jeanne watches from her perch, her eyes trained on the King, expectant.

His hand dislodges the dagger from my own, breaking my trance. The blade clatters to the floor. Finer tendrils of black branch from the main line. The King yells more fiercely, shaking my body as he does so.

I snap my head forward and crack my brow against his, silencing him mid-yell. He leans back slightly, just enough for me to breathe amidst the brief dizziness. With my free hand, I rip a cluster of fangs from his beard.

He barks at the sudden tear. Between my fingers, I let the teeth sift and fall, pinching the largest—the oldest—between my knuckles, and I drive it through his eye.

He lets me go as searing pain takes his focus, and I know it is searing. A fang in the eye is surely no worse than a knife. As he reflexively scratches to remove the tooth, I drop for the dagger. He lurches forward once more. I sever his hand and without pause slice the blade across his neck. The brand scarring his flesh is thick like a callous, but it offers no resistance as the dagger cleanly sinks into it. In the next instant, his skin parts and then gapes, unveiling red.

Blood dashes across my face. The King takes a surprised step back, unable to decide whether poison or blade garners the last moments of his attention. Whatever Jeanne's darts imbued overtakes his face as he falls. I watch them progress as they progressed across Halstaer's chest, although far more efficiently. The infection rapidly crosses his expression, unstoppable. Upon his forearm, it constricts his muscle and skin, swelling beneath until he is flat on the floor, bloated and discolored.

Jeanne steps forward. Blood trickles between my armor and skin, and I try to settle my breathing. She clears her throat, but my eyes are transfixed by the King.

"We need to get out of here," she says evenly.

I keep her in the periphery of my blind eye, knowing I'll leap after her if she remains in my sight. Despite her poisoned darts, she does not register as a priority as I bend to gather the fangs scattered about the King. I move slowly, far too slowly opposed to the encroaching battle outside, but the sharply spreading pain from my ribs impedes my ability to be more efficient. The chaos pushes against the thin walls of the shop as I cut the remaining fangs from the King's drenched beard.

"They're getting closer," Jeanne warns.

Fingers trembling, I tuck the fangs safely away and remove the belt and sheath of my father's dagger from the King. It is an elegant length of leather, meant to be wrapped several times around one's torso. The King has sloppily knotted it at his hip. I carefully tie it around my waist, thinking it might compress the punctures under my ribs. Rather than sheath the dagger, I hold it firmly in hand, terrified it might vanish again.

"*Nhu,*" Jeanne finally bites in frustration. "Come on."

I shoot her a glare that warns against use of my name—not after proving herself complicit over again.

The relief shown in her eyes from the King's death shifts to confusion at my obvious anger. I stand, stooped by the perforations in my abdomen. She takes a brave step forward with the offer of a hand. "I know there's much to explain, but the High Mage won't hold much longer."

Instead of meeting her hand, I tuck the dagger in its sheath, move toward the King, and pluck the dart from his arm.

Jeanne's posture stiffens. "Careful. One prick from that and you're dead."

Careful? I hold it between us, giving her the opportunity to run. It would be easy for her to do so given my current state. When she does not, I limply cross the short distance and gradually knot my fist in her scarf. She stands more steadily than me, and when I lean forward to shove her back, she submissively falls.

Her back smacks against the snapped window frame. Loose books and broken glass tumble out of place.

"How about you beat me up later?" she suggests. "This isn't a good time."

I lift the dart into her view once more, leveling it dangerously close to her face. Not for the first time, her fearful façade effortlessly slips away.

She does me the favor of looking at the dart, then back to me. Her eyes widen, annoyed.

"It's venom," she explains. "From a blackmaw, a rare spider in the Burned Lands. Will kill a man almost instantly but you knew that. Seen it kill before, aye?"

I touch the dart to her skin.

She lets it rest on her pale cheek, unafraid. "I grew up there, you know. Think I fared well in a pack? King threw me into a pit of those spiders when I was six years old. Their venom never took. Pissed him off, but since then, he knew I was useful for one thing: extracting it. Aye, maybe I played a part from a distance, and I'm sorry, but saying *no* isn't an option for me."

I consider testing her claim. She grips my forearm so hard that she begins to gain the upper hand against my hold. Through the window, Surasis has lost ground. Burned men push against their wavering shield, nearing the bookshop with each second, but the pack's proximity does not deter me from Jeanne. I flick the dart away. Glass crunches under my feet as I push her farther. She winces as the tiny shards still fixed to the window frame dig into the back of her thighs.

She exhales sharply, and her eyes flicker toward Surasis's faltering barrier, notably frightened once more. "Where the fuck are your words? Listen..." She grips at my forearm. "Please, Nhu...they made me. Made me bring the venom for their weapons. Boon told them to be quick, that the fairborn was too powerful—"

The magic around my tongue seems to spread down my throat and through every muscle, locking my body in shock at the mention of my father. Jeanne grabs more earnestly at my arm, pulling herself back to me in a secretive manner.

"Let's get out of here," she nearly pleads. "We need to get you out, and then I'll tell you everything."

My answer comes in the form of losing my balance. I can't tell if it's blood loss or shock that tips me forward, but she catches me under the arms.

"Depths," she expels at my weight. "Your legs better fucking work."

Together, me stumbling and Jeanne poorly shouldering my arm, we abandon the shop. Outside, she gathers my strewn axes, reattaching one to the sheath on my back and keeping the other. We haven't taken a step when the High Mage's magic fails. The yellow mist weakens and shifts like several strands unraveling from a tapestry.

Jeanne tugs me in the direction of the wall. The High Mage breaks from their post and slips from the reach of the surging burned men. Instantly, their eyes land on Jeanne and me. It would be much easier for them to run to whatever safety remains, if any, but without glancing in another direction, they sprint toward us.

In unspoken understanding, Surasis takes me under one arm and pulls half my weight from Jeanne. Jeanne hands over my ax and Surasis skillfully lets it fall into their grip. The two of them drag me forward. What strength remains in my legs aids them in hauling me toward the city wall. The High Mage guides us, occasionally arcing my ax backward at the pursuing pack. Magic energy crackles up and around the ax head and lashes off the blade, its destruction apparent in the resulting barks of pain from behind.

Jeanne maintains an unbreakable grip as I begin to sink. Surasis heaves me up, and together, we flee until the wall obscures us in its shade. There, a familiar fire brightens in the dark. Lumin reaches out and ushers us to refuge.

Through the Dark

AS THE DOOR CLOSES behind us, Lumin slams a heavy bar across its width, granting us temporary refuge. If not for the flames on his horns, the space would be entirely pitch. Outside the wall, the sounds of siege are muffled. There comes a pounding from the other side, and I look away, glad I cannot hear voices through the thick stone. I tell myself it is only burned men, but surely not all were able to flee into the tunnels before the path was overrun.

The tunnel dips downward, leading into a sharp curve within. The walls arch inward, not allowing much room for throngs of soldiers. Farther ahead, I hear the procession of footsteps and panicked voices. Some are soldiers, attempting to calm. Others are those of terrified people pushed out from their homes.

Surasis drops my ax, leans heavily against the narrow hall, and places their palms upon their thighs. They lean forward to take a racking breath. I look away from them, unsure of my place in their midst.

Jeanne releases me and steps away in an attempt to give space in a tunnel that prevents it. Lumin eyes her fiercely. She returns his scrutiny with her own.

I press my hand to my abdomen, as though its presence there would heal the wound from the King's claws. As I touch it, I try to exhale, wishing I could breathe through my mouth instead of the air catching in my nose. In the cramped space, I cannot pace to calm my heart, so I shift my weight between legs and clasp my hands behind my head. The more I try to calm myself, the more my airways seem to constrict. All the emotions I have repressed over the last day would come rushing forth had they not caught in my throat. I cough in my attempt to keep everything hidden, and it collides with the back of my teeth, then I cough some more until I cannot breathe at all.

As I double over, two hands cradle my face. They lift me up until I'm squarely looking back at the High Mage. Over their shoulder, Lumin and Jeanne watch anxiously.

Surasis's calculating gaze examines me as critically.

"Stay still," they order me, and holding their hands to either side of my jaw, they hook their fingers underneath. Slowly, they draw their grasp outward, firmly pushing their fingertips into the soft crook of my jaw. The pressure exudes a burning sensation like a sliver from a wound, and then the tension subsides.

The instant the High Mage retracts their touch, they swiftly tilt my face to the side, and I'm overcome with a fit of violent coughs. Air comes through my lips startlingly cold. My throat feels chaffed and raw. I spit onto the floor and begin to dry heave.

Lumin places a comforting hand on my back until I collect myself, then he offers his arm. I briefly clutch at it for support and then break away with a curse.

"*Norveh!*"

At the sound of my voice, Jeanne inches toward the gap in the tunnel. She hunches slightly, like a rabbit looking to bolt, but freezes when I say nothing beyond my swear. If they knew, I'm sure Surasis and Lumin would enact revenge for Jeanne's betrayal, but the way they look at her only conveys distrust, not a desire for retribution. Surasis studies Jeanne no less harshly than Lumin did. In fact, they obviously take Jeanne in from head to toe before angling toward me again.

Similarly, the High Mage reads my expression and follows with bitter words. "Do not look at me as though I am the one out of place in my own damn city."

There is a twinge in their tone, a wince in their last breath. In our moment of calm, I finally take stock of the High Mage's wounds. Their bare arms are streaked with sweat and lesions amidst their many inkings, and exhaustion sinks their eyes. I imagine they were recently much stronger than they appear, perhaps less shrunken in stature and with more color in their gaunt cheeks.

My polished anger prickles anew as I consider what Boon might have done to them.

I clear my throat once more, feeling for my voice, and gesture at my previously locked mouth. "Thank you."

Surasis does not acknowledge me with anything more than the same cautious glare between myself and Jeanne. Anger gradually contorts their expression until they look away entirely and wipe their face within the dark.

"We must leave," Lumin gently urges us. "You are both hurt."

"Give me a moment," Surasis spits.

I pat Lumin's arm to signal my agreement and a desire for space. The instant after he steps away, Surasis slaps a hand on my shoulder and throws me against the door, knocking the air from my lungs. At my back, the thuds of angry men reverberate upon the cold metal. Surasis lets me feel it for a long moment before they speak.

"Lumin tells me you think I let a pack through my walls." They lean in. "You're an elf. Listen through this goddamn door. My people are being slaughtered out there, and you have the gall to think I would let their murderers in?" They slam their hand upon the metal beside my head. The resounding rattle pierces my ears. "My only crime was that I tried to protect *my* city!"

Behind them, Jeanne continues to slip steadily into darkness, pausing only to hear my reply.

"I believe you," I tell Surasis. "I could see that much."

They pull away and look directly at Jeanne. "And who are you?"

She stammers, "I—"

"She helped Lumin and me enter the city," I answer.

Surasis paces, seemingly unconvinced but too preoccupied to care. "Understand that I don't trust either of you, but we'll have to resolve that when we're out. Put one toe out of line in my tunnels, and I'll be sure to escort you into the prison block."

The wound beneath my ribs finally causes me to slide to the ground. Surasis lowers their gaze as I go. Seeing me on the ground at the base of a blood smear seems to appease their anger for the time being.

"Lumin, help her up and let's move," they order. "There's surely someone up ahead who can heal. At least stop that bleeding. Then we'll drive these packs from my walls—Marked included. And you," they say to Jeanne, "you walk in front of me."

"I don't know the way," Jeanne meekly replies.

"You don't know the way through my tunnels but know how to sneak a glim into my city? Move."

Jeanne nervously casts me one last look. Her face blurs in my vision, seeming to remain behind as the rest of her walks ahead of the High Mage. My sight proceeds to shift a moment behind everything else as Lumin picks me up, axes and all. I rest my head against his plated shoulder and shut my eyes.

* * *

My father sits beside me on the Ridgewall, one hand placed lightly overtop the wound beneath my ribs. I glance down and see my blood seeping between his fair knuckles. He appears younger than I ever knew him; his hair black and streaked with silver, and the lines fainter at the corner of his eyes. He wears armor unlike any I have seen, akin to the *vatanukro* in the north.

"Father?" I say, trying to sit up.

"Your mother is here," he tells me. Quietly, so as not to disturb.

"Where?"

He nods his head forward, gesturing at the shadow of a figure standing at the edge of the cliff. Details of her person shift into obscurity as both the setting sun and shadows of the Ridge play upon her back. I recognize her undoubtedly by the obstinate set of her shoulders, arms surely crossed in front, and long braid swept in a light breeze to her hip. Around the edge of her upper arm, her fingers grip, pinching skin between her rings in a controlled anger.

I look to my father. "She's upset."

"I know."

"What did you do?"

"Too many things."

Having known that, I shift and prop myself onto my hands to stand, to go to her.

"You need to stay still," my father says. "You're hurt."

"Can you heal me?" I ask, preparing a wrath equal to my mother's should he say yes.

"You'll be alright."

"Can you?" I repeat, needing to know.

He breaks his gaze from my mother and pins it on me. I flinch, unaccustomed to the sudden fury in the blackness of his eyes. It glints, like a ripple of starlight on the waters of the Deep. It's there, and then it's gone. He looks back to my mother. "If I could heal, she certainly would not be here. I need you to help her, Ashacan."

"How?"

He sighs, defeated. "Help her."

*　*　*

The sound of hushed voices wakes me. I listen before opening my eyes, half hoping to hear my mother or father. Instead, I recognize the reserved, commanding tone of the High Mage followed by Lumin's gruffness. Then, in a different direction, there is an exhale from a horse and the nuzzling of lips smacking for grass. From another, the rustling of leaves, an impatient shifting of boots on grass, and murmurs of uncertainty.

Dim sunlight pushes against my right eye, and as I slowly move my head, I grow aware of the stiffness throughout my body. It is at its worst under my ribs, like a knot of prickling barbs coalescing under my skin.

I open my eyes to a thick canopy of blueish green leaves entwined with thorny vines. The trees are short and stocky, and their roots burrow through rocky ground. Cracks emanate from them as wood and stone fight for hold of Uunshyl. The musk of old bark is undercut by the faint scents of smoke and blood. As my vision adjusts to a landscape far different than the red cliffside of my dream, I hope to see my mother in the haze of fading sleep, but this is not her Wood.

I place myself somewhere in the brambly lands surrounding Piesamur. The voices of my companions continue to murmur, and as I sit up, I see Lumin and Surasis across the way, having a tense conversation beside a large boulder. Several Piesamur soldiers rest against trees in various states of disarray. Swords lean safely within reach upon chests and roots. Helmets, shields, and wrung dry waterskins, are clasped in nervous grips as the soldiers steal minutes of rest or vigilantly keep watch on the surrounding brambles. Amidst them stands an older man holding the reins of Mournstar and Norrl. The two horses' presence motivates me to sit straighter as the direness of our circumstance comes rushing back.

I pause, discovering that my armor has been removed. My filthy undershirt is stained heavily with sweat and old blood. I feel along my abdomen, wincing, and find it padded with a thin layer of bandages.

I panic, remembering that I had bound my father's dagger there and now it is gone. I lurch upward, arms scouring the nearest ground for the dagger. I find my leather armor, bloodied rags, axes and—

It rests beside me. Not far, but half hidden under my armor, as though it too was quickly tossed aside in haste to get to my wound.

Several of the soldiers stir at my movement. Their eyes dart to me, alert and uncertain, but before anyone tries to draw the attention of the High Mage, Criv teases the horses from their foraging, and approaches.

He lifts a calloused hand in greeting. His clothes are darkened by grime and soot stains his brow. A wave of grey hair falls over his eyes. He shakes it away. "Hey now," he says in response to my rigidity. His strained words poorly convey a sense of calm, "Hey, you're alright. Criv, remember? From the stables."

"You brought our horses?" I ask rather than state, my mind still working to organize itself. My voice rubs coarsely along my throat, and my mouth tastes sour.

"Aye," Criv agrees. "The High Mage sent word for them. Seems you need to clear out."

"Where are we? What happened?"

"Better sit still," he hurries to say as I restlessly shift. "Surasis had you healed not long ago. Those scars are hardly closed up."

I take the dagger and stand despite his warning. My body furls forward as my wound hugs back toward my spine. The King's claws dug deep in both directions, almost like those of the caracosh, and the punctures through my back spasm in retaliation. I straighten, trying to accommodate every point of pain, and end up falling forward.

Criv catches me. I let him help. "Easy now," he mutters, "just take a moment."

I blink dizzying spots from my eye and steady myself on his shoulder. Behind him, Mournstar, curiously pokes his nose forward to touch my elbow.

"You've got a fever," Criv notes. "Gods, you're in no state to travel."

I take a moment to let my body tremble in acknowledgement of the fever, and then I make myself straighten. Hands pressed upon Criv's shoulders, I look him in the eyes. "Where's Jeanne?"

His bushy brows furrow in thought. "Mindy's dove?"

"Yes."

He turns with me and motions toward Lumin and Surasis. The glim and High Mage have ceased conversation and are now posed in an interesting position. Surasis sits perched upon a boulder and bends over Lumin's shoulder. They grasp his sharp ear in one hand and tug it backward while working a hunk of metal through his cartilage. Lumin stands stoically, merely blinking as his ear is crudely punctured. He notices me and twitches as though to move, but Surasis yanks him back.

"She's over there," Criv tells me regarding Jeanne. "She was resting but looks like she moved off a bit. See her? Between the brambles there."

As described, I catch pieces of her through the gaps in the thorny arms of a large shrub. If the foliage were not hued by greys and blues, she might have blended in well with her brown attire and dark hair, but I see flashes of her pale skin moving behind the leaves.

"Think she might want some privacy," Criv observes. "Should give her a moment."

I push away from him and with wavering steps, heading in her direction. I locate her deceptively deep within the brambles. In the time it takes me to stumble across the rough ground and through branches that creak at the feeble weight of my hand, I find her sitting. Her shoulder blades press against the back of her shirt as she hunches forward, and her elbows pulse gently as her hands busy themselves with something on the ground before her. I study her back for a moment, surprised by her delicate frame. Although small, she never struck me as gaunt. As my mind catches up to my eyes, I realize why she seems less present than before. Her bulky scarf is missing. An edge of the brown fabric pokes out around her leg, perhaps the object of her attention. Now removed, she appears almost absent from the space around her.

The warm air is muggy in the brush. It heightens my fever and cultivates sweat along the vertebrae of Jeanne's spine. I follow the dotted trail up her shirt, and at the back of her neck find the tangles of her hair parted over her shoulders. There, vivid in the heat, is the harsh scar of a brand.

The mark is long healed and unidentifiable to my eyes. No clear image forms from the ripples of strained flesh. A faint variation in the scar's depth implies the intention of a symbol, but having been pressed too hard, with metal too hot, any clarity was lost in the outpouring of heat. I wonder how she survived such a thing. The burns flood around her spine and creep into her hairline, reaching bare lines of scorched skin up the back of her head.

She did not turn at my arrival, but as I stare at her brand, she seems to sense my presence. She sits up and carefully shifts her hair around her shoulders, flattening it as best she can overtop her neck. She does not look back at me.

Sick and thoughtless, I speak what comes to mind. "You're branded?"

She remains still. "Do not think it makes me one of them."

The clear tension in her posture warns me away, but around my fever, anger burns. "I need answers."

"I know, but you don't sound well. We should discuss it later."

"If not for you, we would all be well, so talk."

"Alright," she quietly assents. Before answering, she rummages at her scarf, and deftly lowers it over her head. Her movement is slow and steady, as though the scarf is barbed. Once flat, she teases her hair from its layers and combs her fingers through it, strategically hiding her scars.

"The brands have different meanings, you know," she says, more fixated on her hair than me. "It all depends on symbols and placement, who brands you, how...women, though, we all receive the same; one brand, on the back of the neck. As a mark of property. If she can survive that long, anyway." Satisfied with the scarf's placement, she stands. "Even if she can survive, there are limited routes of escape. Most ease into death one way or another, but after I survived the blackmaws, the King had a sudden desperation to protect me."

"That didn't seem like his goal," I reply.

"Protection and preservation rarely stem from love."

"That's not true," I say, still not thinking.

She sighs. Her cheek pushes up against the scarf as she turns her chin toward her shoulder. The corner of one deep blue eye looks back. "I can see why you would think that based on how your people fought, but even you only want me for how useful I prove to be."

I can't say my pity for her surmounts the painful memory her words evoke.

"It's okay," she allows. "I never expect more than what I get. I'm sorry it had to happen to you, but I needed an option."

"And Boon gave you one."

She faces me fully. "Aye."

Donned in her scarf once more, she returns to her usual formidable self. I almost feel smaller than her in my current state, leaning slightly forward to favor my healing wound.

She continues on. "I came with the pack on their first outing, and Boon took notice. He thought I presented a unique opportunity to bridge the Burned Lands with Durast and overthrow the High Mage. And that was before you were a factor. No one expects a burned woman just as no one expects a straggling elf."

Skinner slips through her voice at the mention of straggler, and I reflexively wince. Annoyed by my weakness, I harden my tone, refocus. "What happened to the fairborn?"

Her answer is indifferent. "I last saw him in the city by the river. The ruins."

Edgewood? "Was he dead?"

"I'm not sure."

"How can you not be sure?" I demand.

"I took no part in that slaughter," she claims. "I only encountered him by accident afterward. While in the ruins, I took a wrong turn. They had him but..."

I step closer as her thoughts drift. She could easily avert my approach, but instead she remains steadfast in place. I keep an arm's length between us, resisting the urge to grab her by the throat again. After seeing her brand, I hate that I ever touched her in such a rough manner.

She explains secretively. "The venom didn't take."

"The venom you supplied them with, *sai*?"

"I saw the blackness plainly in his veins," she refutes, almost academically, "but it had not progressed as it should have. It was still, and so was he. Looked more asleep than dead."

I stare at her, teeth grinding, wanting to both throttle her and break down entirely.

She steps one foot back, angling to leave. "You should go," she tells me. "The Marked will come for you soon."

I shake my head.

"What?" she muses. "Not done with me yet?"

"No, I'm not."

The corners of her mouth twinge downward. Her eyes widen and relax in an instant, giving me an intimate glimpse of whatever inner turmoil she has thus far kept hidden. Behind her, I see Halstaer leaning against a tree, black lines reaching like fingers from the gash in his chest.

He watches me over Jeanne's shoulder as my gaze returns to her. "Your venom killed many of them." *Including me.*

She tilts her head, oblivious to the Rendaran faces that form behind her in the thorns.

I continue. "You claim to have not taken part in something you sat by and watched."

"And? Are you gonna kill me for it?" she asks. "Kill me, all because I wanted to survive?"

I stare at her, lost, and then there comes a snapping of branches as something large bursts through the brambles. I turn toward the sound in time to see Lumin's claws grip a low hanging branch. He ducks his horns under a thicket above and wrenches the branch from his path. The healthy wood does not cleanly break, and instead splits to reveal a bright green interior as Lumin twists and shoves it aside. His claws leave fine lacerations in the bark. He lifts head and hand at once as he joins us in the clearing. His burning eyes fall first on me and then alight at Jeanne. Sparks leap between his raised claws.

I see traces of fire in his palm and wonder for whom they are kindled. "Lumin?"

The true extent of my question remains unsaid. He must take my meaning seeing how his glare temporarily softens in my direction. "Nhuaela," he says, half out of breath, "I saw..." he stops himself short of explanation and focuses on Jeanne. "This one lies," he condemns.

"I already know," I say, equally surprised and frustrated by his interruption. "I'm handling it."

He makes a contemplative growl in the base of his throat before coming to some conclusion. "You do not know," he decides, and then takes a step toward Jeanne. "Remove your scarf," he orders her.

Caught between them, I glance back at Jeanne, and find her openness toward myself to be replaced by a quiet fury. She returns Lumin's glare vehemently, one hand held flat to the bundle of fabric that engulfs both her chest and neck.

"Your scarf!" Lumin barks. His voice grates as it deepens, revealing a lethality I have not yet heard from him. Its volatile quality sends thoughts of battle and chaos into my mind.

I sense a dire need to calm him. "Lumin," I try again, "Let me—"

The glim ignores me and fully strengthens his flames. "Remove it or I will burn it from you."

Jeanne lowers her hand along the seam of the scarf, her fingers playing at its frayed threads. "You think I fear fire, glim?"

I feel her strike before my addled mind can predict her intention. A searing pain jolts through my ribs as her fist slams into the newly healed wound. Her knuckles bite where the King's claws were buried. I buckle forward, my knees give out, and Jeanne runs.

I try to stand again before the pain has even begun to subside, and I end up back on the ground, doubled over, and blinking around the dots in my vision. Pain slows Jeanne's movement. I see the sole of her boot as she stretches her legs toward the next tangle of brambles. Her hair lifts and flies around her. From behind, Lumin's metal boots grind against the cracked dirt. His fire crackles. No lash of magic whips over my shoulder, but around Jeanne's neck, the scarf blooms in flame.

The first spark ignites just over her hidden brand, and from it rolls a white-hot line that eats the roughspun fabric. The scarf furls like a leaf around her as she darts for cover. Heat singes her hair and licks at her skin as the material burns away, but she pays it no mind. The ashes fall behind her in a trail of swirling flecks. She glances back, and at the turn of her head between locks of hair, I see the lifted bone of my mother's necklace.

There is only the glimpse of an edge, a single piece of uniquely dark dweller bone. It peeks above Jeanne's shoulder and falls at the weight of more. The fragment connects to a strip of leather that encircles her neck and grazes over her brand. It was not there when I encountered her, and then I recall how she bent over some unseen object before returning it to her neck.

Her foot touches ground, and time hastens once more. The ashes spin and flutter. Her hair falls ragged upon her back, and she breaks the wall of thorns. Lumin takes several quick steps after her. He elegantly spins, and in doing so, casts a length of red mist along her path of escape. As it did when escaping Boon, the magic slices through the trees like a blade through flesh. A shockwave of splintering wood echoes upward.

Somewhere above, there is a terrified flapping of wings as birds burst from the branches.

It all settles within seconds. Lumin stands facing the bisected trees, claws at the ready. I've hardly righted myself when several more bodies come rushing through the foliage.

Surasis leads them. The High Mage breathes heavily, eyes alert and conveying a clear panic. "Gods and dragons," they curse at Lumin. "What have you done?"

Lumin finally looks back. He keeps one set of claws aloft. The tired soldiers who accompanied Surasis waver at the sight of him standing at his full height and fuming.

"We must pursue her," he says.

"Pursue her?" Surasis demands. "Who?"

"Jeanne lied," he says. "My god commands—"

"You've just drawn every Marked toward us! That racket could be heard from the city!" Surasis shouts, apparently no longer caring for discretion.

"The Eye gave me sight."

"Didn't give you forethought, did it?"

"I do not need forethought under instruction from my god."

"Fuck," Surasis briefly drops their head in their hand. "We need to move. Now. All of us."

The High Mage delivers a series of orders to their soldiers, sending them off in different directions and warning them to deny association if caught. I shakily stand. Lumin, not seeming to care for the urgency of our situation, disregards the High Mage. He ignores the harried soldiers who scatter to assemble their armor and exchange strategy. I step toward him, momentarily drawing his focus. Upon seeing me wobble on my feet, he notably assesses my weakness with a sharp look, nods at my obvious lack of ability, and ducks through the burst section of brambles after Jeanne.

I put my hand to the wrapped sheath overtop my wound and press. The pressure brings about new pain but simultaneously focuses it, as though to retract its throbbing tendrils to one single knot under my ribs. I sweat at the sensation. My body initially resists instruction to move, but somehow, I find the strength to follow.

The glim does not move fast. When casting magic, he possesses a keen fluidity, but in all other matters, his movements are careful and slow—the only reason I soon catch up to him. Despite his slowness, there is something terribly menacing about him walking through the growth of boulders and vines. As light gathers in his claws, it seems to fade dimly around himself, leaving an edge of shadow around his person through which only the fire shows. He spares no energy and swipes red whips of compressed magic across his path to clear it of obstruction. The fiery energy releases and expands outward. Upon impact, it vibrates the structure of its target, and then cripples it inward with an expulsion of flame. Bark shatters against his form, but he continues to walk, only pausing to search around himself for sight of Jeanne.

"Lumin!" I shout after him, keeping my distance from his chaotic magic.

He stops, completely aware of me lamely trailing him.

"What did you see?" I demand, my voice strained.

"I must continue. The Eye commands it."

Without waiting for my response, he resumes his blight on the surrounding area. He destroys it without second thought, burning, cracking, and utterly decimating anything Jeanne may have touched. Had we been in the Burned Lands or the middle of battle, I might think him reasonable. Even in pursuit of an enemy, his tactic would eventually prove effective. It is a power I covet, one that I wish I had to avenge a thousand wrongs.

Shards of bark fly outward and nip at my skin. The sound of splintering wood is likely the same as what the Rendara heard amidst attack. Visions of burned men begin to creep in around the faces of Rendara in my periphery. A larger chunk of bark strikes my thigh, and rather than bouncing to the ground, I see it morph into an arrow and lodge in my leg.

I shake away the hallucination and move forward through the spray of wood and stone. Lumin pulls an arm back to ignite another spell, and I latch on. The shifting darkness overtop his arm fogs around my touch. I yank him back with all my strength, which is only enough to stagger him, but it distracts him well enough. While I cling to his arm, he ceases his advance and the growing mist in his claws dissipates.

"Stop!" I command. "There's no time for this!"

Lumin lowers his arm so I can place my feet flat on the ground, but still I do not let go. He continues to keep his eyes up and discerning of every shadow. They gleam through the shade that veils his face. "Jeanne must be found," he coldly says. "I should think you would agree."

"I do," I reply, "but now's not the time."

"My god has given orders."

"Did he?"

"A foreboding shadow has been cast through you, Nhuaela. It seems you were never the threat, but she who you came to know."

"And you're going to kill her?"

"Were you not?"

"I don't know what I was going to do, but she knew more. She's not worth killing yet."

"My god has decided."

I yank his arm back down as he moves to lift it. The shadows waft. "You won't find her like this! You'll only get us captured again! She's gone!"

"She cannot be far."

"In the time it's taken you to do all this?" I gesture vaguely at the destruction. "She could be anywhere by now."

He hesitates. His claws flex, but no magic stirs within them. "But she has stolen—"

"I know," I exasperate. "I know, and I want to strangle her for it, but we need to think first. I can't fight right now, and there are Marked searching for us."

He lowers his arm. "I have been given order. I cannot disobey."

"You were also told to find me. What's more important to Lelendelus?"

He considers the question, looking equal parts confused and afraid. The fire on his horns flickers uncertainly.

"You can kill her," I pose, "or you can follow me."

As I wait for his answer, the effects of spent energy cause me to tip forward once more. I lean into the shade encircling his arm and catch my breath. Each intake of air reminds me of my fever and the anger that burns along my spine, prickling at every Rendaran barb in my back. It is the part of me that screams to allow Lumin to unleash havoc.

"Where will we go?" he asks, uncertain.

I recall the terms of my banishment and the command to return. "I have my own orders to complete."

Lumin thinks for an agonizing amount of time as I wait for Marked or more burned men to leap from the bushes. It's not until Criv does so, startling us both, that Lumin breaks from his thoughtful trance, and helps me into Norrl's saddle.

Epilogue

SERIN WOKE WITH A stiffness in his limbs, and as his vision came into focus, so did the pain. It was all over, stricken across his body in what felt like a thousand slashes. Above him was a roof of gaea boughs, and from them hung vines of yellow lacelets. The scent of a nearby fire wafted faintly within the structure. With it came voices. Still waking, he only caught fragments of sentences. They were speaking Dur—humans.

Their proximity spiked the anxiety within him, and all at once, faded memories came flooding back. The camp, the bodies, Nhuaela screaming. And the vashte, shattering into countless pieces. He recalled the burned man at his heels as he slipped between the trees for no other reason than to hide. The man was too large to slink between the trunks, but he tried to reach Serin. He drew weapons and began to hack at the dark trees. That was when the vashte burst, and Serin's world went black.

He regretted waking.

He lifted his head slightly, the movement pulling every thread of pain. He recalled the explosion of bark. The trunks of the vashte cracked from within. A deep groan seemed to rise from their roots, through their hearts, and then they shattered. He remembered the haunting sound, and the scream from the burned man.

Serin let his head rest once more upon the blankets tucked beneath him. His body was bound in cloth. The bandages hugged him neatly, but in some places, he had bled through. His face, largely intact, felt fiery along his ear and the side of his skull. With each second, a new pain came, a new concern; foremost, the humans.

While testing his muscles, he tried to hear their conversation. A man and a woman, he guessed by their pitches. The woman was not happy.

"You think a fucking elf is gonna be grateful for a human's help? Let alone a trespassing human? It's time you leave it," she argued.

"It?"

"The elf."

"That elf is just a kid."

"Please," she scoffed, "has to be at least fifty years old already."

"You know they age differently. Looks no older than my nephew."

"It's *dangerous*."

The more Serin woke, the more he understood.

"Go home, if you want," the man finally replied, sounding indifferent to her decision.

"They'll kill you if they find you. If not for the kid, then for their fucking trees."

"Got nothing to do with trees," he nervously answered, "nothing to do with us."

"They won't differentiate."

The man was quiet for a moment. When he spoke, his voice shook. "I...I don't think there are any left."

"There's always more."

"Just go home."

"And leave you alone?"

"Yes, leave me alone."

A tense silence grew following their exchange, but Serin heard no sound of decisive movement. In the quiet, he tried to budge his limbs. They gradually responded under the tightness of stitched wounds and dry blood. Slowly, he sat up, gritting his teeth to keep from voicing any pain. The shelter he was within was built against a wall of natural stone, so he could not sneak out the back. He searched around himself, looking for his bow before recalling he lost it. Not lost. The burned man had grabbed it. And he let it go.

Stupid rihar, he cursed himself. Halstaer always warned him to never lose his weapon. *Not unless you have another*, he would say. At the moment, Serin had nothing other than the tatters of his clothes.

He flexed his hand overtop the ground. Thinking of Halstaer made him think of everything else and terror came over him. Beneath it was a pain worse than anything physical. He couldn't place it. It was composed of anger and sorrow. He felt something similar decades earlier when his father was killed in the north, but this was not the same. There was no one to console him, not his mother to run her hand over his head or Sil to make him laugh. Halstaer was not there with a bow to distract him with archery.

Serin desperately tried to stave off the flow of recent memories, but one led to another, and soon he could only see his mother and Sil cut through by blades. The vision was backed by Nhuaela's pleading order, her last command.

Run, she had told him—screamed at him as he had never heard her yell before. *Run.*

And so, Serin ran.

Acknowledgements

ASHACAN HAS WAITED SEVEN years to be accurately told. It underwent many critiques and revisions by highly qualified individuals ranging from professors to family members and friends, and I'm grateful to everyone who took even a moment to provide some feedback. First, I must thank my husband, Andrew, for triggering these ideas through a one-shot, casual D&D game that was never quite finished. Andrew, you left me needing to know the end. I also must thank Katie for being my best mate and reading through every story I have ever written since middle school. Katie, this type of fantasy might not be your cup of tea, but I know you'll always find my spelling errors regardless. A massive thank you goes out to my editor, Malyn Berger, for spending time and energy on fine-tuning my writing, and providing clutch advice for several crucial moments in the story. Malyn, this story would be less inspired without you. It would also have way too many italicized words and unintentional rhymes.

Thank you to my family, who supported my writing and indulged multiple read-throughs to accommodate my constant revisions. To my mom, who invested in my writing and disagreed when multiple teachers tried to discourage me. To my dad, who read my book despite the amount of swearing. Thank you, Charlie, Elliot, and Matthew, for creating the foundation of three characters without whom Nhuaela wouldn't have gotten very far.

And to everyone else who ever gave my writing a fair shot—thank you.

About the Author

CATHERINE VINO GREW UP in a small farm town in Michigan, where she cultivated a love for horses and writing. Inspired by the fantasy genre at a young age, Vino began telling stories of her own and stubbornly decided she only ever wanted to be a writer. She went on to receive two degrees: a B.A. in Creative Writing and an M.A. in Literature, which allowed her to hone her craft over the years. What began as short stories about her friends and horses have since flourished into epic fantasies. *The Vhanian Remnants* is Vino's stamp on the fantasy market, in which any reader can find themselves lost in the world of Uunshyl, rooting for the heroine with a chip on her shoulder and an ax in her hand.